HEART ECHOES

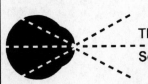

This Large Print Book carries the
Seal of Approval of N.A.V.H.

HEART ECHOES

SALLY JOHN

THORNDIKE PRESS
A part of Gale, Cengage Learning

GALE
CENGAGE Learning·

Detroit • New York • San Francisco • New Haven, Conn • Waterville, Maine • London

GALE
CENGAGE Learning®

Copyright © 2012 by Sally John.

Side Roads Series #3.

Scripture quotations are taken from the *Holy Bible,* New Living Translation, copyright 1996, 2004, 2007 by Tyndale House Foundation. Used by permission of Tyndale House Publishers, Inc. Carol Stream, Illinois 60188. All rights reserved.

Thorndike Press, a part of Gale, Cengage Learning.

Thorndike Press® Large Print Christian Fiction.

The text of this Large Print edition is unabridged.

Other aspects of the book may vary from the original edition.

Set in 16 pt. Plantin.

LIBRARY OF CONGRESS CATALOGING-IN-PUBLICATION DATA

John, Sally, 1951–
    Heart echoes / by Sally John.
        pages ; cm. — (Thorndike Press large print Christian fiction) (Side roads series ; #3)
        ISBN 978-1-4104-4600-8 (hardcover) — ISBN 1-4104-4600-X (hardcover)
    1. Large type books. I. Title.
    PS3560.O323H43 2012b
    813'.54—dc23   2012017664

Published in 2012 by arrangement with Tyndale House Publishers, Inc.

Printed in Mexico
1 2 3 4 5 6 7 16 15 14 13 12

*For my sister
Cindi Cox
and my sisters-in-law
Sandy Carlson, Patti John,
and Patty John*

He heals the brokenhearted and bandages their wounds.

PSALM 147:3

ACKNOWLEDGMENTS

My heart echoes with gratitude for those who came alongside to help create this book.

Thanks to Christopher John, Tracy John, Elizabeth Johnson, Troy Johnson, Anna Younce, Tom Carlson, and Kelly Farmer for providing a myriad of details about trees, the Oregon coast, teenage vernacular and culture, and the military.

Thanks to Anna Rehder for the crash course in law and for so patiently and thoroughly answering my nonstop legal questions. Mistakes are mine.

Thanks to the Johnston, Iowa, high school students for the timely YouTube display of teenage enthusiasm and energy.

Thanks to Karlie Garcia for the blogging tutorial.

Thanks to Margaret Becker, Nicole Sponberg, and Rivertribe for the music support.

Thanks to my readers. You are a constant

source of encouragement.

Thanks to my dream team: editors Karen Watson, Stephanie Broene, and Kathy Olson, along with everyone at Tyndale House who markets, sells, designs, and makes sure the books get into readers' hands.

As always, many thanks to my agent, Lee Hough, who has made all the difference in my work. Thanks also to the whole group at Alive Communications.

And thanks to Tim for thirty-eight years of being there.

CHAPTER 1

Los Angeles, California

At precisely twelve minutes and thirty-five seconds past ten o'clock in the morning, Pacific Daylight Time, Teal Morgan-Adams's world ceased to exist.

She knew the exact time because the NPR radio announcer Dave Somebody said it after his traffic update, which started with, "Slow going westbound on the 10, folks."

Teal snorted. " 'Slow going.' Ha. It's a regular parking lot out here, Dave."

She sat in the thick of it, second lane from the right, windows shut, air on high against the August heat, comfy in her white leather seat. She read e-mails on her smartphone and, in her imagination, dared a CHP officer to zoom up on his motorcycle and ticket her.

"As if moving four miles per hour on the freeway could technically be referred to as driving and thereby breaking the law."

She laughed out loud. If her husband were there, he'd roll his eyes and question once again his sanity for marrying a lawyer. River swore Teal's favorite pastime was looking for a fight. After three and a half years, though, his rolling eyes still sparkled whenever he said it.

The radio announcer wrapped up his report. "The time is now twelve minutes and thirty-five seconds past ten o'clock."

And then the shaking began.

As always, the unexpected movement registered about half a point on Teal's scale of awareness. One eye on her phone, one eye on the Iowa license plate on the minivan in front of her, she inched forward and braked. Her body trembled, as if she were on a train.

"What . . . ?"

And then her coffee mug jiggled and rattled in its holder. Static hissed from the radio.

"Nooo." The mug bounced onto the floor. *Yes.*

"Oh, God!" It was all the prayer she could form at the moment.

Adrenaline surged through her. What to do? What to do?

Duck, cover, and hold on to a sturdy piece of furniture.

In the car? She was in the car!

Teal dropped the phone to her lap, shifted into Park, and grasped the steering wheel tightly with both hands. It shook. Her body quivered. The car vibrated. Her seat belt constricted. The glove box popped open. The world rumbled, a hurtling train on rickety tracks to nowhere.

Her pulse throbbed in her throat. Her thoughts raced in circles. What to do? What to do?

If you are driving, stop. Okay. Okay. *Move out of traffic.*

Out of traffic? Not a chance.

She caught sight of the driver to her right. He clutched his steering wheel, his sunglasses askew, his face scrunched up. Waiting. Holding his breath.

Teal had learned to deal with earthquakes. She and her daughter had lived in Southern California for fifteen years. Tremors came. Teal panicked. Maiya grinned. Tremors went. She walked off the adrenaline rush. Maiya laughed. They talked about what they should have done. Life got back to normal.

These tremors should have *went* by now.

People should be exhaling by now.

She should be out of the car by now, *whew*ing with those Iowa tourists in front of her, exchanging nervous chuckles, talking

13

about Disneyland.

Do not get out of the car.

Do not stop under an overpass.

"Oh, God! Oh, God! Oh, God!"

She stared at the overpass. According to the huge green sign to her right, the next exits at the overpass lay a quarter of a mile ahead. Hers was one of them.

Cars and vans and pickups and semis and SUVs and RVs moved where there was no space for movement. Drivers jockeyed to get out from under the bridge. Horns blared. Metal crunched against metal.

And then the tremors went. The shaking stopped. It was over.

Or not.

In horror Teal watched the chain reactions of vehicles slamming and shoving and sliding into each other not far ahead of her. Straight lanes of traffic were now a massive logjam of cars facing every direction.

And then the unthinkable.

The overpass shifted. It happened in agonizingly slow motion.

The right-side concrete abutment twisted, a giant robot turning, losing his footing, falling, falling, falling. It splayed out over the freeway below. The bridge it had been holding aloft toppled across five lanes of logjam.

The air exploded with shrapnel. Crashing noises reverberated.

Teal burst into tears, released the seat belt, turned off the engine, and ducked. She squeezed herself under the dashboard, covered her head with her arms, and began shaking all over again.

The first aftershock hadn't even hit yet.

CHAPTER 2

River Adams gazed up at the rafters of the garage ceiling. If it had been The Big One, he would be buried under those beams instead of under a mountain of blue plastic storage tubs.

Teal. Where was she? "Please, Lord."

A sharp pain shot through his right side. It had the familiar as-long-as-I-don't-breathe-I'm-fine tug of a broken rib.

Many of the tubs were full of books. Or rather had been full of books before crashing on top of him. The entire set of Anne of Green Gables hardbacks lay scattered about. They belonged to Maiya, his fifteen-year-old stepdaughter, a childhood collection she could not bear to part with.

Oh, God. Teal's panic would be sky high. Maiya would be laughing. *Whoa, dude! Five point nine at least.*

They would be . . . if they were okay.

River refused to follow that line of thinking. His girls had to be okay. In the five years since he had met them, they had become the center of his universe. Teal was the epitome of femininity with her big gray eyes, bouncy personality, and short black hair framing a heart-shaped face. Maiya called him Riv and seemed more his than Teal's in some ways. Her easygoing attitude did not come from her mother, nor her goofy sense of humor.

And the most amazing part of all? They adored him.

He needed to reach his girls.

Taking shallow breaths, River pushed aside what he could from his upper body. The majority of the tubs pinned his legs against the concrete floor. From their weight, he suspected they contained Teal's law books and files. She had put them here when he moved into her house, to make space for his teaching materials in the bedroom she used as an office.

He broke out in a cold sweat and lay still.

"I'd say we're pushing a seven, Maiya. Epicenter . . . really close."

It was the worst he'd experienced in his forty-two years, all lived in the Los Angeles area.

Just before the earthquake struck, he had carried a trash bag out to the garage and put it in the can at the far end. As he walked back toward the door that led into the house, the world started its belly dance. There was nothing in the attached single-car garage to duck under or hold on to. He covered his head with his arms and made a dash for the house.

The dash ended abruptly. The bins struck him, a cannonball shot at close range and full force. *Whoosh,* straight out from the wall where they were stacked. He went down, flat on his back.

Slowly, River pushed aside books and felt for the phone attached to his waistband.

It wasn't there.

He scanned the floor and saw it.

Under the corner of a bin.

Crushed.

He struggled to break free of the trap, his side screaming for him to stop moving, to stop breathing.

They have to be okay! They have to! You owe me, God! You owe me this one!

CHAPTER 3

Crouched as far as possible under the dashboard, Teal sensed an unearthly stillness.

She had seen the bridge go down. The crushing of people and vehicles and concrete and signs and light poles was finished. The world paused for a moment of silence.

She shuddered and gulped for air. "Oh, God. Oh, God. This isn't happening. This can't be happening."

She tried not to do the math, but it nagged for attention. Under the bridge, five lanes eastbound, five lanes westbound. On the bridge, two lanes northbound, two lanes southbound. Traffic at a standstill beneath meant one vehicle per lane times the number that fit under the shadow of the bridge, plus the moving traffic atop it that had not stopped before it gave way. . . .

Inconceivable.

Ten, maybe fifteen minutes later and she

19

would have been under it.

A cacophony erupted. Screams pierced the quiet. Doors opened and slammed. Sirens wailed. Voices rose and fell, a confusion of noise.

Teal struggled up from the floor and out from under the steering wheel, brushing grit from her shins and straightening her skirt. Where was her phone? It must have fallen.

She rummaged under the seat. "It has to be here. It has to be here! Oh, God, please let them be safe. Please let them be safe." She chattered nonstop. Her heart still pounded; her body still trembled.

"Please oh please oh please." She touched the phone, pulled it out, and sat up.

The scene through the windshield came into focus and smacked her breath away.

Half of the overpass was gone.

Vehicles lay on top of it willy-nilly like toy cars abandoned in a playroom.

Underneath it . . .

Incomprehensible.

She could see people everywhere across the freeway, outside their cars, west- and eastbound lanes, on the shoulders, on the median between oleander bushes. They cried, shouted, hugged. Some raced toward the collapsed bridge. Others ran away from it. Some sat on the pavement, faces buried in their hands.

The hot summer sun beat down from a clear blue sky as if nothing had happened.

Teal turned from it all and hit speed dial for Maiya. Her fifteen-year-old always carried her cell phone. Answering it guaranteed she got to keep it.

There was no ring.

Teal stared at the phone. The No Service symbol stared back at her.

"Oh, God."

Her arms ached to hold her baby. Her body ached to be held by River. A hollowness enveloped her. *They have to be safe. They have to.*

She looked at the scene before her.

They might not be. They truly might not be.

No. They were all right. River and Maiya could take care of themselves. He was probably still at home, in the solid 1925 bungalow she had bought ten years before at a rock-bottom price from a grateful client. The neighborhood was flat, not teetering on the edge of a bluff, not at the foot of some boulder-strewn hillside.

Maiya was at her best friend Amber Price's. She had worked last night. Then Amber's mom had picked her up and taken the girls to a late movie. Shauna and JT

Price were as solid as Teal's house. If Teal weren't married to River, she'd write them into her will as Maiya's guardians.

Teal yanked the hem of her powder-blue silk blouse from the skirt waistband and used it to wipe away streaked mascara. There was nothing she could do to reach her family. Absolutely nothing she could do to contact River, Maiya, friends, or coworkers.

But she wasn't alone. No one on that freeway could reach their loved ones.

"Time to put on your big-girl pants, Morgan." The phrase was her old mantra, a survival technique from her early days as single mom Teal Morgan working on a law degree, depending on strangers and mere acquaintances to help.

A banging on her passenger window made her jump. The scrunched face from the car next to hers peered through it. "Are you all right?" he shouted.

She nodded, took the key from the ignition, climbed out, and spotted the attaché in the backseat. Her laptop inside of it would roast. She got back in, cracked open the sunroof, got out, and wondered about looters. Day off or heyday? The car beeped as she hit the locks.

At her left sat two vacant cars. Their oc-

cupants could have been any of the countless people standing or roaming about.
Behind her, two businessmen stood beside
an SUV, removing ties, rolling up sleeves.
She walked forward, toward the minivan
from Iowa. Those people must be going
crazy. Her pumps clicked on the pavement.
She should get the sneakers out of the
trunk. Maybe later. If she had to hoof it
home.

Yes, later. There would be a later. There
would be an end to this horrific moment.

Her steps slowed at the surreal scene
before her. It was like being on the set of
some B movie, a disaster film with obviously
fake props and far too many actors.

She reached the van and gasped. On its
hood sat a chunk of concrete the size of a
desk. A spiderweb of cracks covered the
windshield.

Teal leaned inside, through the open side
door. A woman sat in the front passenger
seat; three kids under the age of ten sat in
the back. All four were quiet and wide eyed.

"Hey." She gave them a small smile.
"Welcome to LA. You okay? I mean, basically overall okay?"

The woman shook her head and then nodded. A butterfly bandage was on her forehead beneath short blonde curls, fresh

23

blood seeping at its edges. She wore her seat belt. "Yes. No."

Teal nodded. "Me too." She eyed the kids, two boys in the center seats and a girl in the far back. They wore swimsuits. "The good news is the beach will still be there tomorrow."

The tallest, a boy, said, "What about a tsunami?"

Teal swallowed. "No worries. The earthquake would have to start underwater, out at sea. I bet this one came from close by. Inland. No big waves."

"What about aftershocks?"

"You're a regular walking encyclopedia."

The corners of his mouth twitched.

She hoped it was a smile and not a precursor to bawling. "Most likely there will be an aftershock. Or a few." As in countless? For days on end? Weeks even? "All the ones I've experienced are smaller than the initial quake. But we still need to duck, cover, and hold on to something sturdy when we feel one."

"Outdoors?"

"Uh, no. Then we just stay away from everything that might fall." She winced. There wasn't anything left to fall except the other side of the overpass.

The little blonde in the back said, "Our

daddy is a doctor. He fixed Mommy's head. Now he's fixing that man." She pointed over Teal's shoulder. "I'm a 'cycopedia too."

"Yes, you are." Teal glanced behind her and saw a man wearing a floral shirt, shorts, and a stethoscope.

The woman said, "He noticed an elderly man in that car and thought he might need some attention."

"That's wonderful. How did you get hurt?"

"My window was down. Something . . . flew . . . in." Her hands fluttered. Teal imagined that under normal circumstances, her skin glowed with Midwest peaches and cream.

"Do you want to get out of the van?"

"Is it safe?"

"I don't know, but maybe safer than that windshield." She blew out a breath. "What we need to do is get out of here. I wonder if . . . Oh." She felt the telltale rumble. "Here it comes. Hold on to your zingie-zangers!"

The kids hit the deck before she did. The woman screamed. Teal hopped onto the seat the oldest boy had vacated, bent double, and covered her head. Nobody asked what a zingiezanger was.

Evidently it didn't matter. They understood, just as her daughter had understood as a toddler. The word probably explained why Maiya still laughed at earthquakes.

The neighbor woman who had cared for Maiya while Teal went to school and worked taught the nonsensical word to her. She used it to warn Maiya about loud noises, running in the rain, zipping down slides, swinging high, uncontrollable giggling, and earthquakes. *Hold on to your zingiezangers!*

Teal ached. She needed to hold on to her family.

The chaos escalated.

Helicopters hovered and whirred and whomped. An amplified voice boomed down from one of them with repetitive, indecipherable messages. Emergency vehicles crept along the freeway shoulders on both sides of the median, moving toward the overpass. Their discordant sirens and flashing lights were nerve-racking.

A slice of America — every age, race, and culture — roamed between parked vehicles. Some people looked like aimless zombies with blank expressions; others sobbed uncontrollably.

Teal did her own haphazard wandering, her breath in ragged spurts, her prayers repetitive one-liners. *Keep them safe. Keep them safe. Help us. Help us.* Her body refused to stop trembling. Walking on pavement she regularly traversed in her car but never set foot on added an eeriness to the entire scenario.

The worst damage within her vicinity was to the van from Iowa; the worst injury, the woman's cut forehead. A quarter of a mile ahead was impossible to comprehend. There would not be enough emergency personnel to help everyone in this one area alone. How extensively had the city been hit?

She and her new best friends hatched an exit plan. The three children and their mother, Carole Swanson, would ride with Teal. Dr. Swanson and the old man with chest pains would ride with Ron, the breath holder, and Joe, a truck driver parked behind him. There was nothing to be done with the out-of-commission minivan. The old man's car would have to stay put. The semi would not be budging for a long, long time.

Behind them a domino effect had begun. In the distance vehicles crept back and forth, back and forth, making tight one-eighty turns. Little by little they inched forward, allowing other drivers to start the turn. A line of traffic snaked toward an exit Teal had passed, perhaps half a mile back, hours ago.

It would take a while before they would have space to turn around. In the meantime, Dr. Swanson from Iowa opened his family's picnic basket and coolers and distributed food and water to the Californians who had not stocked their own cars on the off chance a quake would strike and leave them stranded on a hot summer's day.

Teal drank from her bottle of water because she was sweating and hoped she wouldn't have to get in line at the nearby RV, whose owners had opened their bathroom to the world. She helped the Swansons transfer their things to her trunk and fielded the eldest boy's questions about landslides, seismographs, and fires caused by damaged electrical and gas lines.

It wasn't the most encouraging topic of conversation, but it beat crawling onto her backseat and passing the time in a fetal position.

CHAPTER 4

The concrete floor rumbled beneath River's back.

He eyed the water heater. Strapped securely to the wall, it didn't budge during the aftershock. The wall stayed put as well.

"Thank You, God."

But more aftershocks were likely to hit, jiggling things that had already been jiggled, loosening things like the gas line that led to the water tank. He needed to get to the shutoff valve.

River worked at shoving aside books and plastic tubs, a centimeter at a time, in between the hot knife stabbing at his insides and cutting off his air.

He wondered if the broken ribs had damaged something else. It seemed he would realize if that were true, though, that he would feel worse than he did. Wouldn't he be passed out or screaming in pain by now?

More than anything, River hated being

helpless.

He lay flat again, relaxed his neck and shoulders, and grimaced at the rafters. The last time helplessness engulfed him, it had morphed into a good thing.

It had all started when his sister wanted to divorce her wealthy, philandering investor husband. Jen was her emotionally messy self on steroids at the time. River stepped in as he had always done. Even before their parents' deaths when he and his sister were in their early twenties, he had watched over her.

Jen chose the all-female law firm of Canfield and Stone, specialists in family law and the primo group for taking rich husbands to the cleaners. River imagined a company of Amazons and feared his sister would get carried away with vengeance. Her husband might deserve it, but he knew his sister. Jen would regret her actions.

He tagged along with her to the appointment.

And he met Ms. Teal Morgan.

Helplessness swamped him. She was nothing at all like an Amazon. The woman was everything he didn't know he needed. Life radiated from her face and in the touch of her hand in his. Dried-up corners of his heart soaked it in and longed for more.

"Hi." She smiled. Those luminous, pale-gray eyes rimmed in a bluish slate never wavered.

"Hi. Uh, nice to meet you, Ms. Morgan. I hope you don't mind a big brother butting in?"

"Not at all. And it's Teal. Like the duck."

He grinned. "I'm River. Like the river."

She giggled.

Later, much later, she swore their future was sealed in that moment. She had laughed, tickled with a sudden understanding: ducks could not survive without water.

Yes, a good ending to helplessness.

The shallow breathing was making him light-headed. There was no hope of crawling into his truck; it was parked out on the street. He doubted he could get to his feet. Someone would find him, though. Eventually. Teal or Maiya would come home. Maybe they would feel so bad for him they wouldn't mention the shelves he had promised to build to hold those stacked tubs now fallen on him.

At least Jen was not a concern. Husband Number Two, less of a jerk than Number One, had taken her to Paris for her birthday last week.

Sirens wailed — fire engines, ambulances, police. They grew loud. They faded. More split the air. Far and near. Far and near.

River groaned, dumbfounded at how slow he could be. He was not helpless nor hopeless nor unable to set things in motion.

"Lord, in Your mercy, hear my prayer." He slipped into a cadence that always moved him easily into the presence of God. "Surround my loved ones. For Teal and Maiya, I ask for protection. For our neighbors, I ask for protection. For San Sebastian Academy, I ask for protection. For John, Lynn, Delia, Olie, Mac . . ." He listed his coworkers and then he went on to list every boy who lived at the school, all fifty of them. "And for Jen, I pray she would not hear the news just yet."

CHAPTER 5

"She looks a lot like you," Mr. Smarty-Pants Encyclopedia commented on a family photo Teal had pulled from her wallet as they stood near her car. "He looks like a hippie."

"And what would you know about hippies, Nick?" By now they were all on a first-name basis.

"We have hippies in Iowa." He grinned. The freckles on his nose bunched together. Cute, pesky kid.

"My husband's ponytail does not mean he is a hippie. He's earthy."

"Is River his real name?"

The question no longer bothered her. It came as frequently as the one about how to spell Maiya's name. "His parents were professors at Berkeley in the sixties."

"That explains that."

She shook her head. "You're only ten."

"Eleven next week. What's your point?"

"That you're precocious and annoying."

"I get that a lot. Would your daughter like me?"

"She's too old for you."

"But I'm precocious, and she's a hottie."

Teal slid her sunglasses onto the top of her head and gave him her best glare. "I won't charge you for this piece of advice. 'She's a hottie' is not something you want to say to a mother if you hope to spend any time with her daughter."

He blinked a few times.

She bit her lip, holding back a smile at his sudden speechlessness.

He said, "Seriously?"

"Yeah."

"But it's a compliment."

"Only to hormone-laden adolescents. I thought you wanted to see inside Joe's semi over there."

He smiled and handed her the photo. "I can take a hint. Don't leave without us."

She murmured to his retreating back. "Maiya would eat you up."

Teal retrieved her handbag from the front seat and sat down, her sneakered feet on the asphalt. She shut out the unbearable noise of sirens, helicopters, and crying people and stared at her photo.

It had helped at first, talking with the boy about Maiya and River. But now the apprehension slammed into her again, a literal twisting of her heart. Where were they? Were they all right? How long would this unknowing continue? How long could she take it?

And how long could they take it not knowing about her? River would be having an especially hard time of it.

If he were okay.

He had to be okay.

She noted other people checking cell phones like she had been. Sometimes a signal appeared, but the lines were jammed. There was no getting through. Supposedly no one should even be trying to get through except for emergencies.

She wasn't sure what this was if not an emergency. It wasn't dire, though, at least not for her. She was hot and tired and anxious, but she was walking and talking. She could leave soon in her own car. She was not lying under those tons of broken concrete.

The photo was fairly new. She had done some legal work for a photographer, saw samples of her artistic flair, and decided this year's Christmas card would include a professional family picture taken far in advance. Teal bribed River and Maiya with the promise of homemade chocolate chip cookies. They dressed for the occasion and grinned on either side of her next to a palm tree with the ocean as a backdrop — Currier and Ives, West Coast style.

Maiya's fashion concoctions usually worked. For the picture her black hair was brushed straight back and held in place with a wide tortoiseshell headband. As usual, her vivid green eyes drew attention to themselves. She wore only one pair of earrings — large silver hoops — and a long multicolored neck scarf. Over a white T-shirt hung a loose-knit purple vest and several strands of beads. Black leggings allowed the bun-hugging gray skirt to pass muster.

River, Teal's earthy husband, wore his wavy, nut-brown hair as usual in a low, short ponytail but left the ball cap at home. He had exchanged jeans for khakis and put on a red button-down oxford over a white San Sebastian Academy T-shirt. He smiled, his teeth a slash of white in his perennially tanned face, his cobalt-blue eyes all but hidden behind thick lashes.

Now there was the hottie. Even five years after meeting him she thought so. Totally not her type, though. No one was more surprised than herself when five minutes after he stepped into her office, she was writing down his phone number, and not because he was her client Jenny Nelson's brother.

He worked with at-risk teenage boys. He sat with them during drug withdrawals and at parole hearings and taught them how to plant gardens and say please and thank you. She got regular manicures and haircuts and wore suits and heels. When push came to shove, she raked moguls over the coals until they bled money.

They were an odd threesome.

But they were a threesome, the sort of three-stranded cord that was impossible to break.

Teal put the photo back in her wallet. It was best not to think about them.

CHAPTER 6

River sat on the garage floor, his head between his knees. He had managed to stand up briefly before nausea suggested sitting might be the wiser choice.

It wasn't so much the pain of cracked bones that sickened him. It was a deeper pain, yanked by its roots up and out of its burial place to sneer in his face.

"They're all right." He gasped the words, determined to fight back. "They are all right. Krissy and Sammy are . . . Oh, God. Oh, God."

He was losing his mind.

Teal and Maiya were all right. *Teal* and *Maiya.*

Tears stung his eyes.

What would Sammy have looked like as a ten-year-old?

"Stop."

It was a stupid game to play. Extreme exhaustion brought it on. Sometimes the sight of a towheaded boy in the grocery store. Once his fingers tracing the hollow at the base of Teal's neck sparked it. He could now add earthquakes to the short list.

The boy would be blond and brown-eyed like his mother. All rough and tumble like his father.

Or so River imagined. He'd never held his son.

"Stop."

Would Krissy's hair still be that white-blonde shade at the age of forty?

"Stop it!"

If he knew the answers, then he would not know Teal and Maiya.

Correction. He would have met Teal because he would have gone with his sister to the law office. But he would not have asked for Teal's private phone number. No way.

Had anticipation of dinner with his wife and young son lived inside of him instead of aridity, he would not have looked twice at Ms. Morgan. Had even the impression of his wedding band — then six years gone — been evident to Teal, she never would have made note of his phone number.

In his mind's eye he went to the morgue. The *morgue.* They couldn't locate him right away. He had been camping in the mountains with students. Krissy had been driving in town, on her way to work. Seven months pregnant. An idiot SUV driver on a rain-slick freeway hit her.

Teal most likely had been driving when the quake struck, on her way to the office, on the freeway.

"Stop."

She was okay.

Maiya was with friends not too many blocks away.

She was okay.

River put his arms on a plastic tub and pushed himself to his feet.

He was okay.

They all *had to be okay.*

He took three steps toward the door and sank again to the floor. Rough and tumble disintegrated on the spot.

CHAPTER 7

The hours blurred into one long continuum. The horror came in cold waves, an unending tide of fear and despair with little time to take a breath.

Teal sat in her car with Carole Swanson, both of them unable to stop trembling. Despite the sun beating through the open sunroof, they both held blankets around their shoulders. They listened in silence to the radio news, waiting for the traffic's domino effect to reach them so Teal could make a tight K-turn and drive home.

Home.

To Maiya and River.

They had to be there.

"Teal." Carole touched her arm. "Maybe we shouldn't listen to any more news."

"Maybe not." Instead of turning off the radio, she grasped the stranger's hand and stared straight ahead.

Carole squeezed back.

Newscasters offered only repetitious information in overly pumped tones. "Experts still hold with the initial measurement of 6.8. Ladies and gentlemen, we are talking inestimable, widespread damage in the heart of LA." They spoke of coordinates and fault lines and numbers and tremors in San Diego and Tijuana. None of it mattered to the average person reeling from what had just happened.

"Folks, power outages are everywhere. Remember, gas lines should be turned off and remain off. Once again, the encouraging news is that downtown remains intact. Skyscrapers swayed but held their ground. Indoors, of course, is another story. Offices, homes, restaurants, and stores are a mess." They replayed voices of survivors describing shifting and falling appliances, furniture, groceries from shelves, china from Bed Bath & Beyond.

There would be people struck by those things. People underneath those things. Nobody was guessing at injured or death tolls.

Carole said, "Your husband and daughter should be fine, right? You said they're the other direction."

Teal nodded. River and Maiya were north and east. Even if he had already gone to work or she had already gone to the mall, they were north and east. According to the broadcasts, much of the damage occurred south and west. Maybe . . . maybe . . .

Maybe nobody had checked north and east yet.

She had left home early that morning, pro bono work on her plate, and driven far from the neighborhoods where the majority of Canfield and Stone's clients lived. She met with two women on welfare, walked them through the ins and outs of child support, and headed toward the office. Which put her on this freeway going this direction at this time.

Carole sniffed. Fresh tears trickled down her cheeks. "Do you think God picks and chooses who dies today and who doesn't?"

Teal shook her head. No reason to go there. No reason in the world.

She turned off the radio.

Teal drove Carole and her kids to the Marriott where they were staying. Dr. Swanson would meet them there later, after he and Ron the breath holder took the elderly man to a hospital.

The hotel appeared no worse for wear. Countless guests mingled outdoors, their expressions and voices excited and fearful.

Under the portico, while a porter un-loaded the Swansons' beach paraphernalia, the family and Teal hugged as if they'd known each other forever. Carole took Teal's card. They had absolutely nothing in common other than this one moment in time. It was, at the least, enough of a bond for them to exchange Christmas cards for the remainder of their lives.

Teal drove away, her cell phone practically embedded in her left hand. She had checked it nearly as often as she blinked, but the signal was not there.

The car seemed oddly empty without her friends. The world outside faded into a sur-realistic haze. Traffic choked the streets. Although she was within minutes of her community, getting there at this rate would take longer than she thought she could bear.

But what choice did she have?

The phone rang.

Teal jumped and cried out. "Oh! Oh!" Not slowing to check the incoming ID, she pressed the Answer icon. "H'lo!"

"Tealie!" It was Charlie Yoshida, their neighbor and surrogate grandpa, shouting at his usual volume in order to hear himself. "You answered! Then you're fine! River, she's fine."

44

"*You're talking to River?* What is going — ?"

"Are you fine?"

"Charlie!" She jerked the steering wheel toward a curbside handicapped space and slammed on the brakes.

"You sound just fine." He chuckled. "She's just fine, everyone." His voice grew faint. "We're all just fine. Yes. Cindy! Come here." He spoke his wife's name. "Tealie is fine."

"Charlie!" Teal shouted. "Please!"

"Oh, sorry. We're so happy. Everyone is cheering. The nurses and other patients. River is smiling at last."

"Nurses and patients? Where are you? What's wrong?"

"Sh, sh. Calm down. Didn't I say we're all just — ?"

"Then why isn't River on the phone?"

"Well, he can't talk. I mean, he *can* talk, but they're telling him to lie still and be quiet. Because of the pain."

"What pain?"

"Ribs. We think he cracked some. This place is a zoo, but he needs tests. Oh, hold on. He's trying to sit up and he's cussing. I guess he wants to talk. Here he is."

There was the sound of a labored breath and then, "Teal. Thank . . . God . . . you're . . . okay."

If Charlie had not said he was putting River on the phone, she never could have guessed the voice belonged to her husband. The gentle tenor was nowhere in the hoarse whisper. He paused between each word as if garnering the strength to climb a rock wall.

"Oh, River." She moaned and leaned forward, her head against her arm on the steering wheel. "What happened?"

"Garage . . . tubs. . . . Maiya?"

"Maiya? Didn't she come home?"

"No."

"My phone wasn't working until now. Did you hear from her?"

"Phone . . . same . . ."

What about the house phone? Voice mails? Didn't you check? She let the questions circle unspoken. "Don't try to talk, hon. I'm sure Shauna insisted the girls stay with her until she heard from us. Phone lines are tied up."

"I love you."

She heard the worry and relief in his voice. If he had not been injured, he would have somehow found her stuck on the freeway and come like a knight on a white horse. He could not have sat still waiting, not with those memories of his.

"I love you, River. Let me talk to Cindy so you can rest."

46

"Yeah. Love you."

"I'll be there soon." Wherever *there* was. She squeezed her eyes shut and bit her lip. Blubbering would not help. Cindy would help. Like her husband, she was of Japanese descent but had been born and raised in the States. She filled the surrogate grandmother role, but not in a warm-cookies-and-milk way. A long-retired school principal, she maintained a no-nonsense attitude.

"Teal." Cindy's strong voice came on the line. "Sorry, I was down the hall when Charlie reached you. River sounds worse than he is, so don't worry. They want to do a CT scan to see exactly what's going on. We're at Redman Medical Center. Can you get here?"

"I'm about twenty minutes away. Are you all right?"

"We're a little shaken up, but otherwise fine. There's no obvious damage to your house or ours. Charlie saw River's pickup out front and thought it odd he hadn't checked on us. He went over to check on him. River didn't answer the door, so Charlie used our key to get inside. He found him lying on the mudroom floor. He had crawled in from the garage."

"Oh no."

"Now that's the worst of it. Get your rear

47

in gear and get over here. I've tried Maiya's cell, but it won't connect. Charlie and I will go home and wait for her."

Teal whispered a thank-you as she pulled away from the curb. Her heart pounded with fresh shots of adrenaline. "He's okay. He's okay." She fumbled with her phone and checked for voice mails. There were none. She pressed speed dial for Maiya's number.

An automated voice spoke. No lines were available.

Teal had nowhere to tuck this information into her psyche.

And so she screamed. Once. At the top of her lungs. Long and hard.

CHAPTER 8

Teal kept the tears at bay until her cheek was pressed against River's scratchy one and she heard his whisper in her ear.

"Xena."

Typically she laughed at his ludicrous nickname for her. Now she started bawling. If she were a warrior princess, she would have ordered the hospital staff to attend to him immediately. She would have sent an army out to comb the city for Maiya.

River cradled her face and kissed her as she leaned awkwardly over the high, narrow bed, careful to embrace only his shoulders. Tears seeped at the corners of his eyes and mingled with hers.

There was nothing else to do.

They were in a busy, crowded hallway of the emergency room. It was the only available space. At least River was able to lie down, the least-painful position for him. People with heart issues or major traumatic injuries took precedence. The waiting area was a nightmare of fear and minor cuts and bruises. The news blared from televisions, adding to the tension. Did anyone need to know yet that hundreds of people may have been killed?

Teal thought of the man from the freeway with chest pains. He had been taken to a different hospital. She hoped he was all right. She hoped everyone in the city was all right.

It was too much.

She kissed River's cheek and straightened for her first good look at him. He wore a blue hospital gown and blue jeans. She wanted to crawl up beside him and hold him tightly. "Oh, baby."

He wiped at his tears and tried to smile. "That bad?"

The situation had already etched itself in his laugh lines and crow's-feet, deepening them into crevices. His dark-blue eyes had no sparkle. They matched the circles beneath them.

She brushed his brown hair off his forehead. His skin was clammy. Gently she reached around and removed the elastic band. He always undid the ponytail when he was lying down. "I thought I'd seen you at your worst. Like after those survival campouts with the boys. But you've taken that macho-man disheveled look to new heights. Speaking of the boys, have you heard from the school?"

"Cindy called for me."

"All okay?"

"Yeah. The office?" He winced with the effort of talking.

"I haven't been able to phone anyone yet. Did they give you something?"

"Mm-hmm."

"Let me guess." She held his hand and stroked the platinum wedding band. "You refused everything except one over-the-counter, low-dose-capsule pain reliever." Even that could put him to sleep. If he took two, no telling what would happen. His body seemed incapable of processing drugs without a major upheaval in his system. "You can nap."

"Nooo." The word was an exhale.

She put a finger on his lips. "Stop talking."

He kissed her finger and gazed at her, gratitude written all over him. She saw it in his lean face and strong chin, at rest despite the stress his body was experiencing. "Find Mai."

She took a deep breath, torn between staying with him and tracking down their daughter. "The cell signal won't hold. I have to find a pay phone." If Maiya didn't answer, she would call Shauna. She would check voice messages from their house line, from River's cell, from her cell. She wanted to check in with the office, too.

"Call your family," he whispered.

"Oregon can wait."

His eyes went to half-mast and not because of exhaustion. It wasn't that he disapproved of her choices or that he intentionally dumped loads of guilt on her. He simply never gave up suggesting she might want to be a little more thoughtful toward her family for her own sake.

She said, "But Jenny and Aaron can't wait." At least she had a relationship with his sister and her new husband. "I'll try to reach them in Paris." Teal laid her head carefully on his shoulder. "Listen to me, planning a dozen calls like no one else will be using the pay phones."

He ruffled her hair. A moment later he was snoring.

Maiya did not answer her cell phone.

The Yoshidas answered Teal's house phone. Maiya was not there.

Teal stole a glance over her shoulder. The line for the two pay phones was not getting any shorter. She had waited twenty-five minutes for her turn. People were being polite over the whole thing, not complaining or frowning at her. It seemed the worst scenario was bringing out the best in humanity.

She pressed more numbers, grateful she still carried a business phone card.

Shauna answered her house phone on the first ring, her voice nowhere near its usual calm alto. "Hello!" Teal imagined her friend's sweet face crumpled in worry over her wide range of family and friends.

"Shauna, it's me."

"You guys okay? I've been leaving messages on your voice mails."

"I haven't been able to check any. We're good. Almost." She gave a quick rundown of River's situation. "You're all fine?"

"Yes. We were home when it hit."

"Oh, thank God! Thank God. Can I talk to Maiya?"

"Maiya?"

A deathly silence fell between them, the facts slithering into both mothers' consciences at the same time.

"Shauna." Teal's mouth went dry.

"She's not here, Teal. Why do you think she's here?"

"She spent the night."

"No. She didn't. Amber!" Shauna shouted her daughter's name. "Amber Jaleene! Get in here *right this minute!*"

Teal slumped against the small partition and put an elbow on the shelf. *Dear God. Dear God. Dear God.*

Now she heard Shauna talking to her daughter. "Amber, where is Maiya? Don't give me that shrug. Teal thinks she spent the night here. Why does she think that?"

The conversation quickly disintegrated. Amber wailed loud enough for Teal to hear. She cried that she had promised not to tell. Shauna, a middle school counselor who did not make idle threats, promised to ground her for six months. "Take your pick! Keep your secret or have a life. Teal is about to lose her mind here. Now where is Maiya?"

Their voices grew softer. Then Shauna's breath became audible, a cross between a deep inhale and a sigh. "She says Maiya is with that Jake boy."

"Jake?" Teal's voice rose. "Jake Ford? Since last night?"

"Yeah. They went camping. Up in the forest."

"No!" Her baby spent the night with that delinquent? She was only fifteen! "No!"

"Listen, Teal. We'll sort out all that junk later. Focus on the fact that this means she's most likely fine. There are no reports of damage up that way. Those two are probably scared to death and just trying to get back into the city. Maybe she's home by now."

"He drives a motorcycle!"

"Well, that makes it easier to get through traffic."

"He's nineteen, Shauna! Statutory —"

"Hey, hey. Don't go lawyer on me. We have no clue what happened. Hold on to the good thought that she is safe. She is still your smart Maiya. You take care of River. Amber and I will go over to your house."

"The Yoshidas are there. She's not."

"Well, we'll go and wait with them. I'll keep trying her cell. Now don't worry. We've got you covered. If you want JT to hog-tie that boy until you get there, just say the word and it's done." She referred to her husband, an ex-semipro football player.

Teal halfway considered accepting the offer. "Oh, Shauna. Why would she do such a stupid thing?"

"Why did any of us do such stupid things? Now go. Bye."

Teal hung up the phone and turned to a crowd of expectant faces.

The woman at the front of the line moved toward the phone. "Is she all right?"

Teal shrugged and hurried away.

She understood why she had done such stupid things as a teenager. In a word, she chalked it up to *family.* Why else did kids act out?

But Maiya? What was her problem? Her family consisted of Teal and River, who weren't perfect but they unabashedly loved her and each other. They provided all her needs. To some extent they spoiled her. True, they weren't a traditional family because although they always referred to River as Maiya's dad, he was after all "only" a stepfather. Yet *dysfunctional* had never entered the picture.

Had it?

No matter. It was in the picture now. Familial trust had been ripped apart. Her husband was the one who had brought Jake into their home. He vowed the kid was not dangerous. Her daughter had lied to her about where she had been. Somehow Jake Ford was involved.

Teal could hold it all in for now. But once Maiya showed up and River was alert, she imagined herself going ballistic. Life would never, ever be the same between them again.

Earthquake damage to the support system of a freeway overpass? Tip of the iceberg.

CHAPTER 9

Lacey Janski froze behind the counter, a blackberry pie in her hands. She looked out at the customers in her coffee shop and zeroed in on a white-haired icon of retired local fishermen. "Andy, what did you say?"

The man moved from the table where he had stopped on his way in to greet friends and crossed the room. "Big earthquake down in Los Angeles this morning."

That was what she thought she had heard him say. "Where exactly?"

"I don't know."

"When?"

"Ten o'clock or so."

"How big?"

"Six point — oh, man." His deep voice rumbled. The lines of his weathered face creased into a frown. "I forgot. That's where your sister lives." He stretched across the counter, took the pie from her, and set it

57

down. "You hadn't heard?"

"No." She turned on her heel and strode to the back-room doorway. "Will!" She called out to her husband. "Will!"

He was seated in the far corner at the desk, phone to his ear, speaking softly.

Lacey froze again. How often in recent months had she walked in on Will, phone to his ear, speaking softly?

Softly . . . or furtively?

But it was his business to talk on the phone. They owned the Happy Grounds Coffee and Gift Shop, a small, popular place on the Oregon coast. Ordering coffee and gifts had been a part of their life for twelve years. She hated the telephone. She loved baking. It was an easy division of two major responsibilities. They shared all the others.

"Will!"

He glanced over his shoulder and held up a finger. "That's fine," he spoke into the phone, his tone normal. "I'll get back to you. Good-bye." He hung up. "What's wrong?"

Her heart melted. The question that negated her other one about his phone calls was, how often had she clung to him in recent months like a scared child? He was her rock.

In a flash his arms were around her.

"Lacey?"

"There was an earthquake in Los Angeles." Engulfed in his arms, her face against his denim shirt, she savored the clean scents of laundry detergent and his soap. The weight of his chin atop her head reassured her that he was there. He was there.

Sometimes visitors to the shop were surprised to learn that Lacey and Will were married. At first she thought it was because they were physically mismatched. He was model material for men's underwear ads. Tall, slender with wide shoulders, dark blond, and hazel-eyed, he was — as her mother said — a looker. She, on the other hand, was average in every way, except that she was all nose and mouth and had a coarse, dark-brown horse mane for hair that worked best in a braid when it was long enough.

Her good friend Holly clued her in on what others were saying. "Lacey, you're nuts. People assume you're not married because you and Will are such obviously good friends. Most couples aren't, you know. No way could most of us work together 24-7 like you do. I can't imagine teaching in the same school as my ex."

Lacey did not totally buy into the explanation. If couples weren't friends, why did they bother staying together?

Will kissed the top of her head. "Call her. I'll cover for you."

She nodded and watched him walk into the shop.

It was August, a busy time of year. Two summer employees worked in the gift section, an area that covered the front half of the shop. A waist-high wall separated it from the coffee bar at the back, where there was seating for twenty-two. At three in the afternoon, Will and the college girls could take care of the light traffic.

Teal had not seen the shop since long before Will and Lacey took it over from his parents. Lacey was proud of their homey renovations. She wondered if Teal would think the place more inviting than it had been when they were growing up.

Probably not. It wasn't Teal's style to compliment anything about Cedar Pointe.

Lacey sat down at the desk, picked up the phone, and dialed her sister's cell phone number. Although she seldom called it, she had committed it to memory.

Before it rang, the connection went straight to voice mail.

"Teal, are you all okay? Call me as soon as you can."

She dialed the house number, also at the

tip of her fingers. Again voice mail answered and she left a message. She called Teal's office number. There was no answer.

Lacey whimpered, squeezed her eyes shut, and shook her hands like dust rags. "I can't do this. I can't do this."

Life had become simply too hard in recent months. There was no available nerve ending on which to hang this new stress.

Exactly. She had no place to put this, but others did. And they knew the secret of binding up the stress so that it did not weigh too heavily on their own nerves.

She pulled out the keyboard shelf and moved the mouse. The monitor woke up, and she saw that the computer was connected to the Internet.

She also saw news headlines.

Massive Quake Hits Los Angeles.

She aimed the cursor over the link and hesitated.

Lacey did not need details. She needed help.

She went to her e-mail, composed a short note, and sent it to the addresses of everyone who had ever said to her, "I'm praying for you."

CHAPTER 10

Los Angeles

When Teal returned to River's hallway, she saw someone with a bloodied head bandage lying on the bed.

Her breath caught, but as she neared the figure, she realized it was not River. Where was he?

With effort she waited calmly at the nurses' station until one of them got off the phone. Her effort to remain calm went out the window.

As did the distraught nurse's composure. She informed Teal that River had gone for a CT scan, and no, she was not allowed to follow, and no, she had no guess how long it would take. She also said Teal had no business standing there. The waiting room was the place to wait.

Her heart raced as she made her way back to the pay phone area and stood at the end of the line that now wrapped around chairs and out the door.

Like an unbelievable line for a stupid Disneyland ride.

But maybe it was for the best. Telling River what she had learned from Shauna about Maiya would not exactly comfort him. Reaming him out about that boy Jake would most definitely not comfort him. All of those things could wait until he felt better and she cooled down.

On a normal day she would have chatted with others in line. Today she bit her fingernails and checked her cell phone. Over and over and over.

At last it was her turn to use a pay phone again.

"Hello?"

At the sound of her daughter's fearful voice answering her cell phone, Teal clutched the partition to keep herself upright. "Maiya! Are you all right?"

"Oh, Mommy! Mommy!"

"Shh, hon. We're okay. Where are you?"

"I'm so scared!" Her voice was not lowering from screech level. "I couldn't reach you!"

"I know, but we're talking now. Where are you?"

"I'm coming home, but the traffic is so insane!"

"Mai, exactly *where are you?*"

"Um. Um. I don't know. El Camino and something. At a gas station by that strip mall with Ralphs and Rite Aid." Maiya named an area in the community east of them, typically a thirty-minute drive.

Teal gave up waiting for her daughter to confess. She also gave up aiming for a neutral tone. "Are you on the back of Jake's bike?"

"Oh, Mommy." Things were really bad. Maiya hadn't called her Mommy since she broke her trumpet in the eighth grade. "I'm sorry. I'm sorry."

"Not as sorry as you're going to be, Maiya Marie." *Stupid.* "Honey, I didn't mean that. This is just so awful." She burst into tears.

Then Maiya wailed.

Behind Teal came the loud clearing of a throat. "Hey, lady."

She whipped around and blubbered out, "Hold your horses, mister. I've only been on for two minutes."

So much for disaster bringing out humanity's best.

"Mom! Where are you?"

"At the hospital." Teal glared and turned back around. "River has some broken ribs."

"Oh no!"

"They're doing scans now to make sure

nothing else is damaged inside."

"What happened?"

"The Leaning Tower of Bins fell on him." She took a shaky breath. "Are you wearing a helmet?"

"Y-yes."

"Then just get your rear end home ASAP. Shauna and the Yoshidas are waiting there for you."

"Jake will stay with me —"

"I don't want to see Jake Ford or hear about Jake Ford for a long, long, very long time. He is not welcome in our home. Is that understood?"

"Mom, he's a good guy."

"Maiya Marie, I asked you a question."

"Yeah. I understand, Counselor."

From Mommy to Counselor in less than sixty seconds.

What was going on with her daughter?

Teal sensed that the quake had just exposed a fault line she did not know existed.

Teal found River back in the hallway on a chair, trying to button the filthy short-sleeved white shirt he must have worn to the hospital. His brows went up in a question.

"She's fine."

"Thank God. Is she home?"

65

"On her way." She knelt beside him, pushed aside his fumbling fingers, and buttoned his shirt for him. "What did they say?"

"I'm good to go."

She tilted her head.

He smiled. "Three cracked. No internal damage. If I do something that increases the pain, I should stop doing it. Doc gave me a prescription for pain relievers. The regular stuff helped, though."

"Meaning we'll bypass the pharmacy and go straight home."

"Mm-hmm."

There was no argument to change his mind, so she didn't even try.

She held his gaze for a long moment. His eyes shimmered in a reflection of her own tears.

They were all safe. Nothing else mattered at that moment. *Thank You, God.*

The drive home through empty, dark streets felt eerie. Houses and storefronts appeared intact, but people normally would have still been out and about; shops would have been open.

Teal deflected River's questions about Maiya and told him about her own crazy day. "So now I have BFFs from Dubuque, Iowa, and we have an open invitation to visit them anytime we have a hankering to visit

Field of Dreams or spit in the Mississippi."

"Seriously?"

She caught his little-boy grin. "Uh-oh. I didn't mean to say that part out loud."

"Oh, man." His raspy voice was excited. "Baseball and a phenomenal river I've never seen."

"We'll put it on the bucket list." She slowed and flicked the turn signal as their alley came into sight.

"The garage is full, love."

She glanced at him. "You mean you didn't bother to pick up the plastic tubs?"

His chuckle slid into a groan. "Ouch. Don't make me laugh."

No worries about that once I get hold of Maiya.

The garage opened directly onto the alley. If there was no space inside it, they would have to park on the street out front. Teal drove past the alley entrance and continued on the palm-tree-lined block to their street.

The problem with street parking was that every neighbor had the same kind of old-fashioned, single-car garage and owned at least two vehicles. Car after car after car was parked bumper to bumper along both curbs. She spotted a motorcycle and gripped the steering wheel. If that thing belonged to Jake . . .

"Forget it," she said. "This day just got too long. One way or another, I will make the car fit inside the garage."

"That's my Xena."

"I will not be undone by an earthquake. How lame is that?"

"Attagirl."

A few moments later she reached the garage and tapped the automatic opener. The door rattled up. "Hallelujah, the power is on. Whoa." The headlights illumined empty space. "Do you see what I see?"

"Are we at the wrong garage? Ours never looked this neat."

A few blue plastic bins sat in two short stacks. Elsewhere along a different wall were orderly piles of books and file folders.

They exchanged a glance and said in unison, "Charlie."

Teal blinked her vision clear and drove onto a spic-and-span concrete floor. Her heart felt swept clean as well, free at last of the day's anxiety and anger. They were all okay.

Maybe she would ground Maiya for only half of her life.

CHAPTER 11

River smelled the soup the moment Teal opened the door. Cindy Yoshida's broccoli-chicken-black-bean concoction was a special-event dish.

The woman got that right. Coming home had never felt as special as it did right then.

He followed his wife through the garage door into the house she had welcomed him to share with her when they married. Leaving his bachelor apartment for the warmth of her place had been a no-brainer.

When they first dated, she was in the middle of renovations to the bungalow. Originally the garage had been detached. Teal had it attached by adding a mudroom and family room between it and the kitchen.

He shuffled along behind her, past the washer and dryer and into the family room, a catchall nook for newspapers, books, backpacks, mail, and sweatshirts. It was furnished with a love seat, a couch, and a coffee table. The television was on but muted. River turned from its video of a collapsed overpass lit by garish lights.

A breakfast bar separated the room from the kitchen now filled with the Yoshidas and two of the Prices, a happy, noisy group. Maiya emerged and was immediately lost in Teal's embrace.

His family was safe. His family was safe. *Thank You, God. Thank You.*

He fought back more tears. He did not cry easily. He had a high tolerance for physical pain. Evidently the events of the day had undone him. He sat gingerly on the couch and wiped his shirtsleeve across his face.

His family was safe.

How he loved his girls. He watched them hug, long and hard, rocking back and forth, and was content to wait his turn.

Years ago, Maiya had taken him by surprise. They met when she was a gangly sixth grader with buckteeth who — like her mother — had an impish nose and tilted her head in a cute way, her black hair swinging to one side. She smiled as if she were looking right into his heart, trying to find a spot for herself.

He had one for her. She became the delight of his life. He wished he had known her as a toddler. Now as tall as Teal's five-

70

six, she had outgrown the gawky stage and was finished with the teeth-straightening braces. With adolescence came a budding prettiness and the ability to trip her mother's trigger. River wondered if it was a female thing since he never found himself in her sights.

If he didn't hug her soon, he might start bawling.

From the kitchen, the neighbors smiled at him. Maiya's best friend, Amber, looked terrified. Her mother, Shauna, caught his eye and mouthed, *You okay?*

He nodded.

And then Maiya plopped beside him on the sofa and flung her arms around his neck.

"Oof."

"Riv! Oops, sorry. Oh, Riv! Where does it hurt? Are you all right?"

He winced but held her as tightly as he could. Her long hair was damp and smelled of her shampoo. "I'm fine," he murmured. "So what did you guess, Minnie Mc-Mouse?" It was his special nickname for her, a play on the initials for Maiya Marie Morgan and a reference to their first family outing to Disneyland. "Six point eight when it happened?"

She sat back and stared at him, tears spilling from pretty eyes an unusual shade of dark green. "Mom didn't tell you?"

He sighed to himself. His hunch had been right, then. Teal had been sidestepping talk about Maiya.

His wife was an expert at the ins and outs of truth telling. She would not lie to people, but she chose exactly how much information to reveal and when. It bugged him at times, especially when he was the recipient. She argued it was for his own good, and often in hindsight he could see that it was.

If Teal had withheld something about Maiya, it was because she believed he did not need to hear it right now. She probably thought he was ready to keel over and should go to bed. Tomorrow was soon enough to hear difficult news.

Obviously Maiya could not wait to spill her guts.

A kid needing to talk always trumped personal discomfort, no matter what Teal thought.

He said, "Your mom didn't tell me what?"

"I'm sorry." She hiccupped another sob. "I'm sorry. I'm so sorry."

"About . . . ?"

"Oh, Riv. I didn't feel it."

Her words filtered through grogginess and pain. She didn't feel *what?* The earthquake? No way. Unless . . . unless she had not been

72

where they thought she was. Where she said she would be, at Amber's, a few streets over. Not far from the garage where flying bins had laid him out flat.

It made no sense.

Shauna touched his shoulder. She was an attractive woman with extremely short hair and a smile as big as the outdoors. "I'm glad you're all right." The smile faded. "Amber!" She turned and spoke tersely. "It's time to go."

Amber and Maiya reacted as one and rushed to hug each other. Teal and Shauna watched, their signature glares in place. The divorce attorney and middle school counselor could be scary moms. Their daughters did not stand a chance.

River got the distinct impression that the girls might not see each other again for a very long time. What was going on?

He stood and made it as far as the breakfast bar to say good-byes. Shauna and Amber left quickly; the Yoshidas trailed behind, Cindy still talking.

"I spoke with both of your sisters and several coworkers. Everyone knows you're fine. And they're all fine. So don't worry about returning calls tonight. You need to eat. Have some soup and Shauna's chocolate chip cookies. You'll feel better. I'm coming, Charlie. Okay, good night. We're right next door if you need us." She hurried out the front door and closed it behind her.

River smiled. Cindy always said that when she left, as if they might have forgotten where their neighbors lived. Having grandparent types next door was a hoot and a comfort.

A tremor rolled through the house and the lights flickered.

River met two pairs of frightened eyes. Speechless, no one moved. He stayed leaning against the breakfast bar, Teal stood by the kitchen sink, Maiya at the fridge. It was basically over before it started.

He said, "Two point one."

Maiya's face crumpled and she made a soft mewling sound. She wasn't joining in the game of Guess the Magnitude.

"Whew." Teal unplugged the slow cooker. "Guess the aftershocks aren't over. Well, let's just act normal. Soup, anyone?"

River said, "No thanks."

She looked at him. "You need to go to bed."

He wanted to do nothing else, but exhaustion lined his wife's face and their daughter was having a slow meltdown. He still had not heard where Maiya had been when the quake struck.

Like the aftershocks, the evening was not over.

He walked stiffly across the kitchen. "The most comfortable place I've been all day was the garage floor. Think I'll opt for carpet this time." He touched Teal's shoulder as he passed her. "Let's talk in the living room."

"It can wait." Her eyelids were heavy.

Maiya said, "Yeah, Riv. It can wait."

Ignoring them, he made it to the dining table and held on to a chair as he turned toward the front door. "Maybe somebody could bring me a cookie." He continued past the small entryway and into the living room, another casual space with overstuffed furniture and a fireplace. Windows either side of it overlooked the dark backyard. There were no bookshelves to fall on him.

He lowered himself slowly to the floor and stretched out in the middle of the room. He recalled Charlie's report. He had turned off their gas line earlier, but a neighbor who worked for the power company had checked things and decided it could be turned back on. That meant they had hot water and a clothes dryer. Power was on in their area as well. They were in good shape.

So to speak.

A short while later he had bed pillows

under his head and a plate of cookies within reach. He lay on his back, his feet toward the couch where Teal and Maiya sat at opposite ends. Both of them had changed into T-shirts and flannel pajama pants. Their faces were freshly scrubbed.

River's heart did its funny jig like it always did when Teal's lawyer demeanor dissolved into a sleepy, feminine softness. He loved every side of her personality, but this one most especially made him smile.

She caught his expression. "Don't give me that look. I have never been so angry at you, River Adams."

He blinked. What was she talking about?

"Maiya, tell him what you did."

"Mom! I told you I didn't do anything."

"Oh, good grief. I am not talking about the guy getting to home base. I'm talking about the lie. Your lie. You did not go to Amber's last night after work, did you?"

Maiya's lower lip trembled. "No. I'm sorry," she whispered. "I lied."

"Tell us where you did go and with whom."

Totally in the dark, River bit back an *Objection! Badgering the witness.* Teal knew better than to use this approach. Maiya always balked and they got nowhere.

Maiya pouted. "You know everything.

76

Shauna told you because Amber told her."

"Don't you dare blame Amber for breaking a confidence. I was losing my mind worrying about you. How did I know you weren't lying under some rubble somewhere? I didn't know where River was or that he was hurt. You do realize phones were not working, right? I couldn't —"

"Ladies, please," River interrupted. "Can we cut to the chase? Maiya, where were you?"

Myriad expressions crossed her face, from confusion to defensiveness to a snarl that was all but audible profanity.

He almost wished for another aftershock to scare her into sensibleness.

At last the daughter he trusted showed up, the one who spoke forthrightly and did not hide behind the mask of "cool" when he needed an answer. "I went camping up in the national forest." She pressed her lips together for a long moment and then took a shaky breath. "With Jake Ford."

Jake Ford.

A heavy-duty aftershock would have been good right about now, one that split open the ground and swallowed River whole.

CHAPTER 12

I went camping up in the national forest. With Jake Ford.

A tiny part of Teal had clung to the hope that Amber had gotten Maiya's story wrong. Hearing her daughter admit to it set off a fresh round of explosive emotions: anger, disbelief, sadness, guilt, fear.

Probably every ugly emotion there was to feel.

A female cop lived down the street. She had a rape kit.

But she was probably on duty with every other emergency worker in the city. And besides, Maiya had already bathed before Teal had gotten home.

What was she thinking? This was her *daughter.* This could not be happening.

River's eyes were shut. The furrowed brow expressed a deeper pain than from cracked bones.

Maiya's legs were curled underneath her.

She held a small pillow tightly against her stomach.

Teal kept her voice soft. "Mai, did Jake hurt you?"

"Mom! No!"

"He's nineteen. You're fifteen. Even if you consented, you know what that means."

Maiya huffed. "I know what that means. He knows what that means. It wasn't like that at all."

"What was it like?" Teal cringed, wishing to unsay the quick retort.

"It was like camping with you and Riv. We hiked. We cooked hot dogs. We slept in a tent. In separate sleeping bags."

"You carried a tent and sleeping bags on a two-hour motorcycle ride?"

Maiya's chin went up and she started to roll her eyes but had the good sense to blink instead. "He keeps stuff at a primitive campsite. He knows all about surviving in the wilderness."

Because River taught him. She cut her eyes to the still figure on the floor. His jaw muscle worked.

"Mom, Riv — we just hung out, I swear. I'm not like you, Mom."

Teal steeled herself, but the innuendo hurt. She had made some idiotic choices as a teenager, the typical high school experiments with alcohol and pot. Obviously she'd had a baby out of wedlock at twenty-two. Given that Maiya was that baby, the sex-ed lesson it provided had always been a tight-rope walk. *I never regretted having you, but I regret not waiting for the right man.*

She took a deep breath. "This is not about me. Did he pick you up after work?"

"Stop with the interrogation already! I said I lied. I said I'm sorry. Okay? What more do you want? Jake and I are good friends. That's all. Why won't you believe me?"

"Maybe because you lied about what you were doing last night. Maybe because you broke two of the very few rules we've given you: no motorcycles and no dating. Now answer the question. Did Jake pick you up after work?"

"What does that have to do with anything?"

Teal studied Maiya's defiant expression. She saw her lips quiver. *Oh no.* "You didn't go to work."

Her whole chin quivered now. She shook her head.

"Oh, Maiya."

Her daughter adored her summer job. She, Amber, and another friend worked at The Olde Ice Cream Shoppe, an ice cream parlor owned by the friend's parents. It was a happy place that young families frequented. Customers ordered at the counter; waitstaff delivered goodies to the tables. The best part was the singing. Every so often the staff paused in what they were doing and sang a song together. Sometimes Maiya even played "Happy Birthday" on her trumpet.

"I dropped you off at work." Teal remembered driving through the mall parking lot, winding her way to the entrance nearest the Shoppe's location. Maiya hopped out, dressed in her uniform of blue jeans and colorful striped blouse. She carried her backpack, presumably for the sleepover at Amber's. "You said you were scheduled to work."

"I wasn't," Maiya murmured in a low voice.

Lie number two. Who was this girl?

Teal felt ill. While their daughter was probably in a mall public restroom changing shirts, Teal was swinging by the market to buy halibut for a romantic dinner with River. Being a semi-newlywed with a teen in the house presented challenges. If Maiya was away for the night, Teal went overboard in the romantic department.

She wondered if that sweet memory was

81

gone along with the mother-daughter sense of trust.

"Maiya." River's voice was whisper soft. "How long have you and Jake been dating?"

"We're not dating."

He opened his eyes. "Since when have you been good friends?"

Maiya blinked rapidly. Tears clung to her lashes.

He sighed. "Minnie McMouse, we love you. You can't do anything to make us love you any more or any less. You know that, right?"

She nodded.

She should know it. River told her that so frequently, it should be embedded in her brain.

He said, "This lying isn't like you. Sneaking around behind our backs is not like you. Please, tell us everything so we can figure out what's broken between you and us."

Teal's eyes stung. The sight of him loving their daughter always put a lump in her throat. The response was part gratitude, part sorrow that she had never known such fatherly love.

River said, "Hon, what's going on with you and Jake?"

Maiya pressed the pillow to her face and lowered it. "We-we're friends." She swallowed. "You know, he just gets me. We're in sync. I swear, that's all."

"For how long?"

She shrugged. "Since . . . since . . ."

Since he worked here. Teal completed the sentence.

River said, "Since I hired him to help me do the yard."

Teal wanted to slap her hands over her ears and hum loudly.

Jake had been a student at River's school, one more on-his-last-chance delinquent sent to San Sebastian to either get his head on straight or not.

Of course the *or not* usually showed up after they left the school. Teal did not care about the high success rates. There was always that small percentage who did not make it.

Jake's record included burglary, theft, larceny, drug possession. In his regular high school, he had spent more time suspended than in class. No surprise, his dad was in prison for manslaughter, and his alcoholic mom had been in and out of rehab since Jake was a baby.

Every mother's dream guy for her daughter.

Teal perceived his charming allure, though. He was a friendly kid. Tousled-red-haired-boy cute, once she got past his body art. Tattoo "sleeves" covered his arms, colorful mazelike designs from shoulder to wrist. He was tall, sinewy, and strong as an ox, the perfect choice to help River tear out the front-yard sod and haul in rock.

Teal wished she had never heard of water conservation.

River said, "That was in March. You connected in March. Five months ago."

Teal felt like she had been punched in the stomach. "You've been seeing each other on the sly for five months?"

"He's a great guy!" Maiya said. "You know he is, Riv."

"What I know," River answered, "is that at this point in your life, he is too old for you. Period."

"I'm almost sixteen!"

"He's too old for you." His voice had gotten raspy again. "You have to trust us on this one. Finish high school and then we'll visit the subject again. In the meantime, I can't allow you to see him or talk to him." He looked at Teal. "Sorry if I jumped the gun."

"No. I totally agree."

"But I love him!" Maiya wailed. "He loves me!"

They were just good friends? Lie number three.

River said, "I'm sure you do. And I mean that sincerely."

"Then why can't we see each other? I won't lie anymore. I promise!"

"I'll tell you why." River closed his eyes. "When I was nineteen, I loved a sixteen-year-old. She was one hot chick and super straight. I didn't care if she was still in high school. I was surfing and flipping burgers. I could wait for her to get out of class and do her homework. No big deal. You know what I really wanted, Maiya?"

"What?" she murmured, her tone hesitant.

Like Teal, she probably heard the steel in River's voice. It slipped in now and then, turning his gentle tenor into a lifeless monotone. It was the voice he used to describe something so far removed from their world as to be unimaginable.

Teal felt herself cringing.

River went on. "What I really wanted was to have sex with a virgin."

"Jake's not like that!"

River's eyes opened to mere slits. "That's what this girl told her parents." His smile was repulsive. "I was a great guy."

"Oh!" Maiya sprang to her feet and rushed

toward the hallway. "I hate you! I hate you both!"

Teal sat quietly, returning River's gaze.

Maiya's bedroom door slammed.

He said, "Was that over the top?"

She shook her head and moved to the floor, stretching alongside him, her head in the crook of her arm. "More powerful than my 'you don't want to do what I did' routine." She paused. "Was it true?"

"Mm. Close enough. I'll have a talk with Jake."

"That would be good."

"I'm sorry. I should have been on top of this."

"You said he wasn't dangerous. You've never brought a dangerous one home."

"I've never brought home a convicted felon. They're all potentially dangerous to our little girl."

"Who's not so little anymore. Of course she's had crushes on older boys forever, but this scenario makes no sense. Secretly seeing him and talking with him over the course of five months? And spending the night on a campout two hours from home? What is going on with her, River?"

"I don't know, love. I don't know."

Teal gathered pillows and blankets and

tapped on Maiya's bedroom door. "Slumber party, Mai. Five minutes."

"Popcorn?" came the muffled reply.

"Sure."

" 'Kay."

Teal dropped her armload on the sofa and looked down at River, out cold on the floor. He said he preferred the hard surface to the bed. That was fine with her. After the day she'd had, she would sleep anywhere as long as it was next to him.

She covered him with a blanket and went into the kitchen. While the microwave nuked popcorn, she stood at the breakfast bar with the television remote and channel-surfed.

Videos of the overpass played on every single station.

She heard the shuffle of Maiya's slippered feet across the tile floor. Teal raised her arm and Maiya slid under it, snuggling close.

"I'm sorry, Mom."

"I know." Teal kissed her daughter's cheek, red from crying. "And I'm sorry, but I have decided to reattach the umbilical cord."

"That's not funny."

"You're telling me."

Teal felt something shift between them. A sense of dread crept around her heart.

Ever since Maiya first pressed into misbehavior territory as a tyke, Teal meted out discipline with heavy doses of love and forgiveness. Her days at the office were too full of sad stories about families who never bothered with those things.

Much like her own parents.

But this one scared Teal. This was adult time. Maiya wasn't sneaking into an R-rated movie or disrespecting her or River. She wasn't blowing off homework or stealing her aunt's cigarette and smoking it with Amber.

No. Maiya was setting herself up for un-imaginably deep regret that she would have to live with every single day for the rest of her entire life.

Teal wrapped Maiya in a hug and buried her face in her hair.

For fifteen and a half years this beautiful child had been the only facet of Teal's life that made her own unimaginably deep regret bearable.

And yet . . . she would not wish such a plight on anyone. She would fight tooth and nail to protect anyone from taking the path of raising a child alone.

She cupped Maiya's face in her hands and looked into eyes the color of a spruce tree on a cloudy day. "I love you."

"We did not have sex."

"I believe you." Teal kissed her forehead

and let go. "Butter?"

"And sprinkle cheese."

Wordlessly they prepared two bowls of cheesy buttered popcorn and carried them into the family room. They sat on the love seat, a double recliner, and pulled up the footrests. The newscast was showing a block of storefronts with collapsed roofs.

Teal said, "We should watch something else."

"I couldn't find anything else on my TV."

"You were watching TV in your bedroom?"

"Yeah."

"Hm. That's usually on the banned list."

"Riv didn't say no TV."

"You left the room prematurely. The discussion wasn't exactly over."

"I don't hate you two."

"We know." Teal sighed, eyes glued to the television. "This is such a tragedy. I can't tell you how grateful I am that we are at home. And that Aunt Jen and Uncle Aaron are in Paris and all of our friends are safe. But the city is not going to recover from this overnight. Did they just say three hundred presumed dead?"

"That's what I heard. Lots of them at that overpass. What was it like downtown?"

Teal slowly chewed a few bites of popcorn

and set her bowl on the end table. She wiped her hand on a napkin. The diversionary tactic was not working. She and Maiya could eat comfort food until it came out of their ears, but they could not ignore reality. "I wasn't at the office."

"Then where were you?"

"At that overpass. I —" Her throat closed up. She whispered, "I watched it come down."

Maiya — the little girl for whom she had been so strong for so long — embraced her as if she were a baby. The daughter's shoulder muffled the mother's cries, her shirt soaked up the mother's tears until there were no more.

CHAPTER 13

Cedar Pointe

As if waking up from a deep sleep, Lacey became aware of a shadow blocking the sunlight. She blinked and the coffee shop came into focus, the entire space aglow from rays streaming through the front windows.

The shadow was Will, waving his hand at her from across the noisy, crowded room. He mouthed the word *go.* His brows rose as if the movement could push her away from the counter.

She gave him a petulant look and put a fist on her hip, pretending to be annoyed.

He smiled and turned again to the table where early-morning regulars sat discussing the latest Cedar Pointe gossip.

Lacey glanced at the ornate cuckoo clock on the side wall, wishing the bird would poke out his head and chirp eight times. She had promised herself to wait until then. Seven twenty seemed too early.

But Will had caught her spacing out, her hand stilled on the sliding window of the pastry case as if she intended to open it.

Okay. So she was probably less helpful standing there than not standing there. Will and their two employees were perfectly capable of covering for her. If things got too crazy, a few of the regulars would pitch in and serve the tourists. Andy the retired guy made better macchiatos than anyone.

So why did she hesitate?

Because Teal still intimidated her.

Lacey wiped her hands on the dish towel hanging at her waist and headed into the back room. Worming her way into the graces of the sister she had not seen in nine years was pure ridiculousness.

She sat at the desk and dialed Teal's house number. It rang only once.

"Hello. Lacey?"

The wonders of caller ID.

"Hi, Teal. Oh." She breathed the word, suddenly unable to speak.

"Yeah, I know." Teal exhaled loudly. "But we're okay."

"Your neighbor told me last night, but I needed to hear it from you. I didn't mean to call so early, but I just could not wait another minute."

"No worries. An aftershock got us going

about five this morning."

Lacey listened as Teal told her what had happened the previous day, how Teal had been in the car, out of touch with River and Maiya for hours, River's broken ribs. Her stomach knotted more and more with each horrid detail. "Is it safe to stay there?"

"Who knows? It's earthquake country, as safe as ever, I guess. We're staying home today. The news says the city is basically shut down, what with all the power outages and cleanup."

"The aftershocks —"

"Are scary, but they're lessening in strength and number."

"Oh, Teal! Why don't you come home?"

A heavy silence settled between them.

Once every few years or so, Lacey spouted the question to her sister in a fit of emotion. The first time had been when Lacey was twelve. Teal was in Portland, a college freshman, making plans to spend Christmas with a friend's family in Seattle. It was where Teal had gone for that Thanksgiving.

Another time Lacey asked it, she was seventeen. Teal, twenty-two and long gone to California by then, had phoned to say she had given birth to a baby girl and named her Maiya.

"Lacey," Teal said now.

She braced herself. Teal's responses were always caustic. "If I wanted to be there, I wouldn't be here, would I? I'm raising a child by myself; I do not have the time nor the money for travel. River is my home. I really, really do not care to hear Randi and Owen tell me what a lousy daughter I was and still am."

Which explained why it took Lacey years to gather enough gumption to repeat the question.

Teal sighed.

Sighed? For real?

"I appreciate that, Lacey Jo." It was an old nickname. "I really do. But we'll be fine. We can't run away from the mess right now. Our friends and coworkers and — and, well, the three of us just need to regroup and stick together. Does that make sense?"

"Yeah." What didn't make sense was the hesitancy in her sister's voice. "But if you need to get away at all, Will and I are here. And my friend's aunt bought those cottages just off the 101 on Juniper. She'll give us a deal. Remember them?"

"The Moonbeam Cottages."

She remembered?

They reminisced about the town and all

that had not changed. It was a brief ex-change.

But very, very un-Teal-like.

CHAPTER 14

Los Angeles

Teal set the cordless phone on the counter. Her little sister was an oddball. No matter how many months passed between phone conversations, she always spoke as if they enjoyed a normal relationship. Unlike Teal, she even sent cards for birthdays and every holiday on the calendar, including Passover and Kwanzaa.

"Mom." Maiya stood nearby, stirring pancake batter in a large mixing bowl. "Does this look right?"

"Mm-hmm." She cut open a package of bacon. They were full-on into food with high fat content.

"What did you just call Aunt Lacey?"

Teal bristled as she always did whenever Maiya referred to *Aunt* Lacey. It was too intimate a title for someone her daughter had met only once, nine years ago. They seldom even spoke besides the occasional

96

"Hi, how's it going, here's Mom."

And it was too much like a bucket of guilt being dumped over Teal's head.

Maiya said, "Lacey Jo?"

"Old nickname."

"I get it. For Lacey Joanna. What did they call you?"

They as in the parents? Their nickname would be *worthless, no-good slut.*

Maiya took the bacon package and peeled off slices, laying them in a pan. "Teal Susanna. Hm. Teal Sue doesn't have the same ring."

Teal didn't have the same ring as Lacey in any way, shape, or form. "Lacey called me Tealie Sue."

"Cute."

There had been absolutely nothing cute about Teal's childhood. Even a special name her half sister called her carried a certain amount of pain with it. "Not as cute as Minnie McMouse."

Maiya flashed her a smile. Her eyes twinkled.

Teal felt a rush of gratitude. Not only was her daughter safe, she must be truly, deepdown fine. She could not possibly fake such happiness if she and Jake Ford were intimate. Maiya may have gotten away with lies, but Teal would know if something that profound had occurred.

Wouldn't she?

"Hey." River walked into the kitchen, his hair damp from a shower. He had awakened in much less pain than the night before, and now the forehead creases were all but smoothed out. "I thought I smelled bacon."

Maiya said, "Yeah. Mom's pancakes are coming too."

"Great. I don't remember eating yesterday."

"Did you know she has a nickname? Tealie Sue."

"No way."

"For real."

They both turned toward her.

"What?" she said.

"It's endearing," he said.

Maiya nodded. "Exactly. You should call her that, Riv."

Teal locked eyes with him and willed him to intuit much more than he could possibly know. He and Maiya had been told little about her history beyond "My childhood stunk." Why burden them with sordid details of dysfunction at its finest?

River gave his head a slight shake. "I think I'll just stick with my own nickname for her."

Maiya rolled her eyes and turned her attention to the sizzling bacon. "You mean Xena? Ha. That is so lame, Riv. Lame, lame, lame."

Teal heard the tease in Maiya's voice and saw the warmth in River's smile. Tears stung. She stepped to the counter and turned on the griddle. "Lacey called to check on us."

"That was thoughtful of her."

"She invited us up to get away for a while." Her back to them, she poured oil on the cooker and chose a spatula from the red utensil holder. "Getting away might not be a half-bad idea after all. Maybe we could go camping tomorrow, make it a long weekend."

"Mom, you don't like camping."

"Suddenly it sounds comforting. The camper beats huddling in here, waiting for the next rumble to shake the house. And the three of us alone reconnecting as a family is exactly what we need."

The puzzled expressions behind her were almost audible.

No, she did not care for camping. But River's compact RV, which he kept parked at his school, made it tolerable. Cooking was a hassle and the bathroom a bad dream. Yet sharing close quarters with the daughter who had gone south and the injured husband would be worth every inconvenience.

"Sooo," Maiya drawled, "Cedar Pointe is not a possibility?"

Been there, done that, Teal wanted to snap.

They had visited once. Maiya was six years old, and Teal was a newbie in the area of faith. Overwhelmed with a sense of God's love for her, Teal had been eager to share the grace she had experienced.

There had been no other way to explain her life apart from that. The birth of her perfect baby, the care poured onto them by the neighbor Maiya called Gammy Jayne, Jayne's church, the finances, the ability to finish her law degree, the plum job . . . the release from a lifetime of guilt and shame. Those things were sheer gifts.

Teal still wondered where God had been during that disastrous visit to Oregon. Her mother, Randi, and stepdad, Owen, did not receive Teal or Maiya with open arms. They did not want to hear about Teal's need to escape her past and live in LA. They had no memory of Owen's whippings nor of Randi's knack of looking the other way nor of any alcohol abuse whatsoever.

Lacey was caught in the crossfire, as always an innocent bystander. Teal's remorse over their history grew too heavy. She hugged Lacey good-bye, apologized for being the world's poorest excuse for a big sister, and never went back to Cedar Pointe. She had no desire to ever go back.

But her daughter might. Someday.

Teal felt River's hands on her stiffened shoulders, his gentle touch urging them downward from her ears, which they had crept up toward.

In the throes of emotions still running high, Teal took a chance to find out if "someday" had arrived. She looked at Maiya. "Do you want Cedar Pointe to be a possibility?"

Maiya crinkled her nose in disgust. "Are you kidding me? Grounded in Camp Poppycock, Oregon?" It was Teal's reference to Cedar Pointe. "I remember it as freezing cold and rainy. I bet they don't have Internet or satellite TV or any TV. Probably not even cell service. Aunt Lacey and Uncle Will just stand around all day and make coffee. No thank you. I'd take primitive camping over that anytime. Mom, the oil is smoking."

River reached around Teal and turned down the griddle. "I suggest we stay put for now and not make any rash decisions about anything, not even camping for the weekend. We're all, understandably, a little on edge." He took the spatula from her, nudging her aside.

"On edge" was putting it mildly. Teal had not slept for twenty minutes at a stretch throughout the night. Lying on the carpet between him and Maiya, she dreamed in a half-alert state of the freeway overpass, the Iowans, the sirens, the chaos. She would awaken fully, touch Maiya and River, pad out to the family room, check the TV news, go back, and lie down. Then she would begin the entire process again.

River poured batter from the spouted bowl onto the hot griddle, making six uniform puddles.

She rested her chin against his shoulder and watched him cook. He had not shaved since yesterday. If he skipped another twenty-four hours, his face would darken with the beginnings of a full beard.

She said, "If we go camping, I promise not to mention how I feel about men who hide behind beards."

He grinned his half grin, a yummy expression that made her want to tease him until the other side of his mouth went up, revealing his teeth and laugh lines. "How do you feel about men who can't do much beyond cook pancakes?"

"Love 'em. They would let Xena and Xena Junior drive the camper, chop the wood, carry boxes of food, hook up the wires and pipes and propane and all that stuff."

He laughed.

"Mom," Maiya said, "we can do it the easy way. Take the tent and little grill with charcoal. That's all Jake had at his campsite, and we got along just fine."

Teal held up a finger and closed her eyes.

"What? What'd I say?"

River cleared his throat. "Too much, too soon."

By 8:30 a.m., the day felt as long as a week. Teal considered driving downtown to the office and getting lost in work.

They'd had The Discussion with Maiya. Their pronouncement that, yes — despite the fact that they were all safe and she had not imbibed, smoked, or had sex — she was still grounded indefinitely. The unspecified time limit was River's idea. Teal had wanted to go with a year.

The earlier twinkle in her eye long gone, Maiya had left the breakfast table in a major huff to be alone in her bedroom, about the only activity she was allowed beyond eating and working at the ice cream parlor. They didn't have the heart to tell her kitchen cleanup was still allowed and expected.

Teal sat now on the family room floor next to the couch where River had stretched out. She faced the television, which in spite of their agreement to turn it off, still played nonstop local news.

She said, "Should I hide her cell phone and laptop?"

"No. We need to trust her to some extent. Just put them away in our room."

"What about her television?"

"It's too heavy for you to move. She knows it's off limits. Again, the trust factor comes into play. Though she may need to watch some news today, like we do."

Teal listened to a man on the screen describe how his house became the pile of rubble visible behind him. "I don't understand why I want to watch this."

"Because it's our world. We've all been affected, the entire city. We want to come together as a community and comfort each other."

"We're not being voyeuristic?"

"Are you enjoying a sick sort of fun while this guy talks about everything he lost?"

"No. But I must admit that a part of my brain is registering that there will be a ripple effect in families. The strain is going to push some marriages to the breaking point, and they won't make it. Others are going to decide they need to write that will they've been meaning to for years. Some single dad is going to rethink his visitation rights. All of which means more business for me. Isn't that awful?"

"It's reality. You've never been in the business for the money."

That was true. The income was a necessity, of course, but the law fascinated her. It kept her going. To see it in motion as it helped those who hurt was her passion.

River touched her hair. "Speaking of ripple effects, the earthquake prompted your sister to call."

She turned to him. "Your point?"

"And now we have Tealie Sue. Want to tell me?"

Her throat went dry and she shook her head.

"Love . . ." River pressed with such tenderness. Not responding to his compassion was kind of like telling God to take a hike.

Which she had been known to do on occasion.

River said, "Owen called you that." It was a statement.

Her husband was a smart guy.

When Teal was four, Owen Pomeroy had married her mother. Lacey was born soon after. From the beginning Teal refused to refer to him as her stepdad. He was always Owen, and at some point her mother became Randi, short for Miranda. Owen never adopted her. A huge blessing, in her mind. There would never be any legal ramifications with the scuzzball.

"Yeah." She sighed. "I've told you how Lacey was so cute and funny when she was little. How everyone adored her. Well, she even got a special name, Lacey Jo, from our mom. I was six, not cute, not funny, not adored, so I nicknamed myself Tealie Sue. Lacey liked it. I told everyone at school that was my new name. Owen the moron got wind of it and made it his term of endearment." She smirked. "Which was helpful, in a way. It gave me a heads-up that he was about to ridicule me or smack me."

"Oh, Teal."

"Hey, it's not a big deal. I covered this ages ago. I actually hadn't given it a thought in years." She smiled. "God's honest truth."

River wrapped an arm around her neck and kissed her forehead. "God's honest truth, you are not only cute and funny and adored, you are beautiful inside and out."

He had said the words before, whittling away at those other words planted by her stepdad. On some days she imagined River's were the true ones.

"And one more thing," he said. "I love you."

She laughed and kissed him. Those were the words she could believe any day.

CHAPTER 15

"Mr. Hinson died!" The blonde teen, a friend of Maiya's, announced the news loudly, her dark eyes wide and her chin trembling, right there in the middle of Shoe Place. "A wall collapsed on him!"

As Teal watched the girls whimper and hug each other, she murmured to herself, "Where do I go to resign?"

Just when she thought the earthquake stories could not get any sadder, a new one slammed into her heart with debilitating fury. Mr. Hinson taught math at the middle school. Even now as high schoolers, the girls thought of him with fondness. He was like that.

Had been like that.

The mother of Maiya's friend touched Teal's arm. She couldn't remember the woman's name, but it didn't matter. They exchanged subdued hellos and began the dialogue that had become commonplace the past three days with friends and strangers alike. "Is your family all right? Where were you when it struck?"

Eventually she and Maiya made their way outside to the car with new shoes for marching band and a pair of everyday sandals for school. It was only because of her growing feet that Maiya had been granted a reprieve to exit the house.

Well, that and Teal's stir-craziness. Like most of her coworkers and much of the city, she was doing work from home or putting it on hold. Not that she wanted to stray too far from Maiya and River yet. Aftershocks had lessened in numbers and strength, but they were still strong enough to rattle her nerves.

"Mom —" Maiya spoke over the top of the car — "why can't I drive?"

"Honey, if you say 'Why can't I' one more time, I swear I'm going to lose it. Do you really want me to explain again why you have no privileges?"

Maiya huffed and tossed her head. Her long hair bounced over her shoulder.

Teal got into the car and shut her door.

Maiya slid in from her side. "But you know I have to get in more practice time so I can get my driver's license in October." She slammed the door angrily. "It's like schoolwork. You wouldn't say I can't do homework."

"Those are not the same at all. Driving is a privilege you earn by being trustworthy." She put the key in the ignition and sat back with a sigh to look at her scowling daughter. "Less arguing might convince the jury to commute this part of the sentence."

"Oh, ha-ha." She crossed her arms and stared straight ahead. "From the counselor herself."

Teal studied Maiya's pretty face, so incongruent with the ugly words she had been spouting in recent days. River's insight came to mind: they were all on edge. They needed to cut each other a lot of slack.

But still . . .

"Maiya, rudeness is not winning you any points."

She flounced around to face Teal. "You know what? I'm a little tired of trying to win points with you."

Teal blinked in surprise at the personal attack. Teenage snippy sank to a new low.

Maiya went on. "How could I have told you about my feelings for Jake? Both you and Riv are totally into losers. It's what you both do for a living. But can I hang out with kids who drink or smoke pot? Can I bring home a Goth or a skater? No way."

"Jake's a delinquent."

"Was. He graduated from Saint Sibs with flying colors. He's got a great job. Why can't you give him a chance to prove himself?"

"Because you're fifteen and he's nineteen."

"Honestly, Mom! You're thirty-seven and Riv's forty-two!"

Teal wanted to laugh at the ludicrous reasoning, but she held back, a habit developed through the years. She had always encouraged Maiya to speak her mind and stand her ground if she did so politely.

Despite the lack of *politely* now, Teal had to let her go on. Maiya obviously needed to get some things off her chest.

The very situation Teal had been hoping for, avoiding, and dreading.

"Maiya, if you had told me you had a crush on Jake, I would have said that's natural. You're a young woman, attracted to boys. Crushes and puppy love make us feel alive and happy."

"But you would have said he's off limits."

"Of course. And hindsight now shows us his true colors aren't of the flying sort, which explains why I would have said he's off limits, right? He picked you up in secret on his motorcycle and took you camping overnight. Think about it. A mature guy would have spoken to River, who happens to be his mentor, a close confidant, and said, 'I want to date your daughter.' "

"Like that would have made a difference."

"It would have. Trust me, I'd have been monitoring every single one of your calls and e-mails."

"Is that what your mom should have done so you wouldn't have gotten pregnant with me?"

Keeping up with Maiya's rant was giving Teal whiplash. She shifted mentally from Jake to her pregnancy. "Honey, you know I was twenty-two, way past being monitored by my mom."

"Then you were old enough not to do such a dumb thing."

Teal set her jaw. The crux was always there, and she had no new way of explaining it. "Yes, it was a dumb thing to have sex at that time."

Maiya gazed at her. The deep-green eyes carried shades of Bio Dad's. The confusion in them stemmed from hormones, earthquakes, and a teacher's death.

Teal placed a hand on her arm. "I was independent and stubborn. Sleeping with your birth father was my choice. It was his choice not to be ready to be a dad and a husband. It was my choice to be the best mom possible. I loved and wanted you from the moment I knew you were growing inside of me. The rest did not matter."

"Really?"

She smiled gently. "Maiya, I've always told you that, and I'll say it as often as you want to hear it. Yes, really."

"But he didn't want me."

"He wasn't ready."

"Same thing. You don't have to protect my feelings anymore, Mom. I'm almost sixteen. I get it. Big whoop." The shaky voice undermined the brave words. "Most kids at school come from broken homes. At least they've *met* both parents, though. About the only thing I know is I have my dad's green eyes."

Well, there was no denying that. Teal's eyes were light gray. "Mm-hmm."

"My ears are different from yours too." Biology class last year had provided this new tidbit. She pulled on a lobe. "See? Attached. I must have his."

"Maybe."

"Was he handsome?"

Teal fiddled with the steering wheel, wishing to drive off and leave the conversation squished under the tires. "I've told you before."

"Tell me again. Tell me more besides he

113

was good-looking and you met him on a beach in Oregon. What else?"

"Honey, there is nothing else."

"What beach? Did he go to the same college you did?" Her voice rose and she flounced on the seat. "Where did you go on dates? What color was his hair? Did he play an instrument? Did he like the trumpet?"

"Maiya, calm down."

"Mom!" Her eyes widened. "You could have been killed in that earthquake!"

Huh? "But I wasn't."

"But what if you were? I wouldn't even know my dad's name! I would never ever know his name. I could never meet him."

Teal shook her head. "It's best that you don't."

"Maybe he's looking for me! Maybe he's looking for you. Maybe he still loves you."

Teal breathed in and out, in and out, steeling herself. She would not feed this romantic fantasy. "All right, Maiya. I'll tell you some things I haven't wanted to say because I don't want his character to affect how you see yourself. Does that make sense?"

She nodded.

"He did not love me, hon. And I didn't love him. We truly did not care about each other."

"But you made love."

"We had sex. Call it lust or craving any attention that resembled love. Call it plain old dysfunctional behavior. I'm afraid there was no love involved."

The hurt on Maiya's face tempted her to soften the facts.

But she couldn't. "I did not want him in our lives. He was bad news. Shoplifting, burglary, other so-called minor offenses. Soon after you were born, they finally locked him up for disorderly conduct."

Maiya flinched as if she'd been slapped.

"Honey, there is no romance in the story. He's not a prince or part of a famous family." She reached out and smoothed Maiya's hair. "But hey, who needs a prince when we have River, huh?"

Tears seeped from Maiya's eyes. "It's not the same. Oh, Mommy, it's not the same."

Teal pulled her daughter to herself and hugged as tightly as she could over the console.

And she admitted silently to herself that no, it was not the same, not even with River Adams for a stepdad.

CHAPTER 16

River found Teal on the back patio, aiming the hose at an enormous potted geranium that she had babied for years. He paused in the doorway and feasted his eyes on his wife in shorts and sleeveless top. She was one good-looking woman with feminine curves and, in unguarded moments like this, a vulnerability that made him think she needed him.

Teal moved the hose to a tomato plant and noticed him standing there. "Did you talk to him?"

River smiled and went over to her. "Hello to you, too."

"Sorry." She turned off the sprayer and met his kiss. "Hi."

"Rough day with the caged tiger?"

"I want to go on record as saying that grounding a teenager is ludicrous." She shook her head. "I had to get out of here, so we went shoe shopping. We ran into a friend of Maiya's who told us that Paul Hinson died in the quake."

"Oh no. The math teacher?"

"Yeah. One thing led to another and another, and just now I caved in and let her call Amber, after I okayed it with Shauna. I set the timer for twenty minutes. I hate being a prison warden. Did you talk to him?"

"Let's sit down." They settled onto padded chairs at the round patio table. He tried not to wince at the movement. Driving had been a challenge, but three days away from the school was his limit. Losing immediacy with the boys happened in a heartbeat. In his work, it was not something he could afford.

He saw the strain on Teal's face and stroked her hands clenched atop the table. "Yes, I talked to Jake. He showed up at my office like I asked him to do."

"And?"

"He apologized profusely, claimed he was in love, but promised not to contact our minor daughter. Teal, what's wrong? You're rattled over more than the Jake business and Maiya straining at the bit."

She shrugged, but her leg bounced like a jackhammer and then her face crumpled. "Yeah. She was asking about Bio Dad. More than ever. I guess all this trauma triggered something."

River went silent. Maiya's birth father was a touchy subject between them.

Touchy? It was a major sore spot that usually sparked an argument. The guy's name was not even on Maiya's birth certificate. River's opinion had always been that Maiya should know his name and everything else about him that was age appropriate. Why hide so much from her? And him, for that matter. Keeping Bio Dad a mystery only aggravated Maiya's emotions. It was a miracle she had not acted out more before now.

River pulled at his collar. Heat was definitely growing underneath it.

In the early days he had wanted to adopt Maiya. Shoot, he still did. But that would require Teal to contact Bio Dad and get his permission. She refused. Just absolutely refused. No matter how much she wanted that for River and Maiya, she said it was not possible.

She couldn't find him? No, she could probably find him. Then what? "I know what's best for us, River. Please trust me." End of discussion.

River could not understand it. Obviously the guy had been a part of Teal's life. Or maybe not. He sometimes wondered if it had been a one-night stand. Maybe he had date-raped her. River privately named him the sperm donor. Whatever the whole truth was, Teal kept it to herself.

She said now, "I finally told her about him being in jail."

River exhaled the breath he'd been holding. This much he knew. "She's probably old enough to learn that."

"But I threw it in her face. Worse than the jail thing, I admitted that we didn't love each other, didn't have any feelings for each other. I had to nip her silly romantic notions in the bud. She needs to realize that there was nothing special between us."

River knew that as well. Maiya had been conceived a short while before Teal graduated from college. It was during her years of dark rage, when she fought tooth and nail to leave her family and make it through the world on her own. She was too busy, too focused to be promiscuous. Working two or three jobs, graduating in the top two percent of her college class. The guy remained an inexplicable blip in her tale of gaining freedom and independence

Teal leaned forward and rested her face on the back of his hand. "There was nothing even remotely special between us. What is she supposed to do with roots like that,

River? How can she feel like anything except worthless?"

"She has you and me to convince her otherwise."

Teal looked up at him, her eyes too sad. "I don't understand why you're not enough dad for her. We never even could call you 'stepdad.'"

"Oh, Teal, you know." He touched her cheek.

Since their second date, they had talked about this. It took her a year to completely entrust him with any semblance of playing the stepfather role in her daughter's life. It took her another six months to accept his marriage proposal and let him actually become part of the family. No way would she have unleashed an Owen Pomeroy on Maiya.

He said, "Ninety percent of the boys I work with don't have a relationship with their dads, and that's exactly what they long for most. We always knew that no matter how good my relationship is with Maiya, I could never fill that hole left by her real father."

"*Biological* father." She automatically corrected him, always insistent to never use the term *real* father. "Well, it's asinine."

"What is?"

"That we have such holes. God should rethink all this heart memory hogwash that He wired into us. Fathers abandon kids all the time. We shouldn't have to forever feel like there's something missing."

Whoa. It was the closest she had ever come to admitting that her own father's abandonment affected her. She would only say that she had forgiven him, like it was no big deal.

She wiped her hands across her face as if washing away the day's trouble. "You're the best, hon. You make all the difference in Maiya's life. I am so very grateful that you are her daddy."

He basked in her words, thankful as well for Maiya being his stepdaughter. "Does that mean I'm forgiven for bringing Jake into our safe place?"

"Yes, I forgive you. Like you didn't know that already."

He smiled.

She stood. "I should have caught on. I mean, she worked in the yard with the kid for two days straight. When was the last time she hung out in the yard, let alone picked up a shovel?"

"Or cared where we stuck an azalea?" He stood and held out his arms to her.

She stepped into his embrace.

121

The hug was a good discussion ender. Did he need to add that he did not trust Jake Ford as far as he could throw him?

Nah. He'd keep that tidbit for another time. Or not.

CHAPTER 17

Portland, Oregon

Although she wasn't the only one on a cell phone in the Portland bookstore's coffee shop, Lacey spoke in a low voice. "Maiya's still grounded?"

On the other end of the line, Teal sighed. "Yes. It's not fair, making her start her junior year with no social privileges. I should at least give her a deadline. But I can't. After three weeks, we're back to work, she's back to school, but life is not back to normal."

Tell me about it. Lacey did not speak her initial response.

Habits of a lifetime did not die easily. For as long as she could remember, if she spoke to her sister without weighing her words, either Teal lashed out or their parents lashed out at Teal. Often both. Lacey was not the target, and yet somehow she was guilty of creating the conflict.

She had learned to hold her tongue.

Teal went on. "It's not just us with Maiya's situation. There's this citywide feeling that the other shoe is going to drop at any minute."

"That's understandable."

"But it stinks."

Lacey closed her eyes. It was not her imagination. Teal's un-Teal-likeness continued. She remained as mouthy as ever, but in a way that seemed to welcome Lacey into her sphere. It was the only explanation for Lacey finding the courage to call her five times since the day after the quake struck.

"So, Lace, aren't you going to say it again?"

She opened her eyes, smiled, and said for the fifth time in three weeks, "Why don't you come home and get away from it all for a while?"

Teal laughed. "Thank you. I need something predictable in my life, and I think you're it these days."

Lacey's smile stretched into a grin.

Teal said, "There are moments when I actually consider coming."

"Things are that bad?"

"Things are that bad and your steadiness is that good."

Tears stung Lacey's eyes. "It would be

wonderful to see you."

"You really believe that? I'd only make a mess of things."

"Don't say that, Teal. So many years have passed. We've all changed."

"Well, you for one did not need to change."

She wiped beneath her eyes.

"And," Teal said, "I seriously, seriously doubt that either Randi or Owen have changed directions midstream. I would only upset them, like always."

Lacey tilted the phone away from her chin and sniffled.

"I've changed too, Lace. I've gotten more inflexible about what I will not put up with. At the top of my list are parents like . . . I'm sorry."

Lacey struggled to swallow.

"Are you still there?"

"Y-yes."

"I'm still too mouthy."

"It's not — it's not . . ." Will's voice whispered in her mind. *Be open with her. Give her a chance to be a big sister.* "Teal, I-I lost a baby."

"Lacey! When?"

"Christmastime." Her voice shook. She pressed an arm across her abdomen. The emptiness there still felt like a huge void, as if she were missing half her body.

"Christmastime? That was — what — eight months ago? I didn't even know you were pregnant!"

"I didn't talk much about it. It-it wasn't an easy pregnancy. There were problems from the start."

"Oh, Lace. How far along were you?"

"Five months."

"I am so sorry. I can't imagine how awful that must be. Will you try again?"

Lacey raked her fingers through the thatch of horse-mane hair that worked best when it was long enough to braid. It did not quite reach the middle of her ears. She thought of that morning's visit with the specialist, of the prescription in her bag for estrogen. The crater in her abdomen ached as if literally crying out not only for the missing baby, but for the missing womb.

She could not answer Teal's question.

Teal said, "Forget I asked that. It's way too personal for a long-distance relative."

"You're my sister, not a relative. There's a difference."

"Yeah, well, I'm not exactly the ideal model for either. But I am sincerely sorry for your loss, yours and Will's."

"Thank you." She relaxed, grateful for the out. "Speaking of sisters, Will and I are at

Pine's Bookstore in Portland. Remember when Grandma Jo brought us here? One time you and I spent the afternoon in a corner, and you read an entire Nancy Drew book to me."

Teal chuckled. "I remember that. We had happy times with her, didn't we? I wish she had lived longer."

They reminisced about those few happy visits with the sweet grandmother who had lived in Portland. How she could have possibly been the mother of Owen never made sense to them.

By the time Will joined Lacey, she was smiling, amazed at the first regular conversation she'd enjoyed with Teal since . . . since . . . She had no idea since when.

CHAPTER 18

Los Angeles

Teal closed her phone, leaned back in her chair, and stared at the papers on her desk. They refused to come into focus.

The conversation with Lacey weighed on her. Her sister had been pregnant over a year ago and never mentioned the good news? She had let eight months go by before announcing the bad news of a miscarriage? Something was not right about this.

Not that Teal blamed Lacey. Despite Lacey's efforts to keep a relationship going between them, one did not truly exist and never had. A shared moment now and then, like that long-ago afternoon in the bookstore with their grandmother, did not count. *Their* grandmother? Correction. *Lacey's* grandmother, no blood relation to Teal.

She blamed herself. She was the sister who wanted no part of family ties. Therefore it shouldn't matter whether Lacey clued her in on things. It shouldn't feel like another millstone of guilt had been added to the ones she already wore like a necklace, a string of gems designed and manufactured in Cedar Pointe, Oregon.

It shouldn't feel like that. But it did.

There was a brief knock on her door and it opened. Her assistant, Pamela, leaned inside. "Your one o'clock is here. You okay?"

"Sure."

Pamela's brows disappeared behind her steel-gray bangs. At fifty-five, she was a paralegal and mature enough to be willing to chip in with secretarial duties when needed. Her mother-hen routine was icing on the cake. "You can do this in your sleep, Teal. Just listen to her story and take notes. Then go home."

Teal smiled her thanks. "Give me five minutes."

"You got it. Hannah Walton is in conference room B." Pamela shut the door.

The woman hadn't used the intercom in two weeks, not since the earthquake. She hovered, a quirk everyone in the city seemed to have taken on. It was sweet and disheartening at once. Life at home was the same. In some ways, the three of them seemed closer than ever, yet the emotions were rooted in fear that something bad was about to happen.

Would life ever return to normal?

Teal massaged her neck, where the string of millstones pulled heavily. "Lord, I'm sorry once again for being a lousy sister, but I really can't take on Lacey right now. I just can't."

As if the God who allowed such recent destruction across the second-largest city in the United States gave a hoot about her concerns.

Three minutes into the meeting, Teal wasn't so sure she could take on Hannah Walton, either.

It was at that point when her new client spoke the words *biological father.* Teal stopped taking notes, set down her pen, and clenched her hands on her lap under the table.

The woman was twenty-five and drop-dead gorgeous in every clichéd California beach interpretation of the term. Sparkling, even, white teeth. Long blonde hair. Big blue eyes. Pouty lips. Flawless complexion. A body made for bikinis, evident even in the conservative floral-print dress she wore. Sweet little-girl voice. On top of that, she was quietly confident.

If Hannah stood before a jury of her so-called peers who happened to include seven women of average, mediocre looks and self-esteem, she would lose. It was the way of the world.

"Ms. Adams, what do you think?"

"Please, call me Teal." She gave her a brief smile. "I think . . ." *I think this is my worst nightmare.* "Uh, there are avenues to pursue."

"Have you done this before?"

"Yes, I have experience in similar cases. We all do here."

"Did they work out?"

Teal picked up her pen and leaned forward to speak directly to those big blue eyes. "Hannah, every situation is unique to the individuals involved. Please believe that our goal is to protect your rights and your child's. We will do everything we possibly can to make it work out for you. All right?"

She nodded hesitantly. "I just want to keep my baby away from that man. Do you have children?"

"A fifteen-year-old daughter."

"You're a mother!" Her face lit up. "Then you understand."

Oh, more than you can imagine. "All five attorneys at Canfield and Stone Family Law are mothers." Teal wanted to add that family was their *raison d'être,* but that would be fudging. That would make the firm sound ooey-gooey, fuzzy-wuzzy. Those adjectives did not square with their true pursuit: family *law.*

She sat back and poised the pen over her legal pad. "Tell it to me again, from the beginning."

Five years previously, Hannah had had an affair with James Parkhurst, her older, married boss, a big-name producer. She got pregnant. He wanted nothing to do with her or the child. Hannah quit her job and lost touch with him. The daughter, Maddie, now four years old, lived with Hannah and her husband of two years, Ryan. Out of the blue, Parkhurst was suing for visitation rights.

Hannah's chin trembled. "Everyone kept telling me that biological fathers have rights. That's why we never pursued Ryan adopting Maddie. We were afraid James would have to be told and that he might do something crazy like this. He is a mean, vindictive man."

"Do you have any idea why the sudden interest in your daughter?"

She shook her head, the blonde curls swishing.

"Did you tell him you were pregnant with his child?"

"Yes, when I first found out. He called me a slut and said I cheated on him and he doubted the baby was his." She wiped at the corner of her eye. "I never slept around or cheated on him."

"After that, did you two have any contact with each other?"

"No. I never even went back into work."

"Did you quit or were you fired?"

"I quit. I went to the office one Sunday when nobody was around, put my resignation on his desk, and cleared out my things."

"Did you hear from anyone?"

She shifted in her seat, as if uncomfortable with the question. "No. I did receive a final paycheck with severance. It came in the mail, but that was it. I was sort of, you know, on the outside with the staff. Because of sleeping with the boss."

Teal nodded at the typical scenario. "Have you and Mr. Parkhurst had any contact in the past four years?"

"No, none at all. I met Ryan, and he's as beautiful as Maddie." She began weeping. "He's the best husband and daddy in the world. We have a happy life."

Teal begged to disagree. River was the best husband and daddy in the world. She would have lain down and died if Maiya's biological father interfered with them.

Which was why she could not allow River to adopt Maiya. That would have meant contacting the loser who had never been in their lives from the moment of Maiya's conception. Teal would have had to inform him that he had parental rights that she wanted him to sign off on. Nope. Like Hannah, no way was she walking down that road. It was full of land mines.

She regretted that River could not legally become Maiya's father, but not as much as she would regret the painful ramifications of the other path. Adoption was a piece of paper, a technicality that could not enhance the family ties the three of them now so thoroughly enjoyed.

Teal slid a box of tissues across the table. "Hannah, we have to dig deeper, but from the preliminary information you've given me, I might suggest that we file a counter-suit for termination of Parkhurst's parental rights based on abandonment."

"Meaning he has no rights?"

"He has no rights. He gave them up."

"You can do that?"

"If everything you said is solid, yes, I think so."

"Oh, thank you, thank you!"

Teal had not meant to jump so quickly to a solution. She doubted that all of Hannah's information was solid. There would be extenuating details, dark secrets to bring to light. But the compulsion to offer ooey-gooey fuzzy-wuzzies to a mom whose story resembled her own was just too strong to ignore.

Teal directed Hannah down the hall toward the restroom. She headed to her office to check messages and find an assistant to help with the interview. Her emotions were clouding her thought processes. She couldn't trust herself to listen with an unbiased ear.

On a good day the case would have been tough, but she had handled two similar situations in her ten years with the firm. She should have been able to deal with this one.

She blamed the earthquake. Hyperconcern for her family's well-being permeated every waking moment. River still winced whenever he sat down or stood up. Maiya still pulled at the reins like an unbroken mustang.

Nights brought little relief. Teal got up often and walked the floors and looked out the windows, as vigilant as a security guard on night duty. The sound of sirens gave her a stomachache. She either did not eat or binged. She was falling behind on regular life, not responding in a timely manner to e-mails or phone calls. Even clients were relegated to the back burners.

She thought now of the pamphlet stuck in a kitchen drawer. It was a list of post-traumatic stress disorder symptoms. Some caring volunteer had knocked on the door and placed it in her hand before she shut the door. She had skimmed it, pitched it, dug it out of the trash the next day, and stuck it in the drawer, refusing to believe it described her.

Which was probably a symptom in itself.

As she rounded a corner into the central part of the firm, she spotted Pamela at her desk outside Teal's office, on the phone.

As Teal approached, Pamela turned. Sheer horror distorted her face.

"Teal!" She held the phone out. "It's River."

The large room tilted. The cubicles in the middle section swirled. Teal's feet slogged through thick mud.

"He needs to talk to you." Pamela's voice sounded as if it came from a far distance.

An eternity passed. At last she reached the outstretched phone. "River?"

"Teal, the school just called. Maiya's. It's on lockdown."

Her legs wobbled. "What?"

"I got an automated message. That's all it says. Your cell's probably off?"

"Yeah." She pulled her phone from her jacket pocket, its volume off for her meeting, and read *one missed call.* "What do you mean, lockdown?"

"The doors are locked. Security is doing their thing. Nobody goes in or comes out until — I don't know."

"Why?"

"Why what?"

Pamela waved for her attention. "It's online." She glanced up from the monitor. "It says there's an unauthorized person on campus."

"River, the online news —"

"Got it here, too. Unauthorized person. All right. Let's not panic. It's probably no big deal."

"I'm on my way." She heard the panic in her voice. Her heart resounded in her ears.

"Teal, slow down. We won't be able to get near the school."

"Then they'll direct us somewhere else! I'm on my way."

"I'm closer. I'll get there first and call you, direct you where to go. Turn on your cell."

Teal handed Pamela's phone to her and looked at the cell in her hand. She couldn't remember how to turn the sound back on.

Before she sank to the floor, Teal felt Pamela's arms around her, leading her to sit on a chair.

Teal could take a lot in stride. Watching a bridge collapse and dozens die in their cars, for one. Learning that her daughter had entered a rebellious season, for another. But the image of Maiya locked up on a campus with a crazy person who probably had a gun or two?

Total paralysis.

CHAPTER 19

River stood with dozens of other parents on the perimeter of a shopping center parking lot. Arms crossed and lips pressed shut, he held himself together and gazed from behind dark sunglasses. The panic in the growing crowd was palpable.

He had lived through a couple of his own school lockdowns and faced gun-toting and knife-wielding teenagers crazy high on chemicals. San Sebastian Academy housed boys who had been expelled elsewhere. Some did not easily get the hang of new rules.

But at SSA, with a student-teacher ratio of six to one and a male population focused on being their brother's keeper, rule breaking was next to impossible. A lockdown at Saint Sibs meant somebody was already sitting on top of the out-of-control kid while the other boys were confined to their rooms until the director got to the bottom of the situation.

Life wasn't that way at Tremont High.

He felt a tug on the cuff of his jeans and looked down at Teal sitting on the curb. Her legs had given out twenty minutes ago. No hint of fight remained in her eyes.

As he lowered himself to the ground, his breath caught. He silently swore at the earthquake, himself, and the bins of books. "It's going to be okay." He pulled Teal close.

"You don't know that." Her voice was muffled against his shirt.

"We have to believe it."

"I can't. Not at this moment in time."

He couldn't either. Tremont High was a public school with a solid academic reputation and a blend of ethnicities that added a richness. Maiya loved it. And yet . . .

Metal detectors and police officers were part of the campus decor. Strict dress codes and codes of conduct were enforced. And yet . . .

There were thirty-five hundred students. Some did not play well with others. Some did not play well at all.

River hugged Teal as tightly as he could.

His cell phone beeped, and he unhooked it from his belt. A variety of tunes erupted around him, a discordant ringing of a dozen cells.

"Hello." Before the word was out of his mouth, an automated voice began reeling off good news. The lockdown was over, everyone was safe, parents could leave or pick up their children.

"Thank you, God."

Beside him Teal had her own phone to her ear and was talking.

River felt his smile fade.

"Y-yes." Her voice faltered. "We'll be right there." She clasped the phone in both hands and met his stare. "That was the vice principal. Maiya is in his office, and Jake Ford is in handcuffs."

In the five years River had known Teal, he had seen her fly off the handle at injustices and all but hyperventilate over various things involving Maiya. But she had always maintained an air of control.

Except for once.

And except for today. Today made twice.

The first time, Maiya was in seventh grade and had accidentally been marked absent one day. The school contacted Teal — who had dropped Maiya at the school earlier — and asked if she was home sick. Teal phoned River and the police and went to the school. When he arrived, he heard her voice from the front door at eardrum-shattering decibels. The school nurse entered the fray and informed them all that Maiya was in her office, sick to her stomach. By noon that day, River had tucked both of his girls into bed, Maiya with a stomach bug, Teal with a migraine. He had to make her promise not to sue anyone at the school.

It crossed his mind that this time, he himself could be in her lawsuit sights.

In all honesty, he felt grateful to be out of her line of fire for the moment. He'd much rather be in the back of a police cruiser than inside the school. He'd left Teal there, bouncing off the walls and yelling at the vice principal about his decision to suspend Maiya from school.

He turned to Jake Ford beside him, the goofy kid who had so captivated his daughter. "I don't know what to say."

The lanky boy winked. "Maybe you could say to the cops they should uncuff me?"

"You snuck into a high school, Jake. Be glad they didn't shoot you."

"I didn't sneak in. A friend opened a back door for me."

Thank God that friend had not been Maiya.

Unless they were both lying.

Jake smiled. "I swear again, it wasn't Maiya." His freckled nose and mop of curly red hair easily disarmed others. He wore a denim jacket, but even when his tattoo-covered arms were exposed, people gravitated toward him, people from all walks of life, including the uptight and middle-aged. He was a natural charmer — nothing phony about his charisma — and seemed not to have a harmful bone in his body.

River truly believed he didn't. The kid simply made idiotic decisions that got him into trouble. "You're going to have to rat out the friend."

"I can't do that. It's all my fault. I talked her into it."

Her? A list of Maiya's friends ran through his mind and his stomach twisted. "But it was her choice, and the authorities think that girl was Maiya. They've suspended her."

"No way! Really?"

"What did you expect? She was hiding you in a band room closet."

"We went in there before the lockdown announcement. We just wanted five minutes alone."

"Why, Jake? Why did you do this? You promised me you would not contact her. I trusted your word."

He shrugged. "It's not what I planned. It was just going to be a quick duck in and out. Hand her the flowers, profess my undying love, and split."

"And how was that not breaking your promise?"

"Man, we hadn't talked for two weeks. We needed some kind of closure, you know? I had to tell her good-bye."

"Jake, you're nineteen and intelligent enough to get it: breaking promises will get your friends in big trouble. Breaking laws will land you in jail."

"I was just trying to see my girl."

"*Ex*-girl." River heard the steel in his voice.

"River, I care for her. I really do. I swear I'll stay away, but I miss her. I think she misses me, too."

"Let me tell you something about love. It means you want the best for the other person and you will help bring that about. The best for my fifteen-year-old daughter at this moment is that her mother and I are not upset. Guess what? We're upset. We are very upset." River stopped himself short of heaping hot coals of blame on Jake. He thumped the window with his fist to get a nearby cop's attention to open the door.

Jake said, "Hey, I'm new at this, okay? Can you at least put in a good word for me?"

As River slid out the door he turned to look at the boy. "And what would that good word be, Jake? That you can't keep a promise if it's hard?"

"Come on, man. You know me. I got through Saint Sibs with flying colors. I got a regular job at the garage. I make good money."

River straightened, swore softly, rested his arms on the door, and swore again. Jake's life had been one abandonment after another. If River quit on him now after their mentoring history, the impact would rank just below that of Jake's mom and dad.

The distraught faces of Teal and Maiya flashed through his mind.

He was not in a good space for decision making. He leaned back down into the car. "Jake, you chose the wrong girl to mess with."

The boy squirmed, his hands still uncomfortably handcuffed behind his back. "I'm sorry." There was a new note of fear in his voice. "I'm sorry, Mr. Adams. It won't happen again, sir."

River's heart pounded in his ears. His throat felt tight.

A tear slid from the corner of Jake's eye.

"I can't promise. But I will carefully consider speaking on your behalf." With that he walked quickly away before he caved in.

Nuts. He'd never seen the kid cry before.

CHAPTER 20

Keeping her head as still as possible on the bed pillow, Teal removed the ice pack from her forehead and dropped it to the floor.

River climbed into bed beside her. "Feeling better?"

"Yeah." She turned slowly onto her side and faced him. "Thanks."

He smiled and his eyes crinkled. In the dim light the cobalt blue appeared almost black.

The migraine had sent her to bed before dinner. It was now after ten o'clock. "What did I miss?"

"More tears and apologies. Poor kid. What could she do? The love of her life suddenly appears with a bouquet of roses in an empty school hallway where she happens to be on her way from study hall to the library. We forgot to include this scenario in our 'just say no' lectures."

"How naive of us."

He chuckled. "Just say no to booze, drugs, sex, and guys bearing gifts in the hall during class."

"It lacks a certain ring."

"I'll work on it."

"Do you buy their story?"

"Sure," he said. "Her history class was given library passes the first day of school to work on a project during study halls. It would've been easy for Jake to learn her schedule. It would've been easy for the anonymous friend to find out if she would go to the library today."

"Or encourage her to do so because Jake was coming."

They stared at each other.

Teal said, "Did you ask her that?"

"Didn't think of it. Did you?"

"I only thought of it now. But she insists she did not know his plans or who opened the door for him. Same thing as innocent bystander?"

"Could be, up to that point."

She sighed. "It kind of breaks down when we get to the part about the cops finding them in the band room closet. The officials don't buy that she wasn't hiding him."

"Maiya probably did panic like she said and had no idea the lockdown was about him. No way to prove it, though."

"So we can't fight the suspension."

"No, we can't, Ms. Lawyer. Our focus should be on supporting Maiya while she deals with the consequences of her actions."

"You always take the oomph out of my battering ram, Mr. School Counselor."

His smile came and went. "Her boss called her tonight. He said with school back in session he needs to cut staff. Not enough ice cream customers to keep everyone on, and since Maiya was the latest hire . . ." He shrugged.

"That's not fair. What a lame excuse! That chicken —"

River put a finger on her lips. "The bottom line is she's learning a huge life lesson early in the game. She'll be better for this mess in the long run."

Teal moved his hand and held it. "But what about the short run? I'll take her with me to the office tomorrow, but I can't keep that up. And she can't go with you every day."

"She'd be fine in my office or helping out in the main office."

"But we're talking six weeks off of school. Six weeks of her *junior* year. Six weeks' worth of *zeros* in every class. She needs a tutor to keep up."

"We'll find one."

"River, it's more than that. It's — it's —"

"Sh." He wiped at the outer edge of her eye. "Relax. Take a breath."

She took two. "She needs loads of attention right now. I should be mommying her. I missed out on so much when she was little."

"She's fifteen and she's grounded. Life is difficult."

"I love you," she said.

"And I love you. What's up?"

"Can you say that other part? I need to hear it. 'I love you, da, da, da'?"

He waited a couple beats before saying anything. "I love you no matter what. And for the record, I am in for the long haul."

She smiled. The first time he said he was in for the long haul was the day he proposed for the umpteenth time. That was the time she finally replied *yes*. His words had struck a long-dormant chord within her, and she knew that she had been created to hear such music.

"River, I want to take her to Cedar Pointe for a few weeks."

He blinked. "Camp Poppycock?"

"I think I'll stop using that derogatory moniker."

"Why?"

"Because it's not user friendly. She's not

going to like the idea anyway —"

"No, I meant why do you want to take her there?" He interrupted her, his voice tense. "Why Cedar Pointe, your nemesis?"

"It's complicated."

"Care to uncomplicate it?" His mouth was settling into a grim line.

"Because it's so far off the grid. It's disciplining her with the advantage of getting her away from all the chaos in the city. I don't want her to be continually faced with no social life and no school and now no work."

"All of which is the whole rationale behind disciplinary action."

"But she never should have been *suspended.* Us grounding her from after-school activities is one thing, but this is totally unfair punishment. It'll haunt her for years and have such a major, negative impact on her grades and college applications."

"You're overreacting. You two would leave home and you'd leave work for weeks because she might get an A-minus and have to go to her second college choice? What's really going on?"

Tears pooled in her eyes. She felt all twisted and squeezed inside. "I'm losing it, River. I haven't slept through a night in weeks. I drive crazy routes to avoid others, and still every day I go past rubble. I'm always hypervigilant. Sirens scare me to death. I can't focus at work. I can't stop reading all those obituaries."

"Oh, Teal. Why didn't you tell me how bad it is?"

"Because you'd say I should talk to someone."

"You should. Start with Pastor Lillian."

"I just want to go away."

"To Cedar Pointe." Disbelief filled his tone. "The place you've avoided most of your life, especially the past nine years."

"I have a plan B."

"Of course you do."

"We could all go visit my new best friends in Iowa. See the Mississippi."

"Mm-hmm. Spit in it. Reel in a catfish or two."

"Or plan C: you could come up and fish in Oregon. They have salmon."

He did not reply to her obvious hint.

She knew better. Even if his superiors allowed him time off, there was no way on earth he would leave his boys at the critical start of a new year.

She said, "I'm sorry. That wasn't fair."

"It is what it is. If you feel that this is what you need to do, go. Your mind is made up." Exasperation clipped his words. "Why not

151

rent a place closer? I could easily visit you out in Palm Springs or down in San Diego."

"I don't want a vacation."

"What exactly do you want, Teal?"

She had no words that could encompass the desires she had. They were deep longings that had struck like lightning bolts inside her, burning and splitting. If she didn't do something soon, the thunder would explode and there would be no way out.

"I want to go home."

He gazed at her as if struck himself.

"Everyone should be able to go home when they're in trouble. Right?"

River moved over and gently slid his arms around her.

CHAPTER 21

River listened to Teal's rhythmic breathing. She was fast asleep beside him, weary from events of the past few weeks, undone by forces she could not control.

He hadn't been much help. He should have told her to sleep on this crazy decision to go to Oregon. He should not have debated her.

Not that they were strangers to disagreement. Secure in their relationship, neither was threatened by differing opinions.

So why the racing heartbeat, the sense of doom?

Because Teal had chosen Maiya's well-being over that of their family? No. That was a given, played out in countless ways all the time in their years together. He had joined the game late. Maiya had been ten, well-adjusted for her age, but when kid crises struck, date time with Teal was scratched off the calendar. Not postponed, deleted.

His stepdaughter was still a child, still in need of an up-close-and-personal mother. That biological father void still needed something tangible from the guy himself, not the surrogate.

River shifted carefully, removing his arm from beneath Teal's shoulders, and winced. The pain in his side had subsided but was still there.

Was that it? Was he threatened by the thought of Maiya's finding a piece of herself in Oregon, of even meeting her dad? Oregon was a big state and yet, why not? He conceivably could be there, perhaps in Cedar Pointe itself. But no. Getting something from him was Maiya's right. It would not diminish her relationship with Riv. She was that kind of kid.

Was River threatened by a fear of Teal and Maiya driving into inclement weather like Krissy had ten years before, pregnant with Sammy? Of another driver losing control on the highway and veering into them?

He took a breath, the stab in his ribs keeping it shallow. He took another.

No. That fear had struck with the earthquake, but he had stopped giving in to it some years ago. It was the first time Teal had been late meeting him. She arrived to find him curled in a fetal position on the floor, his heart racing, his body shaking in a cold sweat. At Teal's urging, he had seen a counselor.

Exactly what he had urged her to do and she ignored.

He had learned how not to let the fear debilitate him. In time it all but disappeared, until the quake. Was that it? The quake triggered the old fear . . . No. He sensed a deep ache and understood this was something new.

How was he supposed to live for weeks without Teal and Maiya? As much as he daily lost himself in his work, his girls were his life.

If his side didn't hurt so much, he'd take a deep breath and just get on with life like any other macho guy would.

River watched his neighbor Charlie turn skewers of chicken and beef on the grill. It was Sunday evening, four days before Teal and Maiya's departure. The Yoshidas had invited them over for dinner.

Charlie shut the lid and joined him at the picnic table, his brow still furrowed. "Teal and Maiya will be gone for five weeks? Five?"

River nodded. Somehow the *few* weeks had gotten extended to include most of Maiya's suspension time.

"You probably can't get away from school?"

"Not really." His fall semester was jam-packed already. As the academy's liaison to the community, he regularly took his seniors out to public schools to talk about drug and alcohol abuse. He taught a class on independent living skills. Two campouts were on the docket. Preparations for the big annual fund-raiser filled every other waking moment. "Hopefully I can fly up there for one long weekend."

The old man took a sip of iced tea and the wrinkles below his few wisps of gray hair smoothed out. "Your wife is a strong woman. Cindy and I saw that the first day we met her ten years ago. She'll be fine."

"Yeah." River didn't worry about faking an upbeat tone. Charlie was his sounding board, a great listener who reminded him of his own father. "I'm not so sure about myself."

"We men are a needy lot." He chuckled. "So, she is going home. What about her work and Maiya's schoolwork?"

"You know Teal. She has it all figured out. Her sister, who apparently scored a 2200 on the SAT, has agreed to tutor Maiya. Teal convinced her bosses to allow her to work on what she can long-distance. They divvied up her court dates and other cases. They promised not to fire her."

"What about our lovely juvenile delinquent? Is this commuting her sentence?"

"Her mother thinks not. I, on the other hand, am trying to come to terms with it." He shook his head, still disagreeing with taking Maiya out of the immediate sense of her discipline. "My only solace is that Cedar Pointe sounds like the equivalent of a cloistered nunnery. It won't exactly be a resort experience."

Charlie shrugged. "What else is there?"

River saw through the wise man's nonchalant demeanor. "You mean besides Teal and me being at odds?"

"That should cover it." He put his arms on the table and leaned forward. "A piece of advice?"

"No other reason for me to be unloading on you, Charlie."

"She's rattled. The earthquake shook something loose. Maiya's behavior compounded it. You know Teal has been running her entire life. Especially since Maiya's birth."

River stared at him. "But we got married.

157

We have a solid relationship."

"This isn't about that. This is about her coming to the end of the road. She's tired of running. It's time she found herself."

"She's thirty-seven years old."

"She never had the opportunity before now. She's been too busy surviving."

"But she has me."

"You're not enough. Sorry."

That slender thread of machismo River had been grasping snapped in two. He wasn't enough for Maiya. He wasn't enough for Teal.

Charlie straightened back up and reached for his tea. "You are enough for her to come back to. She'll return. But you might want to consider engaging in a powerful lot of prayer between now and then."

So he was needy and not equipped enough to take care of his family and was in for a rough time of it.

Maybe he should have stayed home.

CHAPTER 22

Highway 101, North of Los Angeles

Teal stole a glance at Maiya in the passenger seat as they sped along the highway. In the four hours since they waved good-bye to River, her daughter had not moved a muscle. She sat slumped down, arms crossed, mouth set, eyes hidden behind sunglasses.

"Hey," Teal said, "Miss Happy Camper."

"Give it up, Mom. This is me until the day we go home. You might as well get used to it."

Teal bit back a snide *In your dreams, pipsqueak.*

They had been at each other for a week, ever since Teal had announced her plans. Neither one of them was happy about the trip, but that was not a factor. They were going to Cedar Pointe.

Maiya said, "Why couldn't you just use your leave of absence and stay at home?"

"Asked and answered."

Maiya puffed out a noise of disgust. " 'Being away is best' is not an answer. So what if you got called into the office now and then? So what if you couldn't find a tutor? So what if my friends are having good times in the same town without me? Big deal. They still are."

She sighed. "Okay, fine. Reduce it to 'I'm the mom and you're not.' End of discussion."

"That is so unfair. You've *ruined* my life." She shifted in her seat to face the window and went quiet, the air thick with her sullen attitude.

Teal sighed again. Thank goodness she had not mentioned her other reason to leave town: that it would allow her to totally focus on Maiya and mommy her. Maiya would dismantle that warm fuzzy in a nanosecond.

Not that Teal felt it anymore. It had passed last Thursday morning, the instant she told Maiya her decision. Her daughter shouted, "No way," but of course no way did she have a choice in the matter. Between Maiya's tears and River's sad eyes, Teal wondered if the idea was indeed truly stupid.

But she asked her bosses for and was granted an extended absence. Heidi Stone and Zoe Canfield were in their fifties and her longtime mentors in personal matters as well as in business. They had hired her when she was a struggling single mom with a boatload of school loans. From the start they loved her and little Maiya to pieces. If not for their support for River, Teal might have dillydallied even longer before marrying him.

Yet they were also successful business owners who had to pay bills. They questioned her overreaction. True, suing the school district would not be a wise thing to do, but being out of the office for almost five weeks? She pushed back, insisting it was like a maternity leave. Of course her paycheck would be smaller, her loss more than theirs. They reluctantly let her have her own way. She figured if they fired her, her choice of Maiya over career was worth it.

It saddened her to think this might be a first. No wonder her daughter had gone off the deep end with a boy.

Preparing to go had consumed the days. River pitched in at home, cooking, doing laundry, and getting the car checked over, the oil changed. He helped them pack and encouraged Maiya as much as possible, never hinting in front of her at his dissenting opinion. With Teal he did not hold back.

His parting words were "You can always turn around and come back."

Already Teal missed him too much. Maybe it was best to stay a little bit mad at him. The thing was, if he hadn't brought Jake Ford into their home, they would not be in this mess. Nothing else would have caused Maiya to push the boundaries as she battled her way through adolescence.

Yeah, right.

A few minutes later Teal exited the highway and pulled into a gas station on the edge of a town. Maiya headed inside to use the restroom. Teal lowered the window and pulled out her cell to call River, hoping to catch him on his lunch break.

"Xena!" he answered on the second ring.

She rolled her eyes. "Hey."

"How goes it, Warrior Princess?"

"I want to come home."

He chuckled.

"Go ahead and say 'I told you so.' "

"Never. What's up?"

While he ate, she described the ordeal of the trip, ending with "She's withdrawn. I'm snippy. This is not working."

"Hm." He swallowed. "Well, the good news is she doesn't see your Oregon adventure as a get-out-of-jail-free card."

"Hardly. But a major reason we left was

so that I didn't have to keep playing the prison guard."

"Then stop acting like one."

"I'm not —"

"You're not what? Being snippy because her behavior is not what you want it to be?"

Teal opened her mouth to deny his accusation and then closed it. He had simply reworded her own description and he had done so in his typically gentle way.

He said, "Guards get snippy when their charges don't toe the line. They're not called to be mommies. Speaking of which, your mommy talk the other night got me to thinking about my mom. You know how she was this top-notch, no-nonsense English lit professor. She had a prison-guard side to her and it showed up at home often."

Teal's defensiveness melted. She traced the steering wheel with her finger and blinked rapidly until her sight cleared. How like River to turn the subject from her own inadequacy as a mommy to a story about his mother. She loved him for it. The fact that he loved her pathetic self still astounded her.

"But," River went on, "every so often, throughout my life, Mom would say, 'For goodness' sake, River, you are not one of my students. Let's play.' And we would play at whatever. A board game, shooting hoops, going to a movie. She'd do it with my sister, too. Sometimes the three of us together."

Teal wished she had known Liz Adams. If even half the stories about her were partially true, she would have made for a great mother-in-law.

River said, "The last time it happened I was twenty-two. It was before she got sick. I'd bailed out on college. Again. We played Scrabble, she beat me mercilessly, and then we went out for hot fudge sundaes."

Teal found her voice, a quiet, low version of the usual one. "You're saying I should play with Maiya."

"Yep. And I will too. I'll text her on your phone right now. We'll —"

"She's lost phone privileges."

"Teal." His tone would have stopped a killer in his tracks.

"We agreed that —"

"Just lighten up. I gotta go. Call me later." She held the phone until a new text message beeped its arrival.

The passenger door opened and Maiya slid inside. "Icky, skigusting bathroom."

Teal smiled at the Maiya-ism, a phrase she coined when she was three, trying to pronounce *disgusting.*

Teal stared at her daughter's profile, a

portrait of three in one. There was the little girl in the rounded cheeks, the hormonal teenager in the too-large silver hoops hanging from her earlobes, and the young woman in the chin tilted as if to forge a way through a complicated world.

Maiya turned to her. "What?"

"Will you please gas up the car while I use the icky, skigusting bathroom?"

"This is your trip."

Teal held herself still, showing no reaction. What was she supposed to do about the lippy response? With no more privileges to lose and angry about being hauled off to Cedar Pointe, Maiya was having a heyday acting up.

What would River's mother do? Forget Xena. What would Liz Adams do?

Play. Ease up on the rules. For now.

It was either that or turn around and go home.

"Maiya, a part of driving is putting gas in the car. If you want to drive, put gas in the car."

Her tilted chin sagged and swung around to face Teal. "I can drive?"

"You think I want to do seven hundred miles all by myself?"

Maiya practically jumped out of the car.

Teal met her at the pump and handed her

a credit card and her phone. "River sent you a text."

Maiya smiled.

Teal smiled back at her and headed toward the station to buy as much of Maiya's favorite junk food as the place offered.

Memories rolled toward her down the 101 like a fog growing denser with each passing mile. Two hours south of Camp Poppycock, Teal had decided to spend the night in a motel rather than finish the drive as planned.

Maybe the emotional fog would rise with the morning sun.

The motel in a Northern California town, naturally, did not compare to the one they stayed at the previous night in San Francisco. Maiya griped about it. Teal bribed her. If Maiya changed her attitude, she could make the drive up the coast, something she would not be allowed in the dark. Maiya could not say enough positive things about the place.

Since Teal's conversation with River, life on the road had improved to a great extent. In a no-man's-land between home and destination, mother and daughter shoved all the nasty stuff under the rug.

Playtime was almost over, though. The rug

had to be picked up, shaken, and put away. They were left with a hardwood floor littered with nasty stuff, issues like River's absence, being grounded, school suspension, strained relations with extended family, and life off the grid.

"Mom!" Maiya squealed now from the driver's seat. "I don't remember this at all!" She turned toward her side window and the vista of ocean far below. "I was only six, but still, you'd think I'd — Mom! Look at that!"

Teal looked instead straight ahead at the highway and pumped her right foot against the floorboard. The two-lane hugging the winding, hilly Oregon coastline was no place for a fifteen-year-old driver to gaze at views.

"Honey! The road!"

Maiya whipped back to attention. "Oh, yeah. It's just so awesome."

Teal blew out a long breath and took a quick peek sideways. A sweet familiarity washed over her. How could she have forgotten the magic? Ocean on one side, mountains and wilderness on the other, a permeating scent of green like a never-ending springtime.

Maiya said, "This coast isn't anything like ours. It's just so *huge!* And all those mega-rocks out in the water. What are those?"

She glanced again at the Pacific with its

167

collection of boulders, some fat and round, some jagged towers. "Sea stacks. They were part of the cliffs at one time, before the ocean eroded away the land."

"Wild."

"Yeah, they are. You'll see all shapes and sizes. Growing up, I called them giants. They kept watch over Camp — I mean, Cedar Pointe." Teal went still inside, thinking how she would sit for hours on end, gazing at her gentle guardians, giving them names, and feeling safe.

They would stop there first, at the spot where she first knew that someone bigger than her stepdad cared about her.

"Mom, is that it?" Maiya pointed at the windshield.

They were still thirty minutes away, but in the distance the land jutted out into their line of sight. Tiny buildings dotted the area. "That's it, the westernmost point on the continental States."

"Cool."

Teal smiled to herself. Somehow Maiya had picked up on River's fascination with geography and nature. Maybe the unusual aspects of Cedar Pointe would help keep her attitude from sinking too low.

It was too much to hope for. Maiya's attitude bottomed out as they descended the

168

last hill and entered the town.

Braking, she groaned. "Please tell me there's more around the next bend. Like a stoplight. Maybe a stop sign. Any hint of civilization."

It did not require much of a leap to see through her daughter's eyes the three blocks that stretched before them.

The speed limit had gone down to thirty. On the left, the land flattened out enough for a small parking lot above the ocean. A restaurant and shell shop bordered it. On the right was a motel. A little farther ahead were an art gallery, a café, a boarded-up storefront, a real estate office, a coffee shop.

"Well, around the bend is your aunt and uncle's coffee shop."

"There's a coffee shop right over there." She pointed.

"Coffee is a big thing up here in the Northwest."

"What about a stoplight?"

"I'm sure Lacey would have told me if one had been put in."

"Stop sign?"

"No stop signs. This is the highway."

"Mom!" Maiya's voice warbled, making it a two-syllable word.

"Turn into that parking lot."

"Unbelievable." She flipped on the signal.

"You're saying this major highway runs right through town and it doesn't get enough traffic for one lousy stoplight?" She overshot the turn. The car bumped up and down a curb. "Whoops. At least they have curbs."

"Hush and park the car. I want to show you something."

Maiya pulled into a slot, or rather two slots. The car straddled a line, but she turned off the engine.

"Maiya."

She rolled her eyes and restarted the car. "Okay, I'll fix it. It's not like there's anyone else here." Evidently the two RVs and one minivan did not count.

"It's Labor Day weekend. It'll fill up."

"Tourists actually stop here?"

Now Teal rolled her eyes. "It's not Disneyland, but it is beautiful, right? You noticed that on the drive."

Maiya wrestled with the steering wheel until she managed to get the car almost between two lines. "Yeah." Her tone grudged.

"You mind leaving the attitude here in the car?"

She looked at Teal, her expression sad. "All right, Mom."

"Thank you. We're going to be okay. Trust me?"

She nodded, her lower lip thrust out, part defiance, part chagrin.

"Maiya, remember: what doesn't kill us makes us stronger."

The corners of her mouth lifted slightly.

Teal laughed. The old phrase had been their mother-daughter mantra for years, probably up until the day she married River. "We may have to start using that again. Often."

Steep, narrow paths led down from the parking lot to the beach, a long stretch that hugged the sweeping curve of coastline Teal and Maiya had just driven along.

It was a wild, wind-whipped place. The beach beckoned more to tide-pool explorers than sunbathers. It was strewn with logs and debris washed up by the surf, peppered with stones and boulder outcroppings.

Maiya did not say a word.

Teal touched her arm. "Let's go up."

She led the way along a grassy path that dipped for a distance and then began to rise. The vegetation soon gave way to rock. The flatness dropped to cliffs on either side. The wind was in her face, the sun on her neck, the land solid beneath her feet, the loud *whoosh* of the sea filling her head. Teal felt again the magic in the majesty of it all.

The path turned vertical, but neither she nor Maiya feared heights. They were climbing one of her giants, which during this time of low tide was not adrift and separated from the shoreline.

"Mom?"

"Yes, to the top." She answered the unasked question, not turning to look at her teen who played the trumpet, watched ball games, and walked no farther than from the parking lot into the mall. "And yes, I'm out of breath too. Get used to it. This is a physical place. Good grief." She huffed, muttering to herself. "We need to join a gym."

"What happened to my mother, the anti-outdoorswoman?"

"I'm only anti–outdoor plumbing."

"What's at the top?"

The crook of the giant's arm. "Uh, you'll see."

It was a hard climb. The trail tapered, requiring attention to keep their feet on it. They passed no one. At last they stood on a fairly flat surface, wide enough for one scraggly shore pine tree, its limbs sheared off on the windward side. A waxy-leafed ground vine covered the area. Sky and water surrounded them on three sides.

Teal said, "A little farther."

"There is no 'little farther.' "

Teal smiled and walked to the far edge.

"Seriously, Mom."

She waved for Maiya to follow, glanced at the crashing waves far below, and turned sideways. "It's right here." Stepping carefully, she went down and laterally a few feet. The boulder became a wall on her left, blocking sight of Maiya. Bracing herself against it, she bent under a slight overhang and moved into a hollowed-out nook.

"Mom!"

"Keep coming. Hold on to your zingie-zangers!"

Maiya appeared and edged her way down. "Whoa, I guess so! This is high!"

"Have a seat."

They eased themselves down on the damp rock, sitting cross-legged.

Maiya whistled in admiration at the view. "River would love this."

Straight ahead was nothing but a few far-flung giants, the horizon, and two fishing boats the size of bath toys. Waves crashed at the bottom of the rock, but even at high tide it would remain far below.

The crook of the giant's arm was just large enough for the two of them to sit squished together. Above them, his shoulder hid them from view. His elbow curved out to the left as if in an embrace.

Teal breathed in the thick salt air. *Thank You, God. I needed this.* "Nice, huh?"

"Yeah, it is. I don't remember it, though."

"I didn't bring you when you were six. It was winter and everything was fogged in for our whole visit." Fogged in, in more ways than one.

"I saw the plaque by the tree. Warrior Rock?"

"Yes. It was named after a band of Indians who made their last stand up here."

"They got chased out here and killed?"

"Yes."

"Sick."

Teal hesitated to go on. How much was too much for a fifteen-year-old? *Sick* permeated not only the first settlement's history but Teal's childhood. "Anyway, I used to come here to be alone. I felt safe up here."

"Because of Owen and Gran Randi?"

"Mm-hmm."

"I don't remember this coastline, but I do remember them. He was one ticked-off dude. All you and Gran did was hiss at each other like a couple of cats."

"I'm sorry."

"Mom, get over it already. You've apologized like a million times. She's probably still a grump, but she always sends me nice birthday cards. And he's gotta be really old and decrepit by now, don't you think? I'm not afraid of a monster who sits around and drools." She made a silly face, her tongue lolling out.

"Mai." Teal's reprimand was halfhearted.

"Just trying to get you to lighten up."

She smiled to herself. There was no need to describe the specifics that sent her racing to Warrior Rock as a kid. She could trust in her daughter's intuition to set boundaries when it came to Owen and Randi's dysfunctional behaviors.

Maiya said, "So how come nobody ever came to visit us?"

"I don't think any of them wanted to, especially not after our trip here. Long before that, when I left for college, we more or less disowned each other and were happy to do so. Not Lacey so much; she was only twelve at the time. But we were never close."

"Then why are we here now?"

"Fair question." Teal took a moment to word her reply, glad to at last have Maiya's full attention. "I wanted to mommy you through this ordeal, away from regular life distractions."

Maiya gazed straight ahead toward the ocean and worked her mouth.

"You don't have to accept or understand that."

Still not looking at Teal, she said, "You could have done that anywhere else in the world."

"That's true. But Lacey kept bugging me and suddenly I had this overwhelming desire to bring you here." She lowered her eyes and traced her thumb along a seam of her jeans. "She had a miscarriage recently, and I guess I wanted to share my baby with her."

Maiya scooted closer until her arm pressed against Teal's. "That's really cheesy, Mom."

"Promise not to tell?"

"Sure." She laid her head on Teal's shoulder. "I can see this working up here. It feels totally safe. It's kind of like climbing into the Incredible Hulk's lap." She touched a patch of lichen. "He's even green."

Teal chuckled and peeked sideways down at her daughter. How she enjoyed the unlined face when it was at peace, like now. The wide-set, forest-green eyes sparkled in reflection of the ocean's deep blue. The little bowtie mouth sported a hint of gloss, a sign that Maiya wanted to look her best to meet the relatives.

Okay. Teal sighed. Maybe it was time she

let go of the past and put on her own lipstick.

CHAPTER 23

"Nervous?"

Lacey jumped at the voice. "Holly!"

"Sorry." The woman beside her chuckled. Dimples creased her face, ringed by a mass of curly, short brown hair. "I thought you were with us here on earth."

"Physically only, I guess." She looked out again over the top of the pastry display case and realized that the Saturday-morning crowd had fuzzed from view.

"Lacey, go outside and wait for them. I'm here to cover for you all day."

"I know. Thanks." She gently elbowed Holly's arm. "They were supposed to be here by now."

Her best friend since third grade elbowed her back. "Teal never was punctual."

Lacey swallowed. Her sister's reputation made it impossible for townspeople to accept that maybe she had changed. "But she's a lawyer. She has meetings and court times. I'm sure she's more punctual now."

"She's probably just as nervous as you are and procrastinating."

Lacey turned to her. "Really? You think so?"

"Oh, Lacey. So what if she's a big-time Los Angeles attorney with movie star clients? So what if Maiya is a spoiled, rich, 90210 ditz? They will be nervous about coming here."

"Teal has only worked with one big-name actress, and she's not super rich. Some client practically gave her the house. Her loans were atrocious, and River is a teacher. And —"

"And Maiya doesn't hang out in Beverly Hills." Holly laughed. "Lacey, my point is they're human just like you. The only difference is you're nice and Teal was always a pain in our tushies."

"She . . ." Lacey shook her head, tired of defending Teal. "Have you seen Will?"

"He's gabbing out back with some guy. I could say he's being your typical male, making himself scarce, but your husband does okay with emotional moments, that's for sure."

That *was* for sure. He didn't have much of a choice in the face of her round of doctors and hospitals. Holly had been a part of it all. "He wanted to give me space, but I think I want him here."

"Then go get him or go out front. You're making me nervous." She turned to two young people approaching the counter, huge knapsacks on their backs. "Good morning. What can I get for you?"

Lacey let her attention drift off again. Yes, she was incredibly anxious about their first meeting after almost ten years. She wanted to be inside the shop when Teal and Maiya arrived so that customers might act as a buffer zone. It would be best for Will to greet them with her, thicken the buffer zone. She tended to hold herself together when others were around.

The bells on the front door jingled. The sound that should have been lost in the din of two dozen people jabbering at the tables and the gift-shop area resounded in Lacey's ears like pealing church bells.

Two shadows filled the glass and then the door opened all the way.

Suddenly she did not want a buffer zone because there stood her favorite person in the whole wide world. Elusive as she had been through the years, her sister remained the central figure in Lacey's life. Her face and her voice colored Lacey's memories more than any other. Teal had taught Lacey how to tie her shoes, how to read, how to comb the beach for treasures, how not to fear the ocean, how to stay out of sight when their parents went off the deep end.

And now at last, here she was, with a ponytailed clone beside her.

Lacey laughed and clapped her hands and flew across the shop, darting between tables and around browsing shoppers.

Teal grinned and held her arms open. Lacey melted into them.

Her big sister was home.

They giggled and hugged tightly. Teal was shorter by a couple of inches; she felt solid in Lacey's arms. Lacey used to be heavier than her sister's average build, more muscular because she was the athlete.

They parted, holding each other at arm's length, looking at each other, smiling. As ever, Teal's eyes held in them the Oregon winter coast, every shade of gray from the sky's ash to the water's slate. There were crow's-feet around them now and purplish circles beneath them, more than age alone would add.

"Yeah," Teal said, "I've aged."

"I love your hair." The bob suited Teal's smooth, black hair.

"Love yours, all casual and scrunched.

The braid's gone. You look younger than ever."

Lacey shrugged.

Teal squeezed her bony upper arms.

Lacey saw understanding in the tilt of Teal's head, in the fading smile, the narrowing eyes. *Later,* Lacey prayed. *Later.*

Teal smiled briefly and stepped aside, beckoning Maiya to approach.

There had been a resemblance between them when the girl was six, but now she could pass for Teal's twin. Same heart-shaped face, same olive-tone skin, same black hair, same height and build. Only the eye color set her apart.

"Maiya." Lacey wrapped her in a hug. "Welcome to Camp Poppycock."

Her niece burst into youthful laughter, a sound of hope and healing to Lacey's tired soul.

In the huge pool of genetics that made up each of them, they shared only a smidgen of DNA from Lacey and Teal's mother, but for Lacey it was enough to claim. This child was family to the childless aunt.

CHAPTER 24

So far, so good. Seated by herself at a small corner table, Teal sipped from a triple-size to-go cup. *So far, so good* meant she had not yet shed a tear. What was there to cry about? Everything she had feared about returning home had gone *poof* the moment she first saw Lacey. That sight triggered emotions so deep, tears could not reach them.

A vaguely familiar man walked by. Dick, Mick, Rick, Nick? An old fisherman by the looks of his cap and weathered face. She returned his smile, struck by the friendly environment of Lacey and Will's place, the Happy Grounds Coffee and Gift Shop.

She sipped her latte and noted again it was nothing like she could get in Los Angeles–area chain stores. No surprise, given that she was in the Northwest, aka Coffee Country. But it was the best she had ever tasted in her entire life, and a teenager had made it. She eyed him now behind the counter. Baker — one name — was a big kid, more pudgy than muscular, and shy. He wore geeky rectangular, black-rimmed glasses. His hands moved with expertise on the espresso machine.

Will slid into a chair across from her and motioned toward her cup. "Good?"

"Way beyond good. We're into heavenly. I want to take him home with me."

Will grinned. "Ivy League schools are after him already, and I want to tell him to forget college. The future is here, keeping my customers happy."

Teal chuckled.

She and Maiya had greeted Will earlier, but when a tour bus unloaded curbside, he went back to work. Lacey declared she had the day off and promptly steered Maiya around the gift shop. Teal could see them now, smiling and chatting over marionberry jams and key rings made from myrtlewood as if they were treasures.

Teal turned back to her brother-in-law. She had always liked Will Janski Jr. well enough. Not that they had ever hung out together growing up, but he was her age. They graduated in the same high school class with sixty-one others. He was an extrovert who never met a stranger, the perfect personality to take over his parents' shop when they retired seven years ago.

With his open face, dark-blond hair, and slender, six-foot-plus stature, he had not aged much, except for the bags under his hazel eyes.

"Will, how bad is it?"

His face sort of folded in on itself briefly, as if a stiff wind had blown by. "She'll tell you, Teal. When she's ready."

"Are you familiar with how children of alcoholics communicate with their siblings? They do not talk about the ugly stuff because if they do, that means it's real. She may never be ready."

Will's chest rose and fell as he breathed deeply before he spoke. "She told you about the miscarriage."

"How many months after the fact? And I never even heard she was pregnant."

"Maiya seems like a great kid."

Teal could have screamed. She leaned forward and whispered, "Is Lacey dying?"

"She asked me not to —"

"Will! Please!"

"They think the cancer is in remission."

Teal sat back as if slapped. She opened her mouth, but nothing came out. Her thoughts swirled. Her guess had been correct. Lacey had cancer. *Cancer.* What kind?

When? Did she have surgery? She obviously had had chemotherapy; she never would have cut off the long hair that Will adored.

It was too much to take in.

She swallowed. "How are you doing?"

He blinked, averted his eyes, came back. "Let's say my knees are well acquainted with the floor, and that helps."

Now Teal looked away. He had every right to be bitter, but it wasn't in his makeup. She liked him more than ever.

Lacey and Maiya made their way across the coffee shop. Lacey stopped at every table to introduce her niece to customers. Maiya carried a small brown bag with handles and green tissue paper. She politely greeted everyone.

By the time they reached their table, Teal and Will were talking coffee again.

Maiya plopped down beside Teal, laid the bag on the table, and began pulling things from it. "Mom, look at what Aunt Lacey gave me. She said I can have anything I want from the whole entire store the whole entire time we're here. I got bubble bath for us. Isn't this bracelet awesome? This clear stuff is beach glass, and these stones are amethysts." She fastened it around her wrist. "Look at that funny joke book. And marionberry jam. I've never even heard of marionberries!"

Teal looked at her sister across the table. "Lace, come on."

"Hey, she's my niece. I get to spoil her. And I own this shop."

Will gave her an exaggerated frown.

She grinned. "*We* own this shop and *we* want to spoil Maiya. A little. I mean, it's not like we carry Gucci or Coach. So give it a break, Teal."

"Yeah, Mom, give it a break."

Aunt and niece giggled in unison.

Teal saw a familiar spark of joy in Lacey's eyes. It hadn't been there earlier. She would have noticed because it was the one Maiya had had since she was a toddler. It was one reason Teal often inadvertently called Maiya by her sister's name.

Maybe this visit was a good idea for reasons she could not fathom.

Teal wheeled her suitcase up and over the threshold and entered Moonbeam Cottage number three. One sweep of her eyes covered the combined sitting, dining, and kitchen areas. A hall led off from the center of the back wall. Three doors opened into it, two bedrooms and a bathroom.

"This is great, Lacey."

"It's all right?"

Maiya walked in behind Lacey. "Eww!" She stretched the word into a long whine. "Aunt Lacey! This is, like, not the Ritz!"

Lacey fluffed her hair and pouted. "Yeah, but, like, does it matter?"

They both giggled.

Teal stared. The two of them already had inside jokes going?

"Mom —" Maiya lowered her voice to normal range — "she really thought I must be a ditz and shopped on Rodeo Drive."

Lacey smiled. "Those are synonymous with Los Angeles. Anyway —" She spread her arms — "this place is clean and does not smell like mildew."

Maiya rolled her suitcase toward the tiny hall. "With seventy-three inches of rain a year, I suppose mildew is an issue." She disappeared inside one of the bedrooms.

Lacey looked a question at Teal.

"She likes to do research." Teal shrugged.

"A dream student."

"Are you sure you're okay with the whole tutoring thing?"

"Definitely okay with it." Lacey sat on the couch, a saggy-looking plaid eyesore with wooden arms, and rested her head against the back.

"Mom," Maiya called out, "Baker's going to help us with trig."

"Baker, the coffee guy?"

Lacey nodded. "Smart kid. Do you think that table gives you enough work space? I asked for this cottage because it had the largest one. I'm afraid there's no wireless. You're always welcome to work at our house or the shop."

Teal glanced around the room. Six chairs fit around the dining table that took up an entire fourth of the space. Opposite it the open kitchen consisted of the basics: sink, stove, fridge, and cabinets all lined up in a row along the back wall.

"The table will be just fine, and I can e-mail with my phone." She sat on the recliner, a dark-yellow Naugahyde, comfy enough.

A braided rug covered the linoleum between her chair and the couch. The sparse furnishings included a coffee table, two lamps, and a television. Sunlight shone through several windows, a homey charm in their cheery yellow curtains and valances.

"It's a comfortable place. Thanks, Lace. Is that a pellet stove?" The cast-iron device next to the hall opening resembled an old-fashioned free-standing television with a chimney.

"Yes. Will said he'd get some pellets for

you today, just in case. Mornings have been chilly."

"Mom," Maiya called out again. "Which bedroom do you want? Blue stripes or green plaid bedding?"

"You choose, hon." Teal crossed her arms and focused on her sister's tired face. "Talk to me."

Lacey's wan smile faltered. "Will said he told you."

"No details, though."

"I just couldn't . . . over the phone . . ."

"It's okay. I know. I haven't exactly been a confidante type of sister."

"No, you haven't. You've been a pain in the tushie."

"It's who I am. You're such a Goody Two-shoes."

"It's who I am."

They stared at each other for a long moment. Maiya's humming and the sound of drawers being pulled filled the space.

"Lace, I really want to hear it."

"We tried to get pregnant for three years. Then it happened. Five months later, I miscarried. The doctor did a D and C. She found a tumor. It was ovarian cancer. Then I had a hysterectomy and chemotherapy. Now my hair is short and I don't surf anymore and I take naps most afternoons.

I'm thirty-two and I have hot flashes. And I buy cookies for the shop instead of baking them myself."

Teal moved over to the couch and pulled Lacey into her arms.

"And I am so sick of crying about it." Lacey blubbered.

Teal felt dampness on her own cheeks. "I'm sorry. I'm so sorry."

"Well, there is some good news. This week's tests said it's in remission."

"Okay." Teal sniffed. "Okay."

"Okay."

It didn't help much. They wept some more.

Maiya squealed from the other room. "Unbelievable! There is no TV in here!"

Teal sat up and wiped her eyes.

Lacey chuckled through her tears. "I'm so glad she got suspended so you felt the urge to come."

"I would have preferred you just told me what was going on."

"Whatever."

Maiya strode into the room. "Whew. There's a TV out here. . . . What's wrong with you two?"

Teal exchanged a glance with Lacey.

Her sister nodded.

"Aunt Lacey has been sick."

"I know. Uncle Will told me. But she's okay now. Right?"

Teal turned to Lacey. "Are you sure you're up for us?"

A softness pushed aside Lacey's tired creases. It was an expression reserved for elderly people who had found their way through years of ups and downs, finding at last a peace with life and death.

It took Teal's breath away.

Lacey smiled. "I am, without a doubt, up for you."

CHAPTER 25

Los Angeles

River clung to the cell phone as if it were a life preserver. He eagerly drank in every sound of Teal's voice. It was less clipped than usual when she told him of Lacey's illness. A silent chuckle underscored it when she described the full-size beds that filled every inch in the bedrooms of the cottage that did not smell of mildew.

"Teal, I didn't think I could miss you this much."

She groaned. "Come on, big guy. I need you to be all right without me there."

"I thought you liked me being in touch with my feminine side."

"Not this month."

River smiled, but his gut twisted as if he'd just run the mile in six minutes. "I'm not all right, but I'll survive."

"Promise me you will go home tonight."

He glanced around his office space, at his

sleeping bag on the floor, the disarray on his desk. The first night Teal and Maiya were gone, he had gone home at the regular time, eaten chili out of a can, an entire bag of Double Stuf Oreos, and a pound of shelled pistachios while watching eight straight hours of television.

Last night he ate dinner in the cafeteria with the live-in staff and fifty boys, gingerly shot some hoops with a group who promised not to elbow him, worked at his desk until ten, then sacked out on the office floor, which was warmer than his camper parked out back.

"River, it's Saturday. Even you occasionally take that one off."

"Um, maybe." At least he'd go home to get some clean clothes. What else was there? At the school he had food, showers, company, a quiet room. "I'm still behind on the auction prep work. It's easier to do it from here than home."

The auction was a fund-raiser for the school, a huge affair that drew people from all over the county. Items were donated by the dozens — everything from cars to computers to Maui vacations — and auctioned off in October. After coordinating it for fifteen years, River had the process down to a science. The earthquake and the injured ribs, though, had thrown a wrench into his schedule.

"How's that going?"

He filled her in on the details of his annual major project. "Hey, thanks for listening. It always gives me a new perspective."

"Here's a new perspective: take care of yourself. You reverting back to your bachelor days worries me."

"You're the one in Camp Poppycock, sitting on the floor beside the front door because it's the only place your phone connects. I'm the worried one."

"Go to church and tell everyone hello from me."

He chuckled. In less than five years, Teal had overhauled his life. Not only did he now sleep in a bed and eat balanced meals, he also went to a church pastored by a widow who had been a television actress back in the day. Most of the congregation remembered welcoming Teal into their midst as an unmarried pregnant grad student. Many of them had babysat Maiya. Along with River's sister, these people had been all the extended family they needed.

Which made the flight to Cedar Pointe all the more off the wall.

"Okay, I will go to church. Any other instructions, Counselor?"

"I'm out of line. I don't mean to —"

"Hey, I'm kidding."

"I'm not. Seriously, River, I'm not *gone*. I am coming home."

He heard the unspoken: *I'm not gone like Krissy.* "I know."

In the silence that followed, there were more unspoken words, tidal waves of pain, relief, utter joy, hope, despair, and in the end, an all-encompassing blanket of love.

"But," he said, "I really, really miss you."

"I miss you too. Really, really, really."

"Truly?"

She laughed. "Maiya wants to talk to you."

His heart leaped at the sentence.

He was in bad shape. Really, really bad shape.

"Maiya!" She spoke away from the phone. "I can't bring the phone to you. This is the only spot in the house. Here she comes."

"I love you, Teal."

"I love you, River."

Maiya came on the line. "Hey, Riv!"

"Minnie McMouse! How's it going?" Again he listened to the day's events, laughing at his teenager's rendition. She sounded happy, at ease.

"River, have you seen Jake?"

He frowned. "Honey —"

"I just need to know —"

"He's fine."

"What's happening?"

Should he tell her what he had not told Teal? Wiser not to. "He's fine."

The truth was, Jake's boss and River had both spoken on his behalf, both promising to spend time with him. The judge set bail and the boss paid it. Jake was back to work and doing well.

Despite what Jake had done to his family, River could separate himself and speak in court as a professional. The kid needed to pay the consequences of unlawfully entering the school, but for nearly two years he had toed the line well.

"Come on, Riv. At least tell me if you've seen him."

"All I'm going to say is that it will be a long time before I trust him again."

"Do you trust me again?"

He melted at the anxious note in her voice. "I think this time away will be good for you, to help you learn about the consequences of your choices. But yes, I trust you." He chuckled. "Mainly because you're my adorable daughter who has me wrapped around her little finger."

She laughed loudly. "NW."

NW. No way. "Yes, way!" He dug in his jeans pocket and pulled out a folded-up piece of paper, his cheat sheet for text shorthand. "Just, well, just . . ." He scanned the list. "Just G-O-I!" *Get over it.*

"W-E." *Whatever.*

"My brain is cramping."

"N-P." *No problem.* "G-2-G anyway."

"G-2 what?"

She giggled. "Got to go."

"Right. I heard you're having dinner with the grandparents."

"Yes. Mom promised she would be civil."

River clenched his jaw and a fist. Nine years ago poor Maiya had been traumatized by Owen's ranting. It still bothered her. Teal's history with the man was appalling.

Maiya said, "So no worries." The little-girl voice carried a grown-up conviction.

He relaxed his muscles and eyed the texting paper. "Shoot. Are you sure? Because I really wanted to say H-O-T-Y-Z-I-G-T-B-A-B-R."

"H-O-T — ?" She burst into laughter. "Good one, Riv. L-Y-L!"

"Love you lots too."

Still laughing, she cut the connection.

River's smile faded. He felt like he had on the garage floor right after the quake, hopeless and helpless with only one thing to do.

Even if Teal held her tongue, they would want to follow the acronym: *Hold on to your*

zingiezangers; it's going to be a bumpy ride.
"God, take care of them."

CHAPTER 26

Cedar Pointe

Teal awoke with a start and sat straight up in the strange bed. Her heart pounded and thudded. Ice water coursed through her veins and perspiration soaked her neck.

What in the world was she doing in Cedar Pointe?

She listened for odd noises, straining to hear a dog bark or a car alarm pierce the quiet. She heard only the rustle of Maiya turning in her sleep in the next room. The faint glow of a streetlight seeped at the edges of the blinds.

Teal shivered and lay back down, pulling the covers to her chin. It had not been sounds or bright lights that had awakened her. No, it was something within herself, a turmoil of junk. Guilt, fear, regret, anger, questions, hatred, unforgiveness, spite.

Oh, the list was endless.

At home she had convinced herself long

ago that she had moved on and held no grudges. The past was past.

But in Cedar Pointe she smelled the cedars, tasted the sweet blackberries that grew everywhere like weeds, saw the awesome sea stacks, and then she resented all over again the parents who had stolen the goodness of the place from her. She looked at the innocent, hurting faces of Lacey and Will and felt guilty for having a child of her own and good health. She stood near the place where her baby had been conceived in an act of vengeance and felt her face redden with a shame that no one else knew about.

"God, I dealt with this nine years ago," Teal whispered aloud. "I was so happy. You were so real to me. I wanted everyone to know that You cared about me, that even a loser like me could make it. I came back to make peace."

During that visit, she had gone from tongue-tied to belligerent in record time. All the good intentions to be gracious had disintegrated when face to face with her family.

She had tried to explain her forgiveness to Randi and Owen. "For what?" they had asked.

She had almost laughed. "For *what?* For

starters, the physical abuse."

"Physical abuse?" they had asked. "You were abused?"

Lacey had been stuck in the middle, as always. Although in private she had cried and hugged Teal, she still had to live in the same town with Owen and Randi. By not entering into the debate, she chose their side. Understandable. But Teal did not live with them. She washed her hands of the entire mess and went home with little Maiya to live happily ever after.

Until now.

Whatever had possessed her to head north?

Duh. The usual reason behind any rash decision she made: her emotions. In the wake of everything, they blinded her to any reasonable thought processes. Going on feelings alone, she decided to split ASAP.

And here she thought she had matured beyond such actions. Right.

She had been a mess, fueled by anger and anxiety, all the post-trauma stuff. Why hadn't River put his foot down?

Teal twisted her lips into a wry smile. He had mentioned she might see a counselor. Why would he go beyond that? In their early days of dating, he had put his foot down once or twice. She stomped on it. She was not about to sign up for a relationship that meant he got the final say when it came to her personal choices.

They worked on the whole equal-but-different stuff and reached a basic conclusion. They agreed to freely disagree. If Teal did not notice a train coming at her, then River would pull her away from the track without hesitation. Over time she learned to respect and trust his voice.

Evidently a train was not barreling down the track in her direction.

Even if it did feel like it.

In her defense, she had been hit with emotional overload. The tipping point was Maiya's behavior. Her daughter needed serious attention. Thanks to Lacey's input, Cedar Pointe seemed an easy, immediate place to make that happen.

Perhaps Teal and Maiya might connect in a new way. A girl from LA should easily decide on her own that Camp Poppycock was at the ends of the earth. Voilà. New insight and appreciation would be born. She would vow to never again feel treated unfairly or lie to her parents.

Except that so far Maiya was having a blast. Aunt Lacey and Uncle Will loved her to pieces. Their coffee and gift shop was now Maiya's own playground. She had her stepfather's delight in nature and had already called him to insist that he visit because she heard there was an amazing river he had never seen and it was full of salmon.

Stepfather? Since when had Teal identified River by that term?

Since a few hours ago when Maiya asked a question and *father* entered the equation like never before.

Taking advantage of their atypical situation — the cozy cottage, going to bed at the same time, no cable television or Internet to distract — Teal had tucked Maiya into bed.

Maiya smiled and hugged her. " 'Night."

" 'Night, honey."

"Mom, can I ask you a question?"

In the dim light Teal looked at her little girl, a *sure* on the tip of her tongue, a *no* shouting in her head.

They had spent the evening at Will and Lacey's house. Randi and Owen's last-minute cancellation had been rude and predictable but honestly made things more enjoyable.

The aunt and uncle from heaven owned a Wii. She beat Will at bowling. Lacey showed her old photos of herself and Teal when they were little. They pigged out on Will's spaghetti and Lacey's cream cheese brownies. Teal even allowed Maiya some Facebook time on their computer.

The whole time reeked of *family* in a good, wholesome way, but Teal feared it.

She had at last replied to Maiya. "Sure. Ask away."

"Is he here? In Cedar Pointe?"

"No."

No. Bio Dad was not there.

"It just feels like my father belongs here. . . ." Maiya's voice had trailed off and she shrugged.

A shiver went through Teal now. How long could she go on pretending that the guy was nowhere near?

Teal sat at the kitchen table across from the clueless mother who had abandoned her just as surely as her biological father had, and she put on her game face. This visit was like questioning a deceitful husband in court. Teal needed to maintain a stony expression, let loose with a rueful smile occasionally. It would serve everyone better than if she flew off the handle.

Randi Pomeroy made small talk with her and Maiya. A hacking cough punctuated most sentences. She was fifty-eight and looked a decade older. Gray streaked her dark-brown hair, still thick and cut in an ancient Barbie-doll-style bubble. Scrawny with birdlike movements, she pulled a cigarette from a pack on the table and flipped open a lighter.

"Randi, do you mind?"

"Give it a rest, sweetcakes. It's my day off." She laughed, coughed, and lit up. "You don't believe all that secondhand-smoke propaganda, do you? They're just trying to take our rights away."

Teal walked over to the sink and opened the window above it.

"Randi!" Owen's voice reached them from the living room, above the drone of a televised baseball game. "Maybe the kid's got asthma."

"Cool your jets. They would have told us."

Teal poured another glass of lemonade for Maiya and sat back down.

Randi squinted through a smoke cloud. "You don't have asthma, do you, Maiya?"

"Nope."

" 'Cause if you did, we could move out to the porch."

"I'm fine."

"You like that lemon pie?"

Maiya nodded and forked her last bite. "It's great."

"It's Lacey's. She keeps us in sweets.

Which is why your grandpa weighs three hundred pounds."

Teal pressed the wince from between her brows. *Grandpa.*

"Two-thirty!" came the reply.

Randi smiled and shook her head. "He can't take a joke."

No kidding.

Teal thought the man might as well be in the same room for as often as he interrupted their conversation, but she was glad for small favors. The voice was less fearsome than the face that had not lost its menacing scowl.

When they arrived, he had greeted them from his recliner with little more than a grunt and told Randi to get him another beer. Always a large man, he had gained some weight, but he had also aged way beyond his sixty-five years. Browned and creased from a lifetime of fishing on the ocean, he was cue-ball bald.

Maiya said, "I love Aunt Lacey and Uncle Will's shop."

Randi snorted. "You call them aunt and uncle?"

"Yeah. Why wouldn't I? They are my aunt and uncle." Maiya did not miss a beat.

Bless her insolent attitude for once. This was her dig at the reference to *grandpa.*

Randi said, "Just curious since Lacey's only half-related to you. You know, we all would've come down to visit you, but to tell you the truth, we never had that kind of money. Lacey and Will have been at that shop 24-7 for years, so they couldn't get away. Owen's out on that boat all the time. That's the way life is here."

"What do you do at the library?"

She tapped the cigarette against a small ashtray. "I've been librarian forever and a day. Well, not officially a librarian. Didn't go to school and get the paper, but I do everything they do."

Teal tuned out their conversation and wondered how long before the walls closed in on her. They were full of memories best forgotten.

She had grown up in the house, a modest two-bedroom ranch in an old neighborhood. It was in desperate need of updating, but the kitchen and living room had been painted in recent years. The off-white color made the house brighter than she remembered it.

"Oh, trust me," Randi said. "Your mother was a hellion in her day."

Teal opened her mouth to protest, but Maiya was already speaking.

"Did she ever get suspended from

school?"

"No."

"Well, I did, Gran."

"No kidding? Guess the apple doesn't fall too far from the tree, eh? Teal, serves you right for all the problems you caused us." Her chuckle gave way to a fit of coughing.

Maiya glanced at her watch. "Mom, Aunt Lacey said she'd teach me how to do the register so I can start working at the shop. We probably should get going."

"Okay." *Wasn't that scheduled for tomorrow?* Teal saved her question for later and scraped her chair back from the table.

Randi protested politely and made vague plans for dinner and a library visit.

Without too much ado, Teal and Maiya headed out the side door, calling a quick good-bye to Owen and bypassing the living room where he sat.

Without a word, they clipped along the old stone walkway around to the front yard, through the overgrown grass, past alder and fir trees that kept the yard in continual gloom. At the street they got into the car and Teal drove away. She lowered the front windows and ruffled her hair. The stench of something other than smoke turned her stomach.

"Mom."

Teal heard a note of panic in Maiya's voice and glanced over. Her eyes were wide, gazing straight ahead. "What?"

"Is Owen my — my — ?"

"Oh! Honey! No!" Teal quickly steered over to the curb and parked. She turned to Maiya and grabbed her hand. "No, no. Owen is not your biological father. He hit me, he ridiculed me, he whipped me with his belt. But he never hurt me that way. He never molested me."

Maiya exhaled a shaky breath. "His earlobes."

"Are attached." Teal pulled her into a fierce hug. "You're obsessing over earlobes, hon. Trust me, Bio Dad is not in Cedar Pointe."

"Then where is he?"

Teal felt Maiya's tears on her neck. "I don't know."

"Where is yours?"

"I've told you."

Maiya straightened to look Teal in the eye. "You don't know either, but don't you *want* to know?"

"Never. He left me. That makes him meaner than Owen. I don't care to learn the first thing about him. And you may not like this, hon, but I feel the same about yours. It's just not worth the trauma to chase them down and confront them, only to have them say what they've been living all these years: 'I don't want to have anything to do with you.' "

"But maybe not."

"Their track record says it all."

Maiya wiped at her eyes. "It's so not right."

"It's not." Teal's heart thudded in her ears. She was shading the truth by lumping the two men together. Her father left when she was three. Maiya's father left the night he impregnated Teal.

She had never been able to bring herself to explain that, to say that out loud.

Maiya exhaled loudly. "Mom, do we have to go back there, to Randi and Owen's? It was awful. It was like being in a dark cave." She shook her head.

Teal stared at her. The sun had been shining through the kitchen window. She remembered seeing it glint off Maiya's new bracelet.

The darkness Teal had always associated with Randi and Owen was not a figment of her imagination.

She smoothed Maiya's hair. "We won't go back there, not ever again in this lifetime."

CHAPTER 27

Lacey felt Will's eyes on her and looked up from where she sat on a stool near the cash register by the front door. There he was, clear across the shop behind the other cash register at the coffee counter, grinning at her.

He winked.

She winked back and felt all tingly inside, awash in gratitude and delight. Teal and Maiya's visit had cheered both of them, a sensation long missing from their lives.

"Aunt Lacey." Maiya stood beside her, intensely studying the cash register. "Where's the doohickey that scans the price? Like at the grocery store."

"We don't need one of those. Happy Grounds is a small business."

"You mean you have to punch in numbers?"

"Yes."

"Cool."

Lacey laughed.

"I never got to do this at the ice cream shop. I only served food and sang."

"You sang?"

"Most of the waitstaff did. You know, for birthdays and anniversaries. Sometimes we'd do impromptu stuff."

"Now that's cool. Maybe we can start singing for the customers here. You and Uncle Will. He's a good baritone."

"How about Baker, the barista extraordinaire?"

They exchanged a smile.

Lacey said, "He doesn't say much, but he'll open up once he gets to know you." She saw an elderly woman walking toward them, a gift book in her hand. "Ready to get to work?"

"No." Maiya moved aside. "I'll watch you for a while."

"I think not. You're like your mom. I bet you jump in with both feet like she does, no matter what."

Maiya giggled. "Well, yeah, I guess I do."

The woman reached the counter. "Lacey, who is this lovely young woman?"

Lacey made the introductions, confident that her regular customer would not mind waiting while she coached Maiya through the transaction. A few minutes later, Maiya walked her new friend to the door and hugged her good-bye.

The girl was a natural. How on earth had she gotten mixed up with a wild boy and suspended from school?

"Aunt Lacey, you have a weird look on your face. Did I do something wrong?"

"No." She grinned. "I was just thinking how comfortable you are in your skin and wondering how you could get mixed up with someone who wasn't exactly the best influence on you."

Maiya frowned.

"Hey, aunts are allowed to poke their noses into nieces' business. It's in the rule book."

Maiya's frown deepened.

"My weird look was because I remembered feeling comfortable in my skin when I was your age. I was athletic and a surfer. I made good grades, I was class president, blah, blah, blah. Not a huge feat with only fifty-eight in a class. Anyway, guess who I had a crush on and invited to the winter Sadie Hawkins dance our senior year?"

Maiya's face smoothed out. "A loser?"

"The biggest. Actually, it was Will's brother, Cody, who I might add is now an upstanding citizen. So you never know how they'll turn out. Oops, don't tell your mom

I said that. She'll think I'm rooting for —
what's his name?"

"Jake." Maiya grinned. "Thanks for not
lecturing me."

"Why would I? I suspect you know J-A-
K-E spells trouble."

Maiya shrugged and nodded.

"End of discussion. Speaking of your
mom, is she okay? She's been on the phone
since you two got here." Lacey looked over
at Teal, huddled at a table strewn with papers.

"That's just Mom on a new case. River
says she's like a bulldog that won't let go of
a bone."

"I thought only retailers like us worked on
Labor Day. She didn't have to come to the
shop with you."

"She said it was easier than sitting still in
the twelve-inch square in the cottage that
holds cell reception. And her Bluetooth
doesn't work there at all."

"Oh. That's going to be a problem for
her."

"It's going to be a problem for you if she
gets ticked off at whoever she's talking to."
Her brows went up. "If you get my drift."

Lacey got her drift, all right. Choosing to
overlook Teal's abrasiveness came with the
territory of hero worship, but she did not

deny its existence. "She'll growl and disturb the customers."

"Yep."

"She's got to be an amazing lawyer. She always could argue the wallpaper off the wall."

Maiya giggled. "River says the paint."

Lacey laughed. "Do you want to go help those ladies over there?"

"What do I say?"

"They're looking at the myrtlewood kitchen products. Maybe they have questions. Since Uncle Will told you all about the wood, you'll have the answers."

Maiya tilted her head and began reciting. "The myrtlewood tree is a broadleaf evergreen, native to the southwest Oregon coast. The leaf can be used as a substitute for bay leaves in cooking. The wood varies in color from blond to black with shades of reds and greens and grays. This is due to the different minerals in the soil where the trees grow. The myrtlewood tree is even mentioned in the Bible — for example, in Isaiah 55:13. And we have, like, a hundred million thousand number of products made from it." She bowed.

Lacey clapped her hands. "You're hired. Go do your job."

She scrunched her face and clenched her

fist. "I think I can. I think I can." She walked off toward the shoppers.

With no other customers in the gift shop area, Lacey took advantage of the opportunity to walk over to Teal's table and sit down. "Hey."

Her sister looked up, no longer on the phone. "Hey, yourself. You look exhausted."

"I've been ill. What's your excuse?"

She smiled. "You've gotten snarky."

"Cancer will do that to a person. Are you all right?"

Her smile faded. "I have a young mom who needs to get a restraining order against her child's biological father."

"How sad."

Teal nodded and glanced across the room with its chairs full of patrons. "I forgot how tourists overrun the town on Labor Day."

"It's great for business. Slow season starts promptly tomorrow at 8 a.m."

"Maiya and I can skip dinner at your house tonight."

"It's not a problem, really."

"We'll do takeout, then."

"You also forget there is no such thing as fast food within forty miles, and the local restaurants will close up early for the holiday. Will promised Maiya his famous hamburgers."

"You're absolutely sure we are not a burden?"

"Are you kidding? We love having you two here." She saw the hesitation on Teal's face and figured she might be searching for a way out. "Teal, don't worry. Mom and Dad are not coming."

"It's only natural that you would invite them."

"But I didn't. Your visit yesterday was hard enough." Neither Teal nor Maiya had said much about it, which spoke volumes. "Besides that, it's a holiday. They'll be bombed out of their minds by four this afternoon."

Teal grimaced. "I'm sorry you have to live with that."

"Well, I don't so much anymore. I have enough of my own problems to deal with. Somehow they both still manage to work. Once in a while they stop in here, sober. I can fix food for them, but I can't fix them."

"Whew, that's the most candid you've ever been on the subject."

"Snarky and candid." Lacey smiled. "Okay, I like it. Thank you for coming to Cedar Pointe."

Teal's eyes filled.

Lacey felt her own sting. She looked over the low wall into the gift shop. Maiya was holding court with the ladies in kitchenware, showing them two small bowls as if comparing the beautiful colors for them. Another customer dawdled near the check-out counter. "I better go help Maiya."

"Is she doing all right?"

"She's amazing. She's so much like you."

"Yeah, right. She can't be both."

Lacey hesitated. They had stumbled into new territory. Never in her life had she candidly told Teal how she felt. Now because of the joy her niece had awakened, words popped out. *She's amazing . . . so much like you?* But it was true. Why not speak it? "You are amazing."

"Come on, Lace. *Candid* means just say what's on your mind and tell me to deal with it. We both know I made a mess of my life. Maiya is amazing in spite of me."

"You don't see it, do you? Teal, you've been my role model for as long as I can remember. I swear I can still picture you peering over the crib at me, singing songs and making faces. You were there in ways Mom should have been. I practically worshiped the ground you walked on."

"Why would you do that?"

"Because you're my big sister. You used to make me cry, but I idolized you. You were always so full of life, so beautiful inside and out."

Teal swallowed. "I treated you like dirt."

"Yes, you did, but in the big picture, that didn't matter. I wanted to be like you when I grew up. Well, minus the grating personality that still puts my teeth on edge."

They stared at each other for a long moment. Teal's eyes grew wide and the corners of her mouth went up and down.

At last Lacey grinned. "Do you think I'm there?"

"Snarky and candid?" Teal laughed. "Yes, you just might be."

Lacey's eyelids grew heavy, but she refused to give up. So what if it was after ten o'clock? Her niece wanted to talk.

The two of them sat in her living room, Lacey in the recliner tilted back. Maiya sat cross-legged on the floor beside her. Teal had left soon after dinner. Will was in his man cave, formerly the back bedroom, watching the History Channel on his big-screen television until Maiya was ready for him to drive her to the cottage.

"Aunt Lacey, is this you in the hooded wet suit?" Maiya pulled a photograph from the pile on the floor and held it up.

"That's me. Do you surf?"

"No way. I like hiking with River when we camp, but that's it for being athletic." She held up another picture. "This looks like Uncle Will. Who are the other guys? They all kind of look alike."

"It's the Emerson blond hair and hazel-green eyes, on Will's mother's side. That's his younger brother, Cody, in the middle and their older cousin, Dylan, on the right. He died in a car accident when he was in his early twenties. It was so sad."

"Is Cody the wild one you had a crush on?"

"*Briefly* had a crush on, before his brother decided to notice me. Actually, I liked Dylan, too, but that was before I noticed Will." She pointed to a photo lying in the box. "Those are my in-laws, William and Nora. They'll be in town next week. You'll get to meet more family."

"They're not my family." A new despondent tone filled Maiya's voice. "I mean, Uncle Will is the bomb, but technically, he's not family. Only you and Mom are. Well, not counting Randi."

Lacey found it curious that her niece seemed bothered by a lack of blood relatives. "Technically, that's right. But having River for a stepdad has worked pretty well for you, right?"

She shrugged a shoulder. "He can't even adopt me."

"But he's been there for about five years now." Lacey forged ahead. "He's your true dad in spirit. And if I know William and Nora, you'll have them for grandparents the instant they meet you, even if it's not all official." She looked at Maiya's bent head and busy hands riffling through photos. "Honey, are you looking for something in particular?"

"Oh . . . I don't know."

"I have more boxes."

Maiya looked up at her. "You do?"

"They don't seem organized, but there is a method to my crazy filing system. If you tell me what you're interested in, maybe I can help."

The girl's shoulders slumped. "I'm looking for my dad."

Her dad? No wonder the sudden interest in old photos and talk about family being official or not. "I don't, um —"

"You don't know. Nobody does except Mom, and sometimes I wonder if she even knows."

"That's hard, Maiya. Um, at least you've got River. Who needs a piece of paper? From what I hear about him, I might ask him to be my stepdad too."

"I would too if I were you. I mean, don't get offended, but I wouldn't want Owen for a dad. I got freaked out yesterday because I thought he might be."

Lacey felt a sudden hollowness. "Why did you think that?"

"His earlobes." She yanked on one of hers. "They're attached like mine, and Mom's aren't. It's a hereditary thing."

"Did you ask her?"

"Yeah, and she said it was not a possibility, no way."

Whew. Thank You, Lord. "I'm glad to hear that. I didn't think he . . ." But how could she know for sure? Owen treated Teal so horribly. "He was not at all kind to her."

"He scared me to death the last time we were here. What was he like to you?"

"Oh, normal, I guess. As normal as any run-of-the-mill dysfunctional dad can be. I sensed that he loved me because I was his daughter, even if he couldn't show it. There were no major traumas. He clearly resented your mom, maybe because she wasn't his. After she left for college, he seemed less angry, but then he drank more."

Maiya busied herself with the photos. "River's cool. But inside I feel like something's not . . . finished." She gazed up at Lacey, her eyes unblinking. "You really don't know who he is?"

"No. Your mom never told me."

"Don't you have a clue? Who were her boyfriends? Who did she hang out with?"

"Honey, I was twelve when she left for college. I seldom saw her after that. She stayed up in Portland most holidays and summers, working and going to school. Then she moved to LA before you were born."

Maiya looked down again and her hair fell about her face, hiding it. "She had to have some friends she kept in touch with here."

Lacey leaned back in her chair, unsure what the aunt's rule book said about revealing a sister's flaws.

To her knowledge, Teal did not have friends to keep in touch with. She never spoke of anyone close at home. If she hung out with anyone, it was with other outsiders. They were like shadows to Lacey; town gossip labeled them wild. The adjective seemed to fit her sister. They came from nearby towns, were older, and had cars so Teal was able to hitch rides and spend very little time at home.

She had been an unhappy, prickly loner who pushed people away. Lacey figured no one was born like that. Owen probably mistreated her from the start, beginning when she was only four years old.

That Teal would get pregnant out of

wedlock seemed a given. The shock was that it didn't happen until she was in college. To everyone's further surprise, she graduated from college six months before Maiya's birth, went on to grad school, and got a great job. At some point she proclaimed a newfound faith in God. Afterward she seemed happy and settled, although still relationally distant from Lacey and their mother.

Lacey shut her eyes and listened to the clock tick. A faint sound of Will's voice drifted down the hallway. Who was he talking to at this late hour? A familiar fear niggled at the back of her mind. Given their nightmare of a year and an uncertain future, she couldn't blame him for looking elsewhere for companionship.

A sudden hopelessness filled her. *Why, why, why?*

She heard a sniff and a soft *splat.* She opened her eyes and saw Maiya wiping a photograph across her sweatshirt.

"Sorry."

"Oh, Maiya. Come here."

The girl scooted closer to the chair and laid her head on the armrest.

Lacey drew her fingers through Maiya's long, dark hair. "Have you told your mom how much it hurts not knowing?"

"Yeah." She took a shaky breath. "She says she'll tell me when it's time."

"Then we have to wait." Lacey leaned over and kissed the back of Maiya's head. "Life stinks, hon. No two ways about it. It just does."

Lacey felt Will's weight sink into the mattress beside her but did not have the energy to open her eyes. "Hi."

"You're supposed to be asleep." He reached for her hand and held it.

"Maiya get home okay?"

"Yes, worrywart aunt. I walked her inside the cottage like you ordered. Teal was still up, working on her laptop."

"What are we going to do about her cell and Internet service in the cottage?"

"Happy Grounds Coffee Shop opens at six thirty with free Wi-Fi and great cell reception." He kissed her cheek. "Maiya says you're awesome."

"She thinks you're the bomb, Uncle Will."

"That's good, right?"

"Almost as good as awesome." She smiled. "Isn't it wonderful having her here?"

"Yeah. She's easy to be with. She seems so familiar."

"She's a Teal clone."

"It's not just her looks. There's something

226

about her." He yawned. "Maybe it's because she's your niece. 'Night, Lace."

" 'Night."

His breathing evened out.

Lacey's did not.

She opened her eyes. The bathroom nightlight filtered into the room. Will's face was at rest. He was such a good guy. Steady and solid.

Her doubts made no sense.

But cancer taught her to live in the moment. There were none to waste, none to fritter away with fear and worry. What was there to lose? It was already gone.

"Will."

His eyelids blinked open. He was instantly alert. "What?"

"Were you on the phone tonight?"

"Phone? Oh yeah. Holly called. She's got next Monday off too. She offered to fill in for you. I said you'd get back to her."

It wasn't the first time her friend had called in the evening after what had become Lacey's normal bedtime.

Holly and Will? Stories like that abounded. The sick wife's best friend and husband get it on. It was almost too hackneyed to consider. Almost.

"Lace, you're shaking. What's wrong?"

"I'm so cold."

He pulled her to himself and held her close. "You're overtired, sweetheart."

Her teeth chattered. She felt herself falling as if into a dark abyss.

"Shh." Will kissed her forehead. "It's okay. I'm here."

CHAPTER 28

Los Angeles

Talking on the phone with Teal, River stood in the garage where the month before he had lain under a pile of bins. "You're going to love them." He referred to the newly constructed wooden shelves secured to the wall.

"How did you finish them already?"

"It's Labor Day. What can I say?" He walked to the doorway, switched off the light, and went into the house. "How was your day?"

"I said, 'How did you finish them already?' "

"Had help." Tucking the phone between his chin and shoulder, he crossed the kitchen, grabbed a piece of cold pizza from a box on the counter, and pulled a plate from the cupboard. "I want you to know I am using a plate for my pizza." He took a soda from the fridge. "And I am going to sit at the table, like a civilized person."

"Why do you keep changing the subject?"

"I'm tired and hungry and would prefer to ease into a touchy subject." He set his things on the table, took a bite, and sat.

Teal did not say anything.

He chewed and swallowed and took another bite.

"Oh, River." Her edgy tone said it all. Disbelief, disappointment, a hint of anger. She had figured out the touchy subject.

He swallowed and plunged into it. "Jake's a good worker and he was available. The school guys were committed to a slew of projects there. You and Maiya weren't here. I saw no problem with him helping me."

"No problem? He gets to carry on his relationship with you and be in our home while Maiya and I have to run away? That's a problem with me."

River shoved pizza into his mouth rather than vent his retort; he popped open the soda can. Running away had been Teal's choice. Understandable in a wacky sense but still, in his opinion, unnecessary . . . if not downright idiotic.

She blew out a breath. "I cannot believe you did that."

He took a swig from the can. "I won't give up on him."

"That doesn't mean you communicate that what he did with our daughter was acceptable!"

"I'm not doing that. He knows he's on a short leash and has to earn back my trust."

"There is no earning it back."

"That's where we disagree. This is how I operate. Been doing it for fifteen years."

"But now you have a family to think about."

It hit him, a punch to the solar plexus. He had had a family before — a wife, plans for children, the first on his way. They were not part of Teal's reality. At times, she seemed to totally forget about them.

She said, "What am I supposed to tell Maiya?"

"That the shelves are up."

"I'm serious. If I tell her Jake is buddy-buddy with you, she'll think the whole incident has blown over."

"She's stuck up in Camp Poppycock. I doubt she'll think that."

"I don't want to talk about this anymore."

Her silly remark goaded. She wanted to talk as long as she heard what she wanted to hear.

He threw out his idea to keep the details from her and said, with too much heat, "Tell Maiya I promised the judge that I'd spend

231

time with Jake when he wasn't working at the garage."

"That's how he got out." There was accusation in her flat tone. "Unbelievable."

She wasn't talking about the judge's decision, but that River would offer such a thing. He forced himself to explain in a neutral tone the rest of the story. "His boss posted bail and vouched for Jake's excellent work record."

She did not reply.

"Tell Maiya I wouldn't hurt her for the world. Tell her this is not about her. It's my job."

"I don't like you."

"Feeling is mutual."

A long, silent moment passed. Her breathing sounded as if she'd run a mile. His own wasn't all that steady.

But she wasn't one of his students. He broke the silence and stated quietly what needed to be said. "But I do love you and I want the best for you. Tell me about your day. Any Owen sightings?"

"River, at the moment, I am sitting on a cushion on a linoleum floor, exactly fifteen inches from the front door that was white when I closed it, but now all I see is red. I think it's best I say good-bye."

"Gotcha. Talk to you tomorrow."

"Good night."

River turned off the phone and smiled grimly. For all of her insistence that they agree to disagree, she hated not bagging a clear win.

That was all right. He could live with her wrath. What he couldn't live with was turning his back on a kid who needed another round of second chances.

CHAPTER 29

Cedar Pointe

"Mom?"

Cell phone clenched in her fist, Teal blinked at the front door and tried to focus through the reddish haze. She had never been so angry at River. How dare he bring Jake back into their home!

"Mom! You okay?"

Teal spun around on the cushion and did not even attempt to smile. "I'm fine. Sorry, did I wake you?"

"I was still reading." She stood leaning at the hall opening, a dark-green fleece throw over her pajamas. "Kind of hard not to hear your hissy voice."

Shoot. She had kept her voice as low as she could. Stupid tiny cottage with paper-thin walls.

"Were you and Riv fighting?"

"Just having a little disagreement."

"About Jake and me?"

Teal sighed. "What did you hear?"

" 'Jake' this, 'Maiya' that."

"It's nothing you need to concern yourself with. River said Jake is doing fine, out on bail and back to work."

Maiya's face lit up, all grin and sparkling eyes. "Sweet."

Teal's heart sank. What did she see in this boy? She reminded her of Lacey as a teen, crazy about a guy who had nothing going for him.

Maiya said, "So what's with the arguing?"

Teal stood and picked up the cushion and carried it to the couch. "Nothing." River could explain his actions to her himself. "He wanted you to know and honestly —" she slid the cushion into place and headed across the room to the table — "I didn't think you needed to know."

"How come?"

Teal plugged her phone into its power cord, shut her laptop, and gathered papers. A little less use of the word *honestly* with Maiya would be a good thing. She did not need to clue her daughter in on every jot and tittle about her and River's relation-ship. "Given the fact that you and Jake are no longer an item, it simply did not seem necessary to tell you."

"It's not like he doesn't exist. It's not like

I don't think about him or don't love —"

"Spare me, Mai." Good grief! Did she need to hear again how in love they were? "It's late." She sat at the table and began organizing the papers. "You should get to bed. I'm almost done here."

Maiya shuffled over to the table, pulled out a chair across from her, and sat.

Teal glanced at her sad face and briefly considered apologizing for whatever put that expression there.

"I miss Riv."

"He'd say the same thing."

" 'Spare me'?"

She couldn't help but smile. "No. That you should go to bed."

"Do you think he'll come for my birthday?"

"Hon, he said he'd try."

Maiya rested her head in her arms atop the table. "You could talk him into it."

Not tonight. Tonight she would not be able to talk him into a romantic candlelit dinner with herself for dessert.

She noticed Maiya eyeing her.

And suddenly she heard the tape of her own hissy voice in her head, fussing at her husband, the daddy to this child who stood on wobbly adolescent terrain.

Teal said in a soft voice, "I will do my best

to talk him into it. We know he wants to come. It depends on his schedule. If he gets the auction prep work under control, he'll feel freed up to take time off."

"I'm going to marry a rich man who inherited all his billions and has nothing to do except give to charitable causes and show me the world."

Thank goodness. That left Jake Ford out of the picture.

"It's raining!" Maiya's whine rang out from her bedroom as a morning greeting.

Teal, working at the kitchen table since very early, called back, "A day late. It's supposed to start on Labor Day."

Maiya emerged from the hallway, still in her pajamas. "Uncle Will said that's an old wives' tale. Labor Day falls on a different date every year."

Teal shrugged.

"Mom, the real rain doesn't start until October."

She shrugged again, eyes on her screen as her fingers tapped out legalese for the countersuit in the Hannah Walton case.

"Mom."

"Yeah? One sec." It took more like sixty to finish her paragraph. Then she looked up and forced herself to pull her hands from the keyboard. She clenched them on her lap. "Good morning."

Maiya was sitting across the table drinking orange juice, her eyes puffy, her long hair sticking every which way. "It's not even seven o'clock."

"I know, and I am impressed to see you up and raring to go."

"I mean, you're working already."

"This part has to be done first thing today."

"Is it related to yesterday's emergency?"

"Yes." Her line of sight drifted toward the laptop.

"Can you tell me about it?"

"Can I ever?" She spotted a typo and mentally corrected it.

"I just want to know what can be so important that you don't talk to anybody."

Teal could take a hint. She shut the laptop and picked up her coffee mug. "Without going into details, the case is about parental rights."

"How old is the kid?"

"Little."

"You'll make sure he gets to be with the best parent?"

"Always." She smiled. "Uncle Will dropped off the bicycle he said you can use." The shop was only six blocks away, but Maiya had told Will she preferred not to walk.

"But it's raining! Hard! Can't I just drive myself to Happy Grounds? It's not like there's any traffic or cops between here and there."

"There are cops, and they don't have much else to do except lie in wait for drivers who are breaking the law."

"Ha-ha."

"Aunt Lacey can pick you up later. Didn't you decide to start with the tutoring this afternoon?"

"But Baker's working now before he goes to school. He said he'd take a look at where I am in my trig book. He wants to ask his teacher for some help."

"Wow. I'm really impressed now."

"What do you expect from a couple of geeks?" She yawned, propped an elbow on the table, and squished her cheek against her palm.

Despite the previous night's bout with regrets, Teal felt again the coziness of their situation. When Will stopped by on his way to work earlier, he helped her start a fire in the pellet stove. It sizzled now and warmed the small area. Lacey had thoughtfully stocked the kitchen for them with juice, bread, milk, cereal, eggs — the basics.

Maiya really was a bit on the geeky side. She had books and her trumpet. They need not go anywhere.

Maiya pushed her chair from the table. "I told Baker I'd be there by seven thirty."

Teal blinked away the cozy image. "I'll take you."

"No, that's okay." She shuffled away toward the hall. "Aunt Lacey said to call her when I got up. She'll come get me."

"I think she's been skipping the early shift since her illness."

"It's okay." Maiya looked over her shoulder and grinned. "She told me it was going to rain today. She'd be ready."

Teal smiled.

It was a tight smile.

As Maiya disappeared into the bathroom, Teal called out, "Do you want breakfast?"

"Are you kidding?" Maiya called back. "Aunt Lacey's got quiche, croissants, muffins, scones, juice, fruit — not to mention coffee, which I may take up . . ."

The door clicked shut.

"Aunt Lacey" this, "Aunt Lacey" that.

A mishmash of feelings struck so violently Teal could not ignore them.

Resentment spoke, loud and clear. What was with this instant superglue bond between Maiya and Lacey? Teal's plans to mommy her daughter were being derailed because Maiya would rather hang out with Lacey.

Teal felt ashamed. She should blame her obsession with Hannah Walton's case for taking her out of the picture. She should be happy that Maiya and Lacey liked each other. The truth was, with Maiya's needs taken care of, Teal could get back to work without further interruption.

She blew out a breath. "This does not make me the world's worst mom."

Enough with the pep talk. She took a swig of coffee and opened her laptop.

Teal was again seated on a cushion less than two feet inside the front door, talking on her phone, laptop open before her on the floor, legal pad on her lap.

The bright white door was shut against the rain that lashed at the window on the upper half of the door. With the yellow café curtain pushed to the sides, the wet pane was visible if she craned her neck. Cold air seeped in around the door's edges.

She listened to her client's rendition of the ex-boyfriend's visit. Hannah Walton sounded less strung out than she had yesterday, which added cohesiveness but also red flags.

Teal looked at her handwritten notes, unable to glean facts that warranted a restraining order. "Let me recap to make sure I have everything I need. First off, without advance warning, James Parkhurst rang your doorbell yesterday about 10 a.m., you opened the door, and he said he wanted to see his child."

"He demanded it."

"Did he threaten you?"

"N-no, not exactly."

"Did you feel threatened?"

"Definitely. He was belligerent."

"How so?"

"Teal, the man is six-four and all muscle. He has a deep bass voice, bushy eyebrows, and beady eyes, and enough money to make anyone kowtow."

"So he always comes across as belligerent?"

"I-I guess. Well, not when I was with him. You know, when we were seeing each other. He was, he was . . ."

"A sweet-talker who made you feel safe."

"Exactly."

"Was it his tone of voice that frightened you?"

"No. He was polite, I guess. He said, 'I'd like to meet my daughter, please.' "

"Did little Maddie see him?"

"No. She was out in the backyard with my mother-in-law."

"All right. So you said to Parkhurst, 'No way.' He said, 'If she's mine, I have visitation rights.' You said, 'Over my dead body.' "

"Yes."

"And then your husband, Ryan, joined you at the door and asked him to leave."

"Sort of. He told him to get the blankety-blank off our property."

Teal figured she was going to like this hero Ryan. "And Parkhurst replied what precisely?"

" 'No problemo.' "

"Then he left."

"Yes. Teal, I was so shaken up."

"Of course you were. Do you feel that he might harm Maddie or try to forcefully take her away?"

"Yes!"

"All right." Teal paused. "I'm not sure that we have enough to go on for a judge to sign off on a restraining order —"

"But he's a threat to us!"

"It feels like he is, but the facts don't show it. And he has no past record of similar actions with you or others. I will talk to his attorney today and inform him that this behavior is unacceptable."

"Okay." She didn't sound happy.

"Hannah, that's just one aspect. We are moving forward to file the countersuit to terminate his parental rights. A no-show for five years after you told him you were pregnant is, without question, abandonment according to the California Family Code."

"What does that mean?"

"It means his abandonment is on record and he doesn't have a leg to stand on. Are you up for going through a few more questions?"

"Sure. I'm sorry that you have to work on your vacation."

"I'm not on vacation. A family emergency took me out of town. I apologize that I'm not there in person, but you know I'm available, and everyone at my firm is at your disposal." She heard a beep. "Hold on a sec, please."

She lowered her cell and saw that River was calling. Answer or not?

He would have to wait. He would understand.

Wouldn't he?

Of course he would. It was their life. They had each married not so much a workaholic as an advocate for the helpless. At times, for short periods, the helpless one was prioritized above the spouse. From the beginning they had realized this about their relationship and agreed not to take it personally.

The fun part of such a crazy lifestyle was the catch-up time afterward. They would abandon themselves to each other. Special dinners were in order or daylong dates that included beach strolls, movies, and museums.

River was fine.

In spite of last night's conversation. In spite of the fact there was no available catch-up time anywhere near on the horizon.

She put the phone back to her ear. "Sorry, Hannah. I just have a few questions." *And a hope.* If the original version of Hannah's story was the complete truth, then they were most likely home free. If not, then Bio Dad — who perhaps did not fit the ogre profile — might get a chance to meet his daughter.

A shiver went through Teal. She blamed it on the rain.

CHAPTER 30

Early afternoon Teal's back and head ached from hours on the cushion, talking and e-mailing on her phone. Besides needing a change of position, she needed wireless.

As she walked inside Happy Grounds, the bell on the door tinkled its happy sound. Two people browsed the gift section and six others sat at tables in the dining area. Teal wondered how businesses like her sister's ever made ends meet between September and June.

Two of the six patrons were Maiya and Baker, the latte expert. Their heads nearly touched over an open textbook.

Teal dropped her laptop and briefcase on the nearest table and met Lacey at the counter.

Her sister handed her a mug of steaming coffee. "I saw you coming."

"Mm. Thank you." She nodded in Maiya's direction. "What's with Mr. Latte here at this hour?"

"He got off school early today for some reason or other. Maiya seemed glad to start math with him even after our full day."

"How did you two do?"

"Great. She has syllabuses for most of her classes, so from those we figured out what to cover in the next few weeks. Health and US history will be fun, but Plato will be a stretch. It's been a while." She smiled. "From the looks of those two, I think we've got math covered too."

Teal noticed that Maiya and Baker were still huddled over the textbook and talking with animation, as if trig were the most fascinating topic in the world.

"Hey, I saved a tuna salad for you. Maiya said you like it."

"You are the hostess with the mostest."

"That would be my mother-in-law. I just try to mimic her." Lacey glanced down at her long-sleeved T-shirt and blue jeans and laughed. "However, the wardrobe would not pass muster."

Teal sipped her coffee and studied her sister. The green shirt with its pine tree and "Green is not just a color" message fit the tender expression on Lacey's face. She would love trees and whales, customers and nieces. Maybe even wayward sisters.

Lacey looked up. "I probably won't wear this when Nora's here next week."

"Nora's coming? When?" The muscles in Teal's neck stiffened again. She remembered Will's parents as being friendly. The thought of relating to more people from her past, though, felt like overload.

"I didn't mention that? I told Maiya. Sorry. Sometimes talking to her feels like talking to you." Lacey smiled. "Nora and William plan to arrive whenever their RV pulls into my driveway, sometime next week."

"Weren't they in town already this summer?"

"Yes, but when they heard you and Maiya were here, they decided to swing by again on their way home to Phoenix." She leaned across the counter. "You know you're the talk of Camp Poppycock."

Teal frowned. "With a population of a thousand, I figured as much."

"But it's all positive. The fact that you're a big-time Beverly Hills attorney impresses us."

"Lace, please. It's Los Angeles, and it's not a big-time deal."

"You're so modest." She giggled. "But you do need a place to work, so Will's getting a store key made for you. It's silly for you to sit on the cottage floor and not be able to come in here after hours."

"That's — that's . . ." She wanted to say "unnecessary," but that would be a lie. "Oh, Lacey. I wasn't supposed to be working so much, but this particular case . . ." She shook her head. "Thank you."

"Sure. Come look in the back. I want to show you what Will did with the desk."

Teal walked around the counter and followed Lacey into the back room. She had been given the tour on the day they arrived and noticed the desk nearly buried under piles and piles of papers.

The windowless room was rectangular, the width of the coffee shop, painted an off-white and glowing from a ceiling full of recessed lights. It was half kitchen, half office. An exterior door led to the alley. There was a recliner in a corner. It seemed out of place. It had been added for Lacey's comfort, for those days when she had insisted on working but needed frequent breaks to rest.

Lacey gestured at the desk. "Will's done for the day. Make yourself at home."

The work space had indeed been cleared. "What did he do with all of his stuff?"

Lacey pointed to two cardboard boxes on the floor beside it. "There."

"I don't mind working in the other room at a table. If you don't mind."

"I certainly don't mind, but I saw people interrupt you yesterday." She put an arm around Teal's shoulder and hugged her. "Suit yourself. I'm just so happy you're here."

Teal returned her hug and stared at the desk so as not to stare at the recliner in the corner.

It didn't matter where she looked, though. Her ears still burned and her mind still visited the back room as it had looked nearly seventeen years ago.

The kitchen had contained old, smaller appliances and cabinets with doors that did not stay shut. The walls had been covered in dark paneling, the lighting dim. There had been no computer atop the desk, no recliner in a corner.

There had been a couch.

And two young people fraught with a passion that had nothing to do with making love and everything to do with expressing hatred.

Teal patted her sister's thin back and felt the sharpness of a shoulder blade. "Lace, thanks, but I don't want to take Will's space. I'll use any available table out front and be just fine."

"Well, if you need privacy, this is here for you."

Teal smiled tightly, unwilling to describe the ghosts that kept the back room anything but private.

It was after 5 p.m. Teal sat in the closed and deserted coffee shop and tried to decide if River should phone her first. Technically he had that morning, but she was talking to Hannah Walton at the time and he did not leave a voice mail. That gave her stubborn side permission not to return his call.

But almost nineteen hours had passed since they last spoke. Suddenly stubborn felt ridiculous.

She pressed the speed dial for him.

His cell rang and rang.

She checked her watch again. Classes were over for him. The boys would be busy with kitchen or other duties and soon sitting down to dinner. He didn't normally schedule counseling sessions for this time of day. He might be —

The ringing stopped. She expected voice mail to pick up and wondered what to say.

"Teal?" It was River, live.

She readjusted her thoughts, a torturously long procedure. "Hi."

"Hi."

She hated being at a loss for words. "I didn't think you were going to answer." She cringed, hating more the reduction of her words to pointlessness.

"I was out in the hall with some guys; my phone was on the desk." He said no more.

She breathed.

"Teal, you want to go first?"

"I'm not sorry for being angry."

He laughed, long and hard.

A smile wobbled into place.

He said, "I didn't think you were. The question is, are we cool?"

It was River-talk for *was she calm enough to engage in normal conversation?* "We're cool. How was your day?"

They engaged in normal conversation, a lengthy exchange that soothed her nerves. Backroom ghosts and Hannah Walton's distress faded from the forefront of her mind. Jake's importance in the overall scheme of their life lessened.

Teal was married to a good man. She was the mother of a wonderful daughter whose hormones would even out in the long run. All was well with the world.

"So," he said, "work sounds like it's becoming an issue. What do you think about cutting your visit short?"

"I think that would totally defeat its purpose."

"That would be your 'mommy time,' which seems to be on the wane?"

Like a mommy bear, Teal felt something primal rise up inside of her. "River, we've only been here four days. Once the counter-suit and motion to dismiss are filed, I can work on the discovery in my spare time. Maiya is —"

"I miss you."

She went silent.

"Teal, I miss you so much it hurts. I physically ache inside."

"Maybe it's your ribs?"

"It's not my ribs."

"I'm sorry, hon."

"I'm sorry for being so deeply in touch with my feminine side." His chuckle fell short. There was no humor in it.

"Look at it this way: less than five weeks to go." She had tentatively set the first of October as a departure date. That would put Maiya back in time for the end of her suspension. "It's not *that* long, right?"

"Only if I don't see you before then. I guess I better buy the ticket I put on hold."

"You're coming! For Maiya's birthday?"

"Yep, for a long weekend."

"What about the auction?"

"I'm learning to delegate. I'll be back in time to fix any screw-ups and finalize things." His tone held little conviction.

As they continued to talk, she heard the strain in both of their voices. As much as he missed her and Maiya, it was a difficult choice for him to leave school even for a few days. He did not mention the cost, but she knew that a flight to the nearest airport — located at Camp Poppycock's twin town up the coast, where few people chose to go — would be priced sky high.

She felt a rush of guilt for causing the situation but quickly reminded herself that maintaining a relationship required sacrifices. Despite his show of a feminine side, he was totally in tune with his masculinity. He would be fine.

She wasn't so sure about herself. Call it pride or whatever, revealing to River the ugly part of her life would hurt. The thought of his meeting Randi and Owen and seeing firsthand the poor, backward town turned her stomach. It was not who she was; it was not the woman he had married.

And yet it was still a part of her.

Before River came into her life, she had grown by leaps and bounds. In the light of his love, though, she had positively blossomed. How else could she have found the courage to return to Cedar Pointe?

And yet she was wilting.

There were ghosts in the back room of the coffee shop. There were ghosts at her mother's house, on the stone walkway where she had clung to her father when she was three. There were ghosts in Lacey's naiveté. There were ghosts of Maiya's bio dad in casual conversation at every turn.

Teal feared that not even River could withstand them.

CHAPTER 31

Los Angeles

River flipped his cell phone in his hands, end over end, staring at nothing.

They were not good at this long-distance relationship.

Why had Teal left him?

If he had been sitting with her, looking her in the eye, he could have told her. "This feels like when I lost Krissy and Sammy," he would have said. "I went through the motions, and after a while, I got used to the motions. I got used to their absence. It hurt less. I don't want to get used to your absence now. But I'm starting to."

He was.

And it scared him how quickly it had happened this time around.

Instead he told Teal that he missed her. Which he did.

He missed her when they were on the phone.

Years ago friends and even his sister had warned him about second marriages. "There is more baggage than you can ever imagine. She has a kid? Oh." Groans. "You'll always take a backseat to the kid. The kid was there first."

They spoke from personal experience. He insisted that still, it must have been worth it, right? Replies varied, the best being "On some days."

But he trusted the light Teal had brought into his life. Their journey together would definitely be worth it. It *was* definitely worth it.

Why had she left him?

For Maiya's sake. Which meant, yes, he was sitting in the backseat. Again. Or still?

Still. In a sense.

He worked with teens who had never known a front-seat ride. Which explained why they had ended up in his care. And yet . . .

And yet, where was the balance? Maiya was his own child in every way but genetically. He gave her plenty of front-seat rides. Short ones, when the situation deemed it necessary.

He should have been part of this decision about her. They all could have dealt with it without anyone leaving town.

But there was more going on here. And if he had been sitting with Teal, looking her in the eye, he could have said the hard thing.

"Guilt is why you went to Cedar Pointe. But all of your good intentions to make up with your family and share Maiya with them will not purge you. It will not fill the hole in Maiya's heart. She needs to know who her biological father is, and you need to tell her everything. It's the only thing that will free you and her."

A thought struck him and the phone tumbled onto the desk.

Maybe Teal was doing exactly that. Maybe Bio Dad lived in Cedar Pointe. Maybe she couldn't deal with River being in on it.

Maybe that was why she had left him.

CHAPTER 32

Cedar Pointe

Lacey sat on a park bench, eyes shut, head tilted to catch the sunlight full on her face. "This is great."

"Mm-hmm." Teal spoke beside her. "Thanks for pulling me away from work."

Lacey opened her eyes and looked at her sister. "It's Sunday."

"Now that's the pot calling the kettle black. Happy Grounds is open seven days a week. Either you or Will or both of you are there before it opens at six thirty and after it closes at three, every single day."

"Sunday hours are shorter. It's our day off. Sort of. When do you take off?"

"When a job is done." Teal turned to her now, the sunlight glinting off her sunglasses. "I guess we're both caught up in meeting other people's needs. Your way is just more obvious. You get to give them coffee and muffins. I write briefs and argue."

Lacey smiled and gazed out over the huge expanse of ocean far below them. The bench was located along a narrow path that ran along the rugged coastline. She felt flooded with a familiar sense of gratitude for all that had been given her. The beauty of where she lived, the privilege of serving the comforts of coffee and muffins, the ability to leave the shop in another's hands while she and Will attended church, and now an afternoon with her sister and niece.

Maiya had hiked off the path ahead of them, through scrubby vegetation and out onto a promontory. She sat out there now, evidently having her own time of quiet. Lacey hoped she was contented with the past week. They had slipped easily into a routine of lessons, work, and evenings of games or DVDs.

Lacey said, "Maiya is extraordinary. I hope you make more babies."

Teal shifted and crossed her legs. "It seems selfish to admit to you that we don't want to."

"No worries." She tried to keep her tone light, but it always hurt to hear such things. *We could have a baby, but we don't want one.* Of course the others hurt even more. *We're expecting our third* or *Our first grandchild is on the way.*

"River and I agreed early on. Given our histories, we're not all that interested. Being a single mom took it all out of me, and River's loss of his family took it all out of him. I suppose we're just selfish cowards." She turned to her. "How about you, Lace? Do you talk about adopting?"

"With my situation . . ."

"But you're good now, right? You're getting stronger every day."

She shrugged. "I've only been cancer-free for four months. We can't really plan much except hope we make it to six months. After that we'll hold our breath waiting for a year. If we get to five years, maybe we'll start to think that we might have a different future. Maybe we could adopt."

"Oh, Lace." Teal removed her sunglasses and flicked a finger beneath her eyes. "I'm sorry. I didn't think — I can't imagine."

Lacey touched her arm. "Hey, it's okay. I can't talk to anyone else like this. Can you imagine? 'A Danish for you, ma'am, and oh, by the way, let me introduce my friend Mr. Death. Yes, he's right here next to me. No, you can't see him.' That wouldn't be so good for business."

Pools of tears threatened to overflow from her sister's eyes.

Lacey smiled. "Seriously, it's all right."

"How can you smile?"

"Because I can't see him either."

"You know what I mean." She picked up the sweatshirt on her lap and swiped it across her face. "Don't you and Will talk?"

"We talk plenty, but he's too close. He gets depressed, and then I lose hope because I can't do this without him. Sometimes I need to unload, though, like I did just now."

"I suppose Randi is out of the question." Her nose wrinkled in a frown. "What about your friend Holly?"

Lacey's mouth twitched involuntarily. She quickly pursed her lips.

"What's wrong?" Her sister was overly observant. It probably made her good at her job.

"Nothing."

"Come on. If we're going to have our first good old-fashioned sister heart-to-heart, we can't hold back."

"You want a good old-fashioned sister heart-to-heart?"

"Sure. We're due, aren't we?"

Lacey grinned. A real talk with Teal? It would be a dream come true. "The sister rule book says that thirty-two years — which just so happens to be my age — is as long as you can go without one."

"Or else what?"

"Poof. You're no longer sisters."

"We better get at it, then." Teal took a deep breath. "So what's up with Will and Holly?"

Her question hit Lacey like that first dive into an ocean wave as she paddled on her surfboard, on her way out to beyond the breakers. The water chilled her to the bone even through the wet suit. Its power frightened her. It knocked the breath from her. Her arms stilled and she lay her forehead and nose against the rough surface of the board. It rocked and she considered turning back to shore.

Then she would recall the exhilaration of riding on top of the water and she paddled again.

She had to trust that this first dive into a heart-to-heart with Teal would lead to good things.

Teal said, "I'll be honest. Holly has always annoyed me, so I am not the most unbiased observer. However, she hangs around the store an awful lot. I thought you two were always close. If you can't talk to her, then something is up."

Lacey swallowed twice before she could speak. "We are the best of friends. When I was sick, she spent every weekend and all of her school holidays pitching in wherever we needed extra help. Mostly, though, it was her emotional support that kept me going through the worst days."

"But . . . ?"

"But like you said, she's always at the store. She calls late at night when I'm normally asleep. And is it my imagination, or is she moony around Will?"

Teal winced and nodded. "What about Will?"

"He's been acting secretive, whispering on the phone and always being quick to get off when I walk in the room."

"So, no proof of anything?"

She sighed. "No."

"Have you confronted him? Come right out and asked him?"

"I don't want to know if it's true. The thing is, I can't blame him. I'm not the wife he used to have. He's had to take care of me and our home and our business for months now. He deserves better."

"Shh. Don't go down that road. Nothing is your fault, okay? Not the cancer nor how it's affected your everyday life. Not any idiotic choice Will might have made."

Lacey nodded. "Thanks, Teal. I feel better."

She laughed. "Lace, I didn't even give you any help yet."

"You didn't?"

"No. The thing is, in my opinion Will has not done anything. It's so obvious he absolutely adores you, the way he looks at you, the way he speaks to you and treats you. The phone calls?" She shrugged. "Maybe he's trying to order you flowers or tickets for a cruise. He doesn't even notice Holly. She's an unhappy divorcée who wants to have what you have."

"Cancer?"

"You know what I mean. Hon, I'm not big on painting rosy pictures. I can offer hope to wives in crises, but I'm weak on the warm fuzzies. So that is my honest opinion. If you'd like, I could even give notice to Holly to vacate the premises."

Lacey smiled. "No, probably not. Thanks, though."

"Anytime."

They sat in a comfortable silence, gazing out over the ocean and toward Maiya.

Teal said, "There she goes. I knew she'd do it."

Maiya walked out on the promontory, a high, rocky bluff surrounded by water on three sides. Lacey watched her and saw the little girl she must have been, so much like her mother, with an adventurous streak. How she wished she had known Maiya throughout the years. They were playing catch-up at the relationship-building.

"Teal, I have to confess something. I told Maiya about Cody and Dylan."

"Cody and Dylan!"

"I thought if she knew I had a crush on delinquent types like she did, I'd establish a common ground." She turned, saw the stoic expression in Teal's profile, and wanted to take back her words.

"Kids don't have to know everything about us. They'll still like us."

"I wasn't trying to get her to like me. I wanted her to understand that she wasn't the only teenager who fell for a loser."

The muscle in Teal's jaw tensed.

Maybe the heart-to-heart was over.

She decided not to mention what else she had told Maiya, that Cody had grown from loser into respectable Marine staff sergeant. Teal knew that. Through the years, Lacey had told her whenever Will's brother did something noteworthy. But to admit she told Maiya could be construed as encouragement to hang in there with Jake.

That had not been her intention.

But what if Maiya heard it that way?

Then Lacey had overstepped her role as doting aunt.

She would have made a lousy mother.

They sat for a while in silence, not as comfortable as before, and watched Maiya dance around on the promontory. Teal began chitchatting again as if she'd swept Lacey's stupidity under the rug.

By then Lacey did not have the energy to care much. She'd blown their first heart-to-heart. Self-reprimand and physical exhaustion were an ugly combination. When it was time to go, she stood on legs about as strong as rubber and plopped back onto the bench.

"Lace?" Teal sat down again beside her. "What's wrong?"

What wasn't wrong? She was messing up her one chance to be a good sister and an influential aunt. She was losing Will. The physical after-effects of cancer and treatments still ruled her life.

Maiya knelt before her. "Aunt Lacey?"

She heard the concern in both of their voices but had nothing left inside her to comfort others. "Call Will." She fumbled pulling the phone from her jacket pocket.

Teal took it from her.

The world began to spin and Lacey climbed on board its carousel. Chaotic thoughts bombarded her. There was no cancer, but the pain in the emptiness where there should have been a womb pierced like a surgeon's knife cutting, cutting, cutting.

"Aunt Lacey, drink some water."

She felt a plastic bottle at her lips and took a sip. Arms came around her and she leaned into Teal.

"He's on his way. Ten minutes."

It would take longer than that unless he drove like a maniac through town and sprinted like an Olympic athlete over the half mile of rugged trail to reach their spot.

On second thought, maybe he could do it in ten minutes.

"I'm such a wimp," she whispered.

"Shh. Shh." Teal ran her fingers through Lacey's short hair over and over. She kissed her forehead.

A faint scent of perfume emanated from Teal. It carried the pure blend of floral and spices characteristic of expensive designer brands. Maybe Will would order some on-line for Lacey. Then she could be the type of woman who had it all together.

"Mommy, she's shivering." Maiya's voice was scared.

It's okay. It's okay, Lacey wanted to say, but it wasn't true.

"Put your wrap on her legs."

She felt the warm press of soft fleece

against her thighs.

No, things were not okay. Her body rebelled against her, short-circuiting energy that should have been readily available. It turned it into stress, the very thing that fed that army of cells that had declared war on her. Could it rouse them from the dead? Maybe they weren't dead as in dead and gone. Maybe they were just lying in wait for new rations.

Muffled voices broke through the fog in her mind. Teal's arms slipped away, replaced by stronger ones.

Will had come. She would be all right now.

"Lacey?" He gathered her to himself. "Can you hold on to me?"

Always. She clutched his shirt with both hands. He stood, scooping her up like an overflowing laundry basket. Her ear against his chest, she heard the rumble of his voice.

"She probably overextended herself hiking out here."

"And," Teal said, "she's been doing way too much for us. She's got to be worn out."

Will, the diplomat, did not reply.

He had warned her. "Pace yourself," he had kept saying. "They can take care of themselves. No, you don't have to stock the cottage with groceries and flowers and DVDs. You don't have to entertain them every single moment of the day and night. Tutor? You're really going to tutor? Are you insane?"

No, just hungry for family. How could she contain herself? This was her sister and niece come to visit!

Will set her down now and helped her into the van. He strapped the seat belt around her, whispering, "Hang in there, Lace. We'll be home soon."

As he moved away, Teal leaned in. "Go home and rest. We won't come for dinner." She looked across at Will now climbing into the driver's seat. "Take care of her."

"Got it."

"No, I mean *take care of her*. Don't you dare let her down."

His sharp intake of breath filled the van. "No disrespect, Teal, but what exactly gives you the right to show up after nine years and tell me what to do?"

"She's my sister."

"She's my wife."

Lacey whimpered. She could hold back the tears no longer.

"Sorry." Teal squeezed her arm, backed out, and shut the door.

Will pulled from the parking space and across the lot, his foot heavy on the gas pedal. "Fruitcake."

Lacey wept. It was the sort of crying jag that drew from a deep, bottomless well of despair. It lasted through the drive home and through Will helping her into her nightgown. It would continue even after exhaustion caused her to sleep.

He tucked her into bed and sat on its edge, dabbing at her face with a wad of tissues. "Sweetheart, you're just tired. Try to relax. Things will look better in the morning. They always do."

Dawn was fourteen hours away.

He said, "I'll apologize to her."

"Will." Her throat hurt to talk, her voice rasped. "I hate this in-between."

"I know."

"I hate it." She blubbered. "I'm not dead, but I'm not alive either, am I?"

"Shh."

"If you want out, I understand." There. She had said it. "Seriously. You didn't sign up for this. You can go."

"Lacey, shh." He climbed over her and lay on top of the covers, still wearing his boots and jeans. "You're as fruity as your sister."

She curled against his long body. She was a small, bony version of the girl he had married, almost lost in his embrace. He rested his chin on the top of her head with its too-short hair and began to sing softly a version

271

of "Amazing Grace."

"Hallelujah, grace like rain falls down . . ."

It was how he had calmed her on the most difficult days. He would kiss her bald head and sing about the incomprehensible grace that got them through each day.

But he hadn't addressed the issue she raised about them.

CHAPTER 33

Awkward had become the byword for life in Cedar Pointe. Teal disliked it intensely.

The previous day's testy exchange with Will at his van — Lacey between them like a sacrificial lamb — had been bad enough. Trying to smooth things over with Maiya, who had, thank goodness, only overheard their tones, was agonizing. But the private, brief session with Will twenty minutes ago at the coffee shop pushed unpleasant to the max. *I'm sorry, Teal. I'm sorry, Will. I shouldn't have . . . No, I shouldn't have . . . Truce? Truce.*

Truce. Right. As long as he kept his distance from that vixen Holly.

"Mom." Maiya looked over at her from the driver's seat.

"Eyes on the car in front of you, please."

She harrumphed and turned back. "Got it under control. It's not like it's a freeway." She flipped her long hair over a shoulder.

273

Hands at nine and three. Teal resisted the urge to say it out loud.

Maiya said, "What I was going to say before I was so rudely interrupted is maybe we should ask Gran out for lunch."

Teal rubbed her forehead. Talk about awkward. They were on their way to visit Randi at the library, where she worked. Wasn't that enough? Did they have to do lunch too?

But she said, "Sure."

"She must have a really hard life with Owen."

Teal rolled her eyes. She could not help it. Where had Maiya missed the part about Teal growing up with the man? "You think?"

"Why are you so snippy?"

"I'm not . . . I'm sorry. Work is on my mind."

"Sheesh. What else is new? Why don't you go back to work? I'll hang out with Gran and not bother you anymore today."

Teal pressed her lips together. Things were spiraling out of control. "Maiya, I don't appreciate your lip. I realize you get it from me, but that's beside the point. No more, got that? We'll invite Gran to lunch and yes, give her a pleasant time, which she does not have at home."

"I'm sorry."

Teal sighed to herself, tired of the sorry this, sorry that.

Will had told them that Lacey still did not feel well that morning and needed to spend the day at home alone, resting. He was sorry — *sorry* again — that she was not up for tutoring.

Although Maiya would have been fine on her own doing schoolwork, guilt got the best of Teal. It was her fault Lacey was exhausted. Will was obviously tired of her company too. Then there was the whole point of the trip, to spend more time with Maiya.

It seemed a good time to rid herself of that other niggling guilt brought on by not seeing her mother since last week.

Not that her mother had made an attempt either.

"Cedar Pointe Public Library." Maiya slowed and pulled into a parking lot in front of a small building with a slanted green metal roof tucked in a pocket of pine trees. "There's Gran waiting for us."

More likely having a smoke, Teal thought but said nothing. As they climbed from the car, Randi waved, dropped a cigarette onto the sidewalk, and squished it underfoot. Her grin stretched from ear to ear.

She appeared even older than she had the

other day. The sunlight shadowed every crease in her face and lit up the gray in her hair. Her black slacks bagged and the baby-blue overblouse hung crookedly.

A wrenching sensation tugged in Teal's chest. Miranda Morgan Pomeroy had lived a hard life.

Maiya bounded from the car and down the sidewalk as if in sight of a long-lost love. Randi met her with arms wide open. Granddaughter and grandmother hugged with a laugh.

Ostracized toppled *awkward* as the byword for life in Cedar Pointe. Lacey and their mother had often held each other in the exact same way that Maiya and Randi were now embracing, leaving Teal out in the cold. Seeing them together unearthed the empty feeling and flung it out of the deep hole where Teal had buried it. Now it sat front and center in her awareness.

Let it go. Let it go. Let it go.

Her daughter and mother turned to her, waving for her to join them.

Teal bit her lip. Like a hunted, wounded deer panting for water, she wanted it. She wanted it so badly.

The moment passed, and she waved back with her cell phone, pointing to it and holding up five fingers. She would be there in five minutes.

They shrugged, again together, and headed inside the library.

Teal got back into the car and spent the five minutes repairing her eye makeup and wondering why she wore mascara in a town where people most likely thought it made her look uppity or like a floozy. Of course, that had been their opinion since long before she bought her first Maybelline product. No reason to try to sway them to think otherwise at this point.

She used up fifteen more minutes talking with the office because, yes, she was a workaholic. No reason to pretend she wasn't.

She spent the two minutes walking into the library apologizing to God for being snippy and a miserable example of His compassion for humanity.

The building was fairly new, with plenty of windows, open spaces, and bright colors. She found Maiya and Randi in the children's section, a separate room at the back. They sat at a table, hunched over a book.

Maiya spotted her approach. "Mom! Gran knows my favorite book by heart."

Randi looked up and smiled. "*Goodnight Moon* was Lacey Jo's favorite too."

"Imagine that." Teal showed her cell

phone to Maiya. "Off."

Maiya gave her a thumbs-up. "The library tour is over and we're hungry. Gran said she can take the afternoon off. There's a new place up in Banbury she thinks I might like. 'Kay?"

Banbury. It was thirty minutes up the 101. Thirty minutes each way. Randi had the entire afternoon open.

But did Teal have a choice?

" 'Kay." She mimicked Maiya's shorthand talk. "I drive."

Randi said, "Shotgun."

Maiya laughed. "You're too quick for me."

Randi joined in. Every wrinkle smoothed and the eyes, blue like Lacey Jo's, sparkled.

They sat in a booth next to windows overlooking the harbor. It was a picturesque scene with rock jetties, yachts and small boats moored at long piers, a lighthouse in the distance.

Randi dipped a french fry in a puddle of ketchup. "The fish-and-chips are not as tasty as the Crazy Scandinavian's in Cedar Pointe."

"But it's still good." Maiya wiped grease from her fingers. "I like the clam chowder better here. It has less potato in it."

"Don't you like potatoes?"

"Nope." She held up a fry. "Unless it comes in the shape of a stick fried to a golden brown."

The two of them laughed. They had been doing a lot of that.

Teal pulled her shirttail from her blue jeans and unsnapped her waistband. "Oof. All I know is that I've been eating way too many fish-and-chips."

Randi said, "Oh, you could stand to put on a few pounds."

Teal wasn't slender. Could this be a compliment? She waited for more.

It did not come.

Randi pointed at the window. "That lighthouse over there reminds me of Dutch."

Fried batter and oil churned in Teal's stomach.

Maiya said, "Who's Dutch?"

"Who's Dutch?" Randi's jaw dropped. "You don't know?"

Maiya shook her head.

"Duane Upton Morgan was your mom's dad. Everybody called him Dutch."

Maiya's eyes grew large. "You know his name."

"Now why wouldn't I know his name, honey? I was married to the man. It's where you got your last name: Morgan, same as

279

your mom's before she married what's-his-face."

"River. I just never —" Maiya glanced at Teal — "uh, heard much about him."

"You both got your black hair from him too. He was good-looking." She patted her chest. "My first real heartthrob. It didn't last long. Obviously. Probably wouldn't have even gotten started if Teal hadn't been on the way, if you get my drift."

"Randi." Teal threw everything into her tone. *Please be quiet! Maiya does not need to hear this! The man has nothing to do with us! I don't care if we have his black hair and last name. Just drop it!*

Her mother pursed her lips. "Sweetcakes, trust me, your daughter is old enough to hear that I was pregnant before I got married." She turned to Maiya and winked. "Both times."

"Did he have green eyes and attached earlobes?" She pulled on one of her ears.

"His eyes were like your mom's. I have no idea about earlobes. He did have them." Her laugh disintegrated into a cough.

Teal's mind hit a blank space. She needed to change the subject fast, but nothing came to her.

Maiya said, "Was he smart?"

Randi took a drink of soda. "Dumber than

a rock. You get your smarts from me. You, Teal, and Lacey Jo. Now those earlobes must come from . . . Oh, for crying out loud. You don't know who he is, do you? You don't know your daddy's name."

The color of Maiya's beautiful, deep forest-green eyes intensified. She blinked, her eyelashes gathering droplets.

Randi made a noise of disgust and turned to Teal. "That is the one thing I am so ashamed of you for."

"For getting pregnant outside of marriage?"

"No. For not telling us who he is." She shook her head. "I am so proud of you for all the rest. You left Cedar Pointe and made something of your life. You put yourself through college. You got your law degree. You raised Maiya all on your own. You got a good job. But that." She shook her head again. "And now come to find out you never even told this little girl. Shame on you, Teal. Shame on you." She slid from the booth. "I need a smoke."

Speechless, Teal stared at her retreating back as she walked outdoors.

Maiya sniffed.

Teal looked at her precious daughter wiping her nose with a napkin. "That was the nicest thing your grandmother ever said to me in my entire life."

"Huh?"

"She's proud of me."

"And ashamed."

"Yes. That's important to hear too. It means she really does care." *Somewhere deep inside her hard shell.* Teal reached across the table and grasped Maiya's hand. "I will tell you when it's time. The thing is . . ." She paused. Was it time to tell her one part?

"What, Mom?" Her voice rose in frustration. "What's the thing?"

She blew out a breath. "Other people are going to be affected. That's why the time isn't right."

"But when will it be right?"

"I'll know when I know. Trust me?"

Maiya gazed back at her for a long moment. Her forehead lost its furrows. "That was really the nicest thing she ever said to you?"

Teal nodded. "Her allegiance was to Owen."

"Why?"

"Because he demanded it. He saw me as a threat."

"Why?"

"He's a-a . . ." *An infantile fool.* "A needy person who never could share her attention

282

with others. Lacey was an exception, although I remember the older she got, the more she was left on her own. If it was his dinnertime, Randi was not allowed to go pick her up or watch her play soccer or anything."

"That's sick."

"It is."

"Mom, I'm glad you're my mom. You say nice things to me all the time. And I'm glad River isn't like Owen at all."

Teal felt dampness beneath her eyes. The mascara was going to get messy again.

CHAPTER 34

North of Cedar Pointe

"Excuse me. Excuse me." On Friday night, River wound his way through the small crowd at the very small Oregon airport. At long last he spotted his girls.

Maiya was jumping to get his attention, her ponytail and arms waving. Beside her stood Teal, smiling but subdued, as if the weeks' separation had taken more out of her than she admitted. She wore her denim jacket, his favorite red T-shirt underneath. She looked amazingly good in red.

"Riv!" Maiya squealed.

He hurried through the security doorway before Maiya breached it and dropped his duffel bag to catch her in his arms.

"Oh, Riv! I would have absolutely died if you hadn't come!"

"Me too, Minnie McMouse. Would have absolutely died." Over her shoulder he grinned at his patient wife, her expression forlorn, brows raised and the corners of her mouth drooping.

He winked at her. Whenever he and Maiya shared a moment like this one, Teal went somewhere else. The first time he caught her at it, he asked her what was wrong. She tilted her head in that way of hers and said nothing was wrong. She was simply grateful beyond words that Maiya had him for a dad.

How could he have even considered getting accustomed to their absence?

Then Teal was in his arms, such a perfect fit, and he kissed her for a long, long time.

"Mm." He looked into those magnificent gray eyes and smiled. "Okay, it was worth it."

She smiled. "You mean the seven hours it took to get here?"

"It was *ten* hours and some change. First the drive to LAX, then the wait time there. Crazy. All that time just to hop up the coast." He kissed her again and forgot about the four-hour layover in San Francisco.

She spoke, her lips brushing against his. "You might as well call it an even twelve since it's a bit of a drive to Cedar Pointe."

"Whatever." Travel time did not matter at this point.

Maiya elbowed him. "Psst. People are watching you two. They think you're weird."

He laughed with Teal, and together they pulled Maiya into their circle, making it a family hug. He felt deeply contented and happy.

And then they discussed dinner, the lack of decent restaurants, especially the lack of decent restaurants open after 8 p.m. Maiya whined that she really would have died on her birthday tomorrow if River had not come. She would be sixteen without any friends to celebrate with her. She couldn't even go to the DMV on Monday and get her driver's license. How unfair was that?

The tension that he'd heard daily in Teal's voice over the phone showed plainly in her bunched shoulders and in the smile that kept slipping. She said her mother had suddenly become sociable, Lacey's in-laws had arrived earlier in the week — nice enough but always around — and she hinted at more issues that they would discuss later.

River wondered if their reunion at the airport would be remembered as the best part of his weekend in Camp Poppycock.

Saturday morning, from his wicker chair on the front porch of the cottage, River spotted Maiya through the screen door. "Happy birthday, Minnie McMouse!" he shouted. "Woo-hoo!"

Maiya, still in her purple flannel pajamas and eyes at half-mast, held up a hand in greeting and shuffled into the kitchen.

Across from him, Teal called out, "Happy birthday, honey!" She smiled at him. "You know if you two hadn't stayed up half the night watching Anne of Green Gables DVDs, her birthday could have started before lunchtime."

"Hey, that was the slumber party she's not getting." He and Teal had been discussing how hard this birthday would be for Maiya away from home and friends and her traditional sleepover. "If we were back home, I'd probably vote for a day off from being grounded. She could have at least spent some time with a few friends."

"But we're not at home."

He sipped his coffee and took in the scenery. It was a beautiful morning. He liked the scent of pine, the crisp air, the blue sky. Three other cottages faced the same green space. None of them appeared occupied, which made for a large, private green space. From what he could see of the neighborhood, there was nothing fancy about Cedar Pointe.

Teal said, "Are we still agreed to hold off Amber's call until tomorrow?"

"Yes." Shauna had phoned Teal the day

before. They had decided to grant the girls a telephone reprieve. The only glitch was that Amber needed to tell Maiya that Jake had a new girlfriend. Not exactly the birthday gift they wanted to give their daughter.

And that was only one of the tidbits Teal had saved for conversation out of Maiya's earshot. She said it was the biggie, though. They'd get to the others later.

It wasn't like Teal to hesitate with him about anything. Except for those airport kisses, though, she had been generally ambivalent on every subject, from what to have for dinner, to whether or not to reply to a work e-mail, to what side of the bed to sleep on.

Maiya came outside, a glass of orange juice in her hand, and sat down on the porch step. "Thanks." She leaned against the railing and yawned. "Can we still go to Happy Grounds for breakfast and then to the beach?"

"Sure," Teal said. "We should still make it in time for low tide."

Maiya had told them the list of things she wanted to do on her special day. It was more like a list of what to show River while he was in town. He felt bad for her, which probably explained why he'd stayed up so late with her watching chick flicks. They could at least pretend she had a slumber party.

Maiya said, "Maybe Aunt Lacey can come with us. She loves minus tide too. Riv, it is so cool. It's like going to the aquarium but in real life."

Chalk one up for Cedar Pointe. "Maiya, what do you really want to do most for your birthday? Don't think about me. You've already seen the minus tide."

"But it'll happen again this morning and I want to go, really. It's awesome. You won't believe all the starfish and anemones."

"Okay. What else?"

She shifted forward, moved her head as if she had a Gumby neck, set the empty glass on the step, and crossed her arms.

River recognized the signs and braced himself. He had lived and worked with guys most of his life. His experience with females was limited.

There were women like his mother and his first wife, Krissy, both fairly stable and even-keeled for the most part. Then there was his sister, so off the wall he rarely took her seriously. And then there was Teal. She was a handful, but in ways that intrigued him, in ways that kept him on his toes and made him want to be a better man.

And then there was Maiya, the hormonal

adolescent, the roller coaster on a track that dipped and curved with little warning beyond the rubberneck move.

Hands down, guys were easier.

"Mom." Maiya looked up at them. "Riv. What I want most for my birthday is to know who my biological father is."

River felt himself sag, a sailboat dead in the water. There was nothing he could do about this one.

Teal's face reddened and then all color drained from it. She opened her mouth, closed it, opened it again. "Not here," she whispered.

Maiya's jaw went rigid.

Teal cleared her throat. "When we go home. I'll tell you when we go home."

River watched them stare at each other like hockey players waiting for the puck to drop between them. It was a women's face-off.

Teal had set herself up for a win or lose. There was no middle ground. If she did not come through, her relationship with Maiya would never be the same again.

CHAPTER 35

Lacey grinned at Will driving the van. Then she turned and grinned at Will's parents in the middle seats. Then she grinned at Randi in the far backseat.

Everyone grinned at her.

Will laughed.

All was right with the world.

She caught the tender look on Nora Janski's face. Like Will and William Sr., she was tall and slender. She resembled the hippie she claimed to have been in her younger years. Prim and proper William denied any such thing occurred. An honest-to-goodness hippie never would have attended the conservative college where they met.

Nora's gray-streaked blonde hair was wavy and usually in a ponytail. She wore long skirts, colorful tops, sandals, and dangly earrings that she made herself. A faint scent of patchouli followed her around.

The woman was one reason everything

was right with the world. Her presence made it so.

They had grown particularly close during Lacey's illness when Nora and William spent more time in Cedar Pointe than in their retirement home in Phoenix, working in the shop they once owned and relieving Will of nurse duties.

Will braked at the curb in front of the semicircle of cottages. "There she is."

Nora said, "The birthday girl."

Lacey felt a flutter of excitement at the sight of Maiya, Teal, and River sitting on the porch at the far side of the green space. The official party was scheduled for dinner that evening, but Lacey simply could not wait until then to tell her niece happy birthday and to meet her brother-in-law.

Maiya spotted them and jumped to her bare feet. Laughing, she scurried across the grass to greet them as they all climbed from the van, shouting, "Surprise!"

Lacey embraced her. "Happy birthday, Maiya."

"I can't believe this." She clung to her for an extra-long hug and whispered, "Thank you."

"You're welcome." Lacey leaned back. "Baker wanted to come too, but somebody had to mind the store."

"He'll be at dinner tonight, though, right?"

"Yes." Lacey was grateful that Maiya had one teenage friend. They had invited several of the regulars who had gotten to know her. The group's average age was seventy.

She stepped aside as the others moved in for hugs. As predicted, Nora and William had adored Maiya from the moment they met and treated her like a granddaughter. Totally unpredictable was Randi's response: she seemed delighted about being a grandmother and spent less time than ever with Owen. Uncle Will, the bomb, carried balloons from the van, completely at ease in his role.

He would have made a great dad.

Teal and River stood in front of the porch. Although she had seen photos of him, he was not what she expected. He was taller than Teal, but not by much, nowhere near Will's height. His ponytail, blue jeans, brown sweatshirt, and flip-flops did not fit her image of Teal's husband at all.

Lacey approached them. Her sister appeared less happy than usual, but Lacey would not blame herself this time. She had talked with Teal about the surprise and received an enthusiastic "By all means," so she was not the root cause.

"Lace," Teal said, "this is what's-his-face."

293

River chuckled. " 'What's-his-face'?"

Teal smiled crookedly. "It's your new name."

Lacey stretched out her hand. "Compliments of our mother, who has trouble remembering her own. Hi, River."

"Hi, Lacey." He ignored her hand and gave her a quick hug. "Nice to meet you at last."

"You too. Come meet my husband, the other what's-his-face."

His smile was warm, making him definitely cute enough for Teal. The five o'clock shadow, though, had the look of permanency. Evidently rugged suited her glamorous lawyer sister.

As Will shook River's hand and took over the introductions, Lacey turned to Teal with wide eyes.

"What?" Teal said.

"He's nice."

"He's perfect and I just seriously ticked him off. Did you bring the muffins for Maiya?"

"Yeah. Why would you seriously tick him off?"

She turned and headed into the cottage.

Lacey followed her. "I mean, he's only here for two days."

Teal opened a cupboard door, slammed

it, and whirled around. "It's better than answering his questions and removing all doubt as to exactly how despicable I am."

"You're not —"

"I am, Lacey. Believe me, I am." She strode to the table, yanked out a chair, and plopped onto it.

Lacey sat down and took a deep breath. "You're a good person, Teal."

She smiled crookedly. "I don't need the rah-rah spiel, Lace."

"What do you need?"

"I need to save a little girl from spending half her time with a man she's never met. I'm not sure if I can do that because I think her mom, my client, may have lied. I'm not sure if she really told the man he was a father." Teal placed a hand over her mouth as if to stop more words from coming out.

"What does that have to do with you?"

Teal blinked. Her shoulders went up and down, up and down. At last she lowered her hand. "I-I never told him."

"Never told who . . . ?" Lacey halted her question as the truth dawned on her.

Teal had never told Maiya's father about the pregnancy or about Maiya.

No wonder she wasn't telling anyone anything about him.

■ ■ ■ ■

That evening, Lacey sank onto her recliner in the back room of the shop, pulled up the footrest, and smiled. Maiya's party, still going at full tilt in the other room, had been a success, but she needed a break.

Nora walked in. "What are you smiling at, Miss Lacey Jo?"

Lacey giggled at the nickname, which she always heard as a term of endearment. It reminded her of childhood days when Nora, aka Mrs. J from Happy Grounds, had special names for every kid in town.

"I'm smiling because Maiya is happy."

Nora rolled the desk chair over to the recliner and sat, her long skirt spreading out. "They don't call this place Happy Grounds for nothing." Her wide mouth seemed always on the verge of a grin.

Although the Janskis denied it, Lacey figured they named the place Happy Grounds thirty years ago because Nora was so full of joy. "Great lasagna. Thanks."

"Thank you for letting me help. I wonder if Maiya said lasagna was her favorite because it would make feeding the twenty people we invited easier."

"She might have. She's not your typical

sixteen-year-old, is she?"

"No. Teal has done a great job raising a conscientious young woman. Your sister has grown up nicely herself, except . . ." Nora paused. "She still seems to have that old barrier in place. It's hard to get close to her."

Without going into the details she had heard that afternoon, Lacey summed it up. "I think it's Cedar Pointe memories."

"Oh, most definitely. We all have issues with our hometowns, don't we?" She laughed her infectious, belly-deep guffaw. "Lord, have mercy."

Lacey smiled. "I'm glad you're here."

"Me too. William was ready to head straight back down to Phoenix, but my curiosity got a little out of control. You know how I am, always wanting to hear about 'our kids.' " She gestured quotation marks. "I couldn't pass up a chance to see firsthand one of the lost ones." She leaned forward, her eyes bright, and whispered, "Can you believe it? She's a mom, wife, and lawyer. Whoa! This is huge."

It was huge for Nora. The woman had not only nicknamed, hugged, and given free sweet rolls to every Cedar Pointe kid who crossed her path for thirty years, but she had prayed that each one would reach their potential.

Until the cancer, Lacey had felt like an answer to that prayer for her. She was a young, fairly decent version of the former Mrs. J of Happy Grounds.

"Nora, I will never fill your shoes."

"Honey, why would you want to when you've got your own that are just the right size?"

Lacey sighed. They'd had the conversation countless times. She felt like Teal had earlier in the day; she was not up for a rah-rah spiel. But she needed to vent. "My shoes are ugly and out of date."

Nora cocked her head. One earring dangled. Its amethyst stone reflected the light. "Have you ordered a new pair?"

Ordered a new pair? "What —"

"Nora!" William's shout preceded him into the room. "Nora!" He appeared in the doorway. "Cody's on the phone and you'll never guess." He grinned. "He's being reassigned to . . ."

Nora clenched her fists, squeezed shut her eyes, and grinned, waiting for what was obviously going to be good news.

"To Virginia!"

Nora sprang from the chair with a squeal and flung herself into William's arms. They danced a jig, clapped their hands, hooted and hollered.

"Come on. He's talking to Will."

They scurried from the room, Nora chanting something about no more trips to Germany.

Cody had served overseas with the Marines for years. It had been difficult and expensive for her in-laws to see him and his family. To have him stateside was great news.

Eager to join this new celebration, Lacey lowered the footrest. It bumped the chair Nora had been sitting in as she listened intently, tuning in to Lacey's heart more than her words. Offering a challenge rather than a platitude. *Have you ordered a new pair?*

The image of her earring flashed to mind, its sparkling purple, its two-inch dangle that suited Nora's long face.

Her earlobe.

Lacey halted her scoot off the chair.

Nora's earlobes were attached.

Lacey shook her head. All kinds of people had attached lobes. Owen, for one. It didn't mean . . .

She began contrasting physical attributes, quickly tossing out one after another. Eyes, deep-green and hazel. Mouth, little bowtie and wide. Height, average and tall. Physique, average and slender. Hair color, black and blonde. Voice, soprano and alto.

There was no genetic connection.

None.

Will handed Lacey a cup of tea and sat on the couch beside her. The party was over and they were home alone. "Earlobes? We can't go to seed on earlobes."

"You're right."

"You sound unsure."

"So do you."

He turned sideways to face her, his arm across the back of the couch. "I don't want to go there."

"Me neither."

"This would mean . . ."

"That she's your parents' granddaughter. That you're her uncle. More than I'm her aunt even."

"She doesn't look like a Janski. There's no resemblance to . . ." He paused. "No, that's not true. Remember the familiarity I first noticed about Maiya? I finally figured out it's my mom. She reminds me of my mom. Do you sense it?"

"Mm-hmm. It's not anything obvious, like hair color or facial structure. And yet there's something . . ."

They stared at each other. Nora was Cody's mother, which might explain the resemblance.

Will shook his head. "I can't imagine a relationship between Teal and Cody. He was your boyfriend, sort of. He was in your class. She was older, away at college, hardly ever in town."

Lacey remembered Nora's reference to Teal, the lost one. Other people would have referred to her as a hopeless loser. But in Nora's economy, there was always hope and there were no losers, only children who had strayed from their true selves. She had firsthand experience with her youngest, which probably made her extra sensitive.

Lacey said, "They were both on your mom's list of lost ones."

He blew out a noisy breath. "It still doesn't seem possible. Why would she not tell him?"

"It can't be him."

"Can't be."

They sat in silence for a long moment.

He said, "Maybe it's our imagination."

She knew deep in her bones that it was not. "What should we do?"

"For all our sakes, I think we need to find out. The best way is to be direct. It should come from you. Just ask her. 'Hey, Teal, is Cody Maiya's dad?' No harm in asking, right?"

Lacey's stomach somersaulted. "And if

she says yes, then what?"

"I don't know. Then she's forced to tell, which opens a can of worms. But it has to be opened sooner or later."

She shook her head. "I can't."

"If it's true, you'll honestly be helping her and Maiya. She's not going to bite you, but so what if you set her off? So what if she gets mad? She'll get over it. And you're never going to lose Maiya."

"This isn't a rational thing, Will."

"Let's practice. Just say it out loud to me. I'll be Teal and get upset."

Lacey looked down at her tea. What had Teal advised her about the Holly situation? *Just ask him.* She had tried in her own way, but like a coward she had beat around the bush. *Were you on the phone tonight?*

The bottom line was that she was afraid of the truth. Truth was cancer and a cheating husband and a sister sleeping with a boy Lacey liked. Truth was a death sentence to her well-being.

Or maybe truth was how to order a new pair of shoes. The old, ugly ones were all about living in fear. About not living like Nora did, embracing the fullness of each moment and trusting that if the moment was her last on earth, she had not wasted it wallowing in anything except God's boundless love.

She felt a tingling sensation, as if her nerves were waking up from a long sleep.

"Lace." Will put a finger under her chin and lifted her face. "You don't have to ask her."

Lacey took a deep breath and let it out. "Well, we'll see. If the opportunity presents itself, maybe I will."

He smiled and kissed her softly. "I love you."

"I love you." She set her cup on the coffee table and gazed at him. "Will, are you and Holly having an affair?"

"What?" His eyes bugged out.

And she knew he was not.

"Oh my gosh, no, Lacey. No. Why would you think that?"

"I've been sick."

"Sweetheart, I would never cheat on you."

"She's moony over you."

"Really?"

Lacey smiled. Will was so much like his mother. Open to everyone, giving to everyone, believing the best of everyone. How could Lacey have imagined such a thing about him? "Yes, really."

"Am I moony in return?"

"No. But . . ."

"But what?"

"There seem to be a lot of late-night phone calls with her. And there's the way you whisper on the phone and hang up when I come in or quickly change what's on the computer screen."

He sighed and pulled her close.

Her heart sank. It wasn't Holly. But it was another woman.

"Lace, I've been part of an online support group for husbands whose wives have cancer." He held her tightly. "I couldn't bring myself to tell you how hard this whole thing is for me. I couldn't let you down. How can I be your rock if I'm asking for help?"

"Oh, Will." She looked up at him.

His smile was self-deprecating and his eyes filled. "Turns out I'm not the only guy who feels this way."

She watched as tears seeped from his eyes. In the past she had noticed his eyes red-rimmed, especially since her diagnosis, but had never seen him cry. The sight now did not upset her.

She kissed his cheek, laid her face on his chest, and cried with him.

The new shoes were feeling just right.

CHAPTER 36

"It was a good weekend." River's upbeat tone floated through the dank air Sunday evening, the night before his departure.

Teal frowned, her face averted. Was he nuts? Or simply in total denial of reality? Doing her best rendition of neutral, she said, "We're out here walking the streets because we couldn't take it any longer sitting in the cottage, listening to Maiya bawl her eyes out."

River took hold of her hand, sliding his fingers between hers.

The touch was their first intimate contact since the welcome hugs and kisses at the airport forty-eight hours ago. No, she could not categorize the weekend as *good*.

He said, "True, but it means she's coming to terms with the Jake news. Hard stuff can be good. It moves us forward."

Whatever! She wanted to huff.

"You feel tense, love." His term of endearment had been AWOL along with the physical touch. "I mean it. The weekend was good."

"I suppose one good thing was that you didn't punch Owen's lights out."

"If I'd spent more than ten minutes with him, I might have." He paused. "Seriously, I'm glad you promised Maiya she didn't have to see him again. I've met enough mean dads to recognize the malicious vibes coming from him."

If River had not insisted on meeting Owen and seeing the house she'd grown up in, she would have skipped both. At least they had spent literally only ten minutes doing so.

"Teal, like I said, I will confront him with what he did to you."

"And what? Demand an apology? No thanks. He's a pathetic alcoholic. The only thing that might get his attention is if Randi leaves him, and that in itself would take a major miracle."

While her mother had not owned up to any dysfunctional behavior on either her or Owen's part, she had been spending time away from him, totally atypical according to Lacey. And whenever she was not with him, she drank less, a plus for everyone.

River said, "Well, if you're sure. I don't

306

want to miss an opportunity to be your knight in shining armor."

"You are my knight in shining armor simply by coming here."

"Nah. I came here to fish with Will and his dad on the Rogue River. Have I mentioned the twenty-one-pound salmon I caught this morning?"

"Once or twice." She smiled. River and his rivers. He'd been as excited as a little kid just to see one he'd never seen before. To fish it was icing on the cake.

He said, "It's not like you need a knight here. Lacey and Will are great people. His parents are great people. Baker's a great kid. That group of retirees who came to Maiya's party last night are good folk. And even Randi has possibilities. You're surrounded by guardians."

With a groan, Teal leaned against his arm as they walked. "It's you, River. You bring out the best in others. I don't."

"Yes, you do, just not in your hometown. Naturally there's baggage here."

Baggage and ghosts.

"But," he said, "these people do care about you. You might try letting them inside."

She unbent herself away from his arm.

He tightened his grip on her hand and

stopped their walk, turning her to face him. "Look, whoever he is, whatever his connection to these people, they will accept you."

She shook her head.

"Yes, they will," he insisted. "Two reasons. One, you're a successful lawyer, an admirable, respectable woman. And two, your daughter has brought a new happiness into their lives."

"You can't understand."

"Then tell me. Explain it to me."

Her heart thumped loudly in her ears. She shook her head again.

River exhaled and let go of her hand.

A wave of loneliness swept through her.

So what else was new in Camp Poppycock?

Ghosts or no ghosts, Teal sat at the desk in the back room at Happy Grounds, facing the wall opposite the one where the couch had once been. The shop — the only one in town open on Mondays — was full of regulars and then some. Its noise disrupted her focus. Well, that plus all the other stuff.

The unsatisfactory good-bye with River earlier that morning weighed most heavily. Their last night together had revolved around comforting Maiya. Then Will called and offered to take River to the airport since he had errands to run up in that neck of the woods anyway.

River accepted the offer with a little too much eagerness. She doubted that was due solely to his wanting to let her get back to work as soon as possible. No. He had emotionally checked out the previous night after ending his pep talk with "explain it to me."

Well, maybe it was after she refused to explain it.

Okay. So she deserved the cold-shoulder treatment.

"Teal." Her assistant Pamela's voice came in loud and clear through the Bluetooth. At least that life-changing device worked in the back room.

"I'm here. What do we have?"

"I'm afraid we have a woman scorned."

Teal's heart sank. Hannah Walton's case had leaped out of its original good mom/ bad dad parameters.

The office had received documents from Parkhurst's attorneys through the process of discovery. She had requested his financial and phone records in order to prove he had nothing to do with Hannah during her pregnancy or since.

Pamela said, "We definitely have a paper trail. On numerous occasions James

Parkhurst phoned a number they say belonged to Hannah at the time. I'm checking into that. He claims he left voice mails. There's also a record of him phoning the hospital on the day the baby was born."

Teal shook her head. The blessing and bane of technology.

"I finished tracking the financial records. He wrote four checks to her. The first was out of company funds in the form of a paycheck, but about four times her normal salary, which could be construed as severance. The others came from one of his personal accounts *after* the baby's birth."

"Did Hannah cash any of them?"

"Just the first one."

"We can't prove she received the others."

"No." Pamela paused. "Want my opinion?"

"Always."

"He may have called her a slut when she told him she was pregnant. But I think the main gist of that conversation was that he refused to divorce his wife and marry Hannah."

"Hence the scorned woman."

"Twenty-first-century style. She tells him to take a hike, she doesn't need him."

Teal thought of Hannah's background. She had not needed Parkhurst. Her parents were supportive and wealthy. They stood by her throughout the pregnancy and birth. They had provided the down payment for the house she and her husband purchased.

Teal said, "What has Parkhurst been up to since?"

"Ironically, he divorced that first wife — there were no dependents — and two years ago married his second, a woman on his staff."

"Ouch."

"Exactly. But Hannah seems to have been perfectly happy with her own choices."

"I agree. She didn't need Parkhurst, and she wound up with a really nice guy. The question is, why now? Why Parkhurst's sudden interest in his daughter?"

"Assuming she is his daughter. DNA tests should come in this week."

"Maybe she's not."

"And maybe the judge will rule favorably on our motion to dismiss and throw out the case because there's not enough evidence."

"And maybe it won't rain in Oregon this winter."

Pamela chuckled. "How is life going up there? How is Maiya?"

Teal slid into chitchat mode, briefly filling her in on River's visit and the Jake saga. "At least Maiya isn't playing the scorned woman, but she has heartbroken down to a T. Besides her doting aunt and uncle, she has a handful of retirees here at the shop eating out of her hand. They all gave her birthday gifts. She'll probably get sympathy gifts now."

"Aw." Pamela cooed. "She's such a lovable kid."

"Most days."

"Come on, Mom. She's only sixteen. Let her have her adolescent drama. We've all been there and done that."

A sudden, disquieting thought struck Teal. Not only had she been there and done that, she was there again and reliving it.

That was not exactly the purpose behind visiting her hometown.

How blind of her not to have foreseen its inevitability.

James Parkhurst's perplexing behavior gnawed at Teal. It rooted her to the desk chair in the back room and kept the ghosts at bay.

The man had been in the movie business for years. He had founded his own production company shortly before Hannah Walton went to work for him. To date he had been the executive producer of several movies nominated for Academy Awards in various categories. Some had won, including last year's for Best Picture.

The guy was on his way up, big time. What did he care about visitation rights with a little girl he had never even met?

Teal thought about Parkhurst's life. On the surface it appeared glamorous. He hobnobbed with movie stars, directors, investors, writers, agents, politicians — anybody who was anybody in the industry.

Yet he put on his pants like everybody else, one leg at a time. He spent countless hours on the phone and in meetings, building his network. He missed meals, sleep, vacations, dates with wives one and two. He was divorced. His closest friends would be his driver, most likely a man, and his hairstylist, who would neither be male nor a barber at the neighborhood shop.

Teal chose the hairstylist route because in general women gossiped more than men. Three phone calls later she was talking to a friend of a friend of the hairstylist.

"It's no secret," the woman said. "Parkhurst is a changed man. He's done a total one-eighty, gone from nasty to nice. Samantha, the hairdresser, says he even tips more. You know when the wallet is involved, it's got to be for real."

"What happened?"

"He found Jesus. Or maybe Jesus found him. I forget how that works. Apparently he talks about it a lot."

Great. Now Jesus had joined the ranks of the opposition.

Teal learned little else except that the faith development seemed recent. With any luck, she thought, it would pass and he would stop trying to right the wrongs of his past.

Sorry, Lord. You know what I mean. It'd make my job easier if this were a conversion of the flash-in-the-pan sort.

She winced. How crusty could she get?

Sixteen years ago, when she first went to church with her neighbor Gammy Jayne and Christ's love tangibly and inexplicably drenched her, her world was turned upside down. It was a supernatural development that defied explanation. Acquaintances from her past never would have believed how different she was.

At times she did not recognize herself in the softness and hope and joy that permeated her life. Instead of an angry law student fighting for her rights, she grew into a woman with a deep compassion for others. Her desire to become a lawyer and to combat wrong remained intact, but it became more about her clients' welfare and less about Teal winning.

Of course God could change James Parkhurst into a better man.

Into a bio dad who should be allowed to see his daughter?

Maiya walked into the room. "Mom?"

Teal held up a finger and pointed to the Bluetooth. "Thank you so much," she said to the friend of the friend, ended the conversation, and pulled the device from her ear. "Ack! That's been in there too long."

"Can you talk now?" Maiya sat in a chair beside the desk, a folded piece of paper in her hand.

"Sure." The reply was in no way connected to her mind, which was busy dictating follow-up notes. She'd clue Pamela in on Parkhurst's newfound religion. They'd brainstorm about its effect on the case. Should they put the firm's investigator onto Parkhurst? Was he affiliated with a church? Which one? If it was a weird radical group, that might nix his chances of —

"Mom!"

"What?"

"You're not listening."

"Sorry." She blinked, took a deep breath, shook her head, and exhaled. "Okay, I'm ready now."

The drama queen rolled her eyes.

Teal smiled. "You said something about Baker."

"He gave me another birthday gift."

"Are you getting spoiled or what?"

Maiya had become like the mascot of Happy Grounds. Lacey, Will, and his parents had heaped gifts upon her, everything from clothes to books to jewelry. That group of regular customers had given her gift certificates to a bead shop and a nail salon. Baker promised her dinner at a pricey gourmet restaurant, an evening out which she insisted was not a date.

Maiya gave a wan smile. She'd been into *wan* all day. It fit *heartbroken* so well.

Teal couldn't help but grin. Yes, her daughter was lovable, even in the throes of adolescence.

Maiya lowered her head and unfolded the paper she held. "If I can't meet my dad, who's the next best to meet?"

The room tilted, Teal's stomach with it, and her smile disappeared.

Maiya looked at her. "My grandfather," she whispered. "Baker found Dutch. It's not that hard to do online." She lifted the paper, the familiar print of Google directions clear on it. "Here's the address. He lives just up the coast, ninety miles. He works at a golf course."

"Oh, Maiya." She shook her head.

"You don't have to come. Baker will take me."

Teal kept shaking her head.

Maiya cried, "He's your dad! How can you not want to see him? Gran told me she couldn't keep in touch with him when you were little. Owen wouldn't allow her to. Maybe Dutch wanted to be in your life, but he didn't have a chance."

"He could have tried harder. At this point, it's water over the dam."

"Mom! At least you can think about it. I know you don't want to, but what about me? Can't you do it for my sake?"

The verbal dart hit its mark. Teal felt a burning deep inside her mother's heart. She cleared her throat. "I will think about it."

Maiya threw her arms around her. "Thank you."

Teal watched her hurry from the back room, her fist high in the air, a resounding yes whispered as she brought down her arm.

Teal had no thought but to get out of the shop as quickly as possible. She ducked through the back door and ran down the alley. As if of their own accord, her feet carried her two blocks to the beach and onto Warrior Rock.

She climbed, panting, her chest burning, her ears ringing.

Go see *Dutch?*

How could Maiya think of such a thing, let alone suggest it? Let alone find the address! How many times did she have to explain it to her? He had never been a dad. He certainly was not about to be a grandfather.

The afternoon wind whipped her hair, the air cool despite the sunshine. Holding her cardigan shut, she crossed the deserted top of the rock to the far side and made her way down to the crook of the giant's arm. She sank onto the damp ground.

And then she fell apart.

What had she done? How much longer could she inflict this pain on her daughter, hiding behind one excuse after another?

The truth was . . .

She wiped tears from her face and stared out at the ocean and forced herself to admit the truth she had been ignoring for almost a week.

The truth was, Maiya had met her paternal grandparents the day William and Nora Janski arrived.

And oh! They were everything Maiya could ever want in a grandma and grandpa. Nora surpassed Randi in all departments, from loving to creative. William was solid and he was there *in person.*

"Oh, God, I am so sorry." She blubbered. "I am so sorry."

Not only was she cheating Maiya, she was cheating the Janskis. She was cheating Will and Lacey.

And she was cheating Cody Janski.

He should have had a clue, though. No, it was not as glaring as the clue Dutch had carried with him for decades, but he had enough dots to connect and see the picture.

Cedar Pointe fed on town gossip. He would have heard the latest. *"Teal Morgan is pregnant. Nope, don't know the father."* That was point B. He could have backed up to point A: *"We had sex."*

Once Lacey and Will dated and married, they would have fed him with family news throughout the years. *"Teal's baby girl is two. Teal's a lawyer. Teal bought a house. Teal got married."* She herself got regular updates. *"Cody and Dylan were in a car accident. . . . Cody is absolutely crazy now. He's in jail for five months. . . . Cody got a military waiver; he's a Marine. He's a sergeant. He's married. He's got a son, named him Dylan."*

Yada, yada, yada.

How could she tell *anyone* before telling him?

Now Maiya had stopped asking to know his name. She was holding Teal to her promise to reveal his identity after they got home.

After they got home. After her daughter had spent weeks with her family, not knowing who they were.

"Oh, God, I'm sorry. What am I supposed to do? What am I supposed to do?"

No answer came.

Why would one? If it were true that God could not look upon sin, then He could not look upon her, could not hear her. She was sin incarnate. A despicable excuse for a human being. If the giant flung her into the sea, it would be a good thing.

Teal pulled her knees up to her face and wrapped herself in the cardigan. The bottom of her jeans and the back of her sweater were damp. She shivered, chilled to the bone, chilled to her very soul. She sat like that, waiting for the tears to stop.

They always did stop, and her giant had yet to toss her into the ocean.

CHAPTER 37

Los Angeles

"Teal, love . . ." Just in the door from the airport, cell phone at his ear, River dropped his duffel bag on the family room floor and sank onto the couch. "You don't have to do this."

"I do."

He stretched out his legs and leaned back. Teal had phoned him as he drove home. He had listened without comment to her talk about Maiya's latest request and their plan to visit Teal's father, Dutch Morgan.

Why hadn't he followed his gut feeling and insisted the three of them get in the car and start driving back that very day?

He said again, "No, you don't have to do this."

"River, it's the least I can do for her."

"Why not do the most? The best?"

Teal said nothing.

"It's simple. You set her down and tell her

the circumstances under which she was conceived. You tell her his name. Anyone else involved is not your responsibility."

Still she did not respond.

Which was fine with him. The entire weekend she'd been aloof, preoccupied, and even nervous. Now on the phone, he had begun to hear a coldness so icy it sent a chill through him.

He wanted to blame the intensity of facing her past head-on, but her voice was not the one spoken in determination. Nor was it her confident business tone that exuded a trace of warmth no matter what.

No, this came from some deep, dark part of herself that he did not know.

That he did not *want* to know.

It wasn't like Bio Dad's identity was all that difficult to figure out. Why the big deal? She had indicated it was because other people were affected.

Which meant Mr. Secret Dude was close to them figuratively and literally, as in the same room. The Janskis fit the criteria.

Only one question remained: was it Cody or the dead cousin, Dylan? Dead would have been easy to tell Maiya years ago. Dylan's parents were not in Cedar Pointe. Dylan had no relationship with Lacey.

Three strikes.

He'd give it one more shot. "You don't even have to tell me. Just talk straight to Maiya before it's too late."

"We'll go up tomorrow."

"Teal." He tilted the phone so it would not catch his exasperated grunt. He raised an arm and let it drop heavily to his thigh.

"Sorry, River, I can only do the least."

He heard the ice in her voice again and bit back a sharp rebuke. What she needed was heat. "I love you. I feel bad that I can't be there, but you know I'll be praying."

"Yeah, thanks. I better go. I have a million things to do before tomorrow."

"I'll call you."

"Bye."

"Good night."

He did not move from the couch. Again he felt like he had on the day of the earthquake when he lay on the garage floor and could not move from the bins on top of him. What pressed against him now were waves of emotions.

He truly did love Teal. He loved her with every fiber of his being. He would never stop giving her one more shot. But he was powerless to convince her to trust him with her grief.

"Lord, take care of her. Please."

Why wouldn't she tell Maiya about Cody?

All that nonsense about others being involved was just a plain old excuse.

Ohhh, no. Something else was at work here.

Apparently none of those others had a clue. Cody did not inform them that Teal's baby was his. Throughout the years, Cody never mentioned it, not even after his major turnaround into the good guy who paid his dues. From what River had heard about him, he would have gone back to pick up the pieces of his life. He would have contacted Teal and said, "I owe you." He would have wanted to apologize to Maiya.

But he could not do any of those things because he *did not know.* Teal never told him.

She was just digging a deeper hole for herself.

And why the fixation now on Dutch? What could she possibly gain from confronting someone who walked out of her life when she was three years old?

River remembered a photo Randi had shown him of Teal as a little girl. She was cute and appeared feisty even then, her head tilted in the way so familiar to him.

Something must have died in her the day her dad left.

Like Maiya, a piece was missing. Maybe once she found it, she could help Maiya find hers. Maybe then she would get off this delusional path where she thought she could control everyone and keep herself intact.

"Did You get that, Lord?"

He shut his eyes. Already the house felt too empty of life. He had nowhere else to turn but to God.

"I want my girls back." Preferably the way they were before the earthquake.

Secrets and all?

"Maybe."

CHAPTER 38

North of Cedar Pointe

According to Maiya, Sea West Golf Resort was a fairly recent development. It was located ninety-three miles up the coast, midway between two small towns, filling a large tract from the highway to the ocean. They should be there in a couple of hours.

Teal drove. The feel of the steering wheel under her white knuckles gave a sense of control on a day that was in reality totally out of her hands.

Not far outside of Cedar Pointe, Maiya must have picked up on the tension. "Hey, no worries, Xena."

Teal grimaced. Xena? Warrior mode was out of the question. Even grown-up-woman mode seemed beyond her reach. Her stomach was a knotted fist. Her mind was shut down, unable to respond to Maiya's enthusiastic chatter. She drove on autopilot.

"Remember, Mom, everyone's rooting for

us. Baker, Aunt Lacey, Uncle Will, William, Nora, Riv, and Gran."

Maiya had told the others the previous night while Teal, alone in the cottage, worked on the Walton case, avoiding everyone's reactions to her crazy decision.

"And Gran!" Maiya said in astonishment. "Can you believe her being excited about this? I bet she probably still loves him in a way. You know, I absolutely hate, hate, hate Jake Ford right now, but I'll always have a soft spot for him. That's love, isn't it?"

"Mai, can we not talk for a while?"

Maiya leaned forward to look Teal in the face. "You okay?"

"I'm a mother who just asked her teenager to quit talking. No, I'm not okay."

"Well, let's just soak in some good thoughts, shall we?"

Teal gripped the steering wheel more tightly. She had heard Nora Janski say that exact same phrase the other day when Randi was going off on some negative tangent.

Maiya popped in a CD of worship music, quit talking, and sang along, her voice as soothing as any mother's to a child.

The two hours passed. Teal's stomach remained knotted, but her knuckles turned pink.

Maiya pointed to a sign. "There it is."

Teal flipped the turn signal, slowed, and considered making a U-turn at the wide entrance. There was no traffic either direction.

Maiya turned off the CD player. "How you doin', Mom?"

Teal blinked and drove onto the pristine asphalt drive. No clubhouse or fairway were yet in sight, just cloudless blue sky and rolling hills of grasses and conifers painted every shade of green. "I'm okay."

"Way to be, Xena!" She chucked Teal on the shoulder.

Teal gave her a small smile. The whole thing could be over and done with in twenty minutes.

At the top of a rise, the ocean came into view, white water and distant ultramarine. A golf course lay above it. Tucked off to one side was a castlelike stone structure with wings.

Maiya let out a low whistle. "Wow. Uncle Will said this place makes him want to take up golf. I get it now. *I* want to take up golf, and it seems like the dumbest sport in the world." She was back to magpie mode. "Mom, valet parking is that way."

"We'll park ourselves." She was not about to give up her keys. The only other thing she could control was being able to make a hasty retreat.

They found their way from the visitors' parking lot along a path through exquisite grounds to the main entrance. Inside was a maze of shops, restaurants, nooks, and crannies.

Maiya squeezed her elbow. "Mom, he's director of golf-tournament sales in a place like *this*. He's gotta be a decent guy, don't you think?"

Teal saw expectancy in her daughter's beautiful eyes and pushed aside her own anxieties. She was doing this for Maiya, but . . . but what if Dutch Morgan was a decent guy? Could there be the teensiest possibility that he would be interested in seeing his daughter? She had never imagined such a thing.

A small bubble of hope fizzed in her chest.

The information desk attendant sent them to a grouping of offices where a receptionist greeted them. She was a friendly young woman wearing a headset.

"Do you have an appointment with Mr. Morgan?"

"No." They had decided against phoning ahead. If he were an ogre, he'd deny them a meeting and they'd miss the chance to at least see him in person. "We're family visiting from out of town and just wanted to pop in and say hello."

"He's in a meeting but should return in half an hour or so. May I have your name?"

Teal hesitated. Her own name would warn him. The surname would catch his attention. "Maiya Morgan."

The woman wrote it down. "If you'd like, there's a coffee shop across the way."

"We'll wait here." If she ducked out now, she'd surely lose the momentum that had gotten her this far.

"That's fine. I'll let him know you're here so he won't head somewhere else. He's a busy man."

Teal smiled. *Evidently for thirty-four years.*

They sat on a couch and tried to act normal. Maiya picked up a golf magazine and Teal breathed one shallow breath after another.

Why had her father never come back? How could he not come back to the three-year-old clinging to his leg? *Daddy! Daddy!*

Memories flooded her. He had strong shoulders, and she rode on them when her legs tired as they hiked up and down the trails and to the top of Warrior Rock. He showed her how to gently handle the starfish exposed at low tide. He taught her to ride her yellow bike with training wheels. He was a good whistler.

She should tell Maiya these things. Maybe after today she could.

Her stomach hurt.

People came and went from unseen offices. Miss Receptionist spoke on the phone.

Teal checked her watch. She straightened her black jacket, her skirt, her mauve silk shell. She picked a piece of lint from Maiya's flouncy brown skirt. They had dressed up for the occasion.

She checked her watch.

An eternity passed.

Thirty-four minutes later, one minute per year of separation, he walked in, Dutch Morgan, in the flesh.

Teal's heart boomed.

He talked with the receptionist, his back to them. He was stocky, not as tall as she remembered. His hair was still black, cut short in business style. He wore an emerald-green polo shirt and khakis. When he turned around, she would see her own gray eyes.

Teal elbowed Maiya, who was already staring at him as if she intuited who he was.

He turned, and she saw her gray eyes and her long nose and her broad cheeks and her easy-to-look-at face.

He walked over to them, a half smile on

his face. "Megan Morgan?" He extended his hand toward Teal. "Do I know you?"

She stood and pointed to Maiya. "This is Maiya." She smiled and held out her hand, overwhelmed with a sudden urge to touch her father, to feel his hand around hers. "I'm Teal."

His hand and his smile dropped. The brows drew together. "Is this a joke?"

"Excuse me? Why would anyone joke about being me?" Teal spoke in her distinct, polite tone of voice, the same one that carried well in a courtroom.

He glanced at the receptionist, who hurriedly looked down, and then he motioned for them to follow him.

She exchanged a curious look with Maiya.

He ushered them into a sizable office, shut the door behind them, and stepped over to stand beside his desk, as if he needed the barrier. Behind him a huge window framed a breathtaking view of golf course and ocean.

Arms crossed, he did not invite them to sit. "What exactly do you want?"

A dozen replies scrambled in her mind, but Teal went speechless.

Maiya said, "I wanted to meet my grandfather."

"And you think I'm him?"

"I know you're him. You're Duane Upton Morgan, my mother's biological father. You were married in Cedar Pointe to Miranda Simpson Morgan Pomeroy."

Teal stared at the articulate, courageous young woman who was her daughter, and she calmed.

He scowled, and his nice-looking face took on years. "I do not appreciate the two of you dropping in here like this."

Teal said, "I apologize for that. I thought — I thought . . ." Tears threatened. She rushed her words. "That after so many years, a face-to-face reunion was in order."

"Well, now you've had it. Is there anything else?"

Maiya said, "Uh, like, maybe we could get to know each other? Go have coffee or lunch?" There was a trace of attitude in her tone, but it was couched in a melodious graciousness beyond her years. "Another time, if you're too busy now."

"I'm too busy now, and I'll be too busy later." He leaned sideways against his desk and turned a photo frame around. It was a five-by-seven of a woman and four teens who looked like a set of twin girls and one of twin boys. "This is who I am. This is my family. And this —" he gestured at the window — "this is my work. Listen, Megan,

I left Cedar Pointe and everyone in it a lifetime ago."

"Maiya. My name is Maiya Marie Morgan." She gestured toward Teal. "Aren't you at least interested in learning about your daughter? She went to college and law school and —"

"I have nothing to offer either of you."

Teal swallowed the hesitation and said the name she had yearned to say since her own lifetime ago. "Dad."

He flinched.

She went on. "We are not here to ask for money or to be put in your will or to interfere in any way with your new family." Without warning an odd happiness enveloped her. She was with her *dad,* up close and personal at long last. She cocked her head and smiled. "No matter how old a daughter is, she always wants to know her father."

"Okay. Genetically, I am most likely your father, but I don't want any part of whatever you think that means now."

His words hit her like shrapnel, one razor-edged shard at a time, paralyzing every nerve in her body.

He said, "Apparently you've done all right for yourself. You appear to be a successful woman. The past thirty years did not have a debilitating effect on you. Now, we've had our meet and greet. I sincerely wish you both all the best." He paused and made a flimsy attempt at a self-deprecating smile. "I'm afraid I really don't have any interest in further contact."

Teal's ears were ringing. Squiggly lines bounced before her; the room lost its distinct outline. They had to leave. They had to get out of there.

"Mom," Maiya whispered, her head near Teal's, "ask him why."

Ask him why what?

Maiya squeezed her hand.

Why. The question that had burned for thirty-four years.

Teal raised her chin and willed herself to focus on his face. "Why did you leave me?"

He shrugged. "I couldn't stay."

Maiya puffed through her lips a sound of disgust. "That is seriously lame, dude." She took hold of Teal's arm and they turned. "We're outta here, Mom." She opened the door.

A teenager stood there, her hand raised to knock. "Knock, knock." She grinned. She was one of the redheaded twins in the photograph.

From behind them, Dutch called out, "Susanna-Bobanna! Come on in."

"Excuse me," she said as they two-stepped around each other.

From the hallway, Teal looked back.

"Daddy!" The girl rushed into Dutch's arms. "You'll never guess!"

"Guess what, sweetheart?"

Maiya pulled her from the doorway and out toward the reception area.

Teal stumbled along beside her, trying to keep up the quick pace. Gleaming white tile flew beneath her feet. It gave way to concrete and then grass and at last black asphalt.

They stopped at the car and looked at each other.

Maiya's face was flushed and she was out of breath. "Unbelievable! A stinking piece of dog doo-doo disguised as a human being!" She ranted, generous with profanities she was not allowed to say.

Teal took the keys from her jacket pocket, where she'd kept them close for the hasty retreat now in progress. She handed them to Maiya and burst into tears.

Chapter 39

"Oh, Riv, Mom's an absolute, total mess." Maiya sounded on edge but not quite free-falling over it yet. "I don't know what to do."

Against school rules, River had answered his cell in the middle of his independent living skills class because it was Teal. He figured she was calling with a report on the Dutch Morgan meeting. She knew his class schedule. She would not be phoning unless things had gone south.

At Maiya's first "Oh, Riv," he snagged a hall monitor and asked him to keep an eye on his guys, a half-dozen working on résumés. He headed outdoors, listening in disbelief to her rendition of what had happened. At the baseball field, he settled on the bleachers.

Maiya said, "She just kept crying but we needed a bathroom and I was hungry so we

337

found a McDonald's and then she up-
chucked in there. She wouldn't eat anything
—"

"Slow down, Mai. Take a deep breath."
He heard her ragged attempt. "Did you
eat?"

"Yes."

"Are you okay to drive back? Can you find
the way?"

"Duh. I head south on the 101. It's just
that Mom — she's sitting in the car now,
like, totally checked out. She said she can't
talk to you. What do I do?"

"Hon, basically she's all right, but she's
probably got a migraine. Some ice will help.
Do you see a convenience store?" He
waited, imagining Maiya searching the strip
mall where she said they were parked.

"Yeah, there's one with a gas station."

"Buy two large cups of ice and zip bag-
gies. Make an ice bag and wrap it in a sweatshirt or something."

"O-okay."

"Do you need gas?"

"Um, I could check."

"Just fill it up." He rubbed his forehead.
"You can do this, Minnie McMouse. Your
mom will sleep the whole way, and you'll be
fine. You're an excellent driver."

"Thanks." Her voice gained strength.

"Riv, I have redheaded aunts and uncles who are, like, my age. Isn't that wild?"

"Wild."

"Not that it matters. I'll never see them again. Do you know what? He didn't even say Mom's name. Not once. He never said *Teal*. And he kept calling me Megan. What a jerk. Such a waste of oxygen. Oh, and get this: he called the girl Susanna. Do you believe that?"

River clenched his fist. "Did your mom hear?"

"Probably. She was standing right next to me."

Susanna. Teal's middle name. River wanted to hurt the man. He wanted to hurt him bad. "Maiya, I'm sorry I wasn't there."

"Yeah, me too. It was pretty awful." Her voice became subdued. "Mom's really special, isn't she?" It wasn't a question. "I don't know how she ever came from this Dutch guy and creepy Owen. Gran's not much to write home about either."

"Your mom made positive choices. Instead of living in self-pity because of how they hurt her, she just got on with her life."

"Until I made her go see Dutch." Maiya cried softly. "Oh, Riv. This had to be the worst day of her entire life and it's all my fault."

He consoled her as best he could long-distance, gave her another pep talk, and reminded her to buy gas.

He did not think he could feel any worse about not being there for his girls, but he did.

Chapter 40

Cedar Pointe

If Lacey didn't know better, she would have sworn Teal suffered from a hangover. The previous day's migraine had ravaged her sister's face.

Teal sipped the latte Lacey had brought over from the shop. "Mm. Baker's working?"

"No. I made it all by myself."

She smiled wanly.

"And I made the pumpkin muffins from scratch. None of that store-bought junk for you today." She took one from the box, set it on a plate, and slid it across the table. "Eat. Maiya said you didn't have a thing yesterday."

"Yes, ma'am." She pinched off a bite, popped it in her mouth, and shut her puffy eyes.

Lacey watched her chew, wishing she could ease her sister's pain. Poor Teal, rejected all over again by her father. Owen might have been absent for Lacey in more ways than not, but at least he hadn't deserted her and Randi.

The previous late afternoon, after Maiya had driven them back, Teal went straight to bed in the cottage. Will had brought Maiya to their house, and the story of the meeting with Dutch spilled from her.

Unable to get beyond tearful empathy, Lacey was glad to have Will, Nora, and William there adding calmer, wiser support.

Teal looked at her. "Lace, I'm all right. Really."

"I just can't believe he could do that."

"Don't cry. Please."

Lacey nodded and wiped her eyes with a napkin.

Teal broke the muffin apart. "It's a positive thing. I can now officially close that chapter. No more wondering what happened to him or where he is or what he's like."

"No more blaming yourself for his abandonment."

"I never . . ." She sighed. "Okay, yes, I have. I've spent my life believing I'm not good enough. If I were, he would have stayed or at least made contact."

"For years my mother-in-law told me that

Dad's drinking was not my fault. My head understood, but not my heart. Then I got cancer and my heart broke. Life came down to just me and God. It was like He filled up all the places that hurt. I don't have to earn His love." Lacey smiled. "I still try to some days, though."

"It's so deeply ingrained in me, I can't imagine ever stopping."

"We can't *think* our way into new ways of living. We have to act first. The mind-set follows."

"As in 'just do it'?"

Lacey chuckled. "Yeah, something like that. Just act like God adores you, no matter how awful you think you are, and after a while, it will become your first thought every day. It will be what echoes in your heart instead of those lies from the hurts."

Teal gave a thumbs-up sign.

Lacey bit her lip and sat back. The obviously sarcastic gesture triggered feelings of defeat that were all too familiar.

Way too familiar.

When was Lacey going to stop overlooking Teal's critical, abrasive demeanor? Was that really an act of love?

She leaned forward. "Teal, do you know that God loves you?"

"Yes, I know that." Her tone snipped.

"Sorry." She softened her tone. "I've told you about the neighbor who took care of Maiya when she was a baby and how I went to her church. We still go to the same one. Jayne and her friends loved and accepted me for who I am until I finally made the connection, that God is like that. I couldn't have done what I've done without believing He loves me."

"And yet you've been trying to earn it."

Teal glanced away. "I suppose."

"For me, the word *love* doesn't cut it. There's so much more to this relationship with the holy Father. I mean, God is absolutely crazy about us. He can't stop thinking about us. He's always watching over us, waiting for us to notice Him so He can show us what new gift He's got in His hand."

Tears puddled in Teal's eyes. "That's the kind of father River is with Maiya."

Lacey smiled. "I noticed."

"I guess we don't get one in the flesh."

"Nope. Not fair, is it?" Over Teal's shoulder she saw Maiya emerge from her bedroom. "Sleeping Beauty is up."

"Mommy!" Maiya rushed across the room and flung her arms around Teal. "Mommy!"

Teal hugged her daughter, eyeing Lacey. "Thank you," she mouthed.

Lacey nodded.

"Mom! Are you okay?"

Teal laughed. "If you don't strangle me."

"Sorry." Maiya let go and sat in the chair next to Teal. " 'Morning, Aunt Lace. Mom, I'm so sorry."

"Honey, I told you: it's not your fault."

"But you were out of it when you said that."

"Well, I'm not out of it now, and it's still true. I was telling Aunt Lacey that seeing Dutch took an enormous burden off me, so I'm glad you insisted we go."

"Really?"

"Really. Now I don't have to wonder about him anymore."

Maiya looked at Lacey. "That's kind of what I said last night, isn't it?"

"Kind of." Lacey held her breath, hoping Maiya would not repeat what she had declared over dinner to her, Will, and his parents about her own father.

Maiya turned back to Teal. "I don't want to meet my bio dad anymore. I decided while I was getting ice for you. Why would I sign up for what you've gone through? I am over and done with him."

So much for that hope. Now Teal was off the hook.

Maiya shrugged. "Nora said maybe mine

is a nice guy. And I said flying the coop is flying the coop. He left. He can stay gone." She lifted the lid off the box of muffins. "Ohhh, pumpkin? Yes! Aunt Lace, you're the best."

Teal met Lacey's eyes again, obviously irked.

Anger stabbed at Lacey and she let it flash in her return gaze. If Nora was indeed Maiya's grandmother, she had every right to encourage her with possibilities about her dad.

Just as she had last night, Lacey wanted to tell Maiya she had it all wrong. She wanted to shout the truth. *But your dad does not even know you exist! His name is Cody Janski, and he is a nice guy who deserves to know. You will like him! Your grandparents deserve to know! They already love you!*

As if hearing the internal tirade, Teal shook her head slightly. Her message was loud and clear: *Don't go there.*

Over the week and a half, Lacey did not "go there" with anyone. It wasn't her place to reveal her sister's secrets to others. And pressing Teal to open up would just press her further into her shell, so she did not bother to try.

However, she figured Maiya was fair game

346

for some subtle influencing. The aunt's rule book said so.

Under the guise of schoolwork, Lacey poked around the subject as often as possible. It wasn't that difficult. Father issues were all over the place, from stories for English to US history to biology. *What's missing in this character's life? How did the childhood of that president affect his choices? What do you think about environment versus heredity in that situation?*

Maiya was not slow. "Aunt Lacey, dads are not the most important people in the world. Why do you keep talking about them?" Her breath caught. "Do you know who he is?"

Lacey looked her in the eye and chose her words carefully. "I've asked your mom, but she refused to tell me. He is an important figure in your life, though, no matter that he is absent, and honestly, I hope that you won't give up wanting to learn about him."

"You weren't there! You didn't see how awful Dutch Morgan is. You didn't see Mom fall apart. Meet my bio dad? Yeah, right. No thank you."

"What if your dad is nothing like him?"

"But he *is* exactly like him because he does not want me. And besides, I have River."

After that, Lacey kept herself in check. She had done what she could to plant doubt in Maiya's heart. Perhaps it would prompt Maiya to ask Teal again for her father's identity, once they recovered from the Dutch encounter. Maiya was the only one who could change Teal's mind about that, and Teal's changed mind was the only way her sister was going to find any true peace.

A week or so before Teal and Maiya's departure, the Janskis left for Phoenix. The good-bye affected Nora harder than usual.

She held Maiya's face in her hands and whispered loud enough for Lacey to hear, "I pray that someday you will get to meet your biological father and that it will be a happy occasion. You never know. He may care very much about you. You may have grandparents and even half siblings who would want to be part of your life."

She watched as Maiya responded wordlessly to Nora, with a curious gaze and a soft smile. It was Lacey's own typical response to her mother-in-law. The older woman's wise words would sink into Maiya's heart, more deeply and effectively than all of Lacey's put together.

During the days following the Dutch fiasco, Teal was subdued, as if still reeling from the event. She all but disappeared from sight and often drove up to a coffee shop in Banbury in order to work, saying it was easier where no one knew her. At Happy Grounds, people always stopped by her table to chat.

At last, with far too much unfinished business still between them, Lacey and Teal said good-bye. They stood with Maiya and Will outside the cottage near the packed car.

The sisters hugged for a long time and then made the eye contact that had shifted in recent days. Lacey decided the "finished" business won out over the other stuff. They had reunited and enjoyed one another's company. Silently she forgave Teal for not telling her what she was not ready to tell her. She forgave Teal for sleeping with her boyfriend.

"Oh, Lacey. Thank you, thank you for everything."

She nodded, a sob building in her chest.

Maiya moved Teal aside and grabbed Lacey in a hug. "Come to LA for Thanksgiving. Please, please, please? We have a guest room. Well, it's Mom's office, but it has a sleeper in it."

Lacey looked at Teal.

She smiled. "I won't let another year go by, let alone nine."

Lacey glanced at a beaming Will, who

said, "We'll make it work."

Maiya yelled, "Yay!"

Teal leaned in to whisper in Lacey's ear, "I love you, Sis."

In that instant Lacey felt she'd reached the end of a long yearning. It was the first time her sister had ever told her she loved her.

CHAPTER 41

They headed south on the 101. Maiya drove while Teal settled into the passenger seat, eyes on the expanse of sky and ocean bathed in sunlight.

A profound sense of release enveloped her. She had gone to Camp Poppycock with two goals in mind: to mommy her daughter and to connect with her sister, who had never given up on trying to build a relationship. Both had been accomplished and then some.

In ways, she herself had been on the receiving end more than not. Maiya had helped her through the most difficult event of her life. Lacey had loved on her nonstop, even when she did not respond kindly. Randi had shown a nurturing side, however briefly, that touched Teal's heart. Overall, the townspeople treated her with respect rather than the eyebrow-raising attitude of bygone days.

"Mom?" Maiya glanced at her and smiled. "Thank you."

Teal grinned. "It was good?"

"Oh yes. I totally adore Aunt Lacey and Uncle Will. Gran Randi is a hoot. I wouldn't want to live with her, but at least I know her now. Baker will be a forever friend. I might even have a crush on him."

Teal laughed.

"And I know firsthand that Cedar Pointe is a nice place to visit once every nine years or so."

"I take it you're ready to get back to our regular life?"

"Am I still grounded?"

"Well, I have to check with your dad, but I think not."

"Yes!" she shouted. "He said the same thing. That means I'm not!"

Teal rolled her eyes. It would be good to be back on the same page as River. "Mai, it goes without saying —"

"Except you are saying, and trust me, I know what it is. Jake is off limits. Right? I swear, Mom, I am so over the dude. No worries."

"Okay."

"Are you ready to get back to our regular life?"

"Absolu . . ." Was she?

Not exactly.

Questions about Dutch had been answered. The rock of bitterness toward Randi had softened into a lump of compassion. Hatred toward Owen was simply gone. She, like Maiya, totally adored Lacey and Will. The business about Maiya's bio dad was shelved again but in a different closet. She would know when it was time to open its door.

Through it all she had let down River, her bosses, Hannah Walton, and other clients. She owed them more than *regular.*

She smiled at Maiya. "I am absolutely ready to get back to our life, but *regular* is history. It's time to step it up a notch."

"Go, Mom."

Teal laughed with a freedom she had never known.

CHAPTER 42

Los Angeles

Teal dropped her briefcase on the family room couch and slid off her pumps. "Honey, I'm home!" she shouted, walking into the kitchen. "Whoa! What is that luscious smell?"

River came around the corner, grinning behind a vase of a dozen red roses. Her husband wore his black suit — his only suit — white shirt, and sapphire-blue rep tie. He wore it because while she adored his ever-present blue jeans, rumpled shirts, and ball cap, she had a thing for him in a suit.

Oh.

His hair was neatly brushed off his face, behind his ears. "Welcome to Chez Riv, Mrs. Adams." He set the vase on the counter and wrapped her in his arms.

Teal chuckled. "That sounds like a Maiya-ism."

"It is." He kissed her soundly. "But everything else was my idea."

"Like what?" She hooked her hands at the back of his neck, gazed into those twinkling dark-blue eyes, and felt a twinge of disappointment. Visions of a romantic evening danced in her head, but with their daughter in the next room, those were out of the question.

"Well, the flowers were my idea." He nodded toward the table behind him. "The candles. The leek soup, asparagus, French baguette, and chicken breasts with fontina and prosciutto."

"Mm."

"There's one more. Maiya is spending the night at Amber's."

She opened her mouth to voice an automatic *no* because they had agreed to prioritize family this weekend. But River smiled his half grin and she turned to mush. "Best idea yet."

"I thought so." He winked. "Since we promised her she could see Amber tomorrow, I figured why not extend it to an overnight? Shauna wholeheartedly agreed. The girls have paid their penance. It's time they got to be best friends again." He kissed her forehead.

"I wholeheartedly agree too. Shall I slip into something more comfortable or help with dinner?"

He laughed. "I'll put dinner on the table by myself."

Teal drifted through the house. Candles were lit everywhere. Lights were dimmed. She removed her jacket and shed the day at the office along with it.

In the bedroom a long robe laid out on the bed caught her eye and she backtracked from the closet.

"Oh my."

She sank onto the bed and touched the beautiful fabric. It was purple, a lavender shade. Inside the robe was a matching nightgown with slender straps. Silky. But it would be polyester. River understood that she did not need expensive —

The tag read 100 percent silk.

But . . .

Teal held the gift close, crossing her arms over it, hugging herself, keeping the sob inside.

River.

She and Maiya had arrived home the previous evening after two days on the road, blowing in like Santa Anas. The three of them ate pizza, exchanged snippets of news that only scratched the surface of their time apart, and made tentative plans for the weekend. They fell into bed, exhausted.

Early that morning — that *Saturday* morning — Teal headed out the door. Depositions were scheduled for the Walton case next week. She needed to go to the office and catch up on a million things.

Frankly, she also was ready for some time away from Maiya. Despite their bonding experience, she imagined Maiya felt the same about her. Six weeks of up-close-and-personal had been long enough. Father and daughter could have a special day together. Husband and wife continued in their holding pattern.

It was an obvious choice. Work and her own needs came first. River could wait. Still. They would meet up again after the depositions. Or after she caught up with her bosses. Or after the other cases on her desk were addressed. Or after, or after.

Was this the stepping up a notch she had imagined during the drive from Oregon?

It had only been twenty-four hours, but shouldn't River have been top on her list? Instead, he took care of Maiya, prepared dinner, waited, did not complain, and bought her silk.

Silk was expensive.

Silk was feminine.

Silk exposed those lies Lacey had mentioned, the ones Teal thought had been

357

silenced. The lies that said her dad would not have abandoned her if she was worthy or if she was a desirable, feminine woman.

Lies.

With this gift, River announced loud and clear that they were lies, not to be believed.

"Hey." He stood in the doorway. "Do you like it?"

She smiled through her tears. "How about we delay dinner?"

He loosened his tie. "It's keeping warm in the oven."

The tapers had burned halfway down to the brass candlesticks. Still Teal and River lingered at the dinner table, the remains of his exquisite meal between them, giving voice to five weeks' worth of daily details.

River said, "Randi actually cried when you said good-bye?"

"For real."

"No way." He teased, but his smile was genuinely happy for her.

"All of a sudden my mother cares. And what am I supposed to do with that?"

He appeared lost in thought, and she was content to watch him be lost in thought. His elbow was propped on the table, his chin cupped in his hand. He had not put on his tie or jacket. His shirt shone a brilliant white in contrast to the shadows cast by the candlelight. What had she done to deserve such a man? Nothing. He was a sheer gift. Just like the lavender silk she wore.

He lowered his hand, his eyes intent on her face. "Maybe it will eventually give you some sense of well-being."

"Yeah, right. It'll take another thirty-seven years and I'll be . . ." Teal's protest died in her throat. It was an old habit. There truly had been a response deep in her bones. A vague twinge when her mother said how despicable Dutch's actions were . . . when Randi clung to her as they said good-bye.

She swallowed. "All right. I admit I felt somehow, uh . . . I guess *soothed* is the word."

He nodded. "It's never too late to start expressing and receiving love. Who knows? Someday even Dutch may look you up."

"Oh, River." She shook her head. "Where do you get such hopeful notions? My last hopeful notion was that Randi would pull out a stash of letters from him that she hid because Owen did not want him in our lives. Those letters do not exist because I have not existed for him since I was three. At least back then he noticed me." She snorted. "Or not. Maybe all that is a figment of my imagination too. Maybe we never did have a

359

relationship."

"What about your middle name?"

"Huh?"

"Susanna."

"I know what my middle name is, hon." She gave him a puzzled look.

He sighed, and his shoulders drooped. "You didn't hear, then. Remember when the redheaded daughter came into his office?"

"How could I forget? My head was pounding by then. I was pretty much out of it. He'd shown us the photo, but the kids are less than half my age, so I thought maybe they weren't his. But I knew that wasn't true the moment I saw her because I was looking at me in a red wig. It was so bizarre." She blinked. "But what's this got to do with my name?"

He winced. "He called her Susanna. Specifically, it was 'Susanna-Bobanna.' Maiya told me."

"Hm." She bit her lip. "Hm. Well." She gritted her teeth. She inhaled and exhaled. She clenched a fist. "Nuts! Just when I didn't think it could hurt any more."

River pushed aside plates and reached across the table and unfolded her hand. "Want my take on it?"

Her eyes stung. "No."

"Listen, love. We can't know what all went into his decision to leave you and your mom. But it's apparent he was incapable of finding his way back to you. As far as we can tell, there were no letters, no money, no phone calls, no visits. What kept him away? Shame, guilt, fear, plain old cowardice, any number of things."

She focused on River's face and his low, gentle voice. It kept the tears from spilling.

"If there was one ounce of humanity in Dutch, he must have been hurting."

"River, trust me. There is not a shred of humanity in that man."

"Imagine him with the teensiest bit of it. How do you turn your back on your precious three-year-old without shutting down?"

"I can let him go, but I am not feeling pity for him."

"I'm not saying you should. Just hang in here with me a minute. So, he was in this unbearable pain and like any macho guy, he reacts by shutting down and moving on. He makes a new life. He even marries again and has children. And he names one of them after you because either consciously or not, he is trying to replace the one he lost."

"Meaning?"

"He really did love his first daughter. He just didn't know how to show it."

"That's a pathetic excuse."

"It is. But it's real life. The point is, we all crave forgiveness and compassion."

"Preach it, brother."

He chuckled. "Make fun if you want. You know it's the truth." He squeezed her hand and began stacking the plates. "It's late, and tomorrow is a big day for Maiya."

Lost in her own thoughts, Teal watched him clear the table. She wanted to remind him that she'd dealt with this business ages ago. She had forgiven Randi, Owen, and Dutch. Shoot, she'd forgiven the whole town. For her own sake, she had let everyone off the hook. Her anger was gone. She harbored no bitterness.

But as in River's scenario with Dutch, she had shut down a part of herself. She had crusted over to stop the incessant hurting. The problem was, closing off her heart annihilated the ability to feel any honest compassion toward them.

She touched the edge of her silk sleeve where River's hand had rested on her hand. Maybe the inability to feel any goodness toward her parents was one more lie to stop believing.

Teal blew out the candles and joined River

in the kitchen to help clean up.

He said, "Maiya has a list a mile long of what she needs to do before school on Monday. She wants to wrap all those bracelets she got for friends and those jars of jam she bought for teachers."

"Do you think that smacks of bribery?"

"Nah." He poured detergent into the dishwasher. "It smacks of forgiveness and compassion."

Teal threw a towel at him.

He caught it midair, laughing. "It shows that she forgives the system for suspending her and feels bad for them because they didn't get to visit Oregon." He shut the dishwasher and grabbed Teal in a hug. "She is a funny kid. Taking her up there was brilliant, Teal. I haven't seen her this chipper for months. Must be the healing power of extended family."

"And the healing power of no Jake Ford in her life."

"That too. Are we glad he got another girlfriend or what?" He held her face between his hands, his expression sobering with his voice. "So, about tomorrow. What do you need from me?"

Sunday promised to be a full day. She was eager to touch base with old friends at church. Laundry was piled sky high. Some down time for the three of them was in order, maybe takeout Chinese — unheard of in Cedar Pointe — and a video.

She said, "Um, run her to the paper shop and buy a bunch of gift bags?"

His brow creased. "I was talking about The Talk with Maiya."

She heard the capital letters. "The Talk?"

"You promised to tell her Bio Dad's identity once you got home. It's going to take some time for her to process it."

Bio Dad's identity? "Is that on her to-do list?"

"She didn't mention it."

"River, I told you what she told me. She does not want to hear it now, not after meeting Dutch. And there's no way on earth I want to tell her. I'm not going to put her through anything remotely similar to what happened to me."

He frowned.

"You disagree."

"Yes, I disagree." He lowered his hands to her shoulders, gave them a quick squeeze, and let go. Stepping back, he leaned against the counter and crossed his arms. "I disagree strongly. You promised her."

"There are extenuating circumstances."

"Extenuating excuses. Come on, Teal. You're the adult. You understand that she needs this information. She has a father wound just like you do. If it doesn't get addressed, she's likely to act out again, which is what the Jake thing was all about." He paused.

She wanted to cover her ears.

He said, "Which is what your behavior was all about, right? Why you slept with him and kept the baby?"

The lies again. Lies about not being good enough. Lies about using others and being used to fill the emptiness, that place that hurt so bad because her dad had bailed. Lies about keeping a baby because then she would have someone who loved her.

No, she was not ready to open the closet. She reached for a compromise. "I'm not telling her tomorrow."

"Okay. It's your decision."

She met his steady gaze. "Okay. We agree to disagree."

He didn't blink or budge.

She loathed and loved how he could do that, nail her with The Look, the one he used with his boys.

It did not mean he was pressing her to change her mind but rather to examine herself. It always sent her thoughts spinning. No one else could do that to her. It was probably what attracted her to him in the first place.

She gave him her own look. *Don't mess with me.*

He was supposed to uncross his arms and shrug.

But he didn't.

Fine. She had done enough self-examination in the past five weeks to last forever. She was in good shape, considering. The family reunion had been difficult, but in the end made a positive impact on her. The Dutch meeting had been less fiasco than wake-up call to let the memory of him go. Maiya had gotten to know her relatives, almost *all* of them, and it was more than enough to fill her emotional tank.

Teal held out her hands in defeat. "Whatever it is you want to say, say it. I can take it."

Although he kept his arms folded, the air about him relaxed. "I'm not asking you to tell me anything."

"All right."

"I want to make sure you fully realize that it's not exactly rocket science to figure out who he is."

Heat exploded in her chest and burned its way up her neck.

He said, "Anyone who saw and heard what I did in Cedar Pointe could figure it out. Lacey and Will for sure. Maybe his parents. Maybe even Maiya."

Her cheeks felt on fire. How could she tell River? It wasn't the identity exactly. It was the circumstances. It was the betrayal of so many people. It was herself, sin incarnate.

Could others really and truly guess who he was?

With difficulty she swallowed. "Please don't . . ."

"Teal, I won't tell anyone. No one said anything. It's just fairly obvious."

"I'm sorry."

"I'm not the one you need to apologize to. And it's not just Maiya that you're hurting. It's her uncle and grandparents." His voice was barely a whisper. "It's her dad who must not even know she exists."

She studied the floor tiles. The flecked beige had been a good choice. A shiny ceramic brightened the narrow kitchen and did not show every speck of dirt. River's bare feet came into her line of sight.

"You needed to hear that."

"Yeah." She looked up at him. "Um . . . I don't know how to get out of this. Can we not go to bed angry?"

"Hey, you." He wrapped her in his arms again. "I am not mad. I hurt for you. You're behaving like a silly, delusional woman, and that is not who you are. I had hopes that you would take off the mask."

She winced, glad that her shameful face was hidden against his neck. She was totally silly and delusional.

But it worked.

CHAPTER 43

"Brake lights, two cars up." River thrust his foot against the floorboard and braced his hand on the dash.

Maiya laughed. "Got it under control, Riv. Hey, did you know there's no brake pedal on that side of the car?"

"Ha-ha." He relaxed as she slowed the car in the nick of time. "Hey, did you know there will be no driving privileges if you insist on kissing the bumper ahead of you at every single stoplight?"

"Hey, did you know there are no traffic lights in Camp Poppycock and absolutely no traffic?"

"You're saying you're out of practice."

"Yes, sir. I'll get back my LA skills in no time." She glanced at him with her best smile of cooperation, an innocent expression she'd developed long before he had met her.

It still caught him off guard, though. He

really was much better with boys. "Did you get a DMV appointment?"

"Two weeks from Thursday."

"Nothing before that?"

"I could get one next Friday, but I don't want to miss the auction setup."

"Maiya, getting your license is a huge deal. You don't need to postpone it any longer. There will be plenty of help, and you'll be there on Saturday."

Although the academy boys worked for weeks on collecting and organizing items for the annual fund-raiser, the day before always became crunch time. It had grown into a staff family event with spouses and children pitching in on last-minute touches. Teal would take off half a day from work and pull Maiya out of school early so they could help.

He said, "Besides that, you've missed enough school for one semester, don't you think?"

"Guess what? We get out early that day because of a teachers' meeting."

River wondered, not for the first time, what it would be like teaching in a public school with all the extra days spent without the students. He'd probably be bored silly.

She said, "You know how much I like the auction weekend. Speaking of kissing . . ."

"We were talking about kissing?"

"Bumpers." Traffic moved and they were off again. She focused on driving, but like her mother, the queen of jabberwocky could talk and do three other things simultaneously. "Jake and the new girlfriend are history."

River did some mental gymnastics and caught up with her train of thought. "Jake's available again and he'll be at the setup with other grads."

Maiya glanced at him. "But I'm not interested."

"But you want to be at Saint Sibs Friday because he will be, and if your mother's not looking, your paths may cross."

"Okay, so I'd like to talk to him. I need some closure, you know? That's all."

"Will this involve kissing?"

"No. That was just my clever segue."

"Cute. Have you been in touch with him?"

"No way! Amber caught me up. She got it from Claire, who got it from Ben, who got it from Heather, who got it from Pablo, who knows him."

It was like an endless begat list from the Old Testament.

She went on. "But what's up with his trial? Nobody knows."

That was good to hear. The details were

as crazy as a soap opera and did not need to get twisted into wilder stories. Some girl unrelated to the whole business had been arrested for something. As part of her plea bargain she outed Jake's now ex-girlfriend as the one who let him inside the high school building that fateful day.

River measured his words. "This isn't for public consumption yet."

"Got it."

"It looks like he'll be put on probation. He hasn't been in trouble since he was a juvenile. He has a good job and work ethic." He stopped himself from further extolling Jake's good characteristics. Talking Maiya into liking him wasn't the point. "Other than that stupid stunt at the school, his record is clear. But about talking to him, you'll have to bring your mom in on that discussion." He wasn't getting anywhere near giving Maiya permission to see Jake. "Or I will. I won't keep secrets from her."

"Nope. Got enough of those going around."

He held in a snap reply. *You got that right.*

She signaled and turned into a lot. "The outlet store is here. They've got the best gift bags and they're cheap."

It was a strip mall, Sunday-afternoon

crazy busy. River let her find a spot by herself.

He had offered to run errands with Maiya; Teal had offered to stay home and do laundry. Although they had gone to church together that morning, he felt they were both more comfortable with some distance between them. Last night's discussion lay heavy on him. The dark circles under her eyes said it did likewise with her.

Fine. If she wanted to wallow in her delusional idiocy, that was her own fault.

Maybe there was some anger in him.

"River."

Her use of his full name got his attention. "What?"

She turned off the engine and looked at him. "Will it hurt your feelings if I say I want to know who my dad is?"

"Maiya, no, not at all. I've told you that."

"Yeah, but I wanted to make double sure."

He nodded and unhooked his seat belt. "It's for double sure. You and I have a good relationship, right?"

"Definitely."

"I'm not threatened, hon. Your heart has room for both of us."

She smiled wistfully. "Kind of like yours with Mom and Krissy?"

Oh, man.

"And with me and Sammy."

"Uh, yeah, I guess."

"You won't leave Mom, will you?"

"Why — ? No, never. I love you two. I hated it when you were gone." He figured her real question had to do with abandonment. Would her surrogate dad leave her like she thought her biological father had? "Minnie McMouse, I promise I won't ever leave her or you."

"But all you two have been doing lately is arguing, and Mom and I were away for so long, and . . ." She shrugged.

This line of thinking was most likely a remnant of conversation with her friend. Amber came from a solid family. Her parents had been married years before the birth of their two daughters. The Prices did not separate for long periods of time. Or even short periods, now that he thought about it.

He gently tugged Maiya's ponytail. "You know your mom and I don't shy away from disagreeing. The lawyer in her won't allow it, and I'm not about to back down from some opinionated Xena just because she's the most beautiful, intriguing woman in the world."

Maiya giggled.

"Listen, this is just life. Granted, being away from each other was a tough one, but we're learning from it. It'll pass."

"If I knew who my dad was, maybe it'd pass sooner."

"This is not your fault."

She shrugged, unconvinced. "But if I knew . . ."

"Didn't you tell your mom you don't want to know?"

She looked away and frowned. "I felt so bad about making her go and meet Dutch. *That* was my fault. She so totally lost it. Seeing her like that really scared me. I can't make her do something else she doesn't want to do. I won't."

River groaned to himself. *I can't. I won't.* Was she Teal's daughter or what?

Maiya said, "And if Bio Dad is like Dutch, I don't ever want to meet him. But —" she turned to him, her eyes wide and her youthful face a picture of hope — "Nora got me thinking. She said maybe he's not like Dutch at all. Maybe he would care about me. Maybe I even have grandparents and half siblings! Imagine that! They'd probably be younger. I'd be a big sister. That would be cool. As long as the stepmother wasn't one of those ugly ones from a fairy tale."

He thought his heart might break in two. He could dispel Maiya's angst in a flash. With one phone call to Will, he could have the man's phone number. In less than ten minutes, Maiya could conceivably be talking to her biological father. She would learn that yes, indeed, he was a decent guy and that she did have half siblings. From the sounds of it, the stepmother might even be wholesome and welcoming.

After that, she could talk to her grandparents. She could say "grandma" and "grandpa" to them instead of "Nora" and "William."

But his hands were tied. This was Teal's bailiwick.

"Riv, do you think he'd like me?"

Now his heart cracked open. He held his breath, willing his chest not to let go of the sob sitting in it.

"I mean," she whispered, "as a fortysomething dad, you might have an idea?" Her forest-green eyes reflected the Oregon pines.

He imagined Staff Sergeant Cody Janski's eyes were that same shade.

"Maiya, I know he would like you very much. What is there not to like?"

"Oh, lots."

"Bunch of hooey." He paused. "Hon, if you want to know who he is, then you have to tell your mom."

"Nooo." She paused. "Will you tell her?"

He shut his eyes and struggled with how

much he could reveal and yet not malign his wife.

"Please, please, River?"

He looked at her. "Hon, I already have told her. So let's give it a rest. Give her time to think about it. Okay?"

Maiya's lips trembled, but ever her mother's daughter, she rallied. " 'Kay. Thanks." She held up her hand for a high five. "WFM."

He slapped her palm. "Works for me, too." *For now.*

Three times a year, River visited the cemetery. In March, on Krissy's birthday. In June, on their wedding anniversary. And today, October 11, the day he lost her and their unborn son.

He sat on a concrete bench in front of a marble block about the size of a large playhouse. The mausoleum still seemed newfangled to him with its rows of marble frontispieces. Eight up and eight across on all four sides. Open to the elements, not exactly a building per se. Only ashes were allowed to enter.

He let the memories come. Those first hours and days after the accident — and no, he would not call it a divine appointment — were hazy. The single moment of clarity was when he said, "Cremation. Entombment."

Krissy had been steeped in practicality. As a liaison for the Environmental Protection Agency, she told people how to dispose of trash. She would laugh, saying no one could get more practical than dealing with garbage. They met when she gave a seminar at San Sebastian Academy.

With her pregnancy, Krissy had gotten more practical than ever. They needed a will. He needed to know that she wanted her body to be cremated. A green urn in a corner of his closet would suffice, or working the ashes into their garden was even better.

But he couldn't. He wanted a place to visit like he had with his parents and so he had said, "Entombment."

He glanced around now, inhaled the dry scent of a sycamore that shaded the area. Krissy would approve, in part, anyway. The drought-tolerant desertscape majored on rock, cacti, succulents, wildflowers. Not a blade of grass was visible around her and Sammy's place.

He looked at their names chiseled on the gray marble square, grateful for his sister's input. Jenny had brought him to this spot before the funeral and pushed him onto a bench. The mausoleum was a fairly new structure; spaces were available in every row on every side. "Eye level," she had said. "Choose where you can see without getting a crick in your neck."

And so he always sat in that same seat and gazed straight ahead, first square on the left, third row up. *Kristina Ann Samuel Adams.* Her dates. *Samuel River Adams, Son.*

She hadn't been sure of the first name. He insisted it was perfect to use her maiden name. She said Samuel Adams was the name of a beer. He said that first and foremost he was a signer of the Declaration of Independence. She said okay, but only if they used River's name in the middle. He hadn't fully agreed to that until it came time for the engraving.

Eleven years had passed. The intensity of the image of Krissy had lessened as time went on. He looked less often at her photo. His imaginary conversations with her grew infrequent. But three times a year he could sit and distinctly recall her face and her voice.

Teal knew everything. His habit of taking half a day off if necessary to visit the site. His emotional upheaval the night before, his need to hold her in the quiet predawn hour. She would walk with him out to his truck, kiss his cheek, and hand him a small bouquet that fit perfectly in the tiny vase attached to the frontispiece. She would tell him she loved him.

That had not happened today. None of it. Teal was up before dawn and out the door soon after, harried, preoccupied. With work or the Cody thing or the unsettledness between them, he had no clue.

He drove Maiya to school, calming her concerns about it being her first day back after the long absence. Would everyone accept her? Had she become a pariah? Would they want to traffic with someone who had caused the school to shut down?

Not that Maiya was aware of the date. But still . . . neither one of them?

Stop your whining, River. It's so not you.

He smiled at the thought of Krissy's voice. She had been good at calling him on the ridiculous.

"It's mourning."

Baloney. It's self-indulgent hoo-ha.

"Give me a break."

She laughed and laughed until he joined in.

"Oh, I still miss you, Krissy. I miss you very much."

He hoped she knew.

Chapter 44

The three men seated across from Teal in a conference room at her law firm on Thursday morning could easily have passed on the street for identical triplets.

James Parkhurst, his attorney, and his attorney's assistant were tall, good-looking, muscular men with square jaws, deep voices, designer suits in black, power ties in red designs, French cuffs, manicured nails, and classic gold wedding bands.

She had addressed the lawyer, Mr. Smith, as Mr. Parkhurst at least twice in the last five minutes. The assistant's name was nowhere to be found in her memory bank. The higher echelons of Hollywood, even in triplicate, did not intimidate her. No. It was simply her mind. It had gone for a hike and had not come back.

As they waited for some technical issue with the video equipment to be resolved, Pamela slipped her a note. *Out. Now. Now* was underlined.

Obviously her assistant had noticed her fumbling attempts at coherent speech.

Teal excused herself and followed her out the door.

She scurried to keep up with Pamela, down the hall, around the corner, and into the ladies' room, where she sank onto a damask chair. It was such a soothing place with overstuffed chairs, muted wallpaper in shades of pink, lavender-scented potpourri, and vases filled with silk flowers. A part of her wanted to stay put until six o'clock.

In contrast, Pamela was in full-on business mode. Mother Hen was nowhere to be seen. Her hair seemed particularly steely iron in color, its blunt angles extra sharp. It suited the expression on her face. "Girl, you have got to get your act together."

"I'll be fine."

She sat in the other chair and leaned forward. "You can't keep their names straight."

"Don't they seem like brothers? Like identical triplets?"

Pamela pursed her lips. "Parkhurst, main guy, reddest tie. Smith, less main, receding hairline. Marxon nicked himself shaving this morning." She pointed to the right side of her neck. "A mark, here."

"Okay, got it." The clues flittered away like moths. "No, I don't. It's because they're so much alike. They're all just *so nice.* Genuinely nice. Not the ogres Hannah portrayed."

Pamela leaned back in her chair and sighed. "I noticed. Give me a jackass any day over nice."

Teal smoothed her black skirt and took a deep breath. "All right. We've identified the problem. We will stay on task and do our job. It's not like the questions have changed. We ask what we have to ask. Reddest tie is the only one I need to address, and his name is Parkhurst. Mr. Parkhurst."

Pamela squinted, critically studying Teal. "You talk big, but your game face is still AWOL. Did you leave it up in Oregon or what?"

Nope. On the kitchen floor. Saturday night. When her husband had seen right through her.

"Teal, if you can't do it, say so. Zoe is available. She'll step in."

Just what she needed. A boss not happy about her long absence covering for her. "No. This is my case. I promised Hannah I would take care of the depo."

"Then go get him, tiger, or else I'll stomp on your tail under the table."

Teal's smile slipped. She was unnerved, almost as badly as in the early days, when she would go home from the office and literally cry on her neighbor's shoulder.

What she needed right now was a good dousing in Gammy Jayne's faith, the kind that acted upon God's immanency. He was right there, right now, available. *Just talk to Him. Tell Him what you want.*

What she wanted was for God to erase Saturday night. To delete that moment when River Adams — the closest physical rendition of God she had ever seen — saw how reprehensible she truly was.

"Teal, you can do this." Pamela's expression softened into an understanding smile.

That got her out of the chair and down the hall.

Back in the conference room, after a few taps of Pamela's toe against her leg, Teal settled into what she knew best.

She asked the questions, the equipment recorded, the court reporter did her job, Pamela took copious notes. Whatever word or facial nuance Teal missed, she could find later. Considering she was probably missing three-fourths of them, this encouraged her, and she fell into a rhythm.

James Parkhurst cooperated, disclosing every fact she already knew. Name, age, address, marital history, work history, finances, the nature of his relationship with Hannah Walton.

He maintained eye contact, not once glancing at his attorney for help. There were flashes of charm, but the gentlemanly sort without smarmy condescension. He smiled when he spoke of his current wife. He winced at his description of himself calling Hannah a slut to her face. He blamed it on fear that the pregnancy rang the death knell of his marriage, which he admitted was all but over anyway. In reality, he said, he probably was more concerned about his money than his marriage. A pregnant girlfriend would muddy the divorce waters.

Slut. Owen had labeled Teal that by the time she was twelve or thirteen. She'd had to look it up in the dictionary and realized what an idiot he was. The definition did not apply to her. After a few beers, Owen would add adjectives, words like *worthless* and *no-good.* She did not need a dictionary for them. Even back then she could have added *despicable* and *reprehensible,* fifty-cent words Owen had no knowledge of.

"Mr. Parkhurst."

He stopped midsentence in his explanation of alimony. "Yes?"

"Do you drink to excess?"

"I am a recovering alcoholic."

"To the best of your recollection, were you under the influence of alcohol when you had this conversation with Hannah?"

"Yes, I'm quite convinced that I was."

"And yet you remember the conversation?"

He sighed. "Distinctly enough to know I behaved badly. She did not deserve my response. I knew she loved me and that she hadn't dated anyone else for over a year. She wasn't the cheating type. Unlike myself."

Teal held in her own sigh. The guy was building a credible case and she had to go with it. "Did you discuss the situation at a later time while sober?"

"I tried several times to contact her. Some of the voice mails I left while sober." His lopsided smile reeked of self-deprecation. "She did not answer my calls. She cleared out her desk one Sunday when she would have known I was on the golf course. I went to her apartment one night, not quite sober, and begged her to let me help financially."

"You and she spoke?" This was news.

"Well, I spoke, and she slammed the door in my face. I can't blame her."

"Did you have further contact after that?"

"No. She changed her phone number to

an unlisted one. I went to her apartment again, but she had moved out. I thought of tracking down her parents, but by then I had caught on that she didn't want me involved."

"Did you give her money?"

"I tried."

She let him go on about his attempts to give Hannah money to help with expenses. His mailed checks were not returned, but neither were they cashed.

He said, "I've put money in a trust fund for Maddie. It will be hers when she turns twenty-one."

Okay. More news.

"Mr. Parkhurst, did you tell your wife — uh, your first wife . . ." She scanned a paper.

As if knowing the typed words blurred before her, Pamela pointed to the name. Janelle, wife number one. Not to be confused with Alison, wife number two.

She looked at him. "Did you inform Janelle about the affair and the pregnancy?"

"Not until later." His cheeks actually took on the color of his tie. "Because it would have given her something else to hold over me. I was concerned it would give her grounds to demand more than half of my money. It was all about the money in those days."

Teal had seen the paperwork. Parkhurst and wife number one had settled out of court for a no-fault divorce after ten years of marriage. She received half of their property and should be set for life. A reasonable woman would not have asked for more. Not that Teal had seen much of *reasonable* when it came to divorce.

She said, "You mentioned 'something else.' Like what?"

He shifted in his chair. "Two affairs. Abuse — mental, emotional, and physical."

Oops. That was a bit more than recorded. Nice daddy material. "You and Janelle did not have children?"

"No, we did not."

Thank God.

"We would've had more kids." Owen's voice crept in again. *"If you'd gone with your own dad, we would've had the money and Lacey could've had a real sister."*

Teal had been sixteen for that one. It was the day she grabbed his belt as he swung it toward her thigh. She swore if he hit her, she would report him to the new neighbor. The friendliest man she had ever met was a sheriff's deputy. Owen believed her. He never whacked her again. A run-in with the guy about property lines must have convinced Owen he'd best not tangle with him.

Her palm burned for days, but it was worth it. His verbal abuse reached new heights, but that she could deal with. She spent as little time at home as possible, going to school, running with other rejects, working at the video store, sometimes even sleeping on the back-room floor there after everyone had gone. She figured out how to get scholarships and grants and go to college.

She might have been a worthless, no-good sister and daughter, but she was no slut. She didn't have time to be.

Parkhurst said, "We never wanted children."

"Neither of you?"

"Correct."

"And now you do?"

"Yes. Both Alison and I do."

"What changed?"

He folded his hands on the table. Much as she studied his handsome face for any sign of the reprobate she wanted to see, there was only an ethereal peace about him.

"In a word, Jesus changed me."

She had hoped not to bring Jesus into the matter. If Parkhurst's experience was the real deal, if the Spirit of the living God had gotten hold of him, then they might as well pack up and go home right now. Hannah might as well invite Maddie's bio dad over for a get-acquainted dinner tonight.

He went on. "First Hannah left; then Janelle, along with half of my assets. I produced three movies that barely made it to cable TV. I drank more." He paused. "Then Alison came to work for us."

Teal had seen photos. The woman was a typical Parkhurst company hire: twenty-something and gorgeous.

He said, "I don't know how to explain it. She was a whiz in the business and refused to let me run it into the ground. I went to AA for her. I went to church for her. Jesus got through to me, probably through her prayers." He shook his head as if in amazement. "This always sounds hokey, but I have to say it. God invaded my life, and I am not the man I was five years ago. I want to be a good father, even if it's only part-time."

"Mommy, Mommy! Gammy Jayne says Jesus loves me, and guess what? He does! He told me!" Teal had laughed at Maiya's big round eyes and four-year-old excitement. "I know, sweetie! I know. He told me too, when you were growing inside my tummy." The little bowtie mouth formed a speechless O. They had danced a jig around the studio apartment.

The knowledge that Someone watched

over them provided a peace that lasted for years and years.

It lasted until an earthquake sent her running to Oregon to be reminded at every turn that she was, indeed, a slut.

"Mr. Parkhurst, I apologize if this sounds indelicate, but why Maddie? Why not move on and have children with your wife?"

His face slackened, he made eye contact, and she knew she had missed something. She had missed requesting a vital piece of his history during discovery.

"My wife can't have children. She has physical issues. We've considered adoption, but for now Alison and I simply want to be a part of Maddie's life. I'm not asking for custody, only for the visitation rights of any father who wants his daughter to see that he loves her very much."

He had her on "I want to be a good father, even if it's only part-time."

What if Dutch had ever said that?

What if Cody would say it if he knew Maiya was his daughter?

"All right, thank you. We're finished here." She abruptly ended the meeting. Before Pamela could kick her, she stood and said her good-byes to the triplets. Mr. Parkhurst. Mr. Nixon. Or something like that. Mr. Jones. Or was it Smith? "Thank you. Thank you. Pamela will show you out."

Teal made a beeline for the ladies' room. She folded herself onto the chair, head on the armrest, arms wrapped around her knees, and decided this time she would stay put until six o'clock.

Pamela found Teal long before six o'clock. She sat in the other chair. "They're going to chew up Hannah Walton and spit her out."

"And manage to do it with the utmost civility." Teal sighed and sat up. "Her version still has holes in it. We need to prep more before her deposition on Monday. Let's get her in first thing in the morning."

"She's on her way now. She'll be here at one. I moved your two o'clock to seven tomorrow morning. Today's three o'clock is now at four thirty."

Teal stared at the woman. "Sometimes your efficiency bugs me."

Pamela smiled. "Lunch is on your desk. Chicken salad."

As more often than not, they ate together in Teal's office, taking little notice of the food while they worked.

Fork in one hand, keyboard beneath the other, Teal scanned her calendar on the monitor. Despite her recent absence, it was full. An endless parade of women needed advice, wills, divorces, separation papers, restraining orders, child custody changes, or to haul a deadbeat dad back into court.

There was so much pain scheduled to cross her threshold.

She muttered, "Maybe I'll open a coffee shop."

Across the desk Pamela eyed her over her own laptop. "Oh?"

"Like my sister. You know, she just makes people happy. They come in, unload their woes, drink coffee and eat sweet rolls, and then they feel better."

"You make people feel better without the caffeine and sugar."

"But this takes so much more out of me than grinding beans and filling the creamer would."

Pamela smiled. "It's been a crazy week. This Walton-Parkhurst case is a rough way to jump back in the saddle, but you'll be fine. Once you got going this morning, you were great."

"Thanks to you. You're a lifesaver, Pamela."

"I'm just your backup, doing my job. By the way, how's Maiya's first week back to school going?"

"Uh, really well, it seems." She brushed aside a twinge of guilt. The truth was, there had been no heart-to-hearts. At best, she could say she had not heard any concerns out of Maiya. River had been taking her to school; Amber's mom usually brought her home. Between time with her friends and homework, Maiya had been scarce.

Just like River and Teal. Her ten-hour days at the office plus two hours of work at home weren't twenty-four, but they did not leave much time for family. River himself was at his most busy season preparing for the auction; he was gone most evenings.

"And how was River's Monday? I forgot to ask."

"River's Monday?" Teal glanced at the calendar again. *Monday. What was Monday?*

"The eleventh," Pamela prompted.

"The elev . . . *Ohhh, nooo.*" She set down her fork.

"You forgot? Teal. Honestly?" Concern filled Pamela's dark eyes.

River had spent the anniversary of Krissy and Sammy's death on his own. Teal had offered nothing to her husband, who understandably still hurt, no comfort from her in the morning or at dinner. Her stomach twisted. "How could I do that to him?"

"Given this crazy week, it's obvious how it happened. You didn't mean to."

"But that's not the point." She pushed

away from the desk and stood. "Oh my gosh. I can't believe it. How could I do this to him?"

Pamela twisted the phone toward her and unhooked the receiver. "I'll call his cell number."

"No. He won't answer. He's in class. Oh, Pamela. I have to go there." She yanked open a drawer and pulled out her handbag. "To the school." Should she take any files?

"Leave a voice message. He'll get it sooner."

Forget the files. She grabbed her jacket from the back of her chair and rounded the desk.

Pamela stood and shut the door before she could get through it. "Teal, slow down and think this through. It's an hour to his school, an hour back. If you hope to spend any time at all with him, you'll lose the afternoon."

"That doesn't matter! I've let this man down far too many times. You have no idea. I swear, I don't know why he's still married to me." Her voice rose and she chirped nonstop like a bird. "Good grief. I left him for weeks. I don't tell him hardly anything about the way my life was before I met him. I won't tell him who Maiya's father is. And now I've let him observe this horrendous anniversary all by himself. He's always playing second fiddle to me and my work."

"He loves you, Teal. He knew he was marrying a workaholic."

"But this is too much. This is too much. I can't ask this of him."

"And what do I say to Zoe and Heidi?"

Her question brought Teal up short.

"Where do I say you've gone to this time? What do I say to your afternoon appointments, those women counting on you to do the equivalent of serving them coffee and sweet rolls?"

"I can't save the world, Pamela. I can't be responsible for this company. I never wanted to be a partner."

"Partner? You might want to think about saving what's left of your job. Your calendar is full of busywork, cases no one else wants. The new hire has a complex divorce going for a bigger name than Parkhurst, and she's in over her head. What you've got there —" she pointed at Teal's laptop — "is straight out of your first year, and you're better than that, Teal. They need you on the difficult stuff, but you keep this up, and you'll completely lose their trust."

"What are they saying?"

Pamela pressed her lips together as if holding back.

"What? So yeah, I've basically been out of it since the earthquake. Most of us have, in one way or another. The whole city has PTSD. Oh, no. They wouldn't really fire me, would they?"

"It's idle gossip. Zoe and Heidi would never say anything to me or anyone else. I'm simply trying to read the tea leaves that you're ignoring. Remember this morning when I said Zoe was available to step in for you?"

"Yeah."

"It was because you appeared frazzled this week. That's what she said. That's why she offered."

Some of the spunk drained from her. *Frazzled?* Zoe and Heidi had always been observant, but to notice her in recent days put them at guardian-angel levels. Not even Pamela had noticed Teal was off until that mix-up with the men's names earlier.

Teal was good at faking cool. All week she had taken special care with her hair, makeup, and clothes. She kept her shoulders squared. She thought before she spoke.

She buried that stupid woman who could not look her husband in the eye and she held on to delusional.

Pamela said, "It's no secret they didn't want you to be gone for weeks on end."

"River didn't want me gone for weeks on end either." She struggled into her jacket. "If it comes down to them or him, there's no question. I choose him." If he was still interested. How long would he put up with silly and delusional? What if this was the last straw?

Pamela touched her arm. "Then choose him, Teal. Only do it so that you both know without a doubt that that's what you're doing."

The loving admonition on her friend's face was almost too much to bear. "Okay." She breathed out the word. "I hear you. Please, you don't have to cover for me today."

"Are you kidding? I love this busywork. I'll meet with your appointments." She grinned.

Teal rolled her eyes. "Take the exam already and get certified."

Pamela laughed at the joke between them. She had a law degree, but not wanting the pressure, she never followed through to become licensed with the state. Like Teal, she was where she wanted to be.

Pamela said, "My main concern is Hannah. No amount of prepping is going to get her ready for the triplets."

"Just help her plug some of those holes.

He went to her home. He sent her money. Did she see the checks? What did she do with them?"

"Why don't I put the investigator onto Parkhurst one more time too?" She went to the credenza, picked up Teal's briefcase, and flipped through a stack of files. "Maybe we missed something. Maybe he's not the Goody Two-shoes he appears to be. Maybe tonight he'll celebrate today's performance, get hammered, and threaten his wife."

"You have a sick mind."

"Thanks." Pamela shoved folders into the case and handed it to her. "You okay to drive now?"

"Yes, ma'am." Without a backward glance, she opened the door and hurried away, anxious to make things right with someone.

Perhaps for the first time ever in her life.

CHAPTER 45

Sixty minutes was a conservative estimate for the drive time to San Sebastian Academy, located in the foothills on the outskirts of the city. As frazzled as Teal was, the trip was going to take longer.

Her usual ability to focus on freeway lane openings and zip in and out of them was gone. Instead she concocted a half-dozen scenarios. Would River welcome her with open arms? Would he be in the middle of teaching and need to ignore her? Would he ignore her anyway? Should she apologize profusely about Monday? Or simply kiss his cheek and go home to prepare her manicotti that he liked so much?

He had seemed fine all week.

Why did she think that? How would she know? They passed in the kitchen, grabbed whatever for dinner, spoke of routine things, gave cursory good-night kisses.

At least they had that one night they happened to go to bed at the same time. What had they done Monday evening?

Monday was her extra-long day. She had arrived home at 10 p.m.

"Oh, God, I'm sorry."

River was such a gift to her, one she had not even hoped for, let alone requested. Did she push him away because he was undeserved? Because why get attached when he would probably leave her?

Like everyone else in her life had, including Cody.

Traffic slowed to a crawl, and in an instant the flashbacks that had faded to almost nothing unleashed themselves with intensity. She braked as images of the earthquake nearly blinded her. The echo of squealing brakes, explosions, crunching metal, people shouting and crying deafened her.

"God, help me. Help me!"

Tears streamed down her face. She wiped at them, unable to see if brake lights were lit or not.

"I'm so sorry. I'm so sorry." The apology would not stop forming.

The blare of a horn startled her. She jumped. It blared again, directly behind her. She froze and for one eternal moment she wondered if she could go on.

With life.

With the secrets.

With the regrets.

With the juggling of roles. Lawyer, mother, wife, friend, neighbor, church member. Now sister. Maybe even daughter.

Had she always listed *lawyer* first?

Yes. Yes, she had. Always.

Maiya was sixteen years old. *Sixteen.* The 24-7 mommy season — the one she basically missed — was long over.

Teal cried harder.

A horn blasted again. She sensed the movement of vehicles on either side of her car. They picked up speed.

There was a tapping at her window, and she turned to see a highway patrolman's face framed in a helmet. He removed his sunglasses and motioned for her to roll down her window.

She fumbled for the automatic button, wiping her face with the front of her jacket, blubbering. What was she supposed to do? In all her years of exceeding the speed limit, she'd never been pulled over. Now, her brake pedal pushed to its limit, a cop appeared.

The window descended.

"Ma'am, are you all right?"

"Y-yes. No. Yeah."

"You need to move. You're blocking traffic. Can you drive if I help?"

She nodded. Flashing lights reflected in her rearview mirror. His motorcycle was parked behind her.

He said, "We'll get to the shoulder. Just follow me, okay?"

"O-okay." Her hands were shaking as much as her voice.

She kept her eyes on the strobelike bursts of blue and white lights from his motorcycle. Vehicles around them parted like the Red Sea. Within moments he was leading her slowly down the freeway and changing lanes until they were on the shoulder.

She stopped, put the car in park, shuddered, and hoped he wouldn't ask if she could drive. She was clinging to the delusion of control by her fingernails. Of course she could drive.

He came back to her window and began the whole process. License, registration, calm talk, his eyes taking in every detail about her. He went back to his vehicle to check on her information.

With each passing minute her fears receded. There had been no earthquake. River was safe at school. Maiya was safe at school. Teal might get a ticket, but she was safe on the freeway.

She had many regrets, but she also had, at

long last, a contrite heart. And God loved contrite hearts. He could work with them in their brokenness. He could offer them do-overs and new dreams.

Maybe He could even delete the echoes. After all, He was God.

"Thank You."

Teal eventually made it to the school's parking lot. For a while she gazed at her face in the visor mirror, coming to terms with the fact that she did not carry enough cosmetics to repair the damage. She slipped on her sunglasses.

The officer had not ticketed her. Instead he chatted and learned of her whereabouts during the earthquake. He said paralyzed drivers like her were not uncommon. He offered to call her husband. She stopped crying and said she would take the next exit and follow side streets the rest of the way. He led her to the exit, braked on the shoulder, and waved as she passed him.

Teal walked across the lot now toward the main building, unsure where to find River. His schedule was fluid. His classes weren't always conducted in a classroom. He took boys camping and to the city. He worked with them on the grounds to prepare for various events.

"Mrs. Adams."

She turned and recognized one of the security guards approaching. "Hi, Mick."

"How you doing?" He stopped and smiled, his eyes hidden behind dark sunglasses.

Like all the security guards, he was a cross between paramilitary and bouncer. Square jaws, square shoulders, squared-off buzz cuts. Pecs and deltoids bulged beneath their navy-blue polo shirts. She did not want to know what these guys had done before joining on at San Sebastian, but she had no problem with them making sure River stayed safe.

"I'm fine." A derisive laugh escaped her. He would have already noted how not fine she appeared. Like him, she wore sunglasses, but fresh lipstick did not hide tear-streaked cheeks. Her hands kept going to her hair, tucking it behind an ear over and over. "Scratch that. I'm not fine today. I am a basket case."

His mouth lost its easy smile. Now he appeared uneasy.

She had seen this before. With the majority of staff, administration, and faculty being male and the student population all male, the academy oozed testosterone. Emoting was a foreign concept.

She said, "You know how it is, living with a teenager and all. How are your wife and the twins?"

"Great." He relaxed again. "They'll be here for the auction next week. You too?"

"Always." Was that on her calendar? She would make sure Pamela put it — No, she would insert it herself. "Do you happen to know where River is?"

"Saw him with a group out at the barns not long ago. I think they're storing items for the auction."

"Thanks."

"Don't forget to sign in at the office."

If not for his watchful eye, she would have skirted around the outside of the main building. The sprawling campus with its rural setting was more open than public schools. The boys didn't need fences. This was a last-chance school. If they left, they'd be sent to prison.

Getting to River had the feel of swimming upstream. No wonder salmon died after their trek upriver. If she didn't get to her husband soon, she might just sit down and quit.

She managed to sign in, make small talk with the office manager, ignore her curious look at the sunglasses she did not remove, drape the visitor ID around her neck, and hightail it outside without falling apart.

The heels of her pumps wobbled on the gravel drive. Nerves wobbled her legs. She was tucking her hair behind her ear still. Her heart pounded in her chest.

She forced herself to slow down. Greeting River in the middle of his day as a floundering salmon was not a good idea.

The place was perfect for slowing down. Surrounded by hills and trees, it was beautiful and peaceful. Adobe buildings housed classrooms, dorm, gym, and cafeteria. There were soccer and baseball fields, barnyards with chickens and goats, a swimming pool. She spotted pumpkins in a large vegetable garden. The October air smelled dry and crisp.

River loved it here. She wondered if he had been happier before he met her than he was now. Back then he practically lived in his camper parked in a lot behind a barn, seldom going home to his apartment. The boys were his life. The dorm parents and other employees were his best friends. They were the ones who carried him through the worst nightmare of his life.

She couldn't even manage to carry him for one day.

He always said that she gave him balance, a necessary balance that truly saved him from the loneliness that his full life could not touch. She had always said the same about him.

But that wasn't true. Deep down she remained unbalanced, stuffing the hours with more work because now Maiya had a dad who pitched in with parental and household duties.

Why hadn't she seen that?

What a silly, delusional woman she was. And no, it did not really work.

The gravel gave way to dirt. She neared the first barn, a traditional red color, made of metal. The odor of hay wafted out through its open doors. She heard activity from inside — boys talking, River's voice in maximum authoritative tone — and halted.

This was not a good time.

He emerged from the shadowy interior, three boys beside him, all deep in conversation. They wore ball caps, academy T-shirts, and blue jeans.

River looked up and saw her. His face registered concern.

"Teal."

She smiled, wanting to communicate that there was no emergency. Well, not the sort that he would imagine right off.

"Hello, Mrs. Adams." One of the boys recognized her. His face was familiar.

"Hi."

A second boy turned his head, but not before she noted that he was weeping.

The third one scowled.

This was definitely not a good time.

River said, "You guys go on ahead. I'll catch up." They walked away and his expression settled into stoic. "What's up? Maiya okay?"

"She's fine. It can wait. You're in the middle of something."

"Yeah."

"We'll talk at home."

"Sorry you came all the way out here, but your timing kind of stinks." He wagged his thumb toward the boys heading toward the soccer field.

"Go. They need you."

"They do. See you later." He spun on his heel and started after the kids.

This was totally not a good time. She had seen him in work mode and understood that his shortness now was not aimed at her. His mind was simply elsewhere, with those boys in the throes of a crisis.

She watched him hustle past the barn, intent on taking care of young ones who would remind him of himself. She loved him so much for his passion and dedication. His was a noble cause. Taking a rain check on her needs was part of that noble cause. They would get through this. They would reconnect and catch up and make up.

Right?

What was wrong with her? He was her husband. She was his wife. They were in the throes of their own crisis. It was long past time to put him first and to slide herself into the number one spot on his list. If he disagreed, then he could spend the night in his camper.

"River!" she shouted and hurried after him. "River!"

He turned and waited for her to reach him, hands on his hips.

Out of breath, she gulped for air. "This can't wait."

His mouth was a thin line and his eyes strayed to track the boys in the distance.

She took hold of his upper arms, forcing him to look at her. "I am so sorry about Monday. I am so sorry."

He shut his eyes. She could almost see a shudder go through him. His face lost its hardness and he looked at her again. "Thank you."

She burst into tears.

When he pulled her to himself, she only cried harder.

Chapter 46

Teal made her scrumptious manicotti, but
at the dinner table she feasted more on
River and Maiya than the food. They gave
her odd glances, as if unsure what to make
of her demeanor.

After her outburst at San Sebastian that
afternoon, a joyful calm surrounded her.
There was no escaping it. She breathed it in
and out, in and out.

"Mom, how was work?" Maiya probed for
clues.

Teal smiled. "Not much to report. I
figured out that people are not always what
they appear to be. And then I left early,
which accounts for this dinner and the
caramel pecan ice cream in the freezer."

"No way."

"It's all yours."

Maiya angled her head. "I have some
research to do online. And I have to talk to
Heather and Ben about our project for his-

tory class. I need to touch base with Baker, too." She blushed whenever she said his name. "He's got a better grip on trig than Mr. J."

"Fine."

"I just, uh, wanted you to know?"

"Honey, you did get the message that you're not grounded anymore, right?"

River chuckled. "You don't have to run everything by us."

"You remember that Jake broke up with his new girlfriend?"

Teal said, "We trust you. Now go. It sounds like you have a lot to do. We'll clean up."

When she had gone, Teal met River's gaze. He said, "I could make a fire outside."

She smiled. They were on the same page. The backyard was the only place for private, uninterrupted conversation if Maiya was in the house.

A short while later, bundled in sweats and a jacket, she joined him on the dark patio beside the terra-cotta fire ring. Under its domed grate, the wood snapped and crackled. The heat felt good in the cold evening. She handed him a cup of tea and sat on the cushioned chair shoved close to his.

"Do you want to tell me about Monday?" she asked.

"I missed you. But I had a good whining session. Krissy told me to get over it and I moved on."

"Get over what?"

"The distance I was feeling from you."

She leaned against his arm. "I'm sorry."

He kissed the top of her head.

"River, I don't want you to get over something like that. There shouldn't be a distance between us."

"I see our life like a forest. I can come looking for you, but if you keep hiding behind the trees, there's not much else I can do except get over it."

"You could leave."

"No, love. It's *our* forest."

"Really?"

He smiled. "Really. You are stuck with me lurking about."

Why did she ever hold back on this man?

"I think . . ." Her breath caught. Her heartbeat thundered in her ears. The joyful calm had fled, but deep inside she knew it was still out there . . . in the open forest. "I think I'm tired of hiding."

"You think?"

"I am. For sure." She resisted the desire to crawl onto his lap and hide her face against his neck. She inhaled deeply, skipped the rehearsed intro, and went straight to the punch line. "Bio Dad is Cody Janski."

No sound or movement came from River, but a tension went from him as obviously as if he had slid from his chair onto the concrete.

Teal waited for her own knotted stomach to untwist. It didn't. Because there was more. "Whew. I never said that out loud to anyone." She tried to smile. "Lucky you, huh?"

He touched her cheek and whispered, "Yes, lucky me."

Okay, so far, so good. "No surprise either, right?"

He shook his head and lowered his hand to her arm. "No."

"Has Maiya guessed?"

"She hasn't said."

Thank You, God.

Teal took another deep breath. "He was Lacey's boyfriend. Well, sort of. They had one date, when she invited him to a dance. She'd been crazy about him for a long time, though. She was so straitlaced, and he was the exact opposite. Mouthy, always in trouble, secretive. He was in her class, but older. There was an air of danger about him. It was a totally idiotic crush. She was a sharp girl. I truly believed it was a joke." She paused. "I'm not making excuses."

414

"I know."

"Later I figured out that she'd had grand visions of rescuing him. If she kissed the beast, he would turn into a prince. Her friends dared her to ask him to the dance. He said yes for one reason only. Randi and Owen gave permission because they were incredibly stupid and inattentive. Which I told them before he came to pick her up." She slowed her speech, letting her anger subside.

"She wasn't your responsibility."

"But she was, River. They were incapable of it."

He squeezed her arm. "You were home from college?"

"It was right before Christmas. I'd gone there to drop off gifts and pick up mine. Weird how we could keep up the charade. I spent the holiday working in Portland." If only she'd stayed away.

The constant pressure of River's hand on her arm encouraged her to release words she had cried to God on the darkest days.

"She came home before midnight." Teal remembered the time. Details like that were etched in her mind. "She was crying so hard, we all woke up. Her hair a mess. Her gorgeous red dress all wet and muddy because she had to walk home. She blubbered that he wanted to have sex. Owen blew up. It took forever for Lacey to get a chance to tell us that no, they did not, and that he had not hurt her. She cried and cried. Said she loved him. That she really could help him change. Then . . ." Teal swallowed a sob and spoke in a monotone. "Then Owen laid into me. Lacey Jo was not a slut like her sister. Lacey knew how to say no. Lacey had dignity. Lacey was a saint. Lacey was a good girl. Lacey was a winner. Lacey could give me lessons. Lacey, Lacey, Lacey."

The accusations echoed again in her mind. His cutting words were memorized, every single indictment proclaimed against her. Owen was angry at Cody, but just as he'd been doing since she was a little girl, her stepdad took it out on her. "I was twenty-two, River. I'd been on my own for years, figuratively and literally. I was going to graduate from college in the spring. I was going to law school in Los Angeles. I should have known better than to believe all that junk."

"He was still your father figure. And, I imagine, he was repeating what he'd been telling you for a long, long time."

She nodded and let out a heavy breath. "I left that night instead of in the morning.

416

First, though, I went looking for Cody. I started at the nearest park in town. It was a popular hangout." Everyone, including the Cedar Pointe cops, knew where the outcasts drank and smoked. As long as the kids bothered no one else, they were left alone.

She said, "I spotted him walking near the coffee shop. We argued. Part of me wanted him to leave Lacey alone. Part of me wanted to get back at her for being the family princess. I hated her in that moment."

River gently wiped under her eyes.

She said, "What did it matter? Randi and Owen believed I was a slut. I'm sure half the town did too. I might as well prove they were right. I told Cody I'd give him what Lacey wouldn't. That I could make him happier than she could. He said prove it."

She went on, rushing her words to get through the worst of it. "It was pouring down rain. He had a key. We went inside Happy Grounds. There was a couch in the back room. He said he wanted a virgin but I'd do. I was angry and he was angry and we —"

"Shh. It's okay."

"River." Teal looked at his face in the firelight. "I *was* a virgin that night."

He stared at her. She saw the surprise in his eyes.

"Teal."

"Doesn't that take the cake? I do it once and get pregnant."

River blinked.

She waited for the light to dawn. "Yeah. One time until you."

He only blinked some more.

"I always just let on that I was experienced. It didn't take much of a leap since I grew up acting tough. And who's going to hire a naive, non-savvy lawyer?"

He shook his head as if he doubted his hearing.

She leaned over and kissed his cheek. "Thank you, by the way, for being sweet and tender and helping me catch on."

He chuckled. "You are . . . I have no word for it."

"A good liar?"

"Complicated. You do know I've always loved you for yourself, not for what you've done or haven't done?" He brushed a stray tear from her cheek.

"Okay."

"Okay. So, obviously you and Cody did not have a relationship. Did you just go back to school?"

"Yes. I hated myself for what I'd done to Lacey, for being the person Owen always said I was. Nobody was surprised when I finally told them I was pregnant. It was easy not to say who the father was. There was no reason to tell Cody. I wanted no part of him or anyone else in Cedar Pointe. But I did want my baby." She smiled. "Suddenly I had my own family, and I could be in control. I could make it what I wanted. Of course what I wanted was for somebody to love me."

"And you never told anyone."

"No. Time and distance did their thing. It seemed pointless to reveal Cody's name. Everyone probably assumed it was someone I met in college."

"But guys talk, Teal. He would have told his buddies."

"He probably did. Honestly, I was a nonentity in town. It wouldn't have been a big deal that he'd slept with a loser of questionable repute. And it wasn't long after that he was in the car accident with his cousin Dylan."

"The kid who was killed?"

"Yes. Dylan was driving, apparently not under the influence. Given Cody's alcohol content, he probably didn't feel a thing. The incident did him in, though. He really started to get into serious trouble after that. He was arrested for disorderly conduct. The story goes that it was the last straw for his parents. They were done bailing him out of trouble. He pleaded guilty and went to jail. I didn't make up that part. Apparently it straightened him out. Afterward he got his diploma and a military waiver."

"I take it Will was not all that close with his brother?"

"No. They were like me and Lacey. Opposites, nothing in common. They would not have talked about that night. Eventually Lacey got over her crush and married Will. Once in a while she would mention what was going on with Cody. He went back to Cedar Pointe about as often as I did." She paused. "It was strange. He was such a distant connection to me, not even a real memory. It was like we had no connection. Maiya was mine."

"And then she grew up."

Teal nodded. "And started asking questions."

The obvious hung between them. Maiya had to be told. Cody had to be told. Lacey had to be told.

Teal said, "I'll get there."

"You will."

"I've hurt so many people. I know it's only getting worse now, the longer I wait. Especially since they've gotten to know her."

He kissed her forehead. "Thank you for

bringing me in first."

"Oh, River, I love you so much. I'm sorry for pushing you away, for hiding behind those trees."

"Hey, how many times do I have to say I'm in for the long haul?"

She smiled. "As many times as it takes?"

"Okay, you got it."

The joyful calm enveloped her again, unfamiliar yet comforting, elusive yet full of promise.

Chapter 47

Cedar Pointe

"Aunt Lacey, you are not going to believe this one!" Maiya's voice rose over the phone line as she went on to describe her latest woe with her history teacher.

Smiling, Lacey settled into the recliner in the shop's back room and pulled up the footrest. She missed her niece something awful. Their frequent phone conversations alleviated the ache to a certain extent, but Lacey was counting the hours until their reunion: Thanksgiving week in Los Angeles.

She disagreed with Will, who thought the lack of dramatics in their life was best for Lacey's energy level. On the contrary, the girl had been a continual source of freshness and joy.

"See, Aunt Lace? I told you I learned more from you in a few weeks than this idiot can teach me all semester. He knows nada about the Civil War."

Aunt Lace, Aunt Lacey, Aunt L. Always with the *aunt* in place. She loved it, although it did remind her not to pass up a teaching moment.

"Maiya, my rule book says to remind you that *idiot* is highly disrespectful."

"Okay, okay." Maiya groaned. "Was that a reprimand?"

"I think so."

"How come I can take it from you and not my mom?"

"Well, that's in the book too. Moms are like emery boards. It's their job to file away at all the rough edges in their daughters."

"But you do it and it doesn't set me off."

"That's because aunts are just plain cool. No other explanation."

Maiya laughed. "Well, Mom's lost her sandpaper personality. She's still into sappy."

When they had last talked on Saturday, Maiya had described Teal as weepy and giggly at the same time, all the time. And River was more mellow than she had ever seen him in her whole entire life.

"Actually, Aunt Lace, I'm beginning to wonder if they remember I live here. The huggy, kissy-face stuff is kind of embarrassing."

Lacey smiled. Obviously something was

going on between Teal and River. The separation must have kicked them into another honeymoon phase.

Maiya went on. "I hope I can spend the weekend at Amber's. Oh, get this. Last night I brought up the Jake thing. Remember he's going to be at the auction on Saturday? I told Mom I wanted to talk with him, get some closure. She just sort of nodded and said, 'Fine.' Do you believe it? Maybe now's the time to ask them for a car."

"You don't want to break the spell. From what I've heard, they're adamant about that one."

"I suppose. So, did you have closure with Cody after that dance you told me about?"

Before seriously considering that Cody might be Maiya's father, Lacey had shared with her some details from that night. Things like he wanted to have sex, that she struggled and her dress ripped before he caught on to the meaning of her *no,* that she walked home in the freezing rain. She figured such brutal honesty might put enough fear into her niece to keep her from pining after Jake.

She said, "Closure? I'm sure I hadn't even heard the word back then. And besides, the incident was such a brief encounter, hardly worth processing beyond, 'Whoa, that was ugly, and good riddance with the crush.' "

Maiya said, "But wasn't it awkward with him later, like when you and Uncle Will got married?"

Lacey measured her words. Given Maiya's September birth date, Teal would have had to have been with Cody around the time of the dance. *If* Cody was the father, which Lacey now believed was true. How much was acceptable to tell the girl about him? That he was a hormonal teenage boy was one thing, but other details revealed character faults that he had overcome. Why go into those now?

Lacey said, "Like I told you, Will and I eloped to Portland. There was no family involved." Thank goodness for her mother-in-law's forgiving nature. Although Nora understood that a wedding with Owen would have been unbearable, she had not been a happy camper about the elopement. "Cody hadn't lived in Cedar Pointe for ages and didn't visit for a long time."

"Kind of like my mom."

"I guess so. Anyway, later he got his act together, joined the Marines, and came home just once before being shipped overseas."

"That all happened after the accident."

"Yes. When his cousin died, Cody went

425

off the deep end. He got into more trouble and left town." No way was she mentioning his jail time. Will and her in-laws never brought up the sad event. Even townspeople no longer spoke of it. The guy was a hero, fighting terrorists.

"So what happened when you finally saw each other?" The girl was relentless. "What did he say to you?"

"Not much, really. He had changed." In fact, he was a new man. Sober, disciplined, caring, likable. "The thing is, what little history we had in common was ancient. He sort of laughed and said something like, 'Didn't you have a crush on me once?' I said, 'In your dreams.' We teased each other. That was the end of it."

"But what about the night of the dance?"

"Neither of us brought it up."

"Didn't Will talk to him about it?"

"Maiya, it was over with. Will and I agreed to let it go."

"Aunt Lacey, don't you think you should finish this business?"

She sighed to herself. "The truth is, I never really cared to talk about it with him, and I don't think he even remembers much about it."

"Well, duh. I bet he can't. He must have been into a lot of junk back then. He was

426

probably wasted that night."

Lacey's heart sank at the correct guess. Once she had outgrown her naiveté, she admitted that Cody had been a wreck, not a mysterious bad boy she could save. He must have killed off a lot of brain cells back in the day. Only answers to Nora's prayers explained his intact survival.

Maiya said, "In a way, you can't blame him for being so mean to you that night. I'm not making excuses. I'm just saying, you know . . ."

Warning bells went off. "Hon, was Jake mean to you? Did he try to force himself on you? Did he hit you?"

"No, none of that. Absolutely not. That's the thing. He's a good guy."

She let out a silent *whew.* "But he's too old."

"Got that after the bazillionth time from everyone. Was your dance in December?"

Lacey swallowed. "My dance?"

"The one you invited Cody to."

"Uh, it was cold and rainy. That could be anytime from November to April."

"Mom was home, though. It was probably a school break for her."

"She would come home at odd times. She never stayed long, and she skipped most holidays with us."

"But you said you wore a formal and it wasn't prom. You probably didn't have formal dances all winter long."

"No. It was a special time."

"So it could have been Christmas."

Lacey imagined Maiya's brain calculating the period of gestation. "I suppose it could have been."

"Your senior year. I was born the next year."

Lacey winced. "Yes."

A long silence ensued. She could think of nothing to say to comfort her niece, nothing that would redirect the conversation. Maiya was smart, and she was hurting.

At last Maiya said, "Aunts aren't supposed to fudge. I have to go."

Her niece was also very angry.

Their good-bye was brief. Not silly. Not warm. Not sweet. Not hopeful. Nothing at all like they had been.

Lacey wanted to call her sister and tell her what an idiot she was to keep them all in the dark.

CHAPTER 48

Los Angeles

Since her heart-to-heart with River a week ago, Teal had gone mushy on all fronts, even where the law was concerned. She resorted to an ooey-gooey, fuzzy-wuzzy approach with the Waltons. For the bottom-line talk, she went to their home.

They lived in a community nicer than hers, farther west than hers. They gave her a brief house tour, and she chatted with little Maddie playing in her room. She was a happy, contented child. Teal figured she would be too if she lived in such a beautiful place. She wanted to go home and redecorate.

Then they seated her in the family room. It had floor-to-ceiling windows and distant ocean views. Redecorating was not going to help a whole lot. Her 1920s bungalow tucked between a street, an alley, and other houses within spitting distance was cozy cute with a potential for cozy cute in different colors.

Teal set her bone china cup on the coffee table and looked at the Waltons seated on the white leather couch. They smiled back, their faces young and fresh and full of optimism. She wanted to crawl under her chair.

Dark-haired Ryan was as handsome as Hannah was pretty. A former lifeguard, he was an engineer who maintained his athletic body and watchful eye, obviously for the sole purpose of caring for his family. Teal had seen him in action. As husband and daddy, he ranked almost as high on the charts as River.

If anything, Hannah was more beautiful than when she had met her. Despite the stressful weeks of lawsuits, delays, a judge's ruling against throwing out her case, and Monday's disastrous deposition that shot more holes into her case, she glowed. Like a . . .

Teal cast her eyes downward. Hannah wore a loose-fitting top. It clung to her midsection. "Hannah?"

She laughed. "Yes! I was wondering when you'd notice."

"Congratulations! When are you due?"

They chatted details. To her chagrin, Teal

sensed a new onslaught of ooey-gooeyness. Her chest felt ready to burst with happiness and sadness. Happiness and sadness? No, it weighed too heavily, gouged too deeply. Joy and sorrow maybe fit.

Good grief. What was wrong with her?

She swallowed the lump in her throat and more coffee and made herself get down to business. "We need to talk about reaching an agreement with James Parkhurst."

Hannah said, "I messed up big time, didn't I?"

"Let's just say things are a little more complicated than we first thought. Understandably you did not want a belligerent, abusive alcoholic near your baby. Of course you hid from him. You had no hope that he would divorce his wife, shape up, and turn into a dream guy like the one sitting next to you."

Hannah and Ryan smiled. On another day, Teal might have thought them saccharine. Today she smiled with them. They were going to be all right. The trick was to convince them they had won no matter the outcome of the lawsuit.

Ryan said, "Will a judge understand it your way?"

"If she's a woman who hasn't told her daughter the identity of her biological father, she might." Teal noticed their curious expressions. "I was like you, Hannah. The guy was a loser. I didn't want him anywhere near my baby. Now she's sixteen and wants to know him." She paused. "She has a right to know him, and he has a right to know her. Blood is always thicker than water, literally. There is no rearranging the physical makeup of either. Genetically, there is a link between father and daughter. It may not lead to anything personally, but that's not for us to decide."

Hannah reached for Ryan's hand. "What are you saying?"

"If James were still an abusive alcoholic, I would fight tooth and nail to keep him out of Maddie's life at this time. But he's not. A judge will most likely set the terms for his visitation rights. Or else we can come up with a plan and try to settle with him out of court."

Hannah's face crumpled. Ryan put an arm around her.

Teal softened her voice. "He's a stranger to Maddie. That doesn't change with signatures on a paper. We'll take things very slowly."

Panic filled their eyes.

"Try to work with me here, okay? Try to imagine a former friend who now regrets his behavior toward you. He knows he's to blame for destroying the friendship. He knows it can't really ever be fixed. But now he wants to have contact with you. Not as a good friend or confidant, but as someone out there on the fringes. Could there be a place for him in your life?"

Ryan held Hannah close, did not say a word, and kissed her cheek. Supportive, allowing her to decide.

She placed a hand on her abdomen, her expression blank as if she were lost in thought. After several moments, she sighed. "Okay, let's talk. Hypothetically."

Teal nodded and nearly sighed herself.

The worst part was over. Like Teal, Hannah cracked open a new door to a frightening unknown. Whatever entered would forever change her world.

After meeting with the Waltons, Teal returned to the office, drained and yet filled up. What she had said to Hannah applied to herself. Bio Dad had rights. Daughter had rights. Mother could not control the outcome.

At least there was no Dutch Morgan in either scenario.

Hannah and Ryan agreed to give things a try. They would meet with Parkhurst and his wife in neutral territory, perhaps a park. They would introduce them like old acquaintances to Maddie.

Like people they did not fear or hate, Teal suggested.

Okay.

If Maddie responded well, perhaps the Parkhursts could entertain her at the playground or buy her ice cream while Hannah and Ryan watched from a short distance. Perhaps when Maddie was older, she could spend time alone with them.

It wasn't much, but it was a reasonable beginning. Tomorrow she would try to sell it to Parkhurst. He would resist, especially when she brought up adoption. The Waltons wanted Maddie to have Ryan's last name rather than Hannah's maiden name. They wanted her secure with Ryan in case anything happened to Hannah.

Details would be tweaked. She might mention that winning the little girl's heart was the key and hope that Parkhurst did not ask how he was supposed to do that. If Bio Dad and wife were unable to figure that one out on their own, then any attempt at relationship would die a natural death.

Ditto for Cody with Maiya. It was his responsibility to connect with her.

And if he did win her heart?

Then Teal would be happy for both of them.

She grinned. Mere hours ago, when she last asked herself that question, she had replied that she *should* be happy for them.

Now as she rode the elevator from the parking garage up to her floor, she closed her eyes. For days a vague notion had played tag with her thoughts. She ignored it, easily letting the urgent push it aside.

Until a short while ago when she saw Hannah Walton lay her hand on her abdomen.

"I want a baby," Teal whispered now. "Dear God, I want a baby."

As the elevator jerked to a stop, she shook her head and put on her game face. River simply could not go there again. The loss of his wife and unborn child left him crippled for life in that area. She knew there was a part of him that he held back even from her. The pain was too deep for anyone to touch.

The doors swished open and she stepped into the office lobby, normally a quiet, plant-filled haven. At the moment some commotion from the back drowned the classical music and drew her past the empty reception desk.

Around the corner she heard her husband and smiled. He must be seated at a desk in the center of a bevy of women, employees who let phones ring and clients wait unattended. It always happened when he stopped in. Not only was he seriously good-looking, he was friendly and intriguing, artlessly flirty, full of stories about life at the academy. Today he would be telling them about that weekend's auction and winning at least half a dozen promises to attend.

She still remembered the first time he had come in, when his sister needed a lawyer. All eyes had followed him even before he cracked a smile or said a word.

Among the women at Canfield and Stone, Teal was not an obvious catch. She was not the most beautiful nor the smartest nor the sexiest. Back then, so crazy committed to being single, she had not been the most available, either. But he chose her.

And she really wanted to have his baby.

She would even consider locking her office door and trying to make one right now.

River stood up, as if he sensed her presence, and smiled. He wore his brown baseball cap backwards, blue jeans, and a white San Sebastian polo shirt.

Smiling, she waved and headed the other direction into her office.

By the time she had removed her jacket and set down her briefcase, he joined her.

"Hi." She stepped into his embrace. "What are you doing here?"

He kissed her. He tossed his cap onto a chair and kicked the door shut with his foot. Then he kissed her again.

Long enough for her to forget what day it was.

He grinned. "Hi. Can we talk?"

"Yes. To whatever it is you want."

"No debate? Aw, you're no fun anymore." He guided her to one of the chairs in front of her desk. "Sit. This is serious stuff."

She giggled and sat.

He knelt before her on one knee and held her hands between his.

He had proposed to her in that exact same position in that exact same office.

It was the time she had said yes.

She looked into his dark-blue eyes and knew that his choice of setting was no accident. What in the world?

"River, remember we're already married? I said yes."

"True, but . . . well, I want to propose something new for us." He paused. His shoulders moved up and down as he took a deep breath. "Love, I want us to have a baby."

She gasped.

"I've always said no way. But something

437

has changed. I can't explain it other than that. I'm okay with it now. More than okay. I'm ready. I want one yesterday. Will you say something?"

"If I can get a word in edgewise." She smiled. "I already told you. I said yes to whatever it is you want."

His knee slipped and he sat flat on the floor, speechless, his eyes filling.

A quiet weeping overcame her, its source a joy beyond anything she could have ever imagined.

The story about her ride up the elevator would have to wait.

CHAPTER 49

One month later, Thanksgiving week
Seated on a chaise longue on Teal's patio, Lacey took her first sip of morning coffee. "Mm."

Teal laughed. "Stop being so polite. It's lousy swill."

Lacey smiled at her sister in the chair next to hers. "It's wonderful because I'm drinking it in LA, on a November day *outdoors.* Flowers are blooming and there's not a single cloud in the sky."

"You kind of like it here, don't you?"

"I love it here." Lacey sipped and pursed her lips. "And I can help you with the coffee."

"And the turkey stuffing?"

"If you take me to Disneyland."

Teal laughed again.

Lacey set her cup on the small table between them.

Although she and Will had just arrived the

previous evening, she did indeed love everything about Los Angeles. Of course, it was more than the lovely weather and palm trees and plants she did not know the names of. It was more than Teal's comfortable home with its odd layout full of corners and French doors leading from three rooms onto the patio. It was more than plans to see the place she'd wanted to see since she was a little girl.

Those all paled in comparison to being with Teal, River, and Maiya.

In recent weeks, her niece had warmed again during their phone conversations. She had stopped asking questions and seemed happy. Lacey wondered if she had let go pursuing her father's identity because romance occupied her thoughts. Not surprisingly, she and Baker had kept in touch. Long-distance, their friendship blossomed. He had even applied to USC for college and declared the East Coast ivies off his list.

Lacey asked Teal, "How are you doing with Baker's plans to move down here next fall?"

"Stop laughing."

"I'm not laughing."

"Yes, you are. You think it's hysterical that Maiya would fall for a guy from Cedar Pointe."

Lacey grinned. "Maybe a little, teensy bit."

Teal smiled. "I deserve it. Anyway, I like Baker a lot. I like his mind and his lattes. In spite of his hometown, she has more in common with him than with Jake."

"I heard she got her 'closure' with him."

Teal fluttered her eyelids. " 'Closure.' Good grief. Yes, she did. You would have been proud of me. I stayed out of sight."

"You didn't watch?"

"I meant I was out of their sight. Of course I watched. They talked. He acted respectful. She kissed his cheek. Very classy. Except for all those tattoos. Bleagh."

"I thought it was his trouble with the law that bothered you."

"It was." She shrugged. "But, okay, I have a bias against body art that covers eighty percent of the skin. Just please don't mention that to Maiya. She'll run out and get a tat the minute she turns eighteen."

Lacey chuckled. "You don't think she knows you're biased?"

Teal laughed. "Let me keep some denial in place."

Much as Lacey enjoyed the one-on-one time with Teal, she wished Maiya had not gone to school. That morning, her niece had begged to stay home. She said she *needed* to spend every possible minute with her aunt and uncle! Teal said no.

Lacey had wanted to beg with her but admitted that she was tired from the previous day's travel. It would be good for her to take it easy this morning. Will had gone with River to talk to his classes about running a business. This afternoon, he would join her for a tour of Teal's office. Teal had apologized profusely for having to go to work today, but she said she had one client she had to see before taking the rest of the week off. The remainder of the week was jampacked with sightseeing and Thanksgiving.

Now she noticed her sister fidget. "Teal, I really am fine home alone. I don't mind if you go to the office. I'll nap in the sun and be happy as a clam."

Teal swung around on the lounge chair, set her feet on the ground, and hunched toward the space between them. Her face crumpled, as if she were in pain. "Lace, we have to talk first."

Lacey felt her breath catch. She intuited what was coming.

Teal raked her fingers through her hair. At last she clasped her hands, sat still, and looked at Lacey. "I'm so sorry."

Lacey waited for more. When none came, she said, "And I'm sorry I'm not going to make this any easier for you."

"Touché. You must be tired of sticking up for me, always thinking the best."

"No, Teal, never. You're my hero, still and always."

"I resented you. Good grief, I probably hated you on some level."

Lacey felt the words like a punch to her stomach. Of course Teal would have felt left out. Her little sister was clearly their parents' favored one. But resentment? *Hatred?*

Teal said, "I didn't mean to." She took a ragged breath. "I had sex one time with Cody, in the back room of the shop, the night of your date with him."

Lacey closed her eyes.

"I got pregnant. Apparently he never put two and two together because of my . . . because of my reputation. Which, by the by, was greatly exaggerated, basically to the point of being false."

False? Lacey looked at her.

Teal went on. "Which, by the by, does not matter. Lacey, I can't apologize enough. I did it to hurt you. Even if you realized that night that you wanted nothing further to do with Cody, what I did was vile. I never regretted that I had Maiya, but I do regret that I've kept the two of you from each other."

Lacey planted her feet on the ground and

443

reached out for Teal and clasped her hands. "I forgive you."

Teal stared at her for a moment. "That was fast."

"Not really. I've been mulling it over since September, you idiot. And it wasn't your fault."

Teal snorted. "Of course it was. We can blame Randi and Owen and Dutch and Cody until the cows come home, but it was my decision to hurt you that night and then to keep on hurting you by being silent and not sharing my precious baby with you."

"You kept her. Why? I still can't imagine how you made it work."

"She was the family I never had. You'll do anything for family." Teal smiled sadly. "Thank you for not giving up on me."

Lacey nodded. "Have you told Maiya?"

"Not yet. Only River. I had to tell you next. You suspected in September?"

"She felt so familiar to both me and Will. And then Nora arrived."

"Yeah, I noticed it too. It's such a subtle thing, something in their mannerisms."

"And the not-so-subtle attached earlobes."

"Maiya and her biology." Teal sighed. "Do you think she suspects?"

"For being such a smart lawyer, you sure do a good rendition of a turtle."

"Okay, okay. But if I put out my head, I have to admit things I don't want to admit. Not yet, anyway. Did you call me an idiot?"

"I did. I've been holding it in for a while."

"Hm. Anything else?"

"You're still my hero, Teal."

"You should get out of Camp Poppycock more often."

Lacey smiled briefly. "Um, speaking of camps, there is something else I need to tell you. Cody is being transferred to Camp Pendleton."

Teal stared at her. "I thought it was Virginia."

"It got changed to California. It's near here, isn't it?"

"Yeah," Teal whispered. "A couple hours or so."

"When are you going to tell her?"

Teal shook her head.

"Teal, she's all but asked me if it could be Cody. I am not the one to tell her. And I am not going to keep dodging the subject and jeopardize my relationship with her." She took a deep breath. The rule book for little sisters said that sometimes they should switch roles with the big one. "Therefore, you are going to tell her, and you are going to tell her while I am here. Got that?"

Teal let go of Lacey's hands and hugged

herself tightly. "On Wednesday. No, on Thursday. On Thanksgiving. First thing."

"Perfect. She'll be grateful for the gift. Okay if I tell Will?"

"Please do."

"And then Cody needs to be told."

Teal grimaced. "It's just too much. This is why I keep postponing. . . ."

"All right. If you can't tell him, Will and I can."

"You act like it's good news."

Lacey moved to sit on the other lounge chair beside her sister. She put her arms around her. "Hon, my cancer wasn't good news, but it was the truth. Without the truth, we would all have to live like turtles — in a shell, always protecting ourselves, hiding from others."

Teal rested her head on Lacey's shoulder. "Getting stiff-necked and cranky."

"Exactly. You've been there and done that. You've probably even used up your lifetime cranky quota."

"Yeah, well, you've used up your tell-me-like-it-is quota."

Lacey giggled.

Teal giggled.

And Lacey savored the moment that freed them from the shadows of their childhood, that freed them at last to be sisters.

■ ■ ■ ■

Later that morning, Lacey and Will toured Teal's office, a scene right out of a Hollywood movie. Muted floral wallpaper softened the traditional masculine decor of dark wood. The ambience continued into her sister's private office, where sunlight streamed through tall windows ten stories above the busy downtown sidewalks.

Lacey and Will sank onto a leather love seat behind a coffee table, sipped decent coffee from bone china cups, and wondered why Teal had insisted they stay to meet her client, now seated in an armchair across from them.

Teal had told them that the widowed Ellen Moore was the late Gammy Jayne's daughter. She was small and somewhat frail in appearance, with white hair cut short in a carefree hairstyle. Her face shone with what Lacey could only describe as ethereal joy.

Within moments, Lacey and Ellen fell easily into conversation. There was an instant heart connection of women who had suffered the loss of a child.

Ellen's loss happened much later in life than Lacey's. Her only child, a daughter, and her son-in-law had been killed in a car accident three months before, on their way home from the hospital with their newborn.

Little Jason had survived. He had no other family except Ellen. Ellen, who had become a mother at the age of forty and was now not in the best of health, hired nurses to help care for the baby. She could not keep it up for long. The expense, her age . . .

The conversation continued. One thing led to another.

"What will happen to Jason?"

"That's why I'm here. Teal has always taken good care of us. I want her to walk me through the adoption process. I want to see Jason placed in a good home. I do not want to go through some agency."

Lacey met Teal's eyes across the table.

Teal nodded.

Lacey said, "You want to do a private adoption?"

"Yes," Ellen said. "I want to know the parents. I want to be near them and continue to be Jason's grandma."

Now Ellen looked at Teal. "You have something up your sleeve." It was a statement, not a question.

Teal smiled. "No. You were both coming in today. I'm just letting nature take its course."

"Or God," Lacey and Ellen said in unison. Will's grin brightened the room.

Heart thumping, Lacey tried to speak. She opened her mouth, closed it, and made another attempt. "My health —"

"Is not the deciding factor," Ellen interrupted. "You've told me about your good prognosis. You've told me about Will's parents and your support group, which sounds like it encompasses the entire town." Her eyes twinkled and she leaned closer to Lacey. "Did I mention that my husband and I raised Jason's mother in Oregon? In Banbury. I've missed it. We only moved down here because she did. I still have a bit of a support group myself up that way."

Teal sat back, an expression of disbelief in her raised brows and mouth askew.

Lacey knew what she was thinking. "Yes, Virginia, there are people who adore the Northwest and small-town life."

The crooked mouth curved into a big grin. "Whatever works."

Will clasped Lacey's hand and squeezed. He gazed at her but spoke to the lawyer. "This works, Teal. This works just fine."

CHAPTER 50

Disneyland was crazy packed the Tuesday before Thanksgiving. Crowds everywhere, long lines for every ride and exhibit.

River staggered alongside Maiya and Will, the three of them part of the noisy throng exiting Thunder Mountain. His legs wobbled from the roller coaster ride.

Maiya punched his arm. "You're not getting too old for the rides, are you?"

"Nah. Never."

Will laughed with them. "This one was my favorite so far. Definitely worth the hour wait. Where to next?"

It was a toss-up who had been most excited about the visit to the theme park — Will, Lacey, or Maiya. Their enthusiasm had convinced River to take the day off and play like a kid with them.

Maiya glanced at her cell phone. "It's 1:10. Ice cream is next. Can I meet you there? I want to go back to that one shop and get the Tinker Bell coffee mug for Aunt Lacey."

"Aren't we going that way?"

"No. You're meeting Mom and Aunt Lace at the Mark Twain, yawn, Riverboat ride."

"Is that what we decided?" His brain was addled from the jerky ride. Or maybe it was the general state of happy chaos that came from hanging out with fifty thousand other people in the magical kingdom. "Okay. See you in thirty minutes?"

She batted her eyelashes and held out her hands, palms up. "Riv, we're talking *shopping.* I need an hour."

"All right. An hour at the ice cream parlor on Main Street."

" 'Kay." She excused her way through the group in front of them and melded into the crowds.

River looked at Will. "Is that what we decided?"

"You got me. This place is a wild ride." He grinned. "Wilder than Mr. Toad's ride." The guy was like a big kid.

"It's a special place for us. We came here for our first official outing as a family." He remembered the day vividly. It was Thanksgiving time then, too, soon after their wedding day. Last week he and Teal celebrated their fourth anniversary, a low-key midweek dinner out. "It would have been about four years ago. I think that was the day Maiya and I really connected." He glanced at Will as they strolled along a wide walkway. Teal had told Lacey, who had told Will that Bio Dad was his brother. "It seems like I should explain these things now that we know about Cody."

"Talk about a crazy ride. I'm not sure where to file that information yet." Will shook his head. "It's obvious you're a great dad to Maiya. She's a wonderful girl."

"She's my daughter in every other way. How do you think he'll react?"

"Let me ask first: how are you reacting?"

River let out a breath. "Honestly, I kind of wish he'd ridden off into the sunset never to be heard from again. It's not that I think I'll lose where I stand with Maiya. And she needs to know him. But it's a wrinkle in our life. A complication." He shrugged. "So, what about him? He's not going to pull a Dutch on us, is he? Or swing the other way and sue for custody?" The groundless fears he had not voiced to Teal poured out. He stopped himself short of asking Will if his brother had ever been in love with Teal.

Will said, "He's nothing like Dutch, and I can't imagine him wanting another child. It's not like he and Teal ever had anything going between them."

That answered that question.

He continued. "Cody has a sweetheart of a wife and three good kids, a job that moves him all over the world. My best guess is he'll take it in stride. He might feel some responsibility and be glad that you're in the picture. He's not the punk he used to be." He slapped River's shoulder. "I'd say no worries, man."

River felt a sense of relief. It was hard to imagine someone stepping in now, sixteen years after the fact, and wanting to barge into their lives, but the thought had crossed his mind once. Or twice. "Thanks."

"Sure."

They eventually spotted their wives. Teal was seated on a bench in the shade of a tree; Lacey stood next to it talking to a young family with little ones in a double stroller. Like Will, Lacey struck up a conversation with anyone in the vicinity. They were like a portable Happy Grounds Coffee Shop, hospitality without the coffee.

Teal's pallid complexion struck him again. She put up a good front with Will and Lacey, but she hadn't been herself in the week leading up to their arrival. Given the stress of needing to tell her sister about Cody and now anticipating The Talk with

Maiya, it was no surprise, though.

She gave him a small smile. "Was it fun?"

"I haven't laughed so hard in ages." He sat beside her.

"Where's Maiya?"

He glanced at Lacey to make sure she was out of hearing. She was introducing Will to her new friends. "Minnie McMouse is buying a gift for the aunt. How are you?"

"I threw up and now I feel better."

"Teal." He put the back of his hand against her forehead. "Are you sick? Do you need to go home?"

"I'm fine." She moved his hand and held it. "But I'll probably make an appointment with the doctor."

"Why? What is it?"

She smiled, a slow, lazy movement of the corners of her mouth. Her eyes twinkled. "Most likely a boy or a girl."

Her voice sounded far away, as if he stood at a distance. The words were difficult to make out. "What?"

"I'm a little slow on the uptake. Nauseous and tired? Ten days late? Duh. Lacey figured it out. I know we haven't been trying for long, but —" she shrugged — "this seems to be how it works with me."

"You're pregnant?"

"I think so."

"You're pregnant!" He shouted so loudly Lacey and Will and their new friends stared. "My wife is pregnant!"

They cheered and clapped.

"She's pregnant!"

Other passersby joined in.

"We're having a baby!" He couldn't stop. His face felt like it might split from his grin. He grabbed Teal in a bear hug.

"Uh, River." She pushed against him and looked up at his face. "We might want to tell our daughter before the rest of the world?"

"What? Oh yeah. I guess. Oh, Teal. I'm so happy. Are you happy? Are you all right? Should we go home? Do you need crackers or something? We should put your feet up."

"Am I listening to the next nine months?"

He chuckled. "Probably."

She nuzzled against him and giggled. "I am beyond happy."

"Me too." He rested his chin on her head. "Me too."

And then, to his chagrin, he began to cry.

CHAPTER 51

While the others headed to the ice cream parlor, Teal headed to a restroom. The happy hordes of people slowed her progress. She still wore a silly grin, but then so did three-fourths of the other visitors. The remaining one-fourth were tired or hungry and most certainly not in the throes of happy pregnancy news.

Funny how she had missed the signs, but it had been almost seventeen years. For Lacey, it had only been a little over one. Her sweet sister was ecstatic. Almost as much as River.

She grinned, although she felt a twinge of sadness for him. The poor guy had cried in public. He said they were tears of joy, but she sensed a touch of sorrow, too. This would bring back all the memories of the joyful time that ended so terribly for him.

How would Maiya take the news? Teal laughed to herself. Her teenager would be happy and embarrassed — her parents? eww! — and attempt to find an in-between space of cool. Teal wanted to tell her right now, privately. What a crazy place to have told River, in the middle of Disneyland. She had not been able to contain herself after Lacey pointed out the obvious while they rode on a make-believe Mark Twain boat on a make-believe river that rolled enough to make her sick to her stomach.

Now Teal reached yet another bathroom, grateful for a short line. Maybe she could find Maiya. She guessed which store she had gone to. But River might feel left out. All right. She would not tell Maiya. She would simply bask in a few moments alone with her, the last moments of Maiya being her only child.

A few minutes later she detoured away from the ice cream parlor toward the shop. Having lived sixteen years in Los Angeles with a daughter, she knew her way around the park fairly well. They first visited when Maiya was three. It became an annual trek, sometimes more when special deals were offered.

Like Maiya, River had grown up visiting the place with his parents and sister. The little boy in him emerged whenever he and Maiya hit the rides Teal avoided.

She smiled, imagining the fun they would all have introducing a new little one to adventure, history, fantasy, music and colors, gentle rides, and . . .

Teal stopped dead in her tracks.

Had she seen what she thought?

A gap opened again in the crowd.

And she saw again.

Ahead, on the left, at the side of the wide, congested walkway stood her daughter. Maiya's back was to her, but she was unmistakable. The black ponytail, the khakis with gathered cuffs, the sleeveless grape-purple tee were her. She spoke to a stranger.

Who was not a stranger.

The man wore blue jeans and a brown T-shirt, but his bearing was clearly military. Thirtysomething, he stood under six feet tall. His shoulders were squared, his slender arms roped with muscles, his hair buzzed to the length of colorlessness, his face lean and weathered, his eyes squinted against the sunlight.

They would be green, not quite the dark shade of Maiya's eyes, but green nonetheless.

Teal would have recognized him anywhere. No matter that the dishwater-blond hair was gone along with the slumped shoulders, the chains, the black clothing. He had haunted her dreams for over sixteen years.

He smiled now. Maiya's ponytail bounced. He laughed. Maiya gestured, her hands painting images in the air. He held out his arms. Maiya stepped into a hug.

From her father.

Teal strode, fast and hard, this way and that, no destination in mind. Her heart pounded in her ears. Her throat ached. The world around her blurred. She bumped into people. They apologized. Her voice screamed inside but did not find its way to her tongue.

Where did one go in the happy kingdom to have a meltdown?

She just kept walking.

How could Lacey and Will have done this to her? Was River in on it? Why had they contacted Cody behind her back and set up such a public meeting? Were they nuts or cruel or utterly clueless?

Poor Maiya! On her own while the others ate ice cream? Teal would have allowed a meeting. She would have.

Sometime. Somewhere. Anywhere else than here and not this week. Certainly not before she had told Maiya that Cody Janski was Bio Dad.

But she would have allowed it. She would have.

"Lady! Watch where you're going!"

Sorry! Sorry!

She had to sit down. A busy restroom was not the place. There must be a first-aid station around. If only she could find a map. If only she could find an empty bench.

Certainly not before she had told Maiya that Cody Janski was Bio Dad.

Maiya did not know him. Will and Lacey did. How had they arranged a meeting? Why wouldn't Lacey at least have introduced them? Had Cody approached Maiya after Will phoned him to say where she was? Had Maiya walked into a trap, not knowing she was going to meet —

No.

No to all of that. River, Lacey, and Will would not have done such a thing.

This was Maiya's doing. She had guessed Cody's identity. Not wanting to ask about him, she and that nerdy Baker had tracked him down, most likely not a problem after hearing stories about him being in the Marines and where he had been stationed. Maiya herself had contacted Bio Dad and arranged . . .

Oh, God.

Her baby had done what Teal had refused

to do for her. Maiya had not been able to count on her own mother.

Oh no. Teal would never . . .

But she had.

She was, in the end, no different from Randi, no better. Maybe even worse.

She sobbed and strode smack into the middle of a furry mass.

"Hey, are you all right?" A woman's voice came from the middle of the enormous body of yellow-orange fleece. A tiny screen in a red vest shaded a set of eyes. "Do you want some help?"

Teal shook her head and gazed up at Winnie the Pooh's face bobbing several feet above her own.

"Oh, bother." The voice from the chest pulled her attention back to the eyes. Giant arms enveloped her. "Just have a good cry. Then we'll go find a honey pot and you'll feel all better."

At that moment, Teal did not have any choice but to do as she was told.

CHAPTER 52

Outside the ice cream parlor on the sidewalk fronted by a make-believe Main Street crowded with pedestrians, River leaned against the wall. He crossed his arms over his chest as if that would stop the wrenching twist inside it.

The first time he had experienced the telltale sign of dread was when the forest ranger approached his campsite, hat in his hand, face pinched as if he were in great pain. *"There's been an accident."*

The breath-catching dread never returned until the day after his first date with Teal. They had taken Maiya with them on a picnic at the beach. Teal refused to call it a date; he disagreed. He awoke the next morning soaked in sweat, the wrench working inside his chest, squeezing and crushing and digging.

From that day on, he understood that to love was to risk losing it all again.

At a gut level, he knew Krissy would have said, "It's worth it, River. It's totally worth it." And so he forced himself to learn to live with it, to tame it, to respond more quickly with a *Fear not, I am with you; give it to Me, give it all to Me.* It was either that or curl up in a fetal position.

But right now he was having trouble forming the words. His pregnant wife had been gone far too long for a bathroom run unless she was sick again. Should he go find her? Then there was his teenage daughter, off by herself in this stupid theme park, at the mercy of who knew how many crazies. . . .

Lacey touched his arm and handed him a tiny paper cup and small spoon. Beside him, Will received another. "Life is short, guys; eat more ice cream. This is a sample of the black walnut. Oh my gosh!"

River followed her line of sight. Maiya was making her way on the sidewalk toward them. The sunlight dappled on her face through leaves. She was smiling, talking to someone beside her, a man. . . .

Lacey rushed toward them and threw her arms around the man.

Beside him Will let out a low whistle. "It's my brother. How in the world did he end up here? And with Maiya?" He squeezed

463

River's shoulder as he went over to greet him.

Speechless, River watched a scene that made no sense but irked him. The brothers hugged. Lacey and Maiya hugged. They all smiled. Lacey laughed.

Cody Janski was small compared to Will, his hair all but shaved off, his frame more wiry than slender.

River could take him, easy.

But what was the guy doing there? And where was Teal?

Maiya came over to him. "Where's Mom?"

"Restroom. What's . . . ?" He really didn't have any words.

Maiya pulled apart his crossed arms and hugged him fiercely.

He hugged her back.

She said, "It's Cody. My dad. I think." She let go and made serious eye contact that he could not avoid. "He seems like a nice guy. Wanna meet him?"

River studied her face, tentative and eager. Her eyes pleaded, her smile slipped. "How did this — how did this happen?"

"I had to, Riv. I just had to. Please don't be mad."

Maiya arranged it? Of course she did. Of course she had to. Her mother had dragged her feet long enough.

She said, "Baker helped me find him. And then I . . ." She shrugged. "I called him. I told him what I knew and wondered if he thought he could be my biological father. He was down at Camp Pendleton. We both wanted to meet. I suggested a halfway point." She shrugged again. "That would be here."

He wanted to chew her out for keeping things secret, for putting herself in an iffy situation with a stranger even if he was Will's brother. But then he saw the sparkle in her eyes and realized how long she had waited for this. He was being as childish as Teal had been. Maiya was the one behaving like an adult. She was taking ownership of her life, making important decisions and acting on them.

He tossed the ice cream cup in a nearby trash can and gave her a tight smile. "Introduce me."

Maiya looped her arm through his and pulled him along. Lacey and Will moved aside so he could shake the man's hand. Will started the introduction but Maiya interrupted.

"Riv, this is my dad, Cody Janski. Cody, this is my awesome stepdad, River Adams."

My dad? My dad?

Something sank inside of River. Compared

with "my dad," "awesome stepdad" fell way short.

Geesh. How old was he? Thirteen? He smiled, hoping it didn't look as forced as it felt.

Cody shook his hand and grinned, a wide show of teeth in his narrow face. "Nice to meet you, sir. I apologize for the awkwardness. Your daughter has an irresistible convincing streak in her."

River felt some of the tension drain from him. "She gets it from her mother."

"I bet she does. Lacey has a similar one." He winked at his sister-in-law. "Well, I guess I have to ask the obvious." He paused. "Is it true?"

River exchanged a look with Lacey. This was Teal's job, wasn't it? Lacey widened her eyes as if to disagree, as if to say this could wait no longer.

Maiya's eyes grew wide. "Riv, please. I could have half siblings! Nora and William could be my grandparents!"

Maiya had always longed for this knowledge of extended family. Had she somehow sensed they were not all that far away?

He could not withhold this gift from her. "Yes, it's true. Teal told me."

Cody said, "No question about it? I am Maiya's father?"

Biological. River relaxed his clenched jaw. "Absolutely no question about it."

Cody turned to Maiya. "Give me five." They slapped each other's hands. "Welcome to the Janski side of your family, Miss Maiya."

There was a brashness to him that reminded River of so many of the boys who had attended the academy down through the years. He was seeing them, kids like Jake Ford, seventeen years from now. They would never lose that audacious manner and might even be able — as in Cody's case — to mold it into creative energy for positive endeavors.

He wasn't convinced it meshed with his Maiya's personality, though.

As everyone else seemed to talk at once, River noticed out of the corner of his eye Winnie the Pooh, one of the larger-than-life characters that roamed the park, waving and looking for kids to hug.

Or women?

Pooh ambled directly toward them, Teal under his arm.

They stopped, and his wife shook Pooh's hand and talked at his chest. River stepped onto the street and approached them just as Pooh lumbered around and walked off.

Teal turned and saw him. His frustrations

at her faded. She looked sicker than she had earlier. How could she handle what was happening behind him?

"Teal." He reached her, blocking her view of the Janskis.

The Janskis. That now included Maiya. Would she want to change her name to Janski?

Teal gasped. She had noticed them.

He held her, his hands on her arms, keeping her still. "Love —"

"Oh, River! I saw them back there." She gestured, a flip of her hand toward nowhere in particular. "A while ago. Oh." She moaned. "What am I going to do? I can't face her. I can't face him. This is all my fault. I pushed her away. I pushed her into this."

"Shh." He bent until his forehead touched hers, willing the rash of words to stop.

"I —"

"Shh."

She whimpered.

"Listen to me, Teal. What's done is done. This is not about you right now. This is about Maiya meeting a sperm donor." River grimaced at the harsh description, one he created years before but had never spoken aloud. Back then he had needed to depersonalize Bio Dad.

But now . . . now the guy was a living, breathing human being.

He said, "He's a human being, and from this day forward she will have a relationship with him. Right now we set the tone for the future. We cannot communicate that he is the enemy or that she is a mistake. She can't hear that for the rest of her life." River straightened to look at Teal. "She's okay, love. She's okay. She did this on her own, and she's proud of it, not angry with you anymore."

"But —"

"Later. You ask her forgiveness later."

There was a footstep behind him. "Mommy?"

He moved slightly, giving his girls enough space to hug each other but keeping them close.

"Oh, Mommy," she whispered. "He's nice, and he likes me!"

River scrapped his plan to ground Maiya for life. His little girl had sprouted wings. She needed to fly.

CHAPTER 53

Like a tottering elderly person, Teal clung to Maiya's arm as they moved with River toward Lacey and Will and . . .

And Cody.

"Hey." He grinned his trademark cheeky grin, still familiar after all these years.

She shook his outstretched hand. "Hi."

"You never write; you never call."

His smart remark transported her back to Cedar Pointe when they attended the combined middle–high school. He had been a mouthy upstart, four years behind her in class. Hadn't he changed at all?

She gritted her teeth in a smile. "Did you want me to?"

He laughed. "No way, José." He turned to Maiya and his thin lips settled into a gentle smile. "Seriously, I would have so messed you up in the early years."

Teal had difficulty swallowing.

He said, "It's best we start now. Whatever

that means is up to your mom and step-dad."

Inside Teal, some iron resolve went to mush. "I was going to call or write."

Cody said, "Guess she beat you to it." He shook his head. "Kids. Whaddya gonna do? But like I was telling Will and Lace, I might not have taken it from you, Teal. I sure wouldn't have agreed to meet you all at Disneyland." He smiled again at Maiya. He seemed to have a special one for her.

Will suggested they find somewhere to sit. River agreed. Lacey herded them toward a small round table outside the ice cream shop and Will went inside to buy ice cream for everyone. They borrowed chairs from other tables and eventually sat.

The whole scenario was bizarre and awkward, but Teal did not have a better idea. Until recently she had never imagined seeing Cody again face to face or even talking with him. She would have told Maiya about him first. Then she would have written a letter to him in Virginia, where he was supposed to be. If they heard back and if he was open to communicating with Maiya, she would have suggested letters and e-mails.

And maybe, just maybe, down the dark, murky road of the future, they would meet when Maiya was married with kids of her own and he happened to be in town.

She longed for her turtle shell.

She scooted her chair closer to River's, leaning against his arm, feeling decidedly clingy. Maiya sat on his other side, between him and Cody. Between her two dads.

Awkward beyond belief. Way, way weird.

Next to her, Lacey squeezed Teal's arm and gave her a small smile as if in agreement.

At least they were spared any ex-flame type of residue. Teal and Cody had never had a relationship. Theirs was such a small school that they knew each other, but he scarcely crossed her radar until Lacey's crush. An independent college student by then, Teal had felt it her duty to inform her half sister that she was nuts.

Then that night . . . That night he was simply a means for Teal to hurt Lacey — to fulfill every prophecy Randi and Owen had ever declared over her.

No, there was no love lost here. No closure needed.

Which made Maiya's story all the more sad.

"Mom, Riv?" There was an anxious crease between Maiya's eyebrows, the one that begged for their approval.

Teal felt River bristle. Or was it her own nerve endings igniting his where their arms touched?

We cannot communicate that he is the enemy or that she is a mistake.

No, they did not want to do that.

Teal laid her hand on the bare skin of his forearm. She needed him to rub off on her. "What, hon?"

"I have two brothers and a sister. Well, half. Just like you and Aunt Lace, Mom."

And you have another on the way! She wanted to shout, but smiled instead. "What you've always wanted. How old are they?" Lacey, of course, had mentioned them through the years, although Teal had not committed the information to memory.

"Dylan is ten, Evan is eight, and Hayley is six. Isn't that cool?"

"Very cool. You can be as bossy as I was."

Lacey laughed. "Knowing Maiya, she may pass you up in that department."

"Hey!" Maiya protested.

"Funny." Teal turned to Cody. "Did you tell your children yet?"

"Yeah. Too soon, I admit, since I didn't know for sure. But that's just me. Maiya got ahold of me while we were all in Texas. They're still there, at my in-laws', until tomorrow. They're excited about having a

473

big sister."

Teal wondered how one told little kids about a one-night stand. "And, uh . . ." She had to ask him. She could not hear it from Maiya. Could not hear his wife's name in the same sentence as *stepmom.* "Your wife? She, uh — ?"

"Erica took the news in stride." He chuckled. "I married a brick with a heart of gold. I did have to talk her out of tarring and feathering you, though, for not telling us sooner."

Teal felt her eyebrows rise.

"I reminded her that we've been overseas most of our married life. We couldn't have really gotten to know you." He looked at Maiya. "Now we'll be living just down the road. They can hardly wait to meet you. If you want."

Maiya grinned.

"And then there are my parents."

He had told them already? Teal felt ashamed and guilty and grateful all at once. Nora must be so angry with her.

Cody shook his head as if in amazement. "I'd call from Germany and it was 'Maiya this' and 'Maiya that.' So I know when we tell them, they'll be on cloud nine. I think they already adopted you."

Maiya's grin stretched until her eyes

nearly shut. "Really?"

He laughed.

At the word *adopted,* a knifelike sensation ripped through Teal. River had never adopted Maiya. He wanted to, but she could not allow it. Contacting Cody four years ago was out of the question. She wasn't risking her newfound happiness by dragging her past into it.

Could it happen now?

River addressed Cody. "What do you propose to do from here?"

"Well, like I said, we'd all love to have Maiya come visit." He shrugged. "For a weekend or whatever. I don't want to disrupt your lives." He gazed at River. "I'm not claiming any rights here, but it seems a good thing for a biological dad to get to know his daughter." He turned to Maiya. "If she wants."

Maiya looked a question at River and Teal.

Teal said, "It's up to you, honey. We can make it work."

"I could drive down to Pendleton."

"Nah, I don't think so." Teal smiled. "Not yet, Miss Just-Got-Your-License. We'll figure something out."

Maiya grinned again. "Okay. I'd like that."

Will walked up to the table carrying a container that held six huge waffle cones filled with ice cream. "Ta-da!" Ever the perfect host, he had remembered everyone's favorite flavor and now served them.

Maiya and Cody discovered they each had caramel pecan.

She said, "That's your favorite?"

"That's yours? Get out of town."

They laughed.

Teal kind of hoped they all could have gotten out of town right then and there. As it was, they would be eating ice cream until nightfall.

River leaned over to eye her cone. "Hm. Strawberry's your favorite?"

His nearness calmed her. She smiled the special smile she had just for him. "Yours too?"

"Get out of town."

Her stomach full of strawberry ice cream and settled for the moment, Teal knew now might be her only chance. "Cody, can we talk?" She glanced around the table. "Alone?"

"Sure."

She squeezed River's arm and he nodded in understanding.

Cody walked beside her through the crowded Main Street. He said, "I apologized to River for meeting like this. I tried to talk

Maiya out of it, but the truth is, I really wanted to meet her and find out the truth from you. It seemed like the best time. I was able to get today off. Tomorrow, when Erica and the kids get here, life will be crazy for a while, till we get settled in."

"I apologize for not addressing things directly with you."

He chuckled. "With Maiya in charge, you didn't need to."

"She's just a kid. I shouldn't have . . ."

"She looks like you, but at the same time she's got my mother in her DNA. I mean, the way she moves her mouth, and there's something about her walk. Do we need to do a paternity test?"

"No. You are her father. There is no other possibility, because I was not intimate with anyone else."

He looked at her. "I thought Lacey was the squeaky-clean sister and you were the, um, opposite."

"I didn't sleep around. Do you remember that night, in the back room of your parents' place?"

He worked his mouth as if unsure what to say. "Honestly, no."

Teal believed him.

They continued in silence. He spotted a vacant bench off to the side and gestured toward it. They sat.

He said, "Look, it's no secret I sowed a lot of wild oats during those years. Most of the details are lost in a purple haze. How did you and I hook up?"

"You took Lacey to a dance."

"Yeah, that I vaguely remember. She wasn't my typical date. I know she wasn't my typical end-of-date conquest."

"No, she wasn't. But you tried, which is what angered me. Then somehow Owen . . . It doesn't matter. The thing is, I tracked you down that night. One thing led to another."

He rubbed his forehead. "Did I rape you?"

"No." She took a deep breath. "Have you . . . ?"

He lowered his hand and winced. "Like I said, purple haze. So far, no complaints. So far, no other offspring either. Thank goodness. Erica wasn't exactly surprised at Maiya's claim, but I don't know how many more she could take."

Teal tried to imagine what kind of woman would marry him. An independent saint?

He said, "You never told Maiya my name?"

"No. Then I would have had to tell Lacey and Will and my mom and your parents. It would hurt them so much. I couldn't give

Owen the satisfaction to gloat." She cringed. Even Owen had factored into her lie?

"That guy was one mean dude."

"The thing is, my sister was in love with you and she adored me. I basically did what I thought would hurt her the most and then I shoved it under the rug and moved on."

"Kind of hard to hide the kid, though. You got pregnant by immaculate conception?"

She shook her head. How silly, but that was exactly the idea she had promoted.

He said, "What *did* you tell Maiya about me?"

"Nothing." She paused. "I told her you weren't ready to be a father, that you didn't want to be with us."

"Your run-of-the-mill tale of abandonment." Cody's voice and mannerisms remained polite, but he wasn't letting her get away with a thing.

In the pit of her stomach, the ice cream rolled into a congealed lump. She wouldn't want to face him on the stand. "Probably half the dads of her classmates are absentee. Abandonment was an easy explanation. It held her off until a couple months ago. Then I told her that right after she was born, you'd gone to jail."

"Kind of picky about what parts of the truth you reveal, aren't you?"

"Yeah. And I still am. What do I tell her about her conception?"

"Why not the whole truth?"

"It's . . . it's . . ."

"Sordid?"

"Unloving."

"And?"

She shrugged.

"That makes you look like what?" he said. "A flawed human being?"

She frowned.

He laughed, not unkindly. "Teal, you are. I am. The entire race is."

"I know that. I just don't want her to feel unwanted."

"I seriously doubt she'd feel that. She's such a good kid. I deal with eighteen-, nineteen-year-olds coming into the Corps. Some of them couldn't hold a candle to her. The maturity and confidence she expressed when we first talked on the phone was unbelievable. She didn't get that from my genes. Despite the fact that you're a lawyer who knows just how much truth to hold back, I bet you've been Mother of the Year for sixteen years running, right? You've taken care of all her needs and then some. You even found a decent stepdad for her."

"River was a surprise. But I have tried to do my best."

"It seems to have worked. What else is there?"

Adoption. "River. Uh." She swallowed. "River wants to adopt her. Maiya and I want that too."

Cody sat back and gazed at her. "That means I give up my rights as her father?"

"It means you wouldn't owe her anything. You wouldn't be financially responsible for her. She would not inherit anything from you unless you were to stipulate that. She doesn't take your name. She could still visit as often as she wants. You'd still have a relationship."

He looked away. His jaw clenched. His lips pressed together. He made eye contact again. "I sign papers, giving up rights and responsibilities, and we base our relationship on abandonment."

"Not exactly. At this age she wouldn't see it that way."

"But I would. I would, Teal. And that doesn't sit well in my gut. Life is about loyalty. Now that I know I have another daughter, I refuse to abandon her. I won't do it."

She bit back a sarcastic retort. Not only had the guy grown up, he'd gone off the deep end. Had she asked for a stupid knight in shining armor to ride up on his white horse? No. She had River for that.

Disappointment washed through her. River would be crushed. Maiya would be . . .

She did not really know what her daughter would be. Especially once she heard the whole truth from her mother.

Funny. All the fearing about Cody fighting adoption had not helped. All the delaying had not helped. Here they were, exactly in the place she thought she had avoided.

She really had been a silly fool.

CHAPTER 54

After returning home from their long day and evening at Disneyland, Teal had hoped to tuck Maiya into bed and surprise her with the baby news. Instead she went right to bed herself, needing River to tuck her in. There hadn't been a chance to tell him about her private talk with Cody. That would have to wait. Perhaps the baby news could wait as well.

She said, "Maybe we shouldn't tell her tonight."

He propped another pillow behind her back. "She'll say it wasn't fair to exclude her. How come we all knew and she didn't?"

Teal did an eye roll. "You can be so annoyingly right on about her."

He stretched to pat himself on the back. "Yes, I can."

"I think we've maxed out on over-the-top emotions for one day."

River sat on the edge of the bed. "You're

exhausted, but we have to bring her in. This is major family business." He glanced at her midsection. "For us four."

She sighed and whispered, "He showed her family pictures already! What if she refers to that woman as her stepmom? What if she says 'Dad this' and 'Dad that'? What if — ?"

He put a finger to her lips. "News flash, love. Cody *is* her dad. Erica *is* her stepmom. We have to accept these facts and get used to them. It doesn't take anything away from us, from what we have together. It's not like anyone is going through a nasty divorce and forcing her to take sides."

She moved his hand away from her mouth. "Why couldn't they have just stayed overseas? Or even on the East Coast?"

"Teal." His low tone was San Sebastian style.

"What?" She snapped the word.

"I adore you. I adore that we are having a baby together. But if pregnancy makes you this whiny, I'll be spending more time at school, and I wouldn't be surprised if Maiya moved down to Camp Pendleton."

"Teasing is not going to help."

"I'm only half teasing. I'll cut you some slack for hormones and exhaustion, but this is off the charts. What else is going on here?"

She shuddered and a sob nearly closed up her throat. "She had to do this all by herself."

"Yes, she did."

"I messed up."

"Big time."

"How can I ever . . . ?"

"Make up for it? You can't."

"How can she ever forgive me?"

He shrugged. "Only one way to find out."

"How?"

"How do you think?"

"Ask for it? Apologize?"

His eyebrows rose.

She gritted her teeth and deleted the question marks. "I ask for it. I apologize."

There was a brief knock on the open door and Maiya came into the room. "Apologize for what?"

"Oh, honey."

Maiya plopped on the other side of the bed, her face scrunched. "My bad. I'm sorry, Mom and Riv. I never should have contacted Cody without telling you two."

Teal exchanged a glance with River, who smiled.

She reached over and took Maiya's hand. "Hon, you had every right to do that. I am proud of you for being brave and doing what had to be done when I dropped the

485

ball. Maybe you should have told us, but I really didn't let you. You knew my response would be what it's always been: 'I'll tell you later.' Thank you for figuring out that 'later' was now."

"I just couldn't wait any longer to find out."

River said, "What made you change your mind? After the Dutch incident, you said you didn't want to know him."

Maiya shrugged. "I was missing Aunt Lacey and Uncle Will and Baker so much. And Nora. I e-mailed her and she e-mailed back. She reminds me of Gammy Jayne, you know, just down-to-earth and not judging me for being me. I guess it snuck up again, that wanting to fill up the empty place. No offense, Riv."

"None taken." He ruffled her hair. "How did our smart cookie put the pieces together? You were putting yourself out there to contact Cody, not knowing for sure it was him."

She blew through her lips. "*Pff.* It didn't take a rocket scientist to figure out it was 99 percent for sure him. I figured I was conceived around Christmastime, when you might have been home from college, Mom. I heard the stories about what a bad dude Cody was. Baker did some research and found out he'd been arrested and went to jail about the time I was born, just like you said my dad was. The way you didn't want to tell me when we were in Cedar Pointe was a red flag. Then there was the awesome way I connected with Nora. And —" she gave them a funny smile — "you saw her earlobes."

Teal sighed. "Maiya, I'm the one who needs to apologize. I'm sorry you had to go through all this by yourself. And from the bottom of my heart I'm sorry that I lied about Cody not wanting anything to do with us when in fact he did not even know you existed."

"But he was eighteen and totally screwed up." She sniffed, on the verge of crying now, her smart-aleck demeanor melting away at the reality of who Cody was. "He wouldn't have cared about us."

"He probably wouldn't have been capable of even trying, but that's moot at this point. I just apologize for everything, honey."

Tears streamed down Maiya's face. "It's okay."

"It's not, but I hope you can forgive me."

"Mom, it's okay. Really." She brushed away the tears. "Yeah, I've been seriously ticked at you, but I never thought about forgiving you. You're my mom. Why would I have to think about that?"

Because I hurt you deeply. So deeply her daughter would not even see the fallout until much later in her life. Something would happen. Perhaps she'd be unable to trust Teal in some way. Perhaps shame would strike out of the blue because of how she was conceived and she would react, thinking herself worthless, engaging in self-destructive behavior.

Cody's accusation echoed through her. *Kind of picky about what parts of the truth you reveal.*

"Maiya, Cody and I were not boyfriend and girlfriend."

"Yeah, I got that. So?"

"So our intimacy was without affection."

"I get it, Mom. You've taught me all about that. How some girls who don't have good dads have sex with guys just to fill up some emptiness. You had Dutch *and* Owen to deal with. Yucko!" Her eyes widened. "Whoa. Is that why you went totally berserk about Jake?"

Teal shrugged. "Honey, don't excuse me for how I let you down. For your own well-being, I hope you can let me off the hook."

Maiya cocked her head.

Teal's breath caught at the mirror image of herself.

"Mom, you did what you thought you had to do to protect me. But it all turned out fine. Right? I got to meet Cody. He's not Riv, but he's cool. And okay, I admit I fantasized about him being a prince, but no worries." She leaned over and kissed her cheek. "I love you. You are not on the hook."

"All right then. I accept that."

"Good. Are we done?"

Teal exchanged a smile with River. "Yes, we're done."

Maiya bounded off the bed and ran through the doorway, calling out, "Don't go away."

River mouthed at Teal, *It's okay.* She took a deep breath.

Maiya popped back into the room holding a bag from Disneyland and slid up onto the bed again. "I have gifts!" She pulled out two small boxes and handed one to each of them. "Happy day."

Teal exchanged a curious smile with River and opened her gift. She pulled out a tiny riverboat Christmas tree ornament and laughed. "Thank you, hon."

River was grinning and inspecting a miniature train. "Thunder Mountain? Thanks."

"Yep. I gave Space Mountain to Uncle Will because he liked that best. Aunt Lace loved her Tinker Bell mug."

River reached over and opened a dresser drawer. "As long as we're exchanging gifts."

Teal said, "Good grief. What was I doing while you two were shopping?"

River winked and gave a shirt-size box to Maiya. While she opened it, he put his mouth to Teal's ear and whispered, "Upchucking."

"Oh yeah."

He smiled. His eyes were sparkling again.

Evidently throwing up was preferable to whining. She'd have to keep that in mind.

"Riv!" Maiya held up a red nightshirt. Minnie Mouse filled the front with her smiling face, pink bow, and pink dress with white polka dots. "Sweet! Thank you!"

"You're welcome, Minnie McMouse."

"Mom, what did you get?"

Teal wiggled the lid off a small box. She wasn't into Disney junk. Why would River . . . ? "Earrings!" She lifted out a pair of beautiful dangly earrings with crystals and not a hint of mouse ears. "River! Thank you."

He grinned. "I had to remember our special day with something special." He leaned over and kissed her.

Evidently too long for Maiya's comfort. She cleared her throat twice. "Okay, I'll be seeing you two."

They laughed. River sat up. "Oh, sit back down for a minute."

She sank onto the bed, a wary expression on her face.

Teal smiled. "I'm happy you have siblings now."

"Yeah?" She sounded puzzled. "Me too. I guess, anyway. I mean, they don't sound like brats."

"You've always wanted one, and now you've got three and another on the way. That makes four. Imagine that. All in one day."

Maiya stared blankly.

Teal saw River's goofy grin and knew hers was the same. They waited, giggling.

At last Maiya squealed. "You're pregnant! You're pregnant?"

Teal leaned forward to receive Maiya's hug. "I'm pretty sure."

"Oh, wow! Oh, wow! Unbelievable!"

River wrapped them both in his arms and they laughed.

Teal breathed a prayer of thanksgiving. Amazing how many over-the-top emotions could be packed into one day.

Teal awoke with a start. The covers were pulled up to her chin. Sunlight rimmed the curtains. River wasn't in bed. She could hear voices faintly from elsewhere in the house.

Why was she still in bed? How had she slept so soundly, not even hearing River get up?

Ohhh, yes. She might be pregnant.

A sense of great joy tickled inside her skin, from the top of her head to the tips of her toes.

As if on cue to prove her thought was indeed true, nausea chased off the tickle and she groaned. With Maiya, it had been the same. Those first months had been gruesome, finishing her final undergrad semester, graduating, packing, all the while nauseated beyond belief. Worse, she had never felt so lonely in her life.

The door opened and River walked in, smiling, carrying a mug and a small plate.

She wasn't alone this time. *Thank You, God.* "Morning."

"Good morning." He set the things on the nightstand and sat. "Peppermint tea and saltines. Lacey's prescription for morning sickness."

"Sounds good. But we don't have either of those things."

"We do now. Those coffee shop people sure do get going early. Want to sit up?"

"Not yet. Want to lie down?"

He went to the other side of the bed and lay on it, fully clothed for work. "How are you?"

She moved slowly onto her side to face him and giggled. "Either I'm pregnant or my mind has tricked my body into thinking I am."

River kissed her. "I vote for number one."

"Me too. Is it time for you to go?"

"Not yet. What did you want to tell me?"

"Did I say I wanted to tell you something?"

"You didn't have to."

"You're pretty good, Mr. Adams."

"Not really." He grinned. "You had a private talk with Cody. I figured you'd clue me in."

"Why? You think you're someone special?"

"Mm-hmm. I know I'm someone special to you."

Her smile faded. She touched his cheek.

River said, "He doesn't want to give up his parental rights."

"He doesn't."

They gazed at each other for a long moment, passing between them a heaviness. As they shared it, back and forth, back and forth, its weight began to lighten.

Teal relayed her conversation with Cody to River.

When she had finished, he sighed. "Not to worry. It's in God's hands. Whatever is best for Maiya is best for all of us. In two years she'll legally be an adult and this won't be an issue."

"I'm sorry I waited so long to tell him." She really was tired of apologizing.

"Like Maiya said, I love you, and you're not on the hook."

"Can you say that again? It's not sinking in."

"Hormones." He chuckled. "I love you, and you're not on the hook." He smiled with a hint of sadness. "Maiya and I could not have been any closer than we've been these past four years. Five and a half if we count from the time we met. She always had that need to know Bio Dad. Adoption would not have taken it away. And Cody's right about loyalty. If he signs off, that's got abandonment written all over it. We don't want that for her."

"But still . . ."

"But still nothing. Who knows? Maybe down the road a piece, she'll opt to change her name. Maiya Marie Morgan-Adams-Janski."

"Lots of hyphens."

"Then I suppose she might add a husband's name. I don't like this growing-up business."

"Me neither, but on a mercenary note, there might be some veteran's benefits to help pay for her college."

"I hadn't thought of that."

"That's because you're not the mercenary in this family."

He kissed her. "I have to go."

"Okay."

"See you tonight." He rose and left the room.

The heaviness crept back into her heart. The damage she had inflicted on River was too much to bear.

If she had addressed things years ago with Cody, when he was in jail, he probably would have given up his rights in a heartbeat. River could have adopted Maiya when he married Teal. Maiya would not have had to track down Bio Dad by herself. Lacey would have loved Teal like she always had and forgiven her. She could have enjoyed aunthood ages ago. After Cody had gotten his life in order, he and Maiya could have e-mailed each other, not really bothering with much else because he had not been a big secret for her entire life.

The bedroom door reopened and River came back inside. He sat on the edge of the bed. "I love you, Xena, and you're not on the hook."

She smiled.

"God told me to tell you He feels the same way and that you might want to let yourself off the hook too." River kissed her cheek and left again.

This time the heaviness dissipated.

EPILOGUE

Thirteen months later

Teal glanced around her living room. Currier and Ives would have been proud. The flames in the fireplace danced around fake logs and the tree was artificial, but the ambience worked.

Colorful lights twinkled on the Christmas tree, decorated with garlands of popcorn and cranberry, Maiya's crafts since preschool, the Disneyland additions from last year, and painted wooden ornaments River's sister had sent from Switzerland. Some gifts, opened a few days before on Christmas Day, still sat under the tree. A picture frame, a book, a sweater.

The fireplace glowed. Pine-scented candles and a single lamp added soft light. Music played in the background, instrumental versions of carols.

The tree held several new ornaments, most of them colorful balls with sparkly blue letters spelling out things like *Baby's First Christmas*. The luscious scent of baking cookies filled the air, compliments of Maiya, who liked spending more time at home than not. Teal's own waistline was an addition of extra pounds, thanks to the best addition of all, now playing on the floor with his daddy.

Bryson Charles Adams cooed and giggled, lying on his abdomen and flailing his arms and legs about like a turtle under water. River cooed and giggled and swam like a bigger turtle.

The baby already had a head full of nut-brown wavy hair. Named after River's father and the neighbor Charlie, the four-and-a-half-month-old provided them all endless hours of entertainment. Teal thought it was amazingly fitting that he'd been born on August 10, the one-year anniversary of the large quake, the event that had set everything in motion to upset their lives. She flipped through the stack of mail on her lap. Four days after Christmas and the cards kept coming. She had sent her own out early, eager to share the newest Adams family photo with sweet little Bryson front and center.

An Iowa return address caught her attention and she laughed. "The Swansons!" She pulled out a photo and a letter and wondered whether the earthquake had set them on a winding side road of life as it had her. Did the aftershocks take them places they had not wanted to go?

Maiya came into the room, plopped beside her on the couch, and handed her a long wooden spoon. "Taste."

She eyed the lump of buttercream frosting and moaned. "Maybe you could get into recipes that include vegetables."

"After New Year's. Taste it. Is there enough vanilla?"

"Mmm." The butter and sugar and vanilla melted in her mouth. "Mm-hmm. Perfect."

"It's Erica's. It's going on her three-layer red velvet cake." Maiya took the mail from her lap. "What have we today?"

Teal caught River's wink. She winked back. It had taken some getting used to, but the blended family was what it was. Several Fridays during the past year, River had left school early and driven Maiya to meet Cody somewhere along the I-5, about forty-five minutes one way for each of them when traffic cooperated. Maiya loved spending weekends with the Janskis, and they loved having her.

Resisting the fact that her definition of family had been turned inside out was pointless. They'd been invaded. Maiya had a stepmom, a dad, a stepdad, a mom, three half siblings at Camp Pendleton and one at home, an uncle, and two sets of grandparents. Bryson had a mom, a dad, and a half sister. The two of them shared Aunt Jenny and Half-Aunt Lacey, Gran Randi, and cousin Jason by adoption.

Lacey had called earlier to tell Teal all about the party they were having today to celebrate the one-year anniversary of Jason's adoption. Teal could not get enough of her sister's baby news and how much fun all of them — even Randi — were having. Lacey and Will had moved little Jason and his grandmother, Ellen, up to Cedar Pointe soon after Thanksgiving last year. To say that the four of them clicked was an understatement. They had been like a family waiting to happen.

Yes, the family tree got complicated. That wasn't even counting Nora and William, who already treated Bryson like a grandchild. They might as well throw in the Yoshidas next door, who thought they were Maiya's surrogate grandparents and were totally gaga over the baby.

Maiya muttered under her breath.

"What's wrong, hon?" Teal asked.

Maiya slapped the mail down and looked up, surprised. "What?"

"You just said a word that I really don't want your brother picking up on."

Maiya usually laughed at that. Instead, she shrugged and shifted around. "Well, the thing is . . . um . . . Okay. Riv, you listening? I guess I should confess something 'cause it's really bugging me."

Teal bit back a sigh. They'd been through enough teenage confessions. The Jake Ford and Cody things were the biggest. They'd been through a few minor incidents in the past year. There was a date that wasn't really a date with someone she'd met at Camp Pendleton. There was the party at Baker's fraternity house. There was the scrape on the car bumper.

The girl was seventeen, a senior in high school. Weren't they about finished?

River said, "What's up?"

Maiya grimaced. "I sent Dutch Morgan our Christmas card."

"Hm."

Teal couldn't even get out an *oh.*

Maiya said, "I just thought, you know, if he sees what a fun-looking family we are and finds out he's got a little grandson now, he might write back. At least send a card. Say hey."

Teal cleared her throat but her voice still came out in a whisper. "Did you send him the letter too?"

"No. I thought that might upset you." She shrugged again. "The picture says it all. We're here. We're real. We're cool. We're related. We should keep in touch."

"Oh, Mai." Teal wrapped an arm around her shoulders. "It's okay to give it up."

"But, Mom. I am so happy I know my dad. I just want you to have that too."

"I appreciate that, hon, but it's his choice, and we can't change him." She kissed her forehead. "Maybe you could change Bryson's diaper, though?"

Maiya grinned. "I guess that would be easier." She slid off the couch and scooped up the baby. "Hey, baby Bry. Say Mai. M-m-mai."

His eyes locked on his big sister's and his face grew serious. He pressed his lips tightly together. "Mmm."

"Yeah! Thatta boy. M-m-mai." They disappeared down the hall, squeals of delight trailing behind.

River moved up and sat on the couch. "They're both corkers." He put his arms around her.

She settled against him.

"Does it still hurt?" His tone was subdued.

"Yeah. He's not coming back." She looked up at him. "Like Krissy and Sammy."

River sighed and held her more tightly. "The hurts make us who we are, Xena. And I do so love you the way you are."

"And I so love you, just the way you are."

"Even when I procrastinate about changing a diaper?"

She laughed. "Even then."

A NOTE FROM THE AUTHOR

Dear reader friend,
The older I get, the more I grasp the significance of what is written in our hearts. Our beings echo with our experiences, with voices of other people, with our perspectives. We live out of all of these, whether they are truth or lies. Sometimes we can't tell the difference.

And so Teal was born, a woman whose unhealthy childhood flowed into unhealthy choices that set the course for a life of hiding and running . . . until an earthquake shook things up.

When devastation strikes, we have a choice to make. We can run and hide — an especially attractive option if that's what we're used to doing anyway — or we can sit up, take notice, learn, and heal. The second option requires everything of us, and then some. It requires a heart ready to receive a new message, a new echo, from the only

One who can speak it.

Thank you for traveling this side road with Teal and River. As always, my prayer is that along with them, you were reminded that God does indeed love you unconditionally, passionately, and wildly.

Peace,
Sally John

E-MAIL: sallyjohn.readers@yahoo.com
WEBSITE: www.sally-john.com
BLOG:
http://lifeinthefictionlane.blogspot.com/
FACEBOOK: "Sally John Books" page

DISCUSSION QUESTIONS

1. Teal embodies what we might refer to as a "control freak" personality, a common temperament in today's fast-paced, over-scheduled society. Many wonder how else to balance the full plates they carry 24-7. Do you identify with Teal's natural bent to be responsible for her family's welfare? In what ways can this be a positive thing? In what ways can it become overdone and more negative than positive? What might cause the shift?

2. River's nickname for Teal, "Xena, Warrior Princess," hints at Teal's tendency to take this natural bent to the extreme. What situations in her past and now — after the earthquake — drive her to cling more tightly than ever to a sense of control?

3. Teal's visit to Cedar Pointe is all about heart echoes, memories imprinted from

childhood. What sorts of things does she hear? Once we meet Lacey, Randi, Owen, and Dutch, what do we learn about Teal's need to be in control?

4. River uses the phrase "father wound" in describing what both Teal and Maiya have experienced. What does he mean by this? Can you identify with the concept? Why or why not?

5. River is a long-suffering soul. Explore his character and the impact left on him by the loss of his first wife and child. What developments in his marriage to Teal did he "not sign up for"?

6. Explore the sister roles. How does birth order affect Teal and Lacey? In what ways can you relate to these characteristics?

7. An underlying tension between Teal and Lacey is the general pattern that family members don't talk about what's going on in a dysfunctional home. Have you or someone you know experienced this? What are some ways to try to break the pattern, especially for the next generation?

8. Why does Teal hide her secret about

Cody? How has the secret affected her? Have you ever harbored a deep secret? What was (or would be) the impact of revealing it? Of keeping it?

9. In what ways does Teal learn from her daughter, Maiya? What life lessons have you learned from your children or other young people?

10. Psalm 147:3 says that God "heals the brokenhearted and bandages their wounds." These wounds may come from the lies we believe about ourselves, lies that echo in our hearts. Often they have been placed there by others, whether intentionally or not. What has been your experience with such things? Has God healed your wounds? How do we replace the lies with truth?

ABOUT THE AUTHOR

When the going gets tough — or weird or wonderful — the daydreamer gets going on a new story. **Sally John** has been tweaking life's moments into fiction since she read her first Trixie Belden mystery as a child.

Now an author of more than fifteen novels, Sally writes stories that reflect contemporary life. Her passion is to create a family, turn their world inside out, and then portray how their relationships change with each other and with God. Her goal is to offer hope to readers in their own relational and faith journeys.

Sally grew up in Moline, Illinois, graduated from Illinois State University, married Tim in 1973, and taught in middle schools. She is a mother, mother-in-law, and grandmother. A three-time finalist for the Christy Award, she also teaches writing workshops. Her books include the Safe Harbor series (coauthored with Gary Smalley), The Other

Way Home series, The Beach House series, and the In a Heartbeat series. Many of her stories are set in her favorite places of San Diego, Chicago, and small-town Illinois.

She and her husband currently live in Southern California. Visit her website at www.sally-john.com.

The employees of Thorndike Press hope you have enjoyed this Large Print book. All our Thorndike, Wheeler, and Kennebec Large Print titles are designed for easy reading, and all our books are made to last. Other Thorndike Press Large Print books are available at your library, through selected bookstores, or directly from us.

For information about titles, please call:
  (800) 223-1244

or visit our Web site at:
  http://gale.cengage.com/thorndike

To share your comments, please write:
  Publisher
  Thorndike Press
  10 Water St., Suite 310
  Waterville, ME 04901